tender graces

**Center Point
Large Print**

**This Large Print Book carries the
Seal of Approval of N.A.V.H.**

tender graces

Kathryn Magendie

CENTER POINT PUBLISHING
THORNDIKE, MAINE

This Center Point Large Print edition
is published in the year 2009 by arrangement with
BelleBooks, Inc.

The text of this Large Print edition is unabridged.
In other aspects, this book may vary
from the original edition.
Printed in the United States of America.
Set in 16-point Times New Roman type.

ISBN: 978-1-60285-582-3

Library of Congress Cataloging-in-Publication Data

Magendie, Kathryn.
   Tender graces / Kathryn Magendie.
      p. cm.
   ISBN 978-1-60285-582-3 (library binding : alk. paper)
   1. Family--Fiction. 2. West Virginia--Fiction. 3. Louisiana--Fiction.
   4. Large type books. I. Title.

PS3613.A3438T46 2009
813'.6--dc22

2009025562

To the Angels:
Our Beloved David, Annabelle, and Granny

Ay, to the proof; as mountains are for winds,
That shake not, though they blow perpetually.

William Shakespeare

Grandma Faith wavers in the mists, the wolf calls, the owl flies, the mountain is. Up up I go on Fionadala's back, her hooves thundering. I see my child's eyes only, through the closet keyhole, dark eyes are open, then closed. Thundering hooves, up the mountain we ride. At the ridge I stop, take Momma from my pack. And there, with mountain song rising, with fog wetting, with Fionadala nodding her head, with the fiddles of the old ghosts of old mountain men crying, with the voices of all I've lost and all I've gained, with the mountains cradling, with the West Virginia soil darkening my feet, with Momma's cry of "Do It!" I open her vessel, and as I twirl, turning turning turning, I let her out—she flies out with a sigh, with forty thousand sighs. As I come to rest, she settles upon me, settles upon the trees and mountain and rock, settles, then is finally stilled. The owl cries, the wolf calls, the mountain is, Grandma Faith nods. Momma is a part of it all now.

Chapter 1
Today

All my tired flies out the window when I see Grandma Faith standing in the mountain mists that drift in and out of the trees. She's as she was before, like one lick of fire hasn't touched her, whole and alive and wanting as she beckons to me. Grandma whispers her wants as she's done all my life.

I put my hand out the car window as Momma used to do, and say "Wheeee . . ." then holler to the owl flying in the night, "I'm Virginia Kate, and I'm a crazy woman." He keeps his wings spread to find his supper. I don't feel silly one bit. I rush headlong into the night in my gray Subaru, a tangible addition to the darkness. The tires seem to hover above the road as if like the owl I am also flying. I could let loose my hand from the steering wheel and my car would find its way to a little holler that lies in the shadow of the mountain. Inside the unused ashtray my cell phone lies silent, for I've turned it off, pushed it into the little drawer, closed it as much as I could. I am in no mood for voices telling me any more bad things.

The last time I allowed it to ring, Uncle Jonah had called and said, "Come home and fetch your momma." I haven't called West Virginia *home* for longer than what's good, but I left before light to do as he said without giving myself time to think too hard on it.

Grandma Faith used to say, "Ghosts and spirits weave around the living in these mountains. They try to tell us things, warn us of what's ahead, or try to move us on towards something we need to do. But most of all, they want us to remember."

Momma never told stories much, since it hurt to do it. She said looking behind a person only makes them trip and fall. I understand why now in a way I didn't as a girl.

I touch the journal Momma sent two weeks ago. I should have gone to her right after I read her letter, but I was too ornery for my own good, always have been. I didn't want her to think she could crook her finger and have me scurry back to West Virginia after she gave me up as she did when I was a girl who needed her momma. I had set my teeth to her words and carried on with my own business.

Momma wrote, *I know you'd want to have this diary from your Grandma seeing how you are two peas in a pod. I made a few notes alongside hers. She didn't have everything written down, so I had to fix parts of it. Come soon. I got lots to talk about. Things I reckon will explain what the notes in the diary won't.*

I wrote back, *Dear Momma, I'm busy. You can mail my stuff to me (I'm enclosing a check that should be more than plenty for postage). You have your nerve writing me after all this time and expecting me to drop everything. That's all I have to say right now. Signed, Virginia Kate.*

I didn't open the diary until a week later. And only then because Grandma took up to poking at me until I had enough.

Now I'm full of regret. Momma didn't tell me she was so sick; how was I to know? And the diary notes would have changed things, changed the way I thought about my momma. I'm almost to the West Virginia state line, but I already know it's too late for Momma and me.

In Grandma Faith's journal is the story of how Momma and Daddy met. How I began. In the pages are tucked pictures—one of Grandma with me on her lap, another one of Momma when she was a young girl of seventeen, and one of my parents after they were married in 1954. The journal burns my right palm warm as I rub the tooled leather and pass the sign that welcomes me to the state of West Virginia. But I don't need the sign to tell me. The pull of my mountain calls me home. Oh, how I've missed these mountains, even when I didn't know I did. They'd been tucked away inside, hiding behind my heart, pulsing with my blood. Waiting for me.

Between Pocahontas and Summers County, where Momma was born, where Grandma Faith lived and then died on her own mountain, I look up

11

and beyond at my heritage. All the mystery, all the secrets, all the loss and gain of our lives.

When Momma was a girl, she ran on the mountain wild and dirty until my daddy came to fetch her away. I can well imagine Momma the day she met Daddy, from Momma's scrawled notes off to the side of Grandma's slanted ones. I see my momma just as clear as if I were there myself. The old house perched on the mountain, and Daddy walking up to knock on their door.

I shake away the memories so I can concentrate on what's ahead. The address Uncle Jonah gave me is easy to find, right off the highway. I park, go inside to fetch Momma, walk with my head up and my feet clomping hard. There's no one else here. I'm alone.

Grandma Faith says, "No, you are not alone. I'm here."

When I see how it is with Momma, I'm relieved she made Uncle Jonah take care of things before I got here. But it makes her even more unreal as I put her in the car with me and set my wheels turning towards the little white house where we all lived for a time, where Momma stayed behind alone when she let us go, one by one. I take her around the curves, down the long weaving road, between mountain and memory. Then I'm there. The two hills stand guard over the holler; my headlights glow before me as I pull into the dirt driveway.

Nothing has changed.

My sweet sister mountain waits, mysterious in the moonlight, rising up as it always did. I get out of the car and take deep breaths of clean summer air, listen to the night insects and frogs call to each other, and remember a lonely girl, who grew up to be a hopeful woman. Holding tight to Momma, I walk into the door of my childhood home and the ghosts of a thousand hurts, loves, wants, and lives rush against me. I hug on to her so I won't drop her, and say, "Momma, I'm home again."

She doesn't say, "Stay awhile."

"You can't send me away this time, Momma." But I know she can. She sent me away twice before.

I hurry through the shadowed house, straight to my room. I'm stunned. It's still the same. I place Momma on my dresser, say, "There Momma. There." I turn my back to her, head out to my car again. Outside, the cool air clears my head. Once my bags are from car to room, I don't bother unpacking. Now that I'm here, I want to leave soon as I can.

I open the window and breathe in earth and child-hood smells. A breeze lifts my hair and plays with the strands. The mountains are shadows in the distance and I shout, just to spite Momma, "Hello! Remember me? I'm home!"

I hear an echoing, "Stay awhile, Virginia Kate." Maybe it's only the rustle of leaves, the blowing of wind, but I smile to possibility. Pretending I'm brave, I open the journal to the page with my parents' picture and read Grandma's slanting words, along with Momma's scrawled additions, by moonlight.

Our mothers and their mothers and the mothers before them do the same things over and again, even if in differing ways. Not me. I close the journal. A blast of wind rushes in, pushes against me, and causes something from the nightstand to fall over. It's the Popsicle-stick photo frame Micah made me. My hands grow warm and tingly. The photo inside is of Micah, Andy, and me, grinning without a bit of sense. The Easter picture. We're all dressed up—with bare dirty feet—and my bonnet is tilted on my head ready to fall off. We look so happy it makes my stomach clench.

Grandma urges, "Go to the attic, little mite. More waits."

I put the frame back, and go out to the hall. The stairs make the same loud scrangy sound as I pull them down, the same rattle as I climb. Daddy's old flashlight still hangs on the nail at the entrance, and I use it to look around. There are Christmas ornament boxes, book boxes, unmarked boxes, and a box with *Easter* written in big black ink.

Inside *Easter*, folded in tissue paper, is Momma's green dress, her hatbox with the wide-brimmed hat, and her white gloves. I recall Momma sashaying down the church aisle while everyone stared at her, dim bulbs in the bright shine of her light. I press

Momma's dress to my face and inhale deep. Shalimar. I still smell it. I put everything back before too many things are remembered too soon.

Shining the light in a corner, I find the dirty-finger-printed white box. My Special Things Box. I pick my way over to it, and cradling it in my arms like a baby, take it down with me. Up and down the rickety stairs I go with pictures and mementos, until I have the things I want scattered about my room. I know now I'll stay until I finish the remembering.

When I open my dresser drawer to put away things from my suitcase, some of my childhood clothing is still there. Underneath the white cotton panties there is more—letters, notes, and smoothed creek stones, tucked away as if I just put them there. Inside the cedar robe are two dresses I never wore unless Momma made me. I pick up the Mary Janes and see my sad in the shine.

The room is filled to overflowing with the past—like a broken family reunion. It's hard to suck in air; the bits of ghost-dust choke me. My eyes water, but I know it's not time to cry. Grandma Faith wants me to remember, not to weep. She knows about truth and the pain it can heap on you if you keep hiding from it. Momma knows now, too, I bet.

I say in my croaked voice, "Crying is for weaklings. Crying is for little girls in pigtails." I know I speak strong to the spirits who are watching me. I want to show them what I'm made of. I do.

I empty my Special Things Box onto the quilt. Inside are items I thought important when I was innocent. I up-end paper sacks, a cigar box, envelopes, *Easter*. I'm a crazy searching woman as I go through years in a gulp. The wind blows in and scatters papers. I hear laughter. Everything is willy-nilly as if there's no beginning and no end.

All around me are child's drawings, Daddy's old Instamatic camera, photographs, a silver-handled mirror and comb set without the brush, school notebooks, river and creek rocks, letters, diaries, a bit of Spanish moss, whispers, lies, truths, crushed maple leaves, regrets, red lipstick, losses, loves, a piece of coal—all emptied from dark places.

Everything will be emptied from dark places, even the urn of ashes full of Momma's spirit that can't be contained. Momma always said she never wanted anyone to see her look ugly, and Momma would think *dead* was ugliest of all. She made Uncle Jonah burn her down before anyone could say goodbye. That's what she wanted, that's how she is.

I stop my mad tossing aside, pick up a photo of Grandma standing next to her vegetable garden. She's holding Momma when she was a baby. The same West Virginia breeze that rustles the secrets on my bed pushes Grandma's dress against her long legs. The sun behind her shows the outline of her body. I can sense the smiles that would be there if she had been given a chance to breathe. She reaches out to me. We are connected by our blood and love of words and truth. She's chosen me to be the storyteller. I can feel her. I can.

I will start with a beginning, before I slid down the moon and landed in my momma's arms, those same arms that let me go without telling me why, or at least a why I wanted to hear.

"The stories are made real by the telling," Grandma whispers.

I smell apples and fresh-baked bread. I inhale them into my marrow.

Gazing out the open window, I wish on falling stars of hope. Far off a flash of lightning breaks through the night—a coming storm? I want to remember my life as falls, springs, and summers. I don't like seeing things in the winter's dead and cold. I'm like Momma that way.

I situate myself cross-legged on the bed and the ghosts guide my hands where they need to go. I dig deep into the secrets. I will begin with Momma and Daddy the day they met. The beginning of them is the beginning of me. I hear a hum of voices, like dragonflies and cicadas buzzing.

I'll record our lives, my life, as Grandma Faith wants me to. I look out my childhood window at the moon and the stars, at my mountain, at the rest of my life stretched before me, and the one behind me. Spirits urge me; a clear path opens, up to the top.

My life begins again.

Chapter 2
Out, out, brief candle!
1954-1961

The air smelled clean and new and ripe. Ghosts of old mountain men looked after lost children, their lullaby whispers blowing through the trees that grew wild and deep into the mountainside. It was a day when nothing bad could happen. A day thick with good things to come. The day my parents, Frederick Hale Carey and Katie Ivene Holms, met and fell deep and hard into each other.

Momma looked as if she came from an ancient palace in Egypt instead of a slanted house deep on a mountain in West Virginia. She didn't belong, even with her thin cotton dresses and dirty bare feet. Everyone knew it. It was in the pictures buried in Grandma Faith's journals. It was in the men's faces whenever my momma sashayed by, leaving her trail of Shalimar and sex. It was in Daddy's face when he met her across Grandma Faith's kitchen table.

She was barely eighteen and he was well into twenty-two when they eloped on a stormy Saturday afternoon. Didn't matter to Grandpa, he was tired of chasing off boys who howled outside his daughter's window as if she was a dog in heat. One less hungry mouth. One less womb to worry about some boy filling while under his nickel,

18

that's what Grandpa always harped on about. Grandma only wanted something good to happen for her daughter. Something good meant anything different. Momma was ready to leave. She was always itchy with a restless spirit.

Daddy had made his way up the old logging trail to sell his kitchen utensils. He cleared his throat and knocked on the beat-up door. Old one-eared Bruiser sniffed his britches, let out a huff, and crawled under the house, his days of chasing away strangers long a memory. Daddy kept his back straight as he tipped his hat to the dark-eyed woman who answered the door. Her face had been pretty once, but life had placed lines of worry and sadness over her pretty. She held one hand on her hip, and the other on the door, ready to slam it against him. Her dark hair came loose from its bun, long thick strands whirling in the breeze.

Daddy flashed his good white teeth to her, said, "Ma'am, before you close the door, I want you to think about the last meal you cooked."

"The last meal I cooked?"

"Yes Ma'am." Daddy used his Gregory Peck voice. He always said no woman could resist The Peck Voice. "I have kitchen conveniences, right here in my case. May I enter your lovely home?"

"Well, I reckon you better come on inside before you drop everything." She stood back, smiled, said, "By the by, I'm Faith Holms."

"Frederick Hale Carey at your service, Ma'am."

He followed Grandma to the kitchen, and flipped the case open onto the kitchen table.

Grandma ran an index finger over the wooden spoons, spatulas, hand mixers, and sharp shiny knives.

Momma came in from the woods and sat in the chair across from Daddy. She tucked one leg under her, and slowly swung the other back and forth, pretending to be bored.

"That's my daughter, Katie Ivene." Grandma picked up a spatula and two wooden spoons and put them aside. "I'll take these, Frederick." From the glass flour jar, she took a small linen bag that held the money she made selling salt-rising bread and apple butter, counted out the right amount, handed it to Daddy with flour-dusted fingers. She tried not to think about how much more bread she'd have to bake or how many more apples she'd have to cook to make enough money to replace what she'd given Frederick. Some things had to be done. Even if it meant a longer wait to cross that door for the last time. Even if it meant one more day, or two, or three—as many as it took. She asked, "Why don't you come back for Sunday supper, at five?"

"I would be honored, Ma'am." Daddy tore his eyes off Momma while he closed the clasp and the sale. "Thank you, and I'll be seeing you on Sunday then."

"And we'll be setting here waiting for you."

Momma swung that leg, a smirk pulling at her full lips. Her black hair spilled over her shoulders in a wild mess, her cheekbones rode high, her eyes dark as an undiscovered pyramid, and her skin when scrubbed clean of mountain dirt was smooth and fine with possibility. There was an electric feel in that kitchen that day and Katie Ivene throbbed with it.

The next day, Grandma took more of her secret money to buy her daughter material for a dress. It was a long walk to town, and the townsfolk didn't much like her kind, but Grandma had a mission, a way out for her best daughter, and that was that. There'd always been talk about Grandma Faith's momma. The whispers of how her daddy had married what they called a mixed breed. When Grandma Faith asked her daddy what her blood was mixed with, he'd only grabbed her in a hug and said, "Why, your blood is mixed with sugar, honey." And he'd tickle her and get her to laughing and she'd forget about her momma being just a little bit darker than her daddy, just a bit. She'd forget how people whispered. Grandma Faith would forget how her momma told her to stop asking questions for things that didn't need answers. Life was supposed to be about mysteries, was what Grandma Faith's momma always said, just like her momma had said to her, same as her momma before her, just like Grandma Faith would tell her own.

Grandma Faith considered the life she led on the mountain away from her long gone parents and knew that crying wouldn't do a soul a bit of good. She sucked up the tears into her body and imagined her insides were drowning, while her outsides cracked open like a dry desert. She concentrated on her task of the moment—finding the perfect material for her daughter's way-off-the-mountain dress.

Momma chose red silky fabric, and draped it over her. Grandma watched her daughter twirl, looked at the price tag and her heart near fell to her toes. She squared back her shoulders. "Do you like that, Katie?"

"Oh, yes! I love red. Can I get some red lipstick, too?" Momma couldn't get her mind off the page with Ava Gardner grinning all pretty and fair-faced. She'd ripped it out of *The Saturday Evening Post* she'd found in her momma's underwear drawer. Momma folded and folded the page until it was small and fit inside her shoe; its pages were wrinkled and fading away. She took it out, smoothed it, showed it to Grandma Faith. Momma wanted lipstick just like that, but more red, brighter red, the reddest red. "See how pretty her lips look?" she asked. "I want to be pretty like a movie star."

"You're already pretty, Katie Ivene."

Momma stuck out her lip and widened her eyes.

"Well, I believe I have enough for some lipstick."

"And red nail polish? I can do my nails and my toes."

Grandma spilled a bit of her money from its pouch, touched the coins, felt how cold they were against her palm, how crisp and dry the dollar bills were as they scraped her skin.

"What about a scarf to match it up? And some high-heeled shoes?"

"Wear the scarf you have. And make do with the shoes you're wearing."

Momma pulled a face, but nodded.

The little bag of runaway money was almost emptied. Grandma worried about how long it would take to save that much again, but she sang mountain songs to my momma as they walked the long hard way back home, ignoring the stares from some who didn't like the mystery of their deep dark eyes, and skin that told of kin that once laid with forbidden love. They thought Grandpa Luke chose wrong, but it was Grandma Faith who'd made the wrong choices. She knew the unfairness of the world, knew that no matter how smart her daughter was, or how pretty, just like it had been for Grandma Faith, it could be for her daughter. She'd not have it.

Before light on Sunday, Grandma wrung her best chicken's neck. She told it, "I'm sorry, chicken." It was the way of her life. She remembered suppers with her parents, how they bought their chickens already cleaned from the butcher. Then her daddy died when his big heart gave out too soon.

Grandma Faith's momma was lost to dark winds that blew her farther and farther away from Grandma Faith. Soon after, Luke had come round from the church to help fix the porch. He was big and strong. He sang songs and played the harmonica. He hid his meanness with skill. He was there with promises when Grandma Faith's momma tore out of the old hurting world to search for what she'd lost.

She put the bird in boiling water to prepare for plucking. On the counter were fresh vegetables; a loaf of bread baked in the oven. While she cooked, she hoped Grandpa Luke would eat and drink just enough to be too sleepy to put his hands on her again. Those hands that fixed porches and stroked her face made stronger statements once Grandma Faith had no one to turn to.

Grandpa Luke had tried beating the babies from Grandma Faith at first. His fists made the first two children, a girl and a boy, come out strong jawed and ornery. He told her the third one was born dead, wrapped its twisted body in his oily flannel shirt, and buried it in the woods. But Grandma thought she heard a pitiful mewling as he left the room and that sound would haunt her to her last thought. While Grandpa scraped the burial dirt from his fingernails, Grandma had cried.

She mourned until Grandpa Luke was sick of seeing her tears. After that, his fists let her be for a spell, and her next three children, two boys and a girl, came out pointy-chinned and pretty, but still ornery—especially the girl babe Katie Ivene.

While Grandma fixed that Sunday supper, Momma scrubbed away the layer of fine West Virginia soil and then put on the new dress Grandma Faith had sewn. It hugged her body, straining against her high breasts. She said, "Will you brush out my hair?"

"You smell like roses." Grandma pulled the silver-handled brush through Momma's thick hair.

"He won't care what I smell like." Momma grinned. Oh, she knew things.

"Men care. Least ways most do."

"He'll be too busy noticing other things, I expect." Momma knew her worth.

That afternoon, Daddy whistled up the path wearing a gray suit and hat, white shirt, dark tie, and shoes shined within an inch of their leather. He held roses in one hand, a box of fancy dark chocolates in the other, and a burning hunger deep in his belly. In his pocket was a small book of Shakespeare's plays. He shouted to Bruiser, "Let slip the dogs of war!" Bruiser licked himself and yawned.

During supper, Grandma watched Momma toss her hair, watched her chew with her mouth closed as she'd been taught. The only sound was the clinking of their forks and knives against the plate, and Grandpa's grunting as he chewed with his mouth gaping. The others watched Daddy with interested darkling eyes. Daddy barely touched his supper, his appetite for one thing only.

Grandma asked, "Frederick, tell me about Shakespeare."

"You want to know, really?"

Grandma Faith considered how Daddy thought mountain people didn't care about such things. She wanted to tell him how mountain people cared deep to their bones, and they read books, and loved, and were strong. They weren't stupid or backwards—the mountains were just like every-where else in the world, with good and bad and what lay in the middle of the two.

In between bites of crispy chicken, Daddy prattled away to Grandma about Shakespeare—it was as if they were all old friends, she and Daddy and William.

After the plates were cleaned, Momma said, "Frederick, take me for a walk."

Grandma stilled Momma with a hand. "Katie, be mindful."

"Oh, don't get yourself all in a worry mood." She led Daddy out the door.

Grandma cried out to Momma, but quiet inside herself, *Wait! You're my little girl. Come back.* But she had to let them go. The mountain ghosts sighed with her.

While Momma walked with Daddy, Grandpa Luke snored under the hickory tree, and the other children ran wild, Grandma wrote, *I thought I would be a school teacher like my papa. I never thought I'd have to kill a chicken with my hands. Please let Frederick be a good man for my Katie.* She knew if Grandpa ever found her words, he'd fall into a bull-snorting-rage. He didn't like it that his wife was smart. He didn't like it when she read books and tried to teach her children better ways.

Before she could stop the shameful thoughts, Grandma Faith let herself imagine she was young again, pretended her life was just beginning with someone handsome and good. Her pen moved across the page with its guilty slanted lines of imagining, while Momma and Daddy slipped into the woods, out of Grandma's view, but not out of her inner-sight.

And there, under a buckeye tree, Momma kissed Daddy until their hearts beat fast and eager.

He said to her, "You're beautiful," and she laughed. She knew she was.

And when they reached the secret clearing that never stayed a secret, Momma unbuttoned the dress and let it puddle to the ground. She wore nothing underneath but her want. She stood before Daddy with her shoulders thrown back, her body tall and proud, her painted toes without shoes. She reached up, untied the red scarf that almost matched the red dress and her hair fell heavy, swinging against the swell of her hips. Her tongue was coated with honey when she said, "Come here, Frederick."

My momma showed him what she'd learned from the howling boys, from the last salesman to sneak by, from the woman in town, from her Uncle Jeeter. Momma had learned so well, that after that Sunday, Daddy came back almost every day, his eyes shining with the grand fortune of it all. He brought chocolates, flowers, fancy writing paper and fancy pens for Momma's brothers and sister, and lots of pretty words—as if he owed offerings in return for Momma's gifts. Unknown to all but Momma, she had already received a secret gift inside her body.

Daddy gave Grandma a Shakespeare book, with a note inside, *All the world's a stage, and all the men and women merely players. Enjoy this book, Faith.* Grandma Faith loved the heaviness of the words, and after Grandpa went to bed, she read it by moonlight.

Another supper, Grandma stopped chopping onions for her special gravy and said from prideful memory, " 'To-morrow and to-morrow and to-morrow, creeps in this petty pace from day to day, to the last syllable of recorded time; and all our yesterdays have lighted fools the way to dusty death.' "

And Daddy finished, " 'Out, out, brief candle!' "

While they laughed, Grandpa Luke grunted and picked through a box of chocolates with his dirty fingers. He didn't care about words or beauty. Momma's sister Ruby stuffed her mouth full next, chocolate oozing from her teeth as she grinned. Brother Hank hurried and grabbed a few for himself. Brother Jonah, Momma, and little brother Ben had what was left. That's how the order went according to who looked or who acted like which parent.

Momma thumbed through the book. "Who's this Shakesfool think he is anyway?"

Daddy thought she was so cute, that very night he proposed, right in front of the Holms' clan.

No more than a flea's breath later, down the mountain Momma followed him, carrying a busted up brown suitcase with two dresses—a blue one and the red one—three pair of cotton underwear, her stockings and high-heeled shoes Daddy bought her, and a head full of big dreams.

In shades of dark and light caught by the camera, Momma and Daddy stood in front of the Statue of Liberty. Daddy's hand slung over Momma's shoulder, his fingers brushing her breast. His dark hair fell into his eyes as he looked into the lens. Momma stared off to the side as if she couldn't wait to get back to the excitement of New York. Her hair was unbound and messy and it suited her best.

After the honeymoon, they stayed in West Virginia, moving into a little white house in a holler not too far from Grandma Faith, but not too close. Seven months later, out slipped Micah Dean. Afterwhile came me, Virginia Kate. Next,

Andrew Charles. Daddy sent Grandma letters and photos. We all visited Grandma on Sundays, eating at the same scarred kitchen table where my parents met.

I loved the visiting.

Until Grandma died in a house fire.

Some folks in town said she soaked the outside of the house in kerosene, lit the brush, then laid inside to wait, her heart heavy from losing her children, one by one, by trick or trade they left. Others whispered their own gossip about mean Grandpa Luke throwing one final ugly stomping fit.

Her last words in the diary read, *Luke found my run-away money. Things are bad. I'll send my secret words to Katie for her to keep.*

And many words were left in the dark. Until I set them free.

Chapter 3
Curtain's closed, Mr. Shakeybaby
1963

From my window, I waved and blew sugar-sweet mountain a kiss. A fat wind blew in and I smelled a storm coming. I ran to the kitchen, sat at the table and grinned up at Momma. She wore her blue housedress and white slippers, and her hair looked like mine, all messy, long, and dark. Andy sat across from me eating a biscuit, jelly smeared around his silly mouth. Momma didn't fuss at him like she usually did. She wiped his mouth and asked me, "Where's our Micah?"

"Want me to go get him, Momma?" I gave her my I'm-ready-to-do-whatever-you-ask look.

She shook her head. "Oh, let him sleep, he'll get up when he's hungry."

When she brought me a cup of milk, I sniffed, but I didn't smell anything funny to bring on her happy mood. I thought the day was going to be smooth as creek pebbles. Until Daddy came in and riled up Momma.

Daddy was already dressed in tan britches and a white shirt, his hair combed back from his face with hair-grease. He poured himself a cup of black coffee and sat by me. Momma winked at him, and put two biscuits and a big glob of gravy in front of him. He cut into his biscuit and said, "Guess I better come out with it."

"Come out with what?" Momma asked, while she finally gave me my breakfast.

Daddy bit, chewed, swallowed, cleared his throat, sipped coffee, swallowed.

"I said, *what*, Frederick."

"Mother is arriving today."

Momma turned to Daddy so fast I thought her head would fall off. "She's coming here? Today? And you didn't let me know?"

"Because you'd pester me about it."

Momma fixed herself a plate, sat across from

Daddy, and stared him down. She said, "She'll pick over every speck of dust."

"I bet she has presents for everyone." He wiggled his eyebrows and bit into his biscuit.

"Oh goody." Momma pushed her plate away.

Micah came in with his hair on end, rubbing his cranky eyes. He fixed his own breakfast and sat down. There was black on his fingers and a bit of yellow on his cheek. He'd stayed up making pictures again. His nostrils went in and out, his sign that things were stupid.

"You can say good morning, Mister Micah," Momma said.

"'Morning, Momma." Micah slapped five pounds of butter on his biscuit.

Daddy hitched up a sigh, said, "Mother adores you, Katie."

"She loves her itty bitty mommy's boy is what she loves." She sucked her thumb, popped it out, said, "Waah Waah, I'm a mommy's boy."

Daddy put his finger in the air, about to say something smart, but Momma didn't let him.

"You bake the cake, Frederick." She got up, opened the cabinet and took something from it I couldn't see, but knew what it was. She poured a bit in her coffee, and said, "That woman rides me to drink."

Daddy gulped his breakfast and left to take his walk down the road to get away from Momma before she could whop him with her mean words.

After the dishes were done, Momma went to her bedroom to primp. I sneaked my feet quiet into her room until I was next to her at her vanity table. Her slip was extra white against her skin and I wanted to touch her, but I didn't. The window was open and Momma's flowered curtains danced, twisting around themselves, then coming apart. I heard my name whispered and cater-cocked my head to listen; no one was there so maybe it was only the wind knocking over Momma's glass swans on the bedside table.

Momma went to shut the window and her slip blew against her body. "My lord it's looking like a bad storm coming. I hope the creek don't flood again."

Outside, my favorite sugar maple looked like a picture on the wall. The leaves waved at me, but I didn't wave back with Momma there. She set up her tipped-over birds, patted her bedspread, and hit the throw pillows until they were big and fluffy. "Last time the creek flooded bad, I found Mrs. Mendel's cat floating in the backyard, drowned dead."

Sometimes Momma said creek like *crick*, and said other things in ways that Daddy made her say another way until she had it right. He did that with us kids, too.

"Your Daddy picked the kitty up and dried it with a towel before he carried it on over to her. Pitiful. Mrs. Mendel cried and cried." She sat back down, picked up her silver brush, and pulled it through her hair. Pieces flew away, as if her hair wanted to run off from her head. She asked me, "What're you staring at?" But she already knew. Everyone stared at Momma. She put down her brush and held my chin in her hand. Her cool fingers made me feel sleepy. "You look like my momma and your daddy. I was hoping you'd look like me."

She patted the bench. I climbed up beside her. "Did I tell you how you come to be named?"

I nodded.

She dipped her finger in the Pond's jar, and then rubbed a dab of cream into her face. "Well, I expect I can tell you again, can't I?"

I leaned against her, hoping she wouldn't scoot away from me. She picked up her tube of lipstick and twisted the bottom until a bit of the color poked up. She liked to keep the tip nice and round. She dabbed the color on one side of her top lip, then the other side, and then pressed her lips to let the red bleed onto the bottom. She patted with her pinkie finger to make it all evened up. I put my lips together—was her lipstick cool and smooth, or sticky and warm? I wished she'd kiss me on the cheek so I could find out.

"You came in the heat of summer. Lord, I thought I'd die." She held up her hair while she opened a dresser drawer and dug around. Momma showed me the picture where she held baby me in one arm. Her lips were open and she looked straight at the camera. "If it'd been up to your daddy, your name would be Laudine Kate. Lord help you." Momma shook her head back and forth. "I decided on Virginia Kate Carey after your grandma Virginia Faith, and me. It's a part of my family bush."

I liked being named after both of them. I grinned and prissed at myself in the mirror.

"Your great grandma named your grandma Virginia Faith after West Virginia and Jesus. Isn't that the silliest thing you ever heard?" She sipped her drink with the lemon slice bobbing around, rolled her eyes and said, "We won't talk about your grandma." She put the photo back in the drawer.

I wanted to say how Grandma smelled like fresh-baked bread and apples. She had puppies under her smokehouse I petted, and she let me pound up the bread dough for supper. I loved her best of all and wished she wasn't so dead, even if she did come visit me when nobody else was around.

"Your daddy called you Baby Bug." Momma patted herself with her powder puff and little clouds of Shalimar tickled my nose. "You're not supposed to be named after a creepy crawly."

I touched some of the powder on my leg and rubbed it in good so I'd smell like Momma.

"If it weren't for babies, I might have gone on back to school and your daddy could've finished college—but we don't regret our kids."

Daddy came into the room, squeezed Momma's

arms, and then kissed me on the top of my head. He asked, "What are you so talkative about?"

"How we came to name Virginia Kate a classical name instead of a barnyard name."

"I do believe that's the incorrect use of the word 'classical'."

"Well la tee dah, Mr. Smarty Britches."

Daddy winked at me. "What's in a name? That which we call a rose by any other word would smell as sweet."

"That's the stupidest shit I ever heard."

"Shakespeare? The greatest writer ever?" Daddy's smile fell away.

Momma pushed me with her shoulder. "So you say."

"Your mother loved to hear me quote him."

"Whoop de doo-eth. You and your Shakesbeard. And what does my momma got to do with any-thing?" She dipped out more cream and rubbed it on her legs. "Leave her be."

"Your mother was a fine woman, and you know it, Katie."

"Yeah, that's why she burned herself up. Argument's over, oh husbandeth of mineth. Zip zippo endo, curtain's closed, Mr. Shakeybaby."

Daddy walked out. Momma stood up and put on the blue-and-white sundress and white sandals Daddy bought for her.

I stood up and did a twirl. "Did you fuss all the time with Daddy before I got born?"

"What kind of question is that? Go brush your hair." She gave me a little shove. "I want all of us looking good when that woman gets here. She picks apart worse than a vulture."

I went hunting for Micah. He was always doing something interesting. When I passed the kitchen, I watched Daddy put ice cubes and a hunk of booze in a glass. After a long swallow, his face turned happy. While he looked out the window, he drank the rest down.

I went in and tugged on his sleeve. Sometimes I felt shy around him since he was bigger than everything.

He smiled down at me, said, "There you are. Want to come outside with me and the boys?"

I nodded.

He picked me up and swung me around. He was the strongest man in the world. I snuggled my face in his chest and smelled Old Spice and that smell shirts get when they've been on the line. He said, "Let's go, Bitty Bug."

Outside, the wind blew my hair behind me. I sniffed the air for Mrs. Mendel's flowers. Mrs. Mendel was our only neighbor in our holler. She had wild hair she tried to keep piled in a bun on top her head. The bun was big enough for her cat to sleep in. The hill on one side of us had an empty house on it, and on the other far side of the hill, an old lady lived alone with her million parakeets. The front of our house faced the long road going out of our holler and the back faced my mountain. My mountain was giant-tall where I couldn't see what was on the other side.

I saw all this while not really seeing it because Micah chased me around the house. The wind kept pushing me back, and my big brother was right on my heels, hollering, "I'm going to catch you!"

I ran until I thought my lungs would bust.

Daddy held Andy on his shoulders and they laughed at us when we fell on the grass, our feet burning from running so fast. A slow rain came and it felt good, until Daddy said, "That's it children, time to go inside." I wanted to stay and let the rain fall on me, see the clouds on the mountains like a fairy story, but I knew Momma wouldn't let me.

When Grandmother Laudine drove up in her shiny black Chevrolet pickup truck with her umpteenth husband she'd asked us to call Uncle Runt, the rain had turned into the skinny stinging kind. I watched out the open door as Grandmother blobbered towards me. She hollered back to Runt and the storm took her words out of her mouth and scattered them to far away places. Runt went back to the truck while Grandmother barreled into our living room. We kids lined up to get a good look at her.

She wore a pink pantsuit with pockets the size of my head, tissues sticking up in one and a bottle of Milk of Magnesia in the other. Her britches stopped above her ankles, and she had on pink bobby socks with lace, and white tenny shoes with pink shoelaces. Her hair wasn't hers at all, but a big poofy wig that held raindrops like sparkly diamonds. When she hugged on me, she smelled like Vicks VapoRub.

When Runt came in looking like a wet chihuahua, holding on to more bags and suitcases, she said, "Don't you look a sight, Uncle Runt." He set their things on the floor and stood there like the rest of us, waiting to see what Grandmother would do next.

Daddy grinned as if he thought she was as cute as a two-hundred-pound kitten.

Grandmother put her hand to her ear. "Don't y'all have some bluegrass playing? Isn't this West By Gawd-damned Virginia?"

Momma put her hands on her hips. "What're you talking about, Laudine?"

"Well, I come near across the world and y'all aren't playing bluegrass music. Isn't that what y'all West Virginians do in the mountains?"

Grandmother turned her back on Momma's eyerolling. We kids were hypnotized by her, like in the movies where the vampire makes people do whatever he wants just by looking at them. She grunted, and stooped over to open the wet bags while my brothers and I crowded in. In the bags were plates with outlines of the states, snow globes, cedar boxes with the towns written on top, pecan rolls, and other doodads. She gave each of us a snow globe from Kentucky and a cedar box from Tennessee.

Daddy said, "Glad you could come, Mother."

"You are too far from home, son."

Daddy was born in Plano, Texas. Momma called it Plain-Old-Texas, but Grandmother Laudine didn't think so. Texas was where she lived and always would, she said with every breath.

To rile Grandmother Laudine, Momma interrupted her stories about Texas by singing a line from our state song, "Oh, the West Virginia hills, how majestic and how grand!"

Our state *was* grand, except maybe in the coal mines. In Daddy's books, I saw the pictures of men blacked up with coal dust. Their lungs were blacked with it, too. I wanted to go down with a wash rag and wipe the coal off their faces, give them a drink of water and a sandwich. Momma said they'd be too proud.

Grandmother settled in my room. I had to stay on a pallet between Micah and Andy's beds with their rootin' tootin' cowboy bedspreads. Before we fell asleep, Grandmother sneaked in and tacked up a picture of Jesus, but the next morning, Momma took it down and stuck Jesus in the junk drawer.

From the start, Grandmother Laudine took over things. She was set to get Momma's goat, especially in the kitchen. She whumped her rear against the table so many times, it scratched up Momma's wall.

"You, daughter-in-law, listen to Laudine. This

here's how you make a man happy—" She eagle-eyed Momma up and down. "—in his stomach area." Using a big wood spoon, she pushed around the onions and garlic cooking in the skillet. "Right, Uncle Runt? I taught him everything he knows."

Runt didn't say a thing.

"You see here what I'm doing, little Virginia Kate?" Grandmother stopped and put her hand on her hip. "Now, you know, Katie, I still don't understand why this girl wasn't named after me. Got my feelings in a world of hurt for a while."

"You'll get over it," Momma said.

Grandmother cut her eyes to me. "See how things are done in the kitchen, Laudine Kate Virginia?"

I nodded, but real slow.

"I know how to cook, Laudine." Momma fetched her pink-and-black circle glass.

"You people up here in the mountains don't season! Right, Uncle Runt? Y'all can't taste your food. Tastes all the same, like nothing."

Momma slammed the cabinet door, rattling the bottles she'd hid before Grandmother came.

"My son is slurping up good old Texas cooking like he's starved." She poked the potato salad, then slopped in mustard. She stirred it around and the potatoes turned a pretty yellow. She said, "I think we'll need more taters, Uncle Runt, this salad is too gold."

Runt picked up a potato and peeled. He looked over at me and crossed his eyes.

"You're so full of *it*, with an *s-h*, Laudine." Momma poured herself a glass of tea with extra help splashed in it, and went off into the living room. Grandmother followed Momma out, her mouth a straight line of ornery.

I was about to follow, when Runt stopped me with a grin that wrinkled up the whole left side of his face. He asked, "Want to taste my secret barbeque sauce?"

I waited, even though I was itchy with want to see Momma and Grandmother fight like two cats in a bag. He gave me a big spoon of it and I smacked my lips.

"It's good stuff, ain't it?"

I smiled and nodded, then ran to the living room.

". . . jealous of Mee Maw, Katie Ivene," Grandmother was saying.

"Mee Maw? Who in lord's name is that?"

She pulled herself up tall. "I am now Mee Maw."

Momma huffed out a breath, then said, "I'm calling you Laudine. Zip Zippo Endo."

"You're so dang-burned stubborn. How my son puts up with that stubborn mouth—" she sniffed— "is beyond me."

Momma hiked up her dress, just to peeve Mee Maw who was formerly Grandmother Laudine, and said, "I think your onions are burning, Mee Mee."

"Uncle Runt'll take care of it." She flopped on the couch and pulled down Momma's hem. "I see

42

why my son's so smitten. Food's the last thing on his mind."

Momma's mouth fell as far as it could, since her mouth had turned-up ends that were always up even when she wasn't happy. She said, "Virginia Kate, go outside and call your daddy and brothers to supper."

I walked slow so I could hear the rest of the fussing, but when I turned around to see what they were doing, Momma gave me That Look. I high-tailed it out the back door.

Outside, Daddy pushed Andy on the swing, and Andy's skinny legs went up and down to try to get the swing to go higher. Micah drew his pictures with his back resting against the maple. My daddy and brothers looked so good it made me happy. I broke the magic by yelling, "Come to supper. Grandmother Laudine is Mee Maw now."

At supper, Mee Maw opened her lips and flapped them stupid with all her silliness.

Andy asked, "MeeMer, why're you so fat?" He was so cute that Momma laughed and snorted during the rest of supper.

The day Mee Maw was to leave for home, Runt cooked a big breakfast. I went in to watch him, since he didn't fuss, and didn't ask me all kinds of questions. He said, "I'm making you a big cat-head biscuit, with a little extra sugar in it." He grinned that wrinkly grin again, handed me a lump of white, said, "Here. Nothing better than a little dough."

It tasted spongy, but sweet.

He patted my head. "You're not loud like most young'uns. I like that in a person."

Mee Maw came in. She shook her wiggy head towards the food. "Can't believe my son's wife won't eat bacon, or pork roast, or any kind of pig. Not natural at-tall. She'd never survive in Texas, not one whit."

"It's cause of Petal Puss," I said. But she didn't let me tell the story of Momma's pet pig that got eaten.

"Not natural," was all Mee Maw answered.

After breakfast, Mee Maw, the Queen of Everything, carried two bags in front of her with her head held high and a bit to the left, as if she really did wear a crown. She set a brown paper bag, and a smaller white one with toilet paper sticking out of the top, on the coffee table and *oh me*'d herself down on the couch. Momma scooted away from her.

From the brown bag, Mee Maw handed Micah a pack of paintbrushes and a tray to mix his paints. "Micah, one day you'll paint your Mee Maw and keep it where y'all can see me every day."

"Thanks, Grandmother Moo Moo," Micah said.

She gave Andy a stuffed rabbit with sewn-in eyes and a pink whiskered nose. "Don't that look sweet? And I'm not fat, I'm healthy."

"Thank yew, Meemer." Andy hugged the rabbit.

Next was Daddy's turn. "For my son, I hope for the day you'll come home where your own people are."

Daddy opened a box with cuff links shaped like the state of Texas. He said, " 'The undiscover'd country, from whose bourn no traveler returns'."

Momma snorted into her special tea.

My present was a soft purse with a quarter inside. I petted it, said, "Thank you, Mee Maw."

"That's real Texas cowhide there, Virginia Laudine Kate."

"Would you quit calling her Laudine?" Momma's face was red.

Mee Maw held out the white bag to Momma. "This is for the woman who married my son away from his people. But I forgive her for it."

Runt left the room.

"I'm happy you've forgiven me, Laudine. My heart's going pitty patter thump over it." She stared at the present as if it was a rattlesnake. Mee Maw shook it in Momma's face until she finally grabbed it from her. When she pulled out the toilet paper and looked at what was inside, Momma's eyes slit up. "You can kiss my West Virginia ass, Laudine." She jumped up and threw the whole bag in the garbage.

"Why I never—"

"Oh, you do, and all the time." Momma left the room.

Mee Maw stomped out the door with Daddy 'I'm sorrying' her all the way. I heard the truck fly off down the road.

Later, when Momma went to bed with a headache, I fished the sack out of the garbage. Inside was a picture of hyena-grinning Mee Maw, and two books—one on how to be a lady with good manners and the other on how to cook when you didn't know a thing about cooking. I hid Momma's presents under my bed until I could think of another hidey-place.

Poor Momma had a headache because she knew Mee Maw liked to make deals that changed things. I guessed we'd have to find out what her deal was when she was ready to make it.

Chapter 4
To flea or not to flea,
that's just a suggestion.

"I don't need my husband climbing up some other woman's mountain, you hear?"

"I don't climb mountains anymore, Katie."

"I expect you might if it suits you."

Daddy wore his snarky grin.

Momma stared at him, tapping her foot.

"Katie, I sell things. I do okay for us, don't I?"

"There's other jobs you can do. Ones that don't take you away from your family."

She didn't give up because she knew he would.

Sure enough, Daddy found a job as manager of the five and dime. He said we'd go to a restaurant in Charleston to make merry over it. It was the first time ever we kids left the holler that far. Momma wore a pencil skirt and a sweater that hugged on her tight. She said I had to wear a dress even though Micah and Andy didn't have to spruce up.

I asked, "Why can't I wear Micah's old britches?"

She brushed out my hair too hard. "You don't have a lick of sense. Go put on your dress and quit whining."

In Charleston, men turned their heads to watch Momma.

"I told you all the men would notice my gals." Daddy winked at me, even though they never looked at me.

Momma patted her teased-up hair. "Oh? They noticed? I didn't see them looking at me one speck."

We kids ate fried chicken and smashed potatoes with gravy. Daddy and Momma ate steaks like queens and kings. For dessert, we had chocolate cake.

After, at home, I tore off my dress and shoes and put on my white gown with the lace that scratched my neck. I was working on getting the lace off, bit by bit. It was halfway gone and Momma hadn't noticed. I hurried to the television so I wouldn't miss Beaver doing something funny, but all that was on was that gum commercial.

Daddy whistled and wiggled his eyebrows. "Oh, those Doublemint Troublemint Twins." Then he tore into a yappity-booze-lips mood. "Well, the sales life is over, end of an era. I've sold kitchen utensils, Electrolux vacuum cleaners, encyclopedias, life insurance. I was even a Fuller Brush Man. It was a fine ride. But, what's done is done." He raised up his glass, sipped a bit, and then bowed. We laughed and pointed at him. It was better than television when he mixed his Peck Voice with booze.

Momma gulped her drink, then mouthed off. "Maybe one of those men in the restaurant wouldn't be whistling at anyone but me."

"For Pete's sake, Katie. I was just kidding around. It's a commercial." Daddy pulled Momma off the couch and gave her a big smooch. Micah pretended he was throwing up. Andy clapped his hands. I laughed loud and happy. Lots of times I felt happy, unless I counted up too many ice sounds dropping in Momma's circle glasses. The ice sounds told me how much laughing or how much fussing there'd be.

While Daddy was at his new work, Momma did chores and we helped. After, she'd lie back on the couch and read *Vogue* magazines full of models prissing around in fashion clothes she said she'd soon buy. She blabbervated to Aunt Ruby on the phone about her favorite perfumes: Shalimar, Tabu,

Je Reviens, Blue Grass, Joy, and Miss Dior. She'd tack up her favorite magazine dresses and perfumes to the living room wall and touch them when she passed. Momma said things were going to be better with Daddy making steady money and coming home every night.

I'd wait for Daddy's Rambler lights to come shining down the road, then I'd run out to him and he'd pick me up and twirl me around. Momma said I was spoilt rotten. When he walked in the door, loosening up his tie and smiling, Momma popped in some ice, poured them drinks, and they'd say, "To us!" Then they'd touch their glasses together. That was one. With supper, that was two.

At first everybody looked smiley and happy when I'd count one, two, three, and just every now and then, four.

For my sixth birthday, Momma baked a chocolate cake, and put a sweet carriage and horse on top, with a Cinderella doll beside it. But Momma said she didn't believe in fairy godmothers coming along and doing sparkly magic stuff. She said it was all wishy thinking. She pointed to the doll. "Look at that silly stupid grin on that blond fool. Look at her pink skin." I couldn't figure why she put it there if it made her mad.

All I wanted was my present. I was about to bust wondering what was in the box setting on the coffee table. Momma turned on her orange radio, the candles burned and dripped, supper was on the stove. I thought it was going to be the best birthday ever. But Daddy ruined it. He came home later than he promised and set Momma off to slamming doors and hollering, and Andy to bawling.

I ran outside to sit under the maple that shaded me green. In the fall, the leaves turned into flames, like a house on fire. I wondered about being inside the fire, the skin burning off my bones. I couldn't stand to think about Grandma Faith eaten up like that. I dreamed about her all the time and in all my dreams she never said why she died. She never said she was sorry she burned.

Micah came out and flopped his arm over my shoulder hard enough to make me fall over. He handed me my present with a look that said he was the best brother in the world.

Inside the box was a dark horse with a silky soft mane and tail. I knew it was a little-girl gift, but I didn't care. I'd seen it in the five and dime and I'd wanted it ever since. "Thanks, Micah."

He punched me on the arm. "I didn't do nothing."

"You did, too."

He shrugged.

"Are they still fussing?"

He rolled onto his stomach and pulled up grass into a pile. "I dunno."

"Micah, how come Grandma burned herself up?"

"Huh?"

"I was just thinking stuff."

"Quit doing that."

"Momma won't let me talk about her. But I got to."

He put his finger on his chin. "Well, Momma said some things hurt worse than living."

"What hurt her worser than being dead and burned?"

He shrugged, and then threw pebbles at me.

I threw pebbles back. "Sometimes I see her."

"See who?"

"Grandma Faith." I stroked my horse's head and decided to name her Fionadala. "She comes to me. I smell the apples and bread."

"Nuh uh. Liar."

"Am not." I put my face in Fionadala's fur.

"It's all dreams. Your head is full of cotton clouds."

"Is not."

"I bet they quit fussing. Let's get cake." He pulled me up and we ran inside.

Later, Daddy said Micah was a prodigy because of how he drew things so strange. He looked at Micah proud. I decided to find my own prodigal, if I had one to find.

Soon after my birthday, Momma and Daddy started up Friday Night Supper Dates. They said it'd help them stop fussing so much.

We kids ate chicken pot pie early and were sent off so we didn't even get to watch *The Flintstones*. Daddy gave us Zeros from the five and dime and we ate them fast, the sticky white all over our faces and hands. I was in Micah and Andy's room so we could play *Go Fish* and listen to Momma and Daddy's date.

While their casserole cooked in the oven, Momma and Daddy watched television. By the end of *Rawhide*, both were drunker than the town drunk, and their fight was louder than the bad guys having a shoot-out with the good guys.

Momma said, "Gregory Peck? Who told you that?"

"Every skirt from coast to coast, is who."

"Ha! They'd tell you anything so's you'd stop flapping that yap about Flakesbeard."

"You'd argue the bark from a dog."

"To flea or not to flea, that's just a suggestion."

"Get down, Katie, you'll break the table."

"You saying I'm a fattie mae?"

"I'm saying you need to grow up and act like a woman instead of a little girl."

It was quiet, like before a storm, when all the birds are hiding and the trees are waiting for the wind. Then we heard a crash, and then another. I opened the door to listen better. I was always too nosy for my own good.

"Vee, you crazy?" Micah grabbed Andy and they jumped in the closet. "Come get in here."

I didn't listen. I sneaked out just in time to see a plate barely miss Daddy. Then flew a cup and a saucer, a serving plate, and even the favorite carnival glass fruit bowl. I rooted to the spot as I watched Daddy duck glass bombs. He said, "Stop! Stop!"

Momma spewed out mixed up old words and new words and all in between, "Good fer nothin' son a bitch'n bassurd! I don' gotta stop nothin'." She grabbed an empty bottle and threw it hard as she could. It whizzed by my head, missing me by two horse hairs. When I screamed, Momma saw me, and shouted, "Gawd dam-nit! Git inna room . . . git back for'n I git yor'n . . . you know'd bettern— *Git*!"

I ran and dived into the closet with my brothers. Andy snuffled. Micah threw his shoes against the wall. Their fuss went on until I went insane. The light from the keyhole hurt my eyes, so I closed them, pictured my mountain, higher and higher until it reached up to where Mee Maw said God is supposed to be. I rode Fionadala up and we sat in the clouds, the wind blew my hair all around. Everything was green and wild and quiet, even the birds hushed up. There was clean-smelling air and I barely heard the storm, far away, far away.

When tires threw rocks up against the house, I was back.

Momma hollered, "Don' come back, inna ain't waitin' fer yew!" There was bumping around, and her door slammed.

Micah counted to ten, slow, two times, before we piled out of the closet. He tiptoed out of his room to have a look-see. I held Andy's hand. Micah came back to tell us the news, "Momma said she's going to soak in the tub with coffee."

We heard her go to the kitchen to boil water for her Maxwell House. It took her a long time since she had to think extra hard on things when she and the slap-happy sauce took up together.

"Is she almost done?" I whispered.

"I dunno," Micah whispered back.

When we heard Momma shut the bathroom door, we sat and waited for the squeak of the tub faucet. Next, the thumping around to get a washrag, towel, and the Dove soap she kept secret for herself. The faucet squeaked off. We knew that squeak would go three times when she put in extra hot water. We knew after she pulled the plug to let the water glug out, she dried off hard, and then put on lotion and powder. That was Momma's after-fight-gotta-get-the-loopy-out bath. Unless she went straight to bed with a sick headache.

The three of us walked through the house, our eyes bugging like frogs. There was broken glass, an empty bottle in the hall, a half-empty one under the coffee table, and the front door was wide open. I went to close it and saw Mrs. Mendel at the bottom of our steps holding a flashlight. "You chil'ren okay?" She looked at me as if I was an orphan left on the doorstep. I nodded and closed the door.

In the kitchen, the casserole was dumped out into

the sink, pan and all. I tried to get it out so Momma and Daddy could have it later, but it was too nasty. Their whole Friday Night Supper Date was ruined. Micah and I cleaned up while Andy cried in the middle of the mess, holding on to his stuffed toy I'd named Fiddledeedee the Tiger.

Micah put the kettle on the fire. I made Momma's favorite sandwich, peanut butter on one side, with slices of butter on the other. I wrapped it up in a clean dishrag and left it on the counter, with a glass of milk beside it. Daddy's sandwich was peanut butter and the last of Grandma's apple butter. I wrapped up his like I did Momma's, and set it beside hers with another glass of milk.

Micah said, "That there milk will go spoilt."

"Nuh uh."

He looked at me as if I was a stupid mule, then he put Daddy's milk in the icebox.

Momma came in wearing her robe and slippers, hair up in a ponytail, with the end wet and dripping. She dabbed a towel at her face. "Whew Nelly, I'm almost human, but my head's still loozy-woozy. I need more joe."

Micah cut off the fire and picked up the kettle of boiling water careful as can be. "I made more coffee water, Momma." He stirred her up a cup.

"And I made you and Daddy a sandwich," I said. "For your supper date."

She unwrapped the sandwich and while she ate it, she sniffled and hitched, like Andy. She poured the coffee into the glass of milk and drank it down. "That was the best supper I ever ate. And you tried to clean up the mess, my best babies. What would I do without you?" She kissed us, then made another cup of coffee, sipping it while she cleaned up the things we'd missed. "Your Daddy, Mr. ShakesPeck, ought to be here helping to clean up, seeing as it's his fault!"

After she put on her housedress, she turned on the radio and sang along while drawing Andy a bath. Micah and I sat on the couch and waited for the next thing. When she came out with Andy wrapped in a towel, the front of her dress was wet and it made her look like a real good momma. Andy smiled big and goofy, smelling like her Dove soap.

After Micah and I finished our special Dove soap baths, Momma found some bluegrass and said, "Here's to Mee Maw, may she lose her Texas talk-box in a yapping accident," and then slapped her knee and laughed.

We kids laughed with her.

"I'm near starving, kids." She ran to the kitchen, came back with a plate of sugar cookies, set those on the coffee table, and skipped back in the kitchen like a little girl, except one with lots of booze in her. She next came back with four glasses of cold sweet milk on a tray. We sat on the floor and ate and drank. It was just on the other side of happy.

Daddy wasn't there to see Momma laughing with

crumbs sticking to her face just like ours. Micah's eyes had a shiny-feeling-happy-about-things look. Andy looked at Momma like little boys look at their mommas. Sometimes she just did that to us, made us forget how things were before and go straight to what was happening then. Later, Momma tucked us in bed like a dream.

The wind blew cool in my window and my good mountain was strong and black against the sky, like it was watching out for me. When Daddy's shoes finally hit the floor, my body let go of the tight I'd been holding. He passed my door; I called out to him real soft so nobody else could hear, especially Momma.

He came in and sat on the side of my bed. "What are you doing awake, Bitty Bug?"

I sniffed him, missing the Old Spice and warm cotton. His white shirt had blood on it and that made me sad.

He tucked the quilt around me. "Remember who made this quilt?" He smoothed down the squares.

"Grandma Faith?"

"That's right. She made it with her own two hands. She'd be so proud of how you've grown."

"Momma said . . ."

"It doesn't matter what Momma said about Grandma. She was a good woman. One of the best." Daddy's voice was soft, same as his face.

"How come she was good?"

"Your grandma worked hard every day and she

loved her children, and you grandchildren. She loved Shakespeare's words, like me."

"She did?"

"Yep." Daddy touched the tip of my nose.

"What else about Grandma?"

"Well, she knew all about plants, trees, and birds. She could sew and make the best apple butter."

"Why'd she burn herself up?"

"Oh Bug, that's a grown-up question." He rubbed the back of his neck. "It was an accident, or something. She wouldn't ever do that to her children. Now, no more questions."

I snuggled under the quilt, wishing Grandma were around so I could show her to Daddy.

"Go to sleep or you'll turn into a warty toady-frog, froggy croaking the rest of your life so that nobody understands a word you say."

"That's silly."

He laughed warm as fuzzy socks, then said, "I'll read *Romeo and Juliet* to you tomorrow night, okay?"

It didn't matter if he didn't remember, right then it was like only the two of us lived there.

He stared out of my window. "I don't want you to feel afraid, no matter what happens."

I snuggled deeper.

"Your momma and I, we just . . ." His whole face turned down in a frown. "I promise to do better so you won't have to hear the arguing, okay?"

I nodded.

He stood up. "Goodnight, sleep tight, don't let the bedbugs bite."

I fell asleep and dreamed I was a princess and Daddy a king. I didn't know where Momma went off to.

A week later he broke his promise when he said he'd be home early so we could eat together. Momma fixed herself a drink while we kids ate our macaroni and cheese with hot dogs. She had another while we ate ice cream. She sipped another when his headlights finally glowed down the road.

When he came into the kitchen, Momma said, "I'm glad you finally made it home, Frederick."

"I'm sure you are, Katie."

"You promised the kids you'd be early."

"I was stuck with a problem."

"Oh, sure, I get it."

"No, you don't, because you don't work, now do you?"

Momma's lips pressed so when she talked, they hardly moved. "Kids, go on to your rooms and play."

My brothers did as they were told, but I ran to watch television. Lassie barked at Timmy, trying to tell him another collie killed some chickens and a cat, not her. I loved Lassie. I had a want the size of West Virginia to put my arms around her furry neck and hug the soft while Lassie sat beside me all proud and sweet. In television, everything worked out dandy. I felt warm goodies in my stomach while Timmy's mother hugged Lassie, and then Timmy.

She was telling Timmy something sweet, but what came out of her mouth was Momma's voice hollering, ". . . then why do you smell like a woman?"

"You're imagining things."

"Uh huh. And am I imagining you coming home late more here lately? Am I imagining that cheap perfume I wouldn't wear? I reckon I'm not."

Daddy stomped into the living room. "Go to your room, Bug. *Right now.*"

I ran to my room, jumped on my bed, and buried my face in Grandma Faith's quilt. Momma and Daddy took their fussing into their bedroom, slamming the door, like that would keep us from hearing.

My brothers came into my bedroom, which wasn't like a real bedroom with a regular closet, but had a cedar robe and a fancy ceiling light I was proud to have like nobody else. The old woman before us called it a parlor for her teas nobody came to.

Andy had tears and snot running. Micah had him by the hand, talking about the Wild Wild West Out Yonder and how much wood could a woodchuck chuck if a woodchuck could chuck wood—that usually made Andy laugh. He plopped Andy next to me. I wiped Andy's face with the bottom of his shirt.

Micah asked, "How's about some Kool-Aid and crackers?"

Andy nodded fast.

Micah opened the door, looked out, and made a face. "Momma and Daddy are in their room wrestling again."

Micah got our snack; we settled on my quilt to eat. Nothing was better than a picnic in the middle of the bed. I thought those were the good days, even with all the fussing. We chewed our crackers and drank the last of the Kool-Aid. The soft noises in the bedroom down the hall stopped and everything was quiet.

Chapter 5
Mysterious ways
1964

I'd never been inside a church, not even at Christmas when Mee Maw said she went to sing happy birthday to Jesus. She sent us kids a picture-book Bible with Jesus, Jesus' momma, and other people standing around with halos on their heads. It had Jesus hung up on the cross looking so pitiful and sad. I didn't understand why Jesus' Daddy wanted him up there. The stories were interesting, but God sounded ornery and was likely to smite anyone for any little thing. I liked Jesus better than God because he was a kind man and almost as handsome as my daddy.

Momma said God never did anyone any good and to believe it was a waste of time. It didn't stop Mee Maw from calling to screech over some fellow named Satan. Momma said, "Mee Maw's afraid that instead of sliding into heaven on a beam of light, she'll be riding down on Satan's coattails."

A fancy new dress changed Momma's mind about getting religion. Momma held the dress in front of her, smiling so wide I thought her lips would stretch out of place. She said, "We're going to church!"

The rest of us stared at her, too dumbed up to say anything.

"What's wrong? Cat got your tongues?"

"What brought this on, Katie?" Daddy asked.

"I want to show off my beautiful new dress to lots of people and church seems as good a place as any." She twirled around pretending she already wore the dress and knew she looked pretty in it.

"Buster said church is boring," Micah said. He had peanut butter stuck on his face. "He said they try to drown you in front of the whole church unless you say you love Jesus." Buster was Micah's best friend who lived down the long road a fair piece.

"Nuh uh. You lie," I said.

"I love Uncle Jesus," Andy said.

"Hush it, you kids." Momma pulled her I'm-thinking-about-things-so-be-quiet look while the rest of us admired her still holding the dress against herself. "There's a Baptist church in town. And being Easter next Sunday, it ought to be packed full up."

Daddy raised up an eyebrow. "As long as our priorities are clear. Right, dear?"

Momma twirled around again and paid no mind to Daddy.

Easter morning, I followed Momma into her room to watch her get ready. She shook off her housecoat, and wiggled into the new dress. It was light green and had a wide belt that she made an extra hole in so it would fit just right. Standing at the mirror, she tilted her head one way, then the other. She unzipped the back of the dress, pulled down the top, took off her bra, and then zipped the dress back up. She hopped up and down a few times. "Not bad for having had three babies," she said to herself in the mirror.

Next came silk stockings she rolled in a ball and then slid up her leg. Holding up her shoes, she said, "Look at these new high-heels, Virginia Kate."

"They're pretty, Momma." I didn't tell her I'd tried them on earlier, tottling about a foot before I fell and busted my fun all up.

She left her hair hanging down her back, but pulled mine into a ponytail since my hair always tangled up underneath at my neck. Momma called it my rat's nest. She pulled and tugged until I went slap dab crazy. When she was done, I swung it around to watch it fly.

Momma held up two tubes of lipstick. "Pink or red?"

I quit swinging my hair. "Red?"

"No, not at a church." She put down the red and opened the pink one, twisting until the lipstick was all the way up.

I said, "Pink?"

She closed the tube with a click. "No, I hate pink. I'll just go bare." She laughed as if she said a good joke, and smeared a bit of Vaseline on her lips so that they shined. She turned to me. "So, how do I look?"

"You look bee-u-tee-ful."

"Prettier than that girl at Daddy's work?"

"Yes Ma'am." I hadn't seen the girl at Daddy's work, but so far, nobody was prettier than Momma.

She pulled on her gloves and hat and walked out of her room, leaving me in a cloud of her sweet smell. She had her chin out like she does when she's feeling proud, or mulish. Daddy whistled when she did a slow turn for him. They headed out the door like movie stars. We kids followed them and waited while Daddy took pictures of her. By the tree she made her lips pout, tilted her head to the right, and put her gloved hands cupped under her chin.

Daddy said, "Get over by the car."

She threw back her head and laughed and Daddy

snapped the picture. Next, she leaned back on the front of the car, and her hair fell on the hood. Daddy asked, "Woman, did you forget something?"

Momma winked at Daddy. While he snapped the last one, his shadow moved away from his feet, as if his insides were spilling into the grass.

Momma fluffed her hair. "What about the kids' pictures, Frederick?"

Daddy looked at his watch. "We'll have to take them when we get back."

I wasn't having as much fun in my Easter clothes as Momma was. I wore a stiff cotton and lace dress with a little bonnet that fit funny over my ponytail, lacy socks, and shiny shoes. Micah's suit matched Daddy's, except Micah's tie was brown instead of green. Andy wore seersucker overalls with a white shirt and white shoes.

Andy was in the front seat where he sat as comfortable as an angel on a cloud. He kept saying, "Is Uncle Jesus dere? Huh, Daddy?" Mee Maw once told Andy that Jesus was like a good uncle, so Andy thought he was a real person. Daddy didn't answer him; he was busy helping Momma so she wouldn't run her stockings.

Micah and I piled into the backseat with our pout mouths. My shoes pinched my toes; the strap cut into my foot. I told Momma, "Jesus won't care about shoes."

Micah said, "I got it worser than you do."

I grabbed at the strap, and pulled my face into ten kinds of pitiful.

Micah pulled the collar away from his neck, sticking his tongue out to the side like a dead cow. His neck was dirty and I wondered how he got by Momma like that.

Momma turned around and pointed her finger at us. "You two hush it."

Daddy said, "You all look so good; I'm feeling extra proud today." He roared up the engine of the Rambler and took off.

We were late to the church. All the Baptist-heads turned and looked when we came in. They watched Momma walk bold as you please to the front. Some of the men had their mouths open, as if they'd said "Oh" and forgot to close them again. The women held their fans over their mouths and whispered.

The preacher stared at Momma's new dress. I stared at him. He had big shoulders and had light brown hair in a crew cut. I didn't know what preachers were supposed to look like, but I didn't picture them kind of handsome like that. We sat in the third bench, and I watched Momma to see what I was supposed to do. Her mouth was open a bit and she licked her Vaseline lips with her tongue. I saw her do that a lot and thought it was a secret thing girls did. She bounced around trying to get herself comfortable on the hard seat. The man beside us made a sound like he'd dived into a cold creek.

A woman big as a piano went to play the organ. That's when it was time to stand up and sing. After songs about bloody lambs (I almost cried about the poor little lambs), Christian soldiers, and rugged crosses, Mr. Preacher stood up and took to preachering. Micah pretend-snored, and Daddy pinched him on the knee, but smiled when he did it. Andy fell asleep on the bench, his head in Momma's lap, not even waking up during the fist pounding. Momma looked right up at Mr. Preacher as if he was Lord of the Baptists.

After the singing, hollering, and pounding were all over, Mr. Preacher king-stepped down the stairs. When he passed us by, he slid his eyes over to Momma, but she kept her eyes on the big cross. Another man stood up and told us to stand with our heads down in prayer. I'd never prayed before, but I gave it my best. I said, "God, please make Momma and Daddy stop hollering. I'm right tired of it."

I heard Micah ask, "God, why did you even make neckties if you're so smart?"

Andy asked, "Where's Uncle Jesus?" He stood on the bench and looked all around. Daddy put his hand over Andy's mouth to get him to stop calling out, "Uncle Jesus? Uncle Jeeeee-suuus!" He must've thought Mr. Preacher was Uncle Jesus.

I tried to think of more things to pray about when someone said "A-men!" and then some of the menfolk took up talking, laughing, shaking hands, and calling each other Brother. The mommas pulled their kids by their sleeves. Some of the mommas looked like they sucked on lemons. I wondered if that was what church going did to a person. The daddies followed behind, holding Bibles with one hand, jingling their keys and change in their pockets with the other. Momma wouldn't leave. She kept staring at the Cross.

Daddy tapped his fingers on the bench. "Katie, let's go. I'm hungry."

Momma ignored Daddy.

Micah said, "I told you it was boring. And nobody even got drowned." His mouth looked soured—and he'd only been in church this once.

I made sure my mouth stayed like it was by grinning real big.

Finally, when almost everyone was gone, Momma left the pew. We followed behind her like ducks, but Momma's tail was the only one wagging.

At the door, Mr. Preacher shook Daddy's hand, telling him what a fine family he had. Daddy said some Shakespeare or maybe he just said thanks, then he picked up Andy and walked outside. Mr. Preacher took my momma's hand. "This must be your first visit among my flock, Mrs.?"

"Carey. You can call me Katie."

"Katie. Yes. I'm Foster, Foster Durant." He grinned like one of those big crocodiles on Mutual of Omaha's Wild Kingdom, then said, "I hope you will see your way back to services again real soon."

"We'll see." She smiled and pulled off the glove on her right hand. "You have a lovely church; did your wife help you fix it up for Easter?" With that hand, she fiddled with the top of her dress.

"Never cleaved to a wife." He stared at her hand, and then looked over at me. "Is this your little girl? What a pretty thing she is—just like her mommy." He patted the top of my head and I tried not to get the sour lemon lips. "She looks all exotical like in explorer books."

"This is Virginia Kate." Momma touched my cheek.

"Such dark eyes. You people In-jun, or Eye-talian, or something, what?"

"I reckon you ask too many questions, Preacher Durant. Is that how Baptists do things?"

"I didn't mean anything forward, Ma'am." He took out a handkerchief and dabbed his face. "I could give you a Bible. I have some extras. I mean, I notice you don't carry one about."

"Oh, gosh." She put her finger on her lips and made small circles. "Hmmm." She pulled her shoulders back. "Gosh, I don't know, Preacher Durant."

"Please, call me Foster." His voice mouse-squeaked. He was even sillier when his face turned blotchy-pink. "We honor the Lord mornings and evenings on Sundays, then Wednesdays with a family supper, and there's a Bible studying group that meets every other Saturday."

"People go to church all those times? My lord. Are you kidding me?" She put her hand on his chest and pushed at him. Without looking at me, she asked, "Virginia Kate, what do you think? Should we come back to this church with this friendly preacher-man?"

He mopped his face and stared at Momma.

I didn't trust shiny men. "No, Ma'am." I hoped she wouldn't get mad at me, but I had to tell the truth when it felt important enough.

"We'll think about it, Preacher Foster." She turned her back on him, grabbed my hand, and called to Micah.

Micah was busy touching a painting that showed a bunch of people drowning in the water, holding their hands up to a boat with their mouths open, their eyes big and scared. Micah's eyes were closed like he was blind as he felt the painting. He pretended he didn't hear Momma.

She went over, pulled his sleeve, and we marched on out.

Outside, Daddy was listening to an old man who wore a suit that was too big for him. We walked up in time to hear him say, "Yeah, I got the 'ritis and the gout something fierce. Sometimes cain't get out of bed."

"That's terrible." Daddy patted my head when I

stood beside him. He still held Andy, who was asleep again, missing everything.

The old man pea-eyed Momma up and down. He noticed me and tried to hunker to my level. "Look at you, all dressed up."

I wrinkled my nose. Micah ran over by our Rambler and picked up rocks to put in his pockets so he wouldn't have to smell the old man's breath.

"You like church, little lady?"

I put my hand over my nose and said, "No, Sir."

The old man laughed, turned back to Momma, opened up his mouth, and let a million words fall out. "Jeremiah here. Born in Oregon and left when I was a little mite, been in two wars, married a good woman like you and then lost her to the cancer ten years gone by. Been in West-By-God-Virginia since 1932!" He horse-tooth grinned.

"Hello, Jeremiah." Momma leaned over and kissed him right at his mouth, her hand held on to his shoulder so he wouldn't keel over. I looked back at Preacher Foster Durant. He stared at Momma, his handkerchief just a-going on his big shiny face.

Daddy laughed when Jeremiah said, "Oh my!"

"Well, Jeremiah, my kids are hungry and tired of church," Momma said.

We all jumped into the car, and Daddy drove off. I turned around in my seat and saw Jeremiah standing right still, touching his lips as if he was under a spell. Preacher Foster Durant held his

71

Bible, his spell with Momma shining up his face.

Back in the holler, Daddy took pictures of us kids before we tore off our clothes. Then we ate roast, potato salad, deviled eggs, and lemon icebox pie. After that, we had our first ever Easter egg hunt. We just never thought to do it before. Daddy gave us each a basket full of Peeps, chocolate bunnies, and jellybeans. We poured it all out on our beds so we'd have a place to put the eggs we found. Daddy and Momma sat on a blanket under the maple and drank blackberry wine. It was a strange and good day.

The next week, Daddy gave me a picture of us. Micah made a frame for it out of Popsicle sticks. He glued our picture to it and used more sticks on the back to make it stand up. On the bottom of the frame, he wrote his name in a way he thought was clever with curly cues and a big dot over the *i*. In the picture, we grinned big-open-mouthed, glad to be out of church. We didn't have our shoes on; those we'd torn off in the car on the way home.

Micah was in a telling-me-stuff mood. "I'm gonna be famous. You wait and see."

I flopped cross-legged on his bed while he put his paints away.

"I'm going to make buckets and trucks of money and live in a mansion on a hill."

"Can I come visit?"

"Sure. It won't be in West Blahginia, though."

"How come?"

"Because I'll be rich and I won't have to live here, that's why." He scribbled on his pad, making a face with lightning bolts coming out of the eyes. "It's stupid here."

"Is not."

"Is too. Stoooopid." He punched me on the arm and pinched my knee until I said uncle. "I have homework, Squirk-brain. Get out."

I grabbed the Popsicle stick frame with our picture, and ran back to my room to set it on the table by my bed. I lay across my bed, chewing a Peep from my Easter loot. My dirty feet were on Grandma Faith's quilt and she didn't care, and neither did I. I thought about Micah leaving me and decided it couldn't happen, since that would be too sad. I finished my Peep and went back to his room. Micah was looking out the window, long and hard and far away. I told him that he could never, ever leave me. I told him loud enough that he quit looking so far away and looked at me.

Chapter 6
It takes two to tangle

Momma visited the Baptists for a while. The rest of us didn't want to go, and she didn't make us. We stayed home with Daddy and did Shakespeare plays. Micah was Hamlet and said, "To be or not to be." I was his momma who was poisoned, Andy killed Hamlet with a sword, and Daddy played the rest.

The last Sunday she went to church, Momma came home mad as a wet cat. She tore off straight to the kitchen, came out holding a circle glass with one piece of ice floating, and drank it down in two gulps. I was coloring and she made me go outside the lines of the pony when she hammered her glass on the table. "That stupid Foster Durant."

When Daddy came in from mowing the grass, he sipped his drink while Momma made meatloaf and cream potatoes with green beans. She didn't say why Preacher Foster Durant was stupid, but I could've told her that before. The whole rest of the day went by without one word of fussing and no more talk about church and preachers. I took a deep breath of happy.

When I went to bed that night, Daddy came in and read to me. He said I was the only one who would listen to his Shakespeare. That made me feel special. Opening up the book, he rubbed the page down smooth, and then took a sip from his glass to clear his throat out. He read, "Of one that lov'd not wisely but too well; Of one not easily jealous, but being wrought, Perplex'd in the extreme."

I was soon slipping into sleep.

It was about time for summer when things went wrong. It started when Momma went to the bathroom and threw up. When she went back to bed, I brought her water and saltines. It happened again the next day, but Momma wouldn't let me tell Daddy she was sick.

This went on until she put on her pointy chin. I followed her to the kitchen. She fetched out the stuff to make salt-rising bread and sweet bread. For the salt-rising bread, she peeled and cut potatoes and put them in a jar along with white cornmeal, salt, sugar, baking powder, and soda. She poured in warm water and scalded milk, put the top on the jar, and put the jar in a pot of more warm water until ready to make the sponge.

While that set, she stirred yeast to make the sweet bread with cinnamon. I smelled Grandma Faith. Then I saw her. She stood by Momma while Momma stirred. Grandma turned and shook her head back and forth real slow. I knew then something was coming to beat us over the head.

When the dough for the sweet bread was ready, Momma said, "It helps to pound the dog spit out of dough. I worry it until it gives up answers." She hit the dough three times. "When the stuff in the jar is fermented, I'll make the salt-rising bread."

"Will you show me how to make it, Momma?"

"I will one day, I reckon."

"Why not now, Momma?"

She huffed a sigh, said, "I'm in a mood today. Now let me think."

It was just Momma and me in the house that Saturday. Daddy was at work. Micah and Buster were down to the creek looking for salamanders.

I'd asked him to get me some smoothed rocks while he was there. Sometimes he would and sometimes he'd forget. Andy was over to Mrs. Mendel's having milk and cookies. Mrs. Mendel made the best oatmeal cookies ever. I was supposed to go, but I wanted to stay by Momma in case she turned sick again.

I asked, "Momma, how come you're beating up on the dough?"

"I told you. It helps me think." She stuck her fingers in the gooey stuff.

"What're you thinking about?"

"I'm thinking about stuff that's none of your bees-wax."

"How come it's not my bees-wax?"

"Go outside and play. I can't think with you jabbering on."

I put on seventy-three pouts of pitiful, but she didn't care.

"I said go. Now!"

I ran back to my room and read a book about Dick and Jane. Then I rode Fionadala all around until I heard Daddy put his keys and hat on the hook.

Momma hollered out of the kitchen, "Fred, I need to talk to you, pronto," before he could hardly get in the door. I opened my door to listen, and smelled the bread even stronger.

Daddy went straight to the icebox. I heard the ice clunk.

Momma said, "I got something to tell you and I expect you aren't going to like it a bit."

When they went to their room and shut the door, I sneaked down the hall and sat outside their door. I brought Fionadala with me in case I needed her.

Momma was saying, ". . . it takes two to tangle, dear husband."

"Tango," Daddy said. The ice rattled.

"Tango, shmango, whatever."

"I thought you kept up with that."

"Yeah, blame me."

A drawer slammed.

"I'm not blaming."

"I'm having babies before I have time to breathe, just like my momma."

"What's wrong with that?"

"What's wrong is I'm tired. And you never spend time with them. Off doing lord knows what with that *Keemburlee.*"

"I'm not interested in Kimberly. Can I say the same thing about you and that preacher?"

"You just shut up, you hear? Shut up!"

Something banged against the wall and I jumped.

"I think the pot is calling the kettle black." Daddy sounded sad instead of mad.

"Uh huh. That so, Fred."

Micah sat beside me and about scared me half to death. He had come in quiet as a prowling panther. "What's happening, Vee?"

"I don't know," I whispered.

Momma's voice had that whiny-baby sound to it. "I'd like to keep my figure. I'd like to have my hair fixed up sometime. I'd like to go out and dance without worrying over who'll watch the kids." I imagined Momma counting off what she wanted, looking mad at Daddy in between each raised finger.

"Oh for god's sake. There's no use arguing. It's done."

"I've asked Ruby for her special tonic."

"What?"

"I got to get this out of me. I can't do it, I can't. I'm sick of children."

My toes curled, and there was a buzzing around in my head, like fifty-two bees were in there—big mad kind of bees, like hornets. I looked at Micah, but he stared at his feet.

Daddy's voice rose up. "Have you lost your mind? That's our little baby in there."

"You really are a stupid man, Fred."

"What are you saying?"

"I need me another one of these." Ice rattled and footsteps came towards the door.

Micah and I ran outside. I knew how to open the side screen door so it wouldn't make any noise. We eased out and sat on the steps. I studied Micah's face to see what he felt, but he looked far off. His back went broomstick straight when Daddy slammed out of the front door and Momma threw something across the room. I wanted my brother to say everything was okay. Instead, he rubbed his hands on his legs as if they were sweaty, then let his arms hang down between them. I stared at the scabs on his knees.

He blinked, and he didn't want me to see him cry, so he ran off.

I ran to my brothers' closet, closed the door, shut my eyes, and rode away on Fionadala's back. Her mane flew in my face while we climbed higher and higher. Sister mountain laughed when we tickled its sides. All I saw was misty clouds. All I felt was wind and horse hair pushing up against my face.

The next week, Momma was more worrisome. She went around the house, back and forth, talking to herself, drinking from a pickling jar filled with something that looked like mud with bits of grass swirled in it. Three times a day she jumped off the steps and ran around the house five times. Sometimes Andy ran with her, giggling as if it was the funniest game.

Daddy stayed at work later and later. One night, he grabbed Momma by the shoulders, his face close to hers, and asked, "What have you done, Katie?" He poured his own tonic and went up to the empty house on the hill. I barely could see him up there. Micah said he caught him crying up there one time, but I couldn't picture my daddy crying.

Just when I thought we'd all go insane with the craziness, Momma held onto her stomach as she dialed. She said, "Ruby, come get me. I think I done it," then leaned her head on the wall. "Well, if it don't, then I'll do that other thing." She hung up, and dialed up Mrs. Mendel next. "Can you come watch the kids after my sister gets here? I need to go up to the hospital."

My brothers stayed out of her way. I had the buzzing hornets stinging my head something fierce, but I stood by her bed as she put clothes in a suitcase.

She looked at me, her eyes red and puffed up. "Virginia Kate, I got to go up to the hospital. Mrs. Mendel will be here. You kids better behave." She grabbed her stomach and cried.

"Why you going to the hospital, Momma?"

She didn't answer; she just pushed me out of the way and went to the window with her suitcase to watch for Aunt Ruby.

On the living room couch, Andy had his legs stuck straight out in front of him, and Micah had his arms crossed over his chest.

When Aunt Ruby honked her horn, Momma dialed on the phone again. "Frederick, I'm going up to the hospital." She hung up and walked out the door. When I tried to follow her, she screamed at me to get my butt back in the house. I went to the window and my brothers came to stand with me to watch as Aunt Ruby drove away with Momma lying in the backseat.

Mrs. Mendel took care of us while Momma was

gone. Daddy stayed gone, too. It was quiet in the house. Andy didn't carry on as much as I thought he would. Micah sulled up and drew pictures of ugly things. I stayed in my room, crying in Grandma Faith's quilt. I cried until I was tired of it and decided I wasn't going to cry anymore. I'd dry up every tear since crying didn't do one bit of good. I told Grandma Faith, "No more crying." But I heard her cry.

Not long after, Daddy brought Momma home and she was plumb wore out. Their faces were puffed and red. Momma went straight to bed and Daddy went back up to the house on the hill with a box in his hand. Nothing was ever said about what happened. No baby ever came. It was never talked about again.

After that, there wasn't much happy laughing going on, and booze bottles lined up one, two, three, four, and more.

Chapter 7
Today

Digging through the memories has left my back stiff and sore. My heart is sore, too, taken out of my chest, stomped on, and shoved back in. I get up and stretch, looking at the Popsicle-stick frame holding our faces. That Easter changed everything, but maybe everything would have broken into pieces anyway, with or without Easter dresses and preachers and booze and lost babies. I go to the window and see old moon grinning. Moon doesn't have a lick of sense tonight.

A gust of wind hits my face and sweeps papers from the bed onto the floor. I roll my eyes. "I know, Grandma. I still have work to do."

On the way to the kitchen to make coffee, I like how the old worn floor feels cool on my feet. On the kitchen counter is the red-and-white rooster-handled sugar and creamer, alongside the flour jar that matches Grandma Faith's. Everything is just as Momma left it. Even her cup is rinsed, dried, and left by the sink. I pick it up and rub the cool porcelain. As the cup warms in my hands, I see Momma sipping from it, making that oh-it's-hot-but-good face. I put the kettle on the fire, and then look around.

Near the corner to the left, at attention, stand the liquor bottles. Beside them is an ashtray full of cigarette butts—the red lipstick-tipped filters make it seem as if Momma's coming right back to have coffee with me, as soon as she puts her housedress on. I smell her Shalimar and tobacco.

I say, "Momma? I'm not afraid if you want to come to the kitchen with me." But I really am afraid she'll float into the room, pour rum into her coffee, and start telling me secrets.

I have a sudden urge to sweep the bottles onto the floor, watch them bleed their liquid until they're emptied. Instead, I take a circle glass from the cabinet, pick up the rum and pour a bit into it. I sniff it and the smell makes my stomach clench. I've had wine and beer, and bubbly champagne on the day of my I-thought-this-would-be-forever wedding, but I never cared for the strong stuff. There must be sparkly magic to it, though, since it kept Momma coming back for more. Daddy knew its magic, too. But he learned it's the bad kind of trick before it destroyed him for good.

I take a big gulp. It's fire across my tongue. The frog in my gullet coughs out, "Momma, how could you drink this stuff?" I dump out the dark rum and pour in a splash of vodka. When I swallow the clear liquid, the frog laps it up with a greedy grin. It makes me mad how liquidly smooth warm it makes my tongue, then my throat, then my stomach feel. I glub the rest of it in one throat-heating gulp. I wonder if my chin is getting pointy. Rinsing and drying the glass, I put it back in the cabinet, and leave the bottles where they are, for now.

Momma's checkered curtains blow on either side of the open window, letting the coolness enter the room. I look out to see a light in Mrs. Mendel's house and wonder if she's still awake. She always did turn up on our doorstep when she thought we needed her. But she never meddled. That's just how things were; mountain people minded their own business much as they could.

From the living room, I step outside. The dark

puts its arms around me. The wind is blowing hard; no rain's come yet. Everything feels velvety and close, like my favorite shirt. I step in the cool grass, feeling the blades under my feet, the springiness of the damp earth.

I get moon-sick-crazy, as I twirl around the yard towards Mrs. Mendel's garden, whirl until I'm dizzy as a drunk. I lie in the grass and gaze up at my friend moon staining the sky pale, staining the mountains with mystery. When I get too chilly, I stand and put one foot in front of the other right where I'd stepped before. At the door, I glance back and a shadowy face is looking from Mrs. Mendel's window. I wave and the shadow waves back.

Back in the kitchen, I see us all at the table. I imagine laughing and giggling and smiling. I put Momma in her blue housedress, Micah with his baggy pj's and inky fingers, Daddy's hair combed back—a plate of biscuits and gravy in front of him, Andy grinning with jelly on his face, and me pushing back my messy hair to watch everyone. It's as pretty as the old television shows they used to make. The marks on the wall made when Mee Maw's big rear end hit the table are still there. Nobody bothered to cover them up. Things like that have a way of becoming a part of the room until a change happens to make things stand out like red against black. Empty against full. Alive against dead.

Before I left Louisiana, I called my brothers to tell them about Momma. Micah didn't answer, so I left a message. I remembered how he said he'd never return to the holler, so I didn't expect him to come.

Andy said, "The bookstore's hopping crazy."

"I know you're busy, Andy, but I want to have a memorial. Won't you come?"

"I can't see how."

"I understand."

"You sure?"

"Yes." I rubbed my eyes. "I've called Adin, but will you call Dad?"

"I'll make the calls." I heard my brother's breathing. Then, "You'll be okay, Seestor?"

"Yeah. Don't worry. I'm fine. It's just . . . I have to do this."

"I know you do."

We then disconnected our lines.

There's a feeling as if someone is in the room with me, and the hairs on the back of my neck stand up, but nothing happens and the feeling is gone. Ghosts. When I opened the door, I must have let someone in. I decide it doesn't matter. They can't hurt me anymore than they did, and they can't love me anymore either.

The kettle is whistling like crazy, so I cut off the fire, and unscrew the lid to the instant Maxwell House. Momma took lots of cream and two teaspoons of sugar. I stir in the sugar, a heaping teaspoon of Maxwell House, and—there's no cream. I sip the sweet-bitter.

I settle down at the table and think about the mornings I drank coffee with my daughter. We faced each other, just as my momma and I once did, eyes watching over the rim of our cups. I had searched my momma for answers to her mysteries. My daughter and I searched each other for resemblances we knew would never be there. I smile thinking about my only child. My adopted daughter. Momma never met her but I wonder if they'd have liked each other. Without thinking about it until I do it, I hold my womb, the empty place that remained empty no matter how much I screamed at the unfairness. Adin filled my life in the way that stranded children do, with desperation and then with acceptance and then with love. I know about it. I do.

Through the open window, wind slips in to tickle strands of hair against my face. I have to rub the itchiness out of my eyes with thinking on the moments so hard, the taste of it on my tongue. The smell in my nose. The steam from the cup rising up like a tiny ghost.

"Oh, Momma!" I call out. But she's not talking. That's how she is, back and forth with her moods. Taking deep breaths of the cool air stops the crying from taking over—the joy cry for my daughter and the sad cry for my momma's daughter.

The cup is empty, so I prepare another to take

with me back to my room. Coffee, cup, sugar, hope, ghosts. But, no cream, no Momma.

In the living room, I put down the coffee and open the windows to let the air come in and the ghosts go out, if they've a mind to. I smell earth, evergreen, moon vapors. I can't see them, but I know ancient things are out there, and the mountain laurel, the wolf, bear, the sleeping cardinal and grosbeak, all the hidden and the found.

The brown couch still has the indent where Momma liked to sit at the right side. The big pointed star clock is stuck on five o'clock. A magazine with prissing models is open on the coffee table. The orange radio is still on the end table. I fiddle with the knobs, and staticy whispers waft from the speaker. It only plays ghost music now. But I remember the dancing and singing Momma did to that old thing. Even when it was forced out of Momma's sad lips, she liked a good song. Moon mood music is what I need to block out the quiet, or is it to block out the whispers that break up the dead's quiet? I bet Momma has a radio that works in her room, but I change my mind. Instead, I take my coffee and listen to spirit feet patter with me back to my room.

I say, "Who's here with me?" But I know they won't answer. It's not their time yet.

My brothers' room waits for me. And Momma's room—how will I ever go in there and face the empty, the un-Momma of it? The clouds of powder, the twisting curtains where the wind rushes in, her chattering moods that came when she was feeling happy. I head right on back to my room, humming a song, some old song I heard long ago. It comes up from deep inside of me and tickles my lips as it rushes out.

I do a twirl to my own music, then say, "Hear that, Grandma Faith? I bet Momma's wishing I'd hum something she can do a jig to."

I hear Momma snorting.

I stop my twirl, close my eyes, let my hand wave over the things on the bed, hovering until my fingers feel warm and tingly. I open my eyes. One of Momma's fancy department store bags is under my palm. I put my hand flat on it, press down to feel the heat in my fingers and across my palm, and then I open it. Inside are photographs, and cotton balls that held the perfumes Momma loved. Channel No 5, Tabu, Shalimar. I spill out the memories.

A photo of Andy, Micah, and me lands on top of the rest. We are grinning so big our mouths hurt, Popsicles held in our hands, the juice staining our arms. The photo is black and white, but I know that I had cherry, Micah had grape, and Andy had orange. I have on a sunsuit, Micah has jeans rolled up at the ends and a striped shirt, and Andy, only shorts. I remember playing in a summer rain, slapping each other with wet towels. Hide and seek. Cold Kool-Aid and crisp Saltines. Lying back on the grass to guess the cloud shapes. Naming Grandma Faith's puppies, first picking them up and smelling the puppy breath as their little heads wobble back and forth. Our feet green after the grass was fresh-mowed. I see it all, from this one photograph. See how slip slap happy we were in that time *right there*. How it could have always been. If only. I don't like *if onlys*, but here they are anyway.

Under that picture are a few of Daddy when he was a boy. What was it like for Daddy growing up with Mee Maw Laudine? Four little pictures are my clues. I hold up the one of him when he's a bitty thing, playing beside a well. Beside him is his one brother who was three years older. I know that Peter died from a fever when Daddy was thirteen. In another picture, Daddy's about five, swinging on a tire swing, his face pulled into a scowl.

In the last picture he stands beside a man. Daddy's arms are crossed over his chest, a shadow covering his face so I can't see what his eyes hold. On the back it says, "Frederick, 15, and his new father." So many mysteries to Daddy and to Momma. I won't be a mystery to Adin; she'll know it all because I am writing it all down, just as Grandma Faith did for me. Just as Momma tried to do with her scrawled additions?

I study a photograph of my momma, Aunt Ruby, and their brothers, standing in front of an old beat-up truck, barefoot with untamed hair. Aunt Ruby has an ugly frown on, bent down a little, scratching at her big old leg. My uncles stare out at the camera, their faces full up with mischief. Uncle Hank's the oldest; I never did get to meet him. Nobody knows where he took off to. I imagine he's living in the forests deep, drinking out of the creek, and stealing people's chickens to eat. It makes me both sad and happy to picture him running wild and free. Uncle Ben grins lopsided at Momma as if she's the maker of the stars. He has a moon-in-the-eyes look. I wish I'd known my lost uncles better. More *if only's*.

Uncle Jonah stands right by Momma. He has his hand on her shoulder, as if he's keeping her from floating off into the blue yonder. And Momma, she's striking even under all that wind-swept hair and West Virginia dirt. She has her hands on her hips, one hip jutted out. Her head is tilted back so that she's staring right at the camera with her eyes half-closed. I've never seen anyone like her, my momma.

Rain patters the roof hard, then harder, until the sound is roaring over my head and all around me. The storm is here. It drowns out the whispering as I push my hands into the memories to select the next one.

The snapshot I am guided to jerks me up by surprise and sets my hair standing on end. Micah's face is swollen and he has bruises on his arms and legs. I'm bruised, too, and my hair is whacked into a whopping mess of ugly. Our mouths are turned down and it's as if all our spirit is sucked right on out of us.

I turn it over to read, "Look what I done to your young'uns, baby sister! Ha! That's what you get for stealing Jackson from me."

I taste pennies and sour nasty churns up my throat when that summer slams up against me. The picture makes me madder than a nest of hornets.

All a sudden, I want to burn the whole mess of memories into ashy piles of nothing. I could just spit fire and burn this damn house down with everything in it. I could walk away, wait for the rest of my life to happen. The curtains dance, the wind rushes to rustle the papers, the moon shines on all the evidence. I sass out, "Stop it, Grandma. I'm doing the best I can!"

I stomp my foot. I shake my fist into the air. I'm a woman who'll howl at the moon. I slam the door hard as I can slam it. It shakes the doorframe; it shakes the rafters, the house and the ground beneath me rumbles and roars. I holler out, "I hate you! Rot in hell!" I'm a little girl all over again with no more sense than to scream at ghosts. But I'm a grown little girl with the power to scream out my mad. I've had that scream in me for far too long. I have.

I stand in the middle of my room and wait for something to happen. I sense Aunt Ruby laughing at my messy hair and clothes, my liquor-coffee breath, my sweaty-flushed cheeks, my memory-struck face. I lean out the window, let the storm cool me, soothe me, the mists bathe over me, then I turn in a strong full circle, stamping my feet. When I stop, I'm alone.

No ghosts dare face me now.

Chapter 8
That woman is a terror

I was feeling cat-lazy, flopped on the hallway floor doing a connect the dots puzzle, half listening to Daddy putting ice in a glass and Andy giggling to himself in his room, when I heard Momma's whiny baby voice.

"Fix me one, too. I'm hot and tired."

"Coming right up." Daddy had his I'm-happy-even-though-I-hardly-smile voice.

"Hurry up. I got an idea that'll settle our worry-bones."

I slid on my stomach to the doorway to peep and listen.

Daddy put Momma's glass on the coffee table and sat on his green chair. "What's up?"

She took a big swallow, fell back on the couch, and put the glass against her forehead. "I don't have a speck of time to myself around here."

"Oh come off it."

"And you're always gone off somewhere."

"I'm home every night in time for dinner."

"Oh whoopee dee doo! My husband comes home for supper. Oh, I mean *dee-ner*. Didn't mean to get all hicked up." Momma crossed her eyes. "He-yuck he-yuck, I'm from Wes' Virgeener."

"Katie . . ." Daddy ran his hands through his hair making it stick straight up.

"I'm stuck here alone with three kids."

"And I work all day."

"We used to have fun." Momma flapped her legs open and shut, then lifted her skirt up and down, fanning herself.

"What do you want me to do about it?" Daddy stared into his glass.

Momma sat up straight. "Let's send Virginia Kate and Micah up to Ruby's for the summer. Her boy's gone off to some camp for stupid kids."

I froze right up, inside and out.

Momma said, "She won't take all three, but she can handle the two older ones, after I reminded her I took care of Pooter-Boy when she had *her* vacation."

Daddy finished his drink and stood up. "That woman is a terror."

I took in a big breath, left it there, waited for what would come next. Aunt Ruby was mean when she boozed herself into stupidity. Any little thing fired her off. She cussed and screamed at Pooter-Boy. If she was extra mad, she'd backhand him a good one.

Momma went on, "Mrs. Mendel said she'd take

Andy for a week so we could go on a proper vacation. After that, she'll keep him a few hours a week
for the summer, so we can spend some time
together while the two older ones are gone."

"I don't like it."

"We need to work on our marriage, Frederick.
Don't you want me anymore?" Momma stood up
in front of Daddy.

He held out his hand, dropped it, shook his head,
and then turned away. "I'm going out."

"Don't you walk out that door, Frederick Hale!"

"Try and stop me, Katie Ivene."

She threw her empty glass at him, just missing
his head by a dog's flea as he hightailed it out the
door. The glass pieces flew all over the room where
it left slivers that I knew would find a way to my
feet many a time.

I scooted away from the door, sneaked back to
my room, shut my door, and lay under Grandma's
quilt to read *Grimm's Fairy Tales*. I waited for what
would come next.

When Micah came home, he went to his room. I
heard him talking to Andy, sounding all happy
about playing at the creek with Buster and his dog
Pokie. I wanted to, but I didn't go in and tell him
what Momma told Daddy.

After a supper of scrambled eggs and cinnamon
toast, and after I had my bath and put on my yellow
gown, Momma sat on the side of my bed wearing
her prettiest red nightgown and smelling clean and

sweet. She touched my chin. "Isn't that something how your daddy nicknamed you Baby Bug?"

I breathed in Momma, and hoped she'd stay a while. "What do you call me, Momma?"

"Virginia Kate. That's your name and a good one." She picked up the Easter picture and stared at it. "Lord, church is stupid. That preacher was a ugly liar." She made a sour face, then it went away as she said, "So, summer's here, I reckon. No school."

My stomach tumbled around.

"And your daddy and I want to take a proper vacation." She smoothed the quilt. "I expect it'll help our nuptials."

I stared at her.

"You know, our marriage?" She kissed my forehead and her hair fell over me in a dark waterfall. Her breath tickled when she asked, "Don't you?"

I shrugged.

"You bet it will! Grown-ups need time alone. They don't fuss so much after they have grown-up vacations. Right?" She nodded her head until I nodded mine. "See! We think on it the same way. You're a good girl. Never give me a speck of trouble."

"Momma?"

"Hush now. Time to sleep." She tucked the covers around me and stood to leave. "You're the bestest daughter in the wide-world." At the door, she blew me a kiss, turned out my light, and moved down the hall to Micah and Andy's room to talk to them. She next went to the kitchen and ice rattled cold. Then soft music floated into my room and a woman sang deep and rusty, like summertime.

I sneaked to watch around the doorjamb. Momma twirled with her arms out and her night-gown swirled. She was lit up from behind by the lamp and her body showed through the gown. She didn't look like a momma who had three babies. She was like a momma with no kids at all. She rose up on her toes and bent backwards a bit. I wanted to be her then, grown up and beautiful, dancing. I thought most everything Momma did was as mysterious as the moon and as bright as the sun. I went back to bed, snuggled under Grandma's quilt, and fell asleep listening to the music.

Daddy's clomping shoes woke me up. I waited for the fussing to start up again. Instead, I heard Momma talking soft to him, more ice tinkling in the kitchen, and then the Naugahyde made that crinkly sound. I smiled in the dark and was almost asleep again when I heard Daddy make a growly noise. Soft steps headed to their bedroom. The bed squeaked and Momma giggled. When I heard, "Oh my god Katie. Don't stop!" I put my pillow over my ears and fell asleep that way.

The next morning, Momma hummed as she cooked Daddy a breakfast of eggs, fried potatoes, and biscuits. She looked as if she'd lapped up a full plate of cream. When she rubbed her hand through his hair, he closed his eyes. I kept an eye on Momma while I ate. Micah made his nostrils wiggle. Andy thought it all grand, and laughed the whole morning.

A week later, we were dropped off at Aunt Ruby's house. Momma drove us while Daddy was at work. She stopped the car and waved to her sister standing on her front step. Aunt Ruby's orangey-red hair was cut into tight curls in the front of her head, and the back was a fuzzy mess to her shoulders. Her pink-and-purple cotton dress hiked up on her hips and halfway up her legs—she had real pretty knees. When she waved, the underside of her arm waved, too. The only way she was like my momma was the way both their mouths turned up at the corners to where no one could tell if they were planning something, or being ornery, or getting ready to grin.

Micah and I slipped out with our suitcases and stood by while Momma drove off, plumb forgetting to kiss us goodbye. I hoped hard she would turn around, but she just waved her hand out the window. Or maybe that was her hair flying out instead; the dust from her tires made it hard to see.

Chapter 9
They's stupider than worms

Aunt Ruby told us to put our suitcases away. After we'd done that—I was staying in a smelly room she called the guestroom, and Micah was staying in Pooter-Boy's smellier room—she stood in front of us with her hands on her hippy hips, said, "I think switches are the bestest thing to keep young'uns toed on they's line." She turned her back on us and said over her shoulder, "Look out yonder, out the back winder." We followed her and looked where she pointed to the woods. "You see all them trees?" She stared us up and down until we nodded. "There's pee-lenty of them to wear out pee-lenty legs. Just rememorize that and we'll be fine."

Micah and I floated around the house like ghosts so we didn't get Aunt Ruby riled up. If I spilled my milk, I was switched. If Micah left the spoon outside after he finished eating the peanut butter off it, he was switched. If we talked too loud, walked too loud, or looked at her cross-a-ways, we were switched. She was right, there was pee-lenty switches to wear out on legs. When she moved near me, I covered up my head. That's because Aunt Ruby also liked to pop us upside our heads before we knew what was coming or why.

I thought my head would split right open and spill my brains onto the floor. I went to bed in the middle of the day and let the hornets go about their stinging business. Aunt Ruby gave me baby aspirin and said, "Just chew on them aspreen, titty baby." When the aspirin didn't work fast enough, she stood over me, hollering, "What in tarnation's wrong with a kid that flops around in bed holding on to her head like she's dying? Orter be out playing." She'd shake her half-curled up head and slam out the door. Momma had said Aunt Ruby was just like Grandpa Luke and I believed it.

Then we broke Aunt Ruby's lamp. The lamp was ugly as a monster's butt and as big as one, too. She said her special beau gave it to her and she was always shining it up. The lamp stood on a table by the side of Uncle Arville's easy chair. It was green, yellow, and gold with a big gold lampshade on it.

Micah and I were fussing over a Superman comic book, and when he pulled it from me, I punched his arm hard as I could. That made him a whopping mass of mad. He gritted his teeth and shoved me just hard enough that I fell back against the table. I felt the air moving behind me, then the noise of lamp pieces scattering across her linoleum floor and Aunt Ruby's screaming.

She stood over us like the pterodactyls in Micah's picture books, her beak opening and closing as if she'd tear us up one bite at a time. Nothing she hollered made sense, just a bunch of cussing and spit flying out of her mouth. Micah bent to pick up the glass pieces, while I tried to unbend the bones of the lampshade.

She slapped Micah on the back of his head, her eyes teeny slits of mean. "You little shitters! I got that lamp from Jackson!" She kicked Micah in the leg, and he bit his lip so he wouldn't cry. "I'm sick of you bastards!"

"We didn't mean to." I stood up, still holding the lampshade.

Aunt Ruby turned to me and raised her arm. "Shut up!"

My stomach turned like a ferris wheel.

Micah stood by me. "I'm glad it's broke. It's ugly, just like you!"

Aunt Ruby hit Micah in the stomach. He bent over and spit came out of his mouth.

I thought how he tried to be a good brother almost all the time, but how Aunt Ruby was mean to him anyway. I thought of how she switched and slapped us for stupid reasons. I was filled to the top with an ugly mad. It burned up from my stomach to my head and then spread all over my body like fire. I ran and pushed her as hard as I could. Might as well been trying to move a boulder.

She gritted her teeth, grabbed her own hair and pulled, spitting out a holler that curled my toes. I tried to send Micah mind messages to run, but we stood like scared lambs. In Aunt Ruby's eyes I saw the devil that Mee Maw had shown me in her church book. Her face was purpley and her hair was every which-a-way. Without saying another word, she grabbed me up by my ponytail and shook me until my scalp burned.

Micah ran between us, and this time Aunt Ruby hit him hard enough to send him flying across the room. I didn't see him land, but I heard a *whump* against the wall. She pulled me by my right arm through the living room and into the hall. I made squeaky sounds; my head had drums beating inside it. Even though I didn't like him, I wished Uncle Arville would come home and tell her to take a cold shower and stop being such a Bitchly Bitch.

Micah limped after us. He had a big knot coming on his cheek and his eye was squinting up. She told him, "You stop or I'll snap off her head, you hear me, boy?" He stopped.

She shoved me into her stinky bathroom and I fell on the floor. Slamming the door nearly off its rusted hinges, she screamed, "Fat little bitch! Not s'big in the britches now, huh?"

Micah pounded on the door. "Aunt Ruby! I'll behave. Aunt Ruby!"

She opened the medicine cabinet, picked up a pair of scissors. I waited to feel the hurt while she killed me. Grabbing me up by the shirt, she cut at my ponytail. She stuck my head under the faucet and held me there.

Micah's voice was far and away. "You okay? Vee? I'm sorry—"

Ruby pulled my head from the sink. "That

101

momma of your'n don't want you or your brothers." She turned to the door. "She ain't coming back for you. Stole my boyfriend, stole my clothes. Fucking whore. Thinks she's better'n me." She grabbed me by the arms and shook me until I thought my head would snap off. She spit out, "Kilt her own baby. Shoulda got rid of the lot of you while she was at it."

Micah rattled the knob. "You're a *damn liar*. It's not true. Not!"

She let go and I dropped in a puddle. As I lay my cheek on the cold tile, she said, real sweet, "You shut up, boy. Ain't you had enough? Think your sister wants s'more? Huh?"

"No ma'am," Micah said.

"Say you're sorry for all the worry you done caused me."

I hoped he wouldn't. I wanted him to tell her to shut up and to stomp his feet to shake the house down, even though my stomach did eighty-nine flops about it.

She said, "I'm waiting, little shitter."

"I'm sorry for causing all the worry."

Her big fat feet turned towards me. "You next, Fattie mae."

I didn't say a thing.

"Well, then maybe brother needs a hair-styling. Maybe I'll cut his head off'n his shoulders."

I talked to the pee-floor-tiles. "I'll behave."

Her feet moved away. "That's better. Now, Aunt

Ruby's got things to do." She opened the door, pushed Micah to the side, and stomped down the hall.

Micah jumped in and looked at me on the floor. "You hurt bad?"

"Nuh uh."

He helped me stand up and gave me some toilet paper to blow my nose, even though I know I wasn't crying one bit. In Aunt Ruby's mirror, I saw my chopped up hair and scratched up red face. Momma wouldn't want to look at me anymore, I was so ugly. Micah grabbed my sleeve and pulled me out of the bathroom. He said, "Oh oh, leetle seestor, you look bleestored." He made a funny Popeye face with his scrunched-up eye.

Aunt Ruby yelled from the kitchen. "Sweep up the glass and then come in here to eat."

While we cleaned up the lamp mess, Hank Williams yowled about cheating hearts.

Aunt Ruby had made macaroni and cheese, with banana pudding for dessert. She pointed her finger at us. "You two better eat after I gone to the troubles." She smiled just like the bad guy on *Bonanza*. The one that Hoss beat the hog snot out of. I wished Hoss were around, he'd know what to do with Aunt Ruby. She shook her wooly bully head. "I'm sorry, kids. I get so durn mad sometimes, don't know what gets over on me." She pointed to the table. "Eat."

We ate our supper, and then dug into the pudding.

I hated how it tasted so good. When Aunt Ruby wasn't watching, Micah opened his mouth to show me the chewed up cookie and mushed banana, and I put my hand over my mouth to quiet-giggle. We pretended that we forgot everything. When we finished, Aunt Ruby brought us to the living room and made us stand still while she took pictures. She snapped away, grinning, telling us our momma sure was going to love the nice pictures of her babies.

Uncle Arville came back from his fishing trip, looked at us, grunted, and went out to his shed. I didn't like him. He smelled like grease and old cigarette smoke, and that was the good parts. And he always told the same stories, like, "I was borned in a swamp in Florida, while my mam hunted gator. She just slung me on her back and finished up hunting."

Aunt Ruby ran out to the store to get stuff for supper, and while she was gone, Micah called home, but no one answered. He hung up and went on out the back door without looking at me.

I sat at the kitchen table and waited.

Aunt Ruby came in toting a sack of groceries. "That man ain't worth the trouble." She put them down, opened the freezer, took out a bottle, and filled up a big glass without ice. After gulping half down, she said, "Ahhh, now that's what I call a warm and cozy feeling." She drank the rest and poured another.

She cooked fried chicken, smashed potatoes, and cherry pie and every time her foot landed on the floor in time to the beat of the radio music, her rear end jiggled inside her cabin boy britches like a big bowl of Jell-O. I held my hand over my mouth so I wouldn't giggle and get a switching, or worse.

I watched her, wondered what it felt like to put the chicken in the popping grease, then stand back until it settled down. Or to stir the potatoes with butter and cream until they were gooey. To roll out the pie dough and fill it with different fruits or nuts or creams. Aunt Ruby looked almost sweet when she was fixing up food—and her food tasted good. It didn't make sense how someone that mean could roll out dough just right and get her chicken fried up until it was crispy brown without any burnt spots. I wanted her to show me so I could do it for Daddy. But she didn't let me help any more than Momma did, except when it came to washing up the dishes.

When the chicken was ready, she opened the screen door to call in Uncle Arville and Micah to supper. They didn't answer and Aunt Ruby's mouth straightened out as far as it could with those turned up ends. She said, "Stupider'n my big toe."

Just like Momma, she had changing moods. In her happy times, Aunt Ruby showed me how to sew on her Singer. She said she sewed all her clothes, ever since she was a schoolgirl. And when we'd get the clothes off the line, she taught me how to fold towels just right. She'd snap the towels and jabber about beauty secrets. How she rubbed egg white on her face, slooped mayonnaise and raw egg in her hair. I liked listening to her when she wasn't drunk-mean, except when she talked about Momma, like she started on right then.

She covered the chicken and put on her girls-have-secrets look. "Men don't know jack-flat shit, girl. You rememorize what I tell you."

I nodded.

"Yep, and they's stupider than worms. Don't you be letting men get at you, you hear? Aunt Ruby knows all about men." She stared at me with one eyebrow raised up so high I thought it had crawled up in her hair. "That momma of your'n could tell you a thing or two about nasty men. They's been on her since she was your age."

I looked out the screen door for Micah.

"Just like your momma, you'll end up flat on your back humping men from now 'til Kingdom Damn Comes. Whether you ask for it or not." She reached over and pinched my cheek. "I almost feel a mite sorry for you." Then her mood topsy-flopped again. "Now, go get your wild brother and that sorry husband of mine in t'supper. I been working my ass off, so git!"

I headed to the door.

"Don't you be dwaddling 'round either."

I went by the woods and hollered for Micah. I

didn't want him missing supper again. Aunt Ruby's food made everybody sleepy and quiet, even Aunt Ruby. I opened my mouth to yell again, but Micah's whisper pulled me up in a knot.

"Vee, I'm up here."

"Where?"

"Up in the crab apple tree." Branches rattled. I looked up to see his legs hanging from a limb.

"What're you doing up there?"

"I'm hiding."

"Come down, Aunt Ruby'll get mad."

"I'm coming."

When he came down, I asked, "Why're you hiding?"

"Can't tell you."

"Well, Aunt Ruby wants us right now. Come on." I grabbed his hand and pulled. Micah stopped, so I rolled my eyes and pulled. "Come *on*, Micah."

I'd never seen him look so woogly. "I feel sick, Vee. I think I gotta vomit." He pushed his hand in his hair. "I don't want to eat."

"Aunt Ruby said to come." I pulled him again. "Aunt Ruby said to get you and Uncle Arville to supper. She said *now*."

He looked at the shed. "Can't get him."

"We can bang on the door, stupid idiot."

"He can't hear you."

"Are we in trouble again?" My lower lip shook so I bit it.

Micah whispered. "We might be."

"What'd we do, Micah? What?" I bit my lip harder and tasted blood.

"Go tell Aunt Ruby you can't find Uncle Arville, 'kay?"

"But, I don't—"

"—go do it!" Micah pushed me, then ran to the edge of the woods and leaned over.

A stream of vomit came out of Micah's mouth, and I felt cold cold inside. I stepped to go to him, then I stepped to go to Aunt Ruby, then I stepped to the shed where the radio played loud country and western. I pushed the door, but it was locked. I had a weird whispery feeling come over me. The shed grew brighter and brighter. My head filled up with Grandma's voice saying, "Get Away From There! Now!" I turned to Micah to see if he heard, but he was coming at me with his hair stuck up on end, his mouth going "No, Vee, no, no."

I ran to the back door like Micah told me to in the first place, and said through the screen, "Uncle Arville won't come to supper and the door's locked."

She flew out cussing up a black storm and ran to the shed. Micah looked at me with Rambler hubcap eyes.

Aunt Ruby reached under a rock, grabbed the key, unlocked the door, and went inside.

The whisper in my head said, "It's going to be

okay. It's all going to be okay," and it was a sweet lullaby. My whole body felt warm. I grabbed Micah's hand so he could feel it, too.

Aunt Ruby ran out with blood all over her hands and the front of her dress. She screamed, "He's dead! He's dead! Lord God Almighty, help me." She fell to the ground.

Micah said, "Don't go in there, Vee. You hear?"

I nodded, and I meant it.

He ran off around the house and was gone. My feet stayed stuck as I stared at Aunt Ruby on the ground shaking her head back and forth. I listened for Grandma's whisper again, but all I heard was the knocking of a sapsucker.

Micah came back with a big round man. He went to Aunt Ruby, and Micah stood by me again. Our arms touched; his was cold. Aunt Ruby pointed to the shed, her mouth opening and closing. When he helped her up, there was a spot of blood on the grass I couldn't keep my eyes from. The man helped Aunt Ruby into the house, came back out and went into the shed. From inside, I heard, "Oh shit and mercy!" He came running out, wet up with sweat. "Don't go in there, kids. Christ Jesus." The round man closed the door and leaned against it while talking to himself.

Micah said something low, but all I heard was, ". . . an accident."

I looked at him.

There were ghosts in his eyes.

The man came over to us, scrubbing at his face. "Both of you come inside with me."

Micah looked as if all the blood went right out of his body and into the ground. He bent over and vomited right on the man's shoes. He straightened and wiped his mouth, said, "I'm sorry, Mister."

"It's okay, son." He handed Micah a handkerchief.

We trudged into the kitchen while my stomach loop-de-loo'ed with thinking how Aunt Ruby would surely blame us for whatever happened. She was wailing up a river in the living room.

With a grunt, the man got on his knees in front of us. He touched Micah's eye. He looked at my hair. His mouth made a straight line that he pushed the words through. "What in Lord's name?" Looking towards the living room, he wiped his mouth with the back of his hand, then said, "We'll get your parents here."

My heart flew up to the sky like a bird.

Micah said, "Yes, please."

The man stood up and talked to himself again. "I knew things was wrong over here."

"We could stay with you, if you can't find Momma and Daddy." I put on my best face.

"My God. Lord above." He grabbed the phone and dialed, said, "It's me, honey." He wrapped the cord around his hand. "Call them boys, then come over quick." He hung up and we followed behind him to the living room where Aunt Ruby lay on her couch, drinking straight from the bottle. The man stood over her with his arms crossed over his chest. "What happened here?"

She glugged from the bottle, burped, then said, "I sent my sister's girl out to fetch him so his food wouldn't get cold. Oh my lord, Boyd."

Boyd said, "I got the po-lice called over to this crazy house."

Micah made a mouse-squeak sound.

The door opened before Aunt Ruby could spew cusses—I saw the way the corners of her mouth turned, saw her eyes shoot x-ray beams on Boyd, then on us. A woman with brown eyes and spit curls walked in. I thought she looked like the best grandma, one where all the kids sat on her lap and ate her homemade sugar cookies. Like Grandma Faith would be, except my grandma was prettier, even if she was a ghost.

The woman looked over at us. "What in the world's happened here?"

Boyd went to her and whispered in her ear while she stood with her mouth part-a-ways open.

He turned to Aunt Ruby, "Ruby? You going to explain?"

Ruby curled her lip like a cur dog.

Boyd came over and touched Micah and me on the shoulders. "Go on with Helen, wee ones, and let her fix you up a plate of food." His hands were big and scratchety. I pictured him cutting wood for the fire while Helen cooked good food. I pictured them eating it together, holding their forks with one hand and each other's hands with the other. "And call their parents."

Helen led us to the kitchen, tsk-tsking under her breath. She didn't call at first; she was listening to Aunt Ruby carry on, same as me.

The bottle thudded on the table. "Dead! Up and dead on me! He was drunk on that damned Old Crow."

Boyd said something I couldn't hear. Micah stared out of the back door at the shed. Sirens screamed up the road.

Aunt Ruby was saying, ". . . and he must-a fell off'n the second level. He landed on that old rusted-out pole. Weren't any tires on it to stop it from going right through his belly. I could see his guts, oh lord help me! His eyes was bulgy and blood coming out his mouth and nose and ears! Oh, what will I tell Pooter-Boy?"

The sirens were right outside. The police only needed to look for the ugliest house with broken-down cars in the front.

Helen turned around and asked, "Micah, that's your name isn't it?"

The sirens stopped.

"Yes Ma'am."

"Do you know your phone number? And tell me your last name."

Micah told her and she dialed.

My breath stayed inside, filling up my head until it was light. Momma or Daddy had to answer.

Someone was knocking at the door.

Helen said, "Mrs. Carey?"

I let out all my breath. Momma had answered the phone. She was at home.

Boyd went outside. Micah and I sat with our hands in our laps, waiting.

Helen said, "You need to come quick. Arville's been in a horrible accident." She looked at us. "Yes, so to speak." Then she hung up.

While Boyd was outside talking to the police, Micah shook like I'd never seen him, even when Momma and Daddy were in the worst fights. Helen went over and hugged him hard. She said, "You precious things look like you've been in a heap of hurt."

I nodded. I wanted Fionadala to hold on to.

She sighed and held on to Micah.

"We're okay," Micah said, but he didn't push Helen away.

Boyd came back in the kitchen. "Bob and his boys are here."

Helen smiled at us and I saw how crooked her teeth were, but I didn't care. She said, "Well, I'll get some supper warmed."

Another siren screamed, and then the noise stopped outside. Aunt Ruby gabbered to nobody and burped some more. Boyd went outside again, and I went to peek out of the screen door.

Policemen and other men went in and out of the shed.

"Sweet girl, you come help me," Helen said.

"Me?"

"Yes, you."

I grabbed a spoon and stirred the potatoes until they were steamy again. I picked up the pie and set it on the table. Micah stuck his finger in the cherry filling, looked at it, and then wiped it on his jeans. There was a pot of green beans getting hot and bubbly, so I put butter in, like I'd seen Aunt Ruby do. I sliced up the bread. Helen made sure I didn't cut myself. Boyd came in and told Aunt Ruby to go outside with him.

She said, "I ain't got nothing to say. I'm tired. Want to stay on the couch."

Boyd said with a crunchy gravel voice, "Get up, woman."

Aunt Ruby whooshed out her air, said, "I'm coming; you ain't got to be such a sonuvabitch."

I took the beans to the table and when I turned, I saw men come out of the shed with a covered lump. Helen closed the door, even though it would get hot with no air coming inside. She said, "Let's get this table filled up." While I put the plates on the table, I heard Aunt Ruby outside, hollering. "You taking him now? Taking him away?" She bawled like a banshee.

Boyd came back, washed his hands in the sink, and sat back at the table without saying a word.

Soon as the sirens headed away, Aunt Ruby was back inside in a flash; bumping around a bit before she was finally quiet.

We were busy with food, hands and plates going everywhere. I hoped Aunt Ruby stayed in the living room so we could be with Boyd and Helen. I had my hope. None of us hardly touched the food, but we tried. Micah sat and stared at the grease soaking into the potatoes. All I cared about was Momma and Daddy coming. Everything would be good since Momma and Daddy had their vacation to fix what was broken.

I was a stupid little hick girl with no good sense.

Chapter 10
I'll be waiting

Boyd and Helen waited with us until Daddy came, alone. He looked itchy standing in Aunt Ruby's living room. Aunt Ruby didn't stir at all while Daddy, Boyd, and Helen all whispered by the door.

Daddy finally turned to take a look at us, and his eyes went round. "What in the hell happened here?"

"What I said." Boyd stuck his hands in his pockets. "We're leaving. Let us know if you need anything."

All a sudden, I wanted to go home with Helen and Boyd forever. Helen came over to hug us hard before leaving. As the door closed us in, I heard her say, "Oh, those poor babies . . ."

Aunt Ruby almost fell off the couch trying to get up. She gave up and stayed partly flopped over. "My husband's dead. Horrible dead. Blood ever-where. See! It's still on my shirt. Guts ever-where."

Daddy stood over her. "What did you do to my children?"

"I ain't got time for them young'uns now. I got a funeral to see after."

Daddy bunched up his fists. "What did you do to them, you crazy bitch?"

Aunt Ruby snarled back like a dog. "My husband got hisself gutted, that's all I got to worry over."

"You hell hound! Look at them, look at my children." Daddy pointed to us while we stood trying not to look back at the big lump of Aunt Ruby sprawled on the couch.

"You want to start up with that when you and my sister dumped them brats on me? I don't have time for this shit. I got the life-insurance people to call." She stared back at Daddy and burped long and nasty.

I wanted Daddy to scream at Aunt Ruby. I even wanted him to hit the dog snot out of her.

Instead, he huffed out his air, and said to us, "Come on. Let's get out of this dump. Leave your stuff here."

"You better get out. And I'll be throwing all that shit away soon as you leave." Aunt Ruby wobbly-stepped down the hall.

116

Daddy turned fast and hard and walked out the front door.

I ran to get my things so Aunt Ruby wouldn't throw them away. Micah followed me, whispering, "Leave it, Vee!" But I didn't want to leave everything. He helped me, then we pulled his stuff together. We kept waiting to hear Aunt Ruby running down the hall to get us. When we were back to the living room, she was looking through an address book while talking to herself. "I better call his Mam and Pap. Then his brother." She looked up at us, "You two shitters still here?"

When I hurried to open the door, Micah went over to her and slapped the address book out of her hands. It flew across the room and hit the wall. His voice was like it came out of a drum full of water. "Uncle Ar-vile's burning in hell and you will too, you mean whore."

I couldn't believe it. Aunt Ruby couldn't either. Her mouth opened, then shut, opened and shut, like a big ugly fish. Micah turned around just like Daddy had and walked out the door. I ran out behind him while Aunt Ruby screamed that she'd kill us if we ever came back.

Micah said, "I'll never come back, ever."

I grabbed his arm as we ran across the yard, dragging our suitcases.

Daddy was half out of the Rambler. "Get in this car, you two. *Now.*"

We dived in the car.

Daddy took off down the hill, leaving a big dust cloud behind us.

I finally let out all my breath I'd been holding.

Daddy drove with one hand, the other he tapped beginning with the little finger and working his way to the thumb, over and over. He kept looking at Micah in the rearview, waiting for him to say something. When he didn't, Daddy said, "What went on back there?"

"Nothing."

"Don't give me that."

"Give you what?"

"Don't be smart. This is serious." Daddy looked over at me, and I touched my hair. He said, "That Aunt Ruby is a nutcase."

Micah said, "So why'd you and Momma make us go there?"

At first Daddy didn't say anything. Then he said real quiet, "I don't know, son. I don't know." He ran his tapping hand through his hair, leaving it on top of his head, holding in the thoughts he didn't want to let out.

I held my breath in again, and let it out slow. I knew if I let one tear fall, the rest would rush on out. I wasn't going to be a baby.

Daddy traded hands, tap tap tapping. "How about we stop for some hamburgers, put all this Ruby stuff behind us, huh?"

I nodded, but I don't know what Micah did.

We stopped at a diner mixed with a hotel. Daddy

ordered hamburgers and fried potatoes with root beer floats. I felt like I was in one of my bad dreams that all a sudden turned good. Micah must have, too, since he looked the same as me. My brother gobbled down his food like he was starving. I laughed at his chipmunk cheeks until I remembered how many times Ruby had made him go to bed without supper.

Daddy sucked up his float with a loud sloopsh sound, then asked, "Isn't this nice?" He sloopshed again.

"Yes, Daddy." I wanted him to feel better. "It's good."

Micah didn't talk.

When Daddy went to the bathroom, Micah asked, "Seestor, can I have the rest of your ta-toes?"

I handed them over, watched him cram a bunch in his mouth.

With his mouth full, he said, "Thanks for the po-taters, Vee-Katers." He reached over and put me in a headlock. I thought I smelled Uncle Ar-vile's hair grease.

Back in the car, I right away fell asleep and dreamed I was trying to climb my mountain while Aunt Ruby screamed and cussed and chased me. Every time I climbed up away from her, I'd start sliding back down. Then Grandma Faith sat beside me. She kissed me on the cheek and said little mites like me shouldn't have to hurt. I leaned against her, feeling happy she'd run off Aunt Ruby.

I woke when we were at the end of our long road. Daddy drove up to the house, stopped the car, and left it running. He sat holding onto the steering wheel. Micah hurried to get out and the slammed car door made me jump.

I asked, "Daddy? Aren't you coming in?"

"No, Bug."

"Are you going to the store to get some milk?" I showed all my teeth.

I couldn't see his eyes in the dark. "Bitty Bug . . ."

"Okay, Daddy, you go on to the store and I'll be waiting." I grabbed my suitcase, opened the car door slow, to give him time to tell me the truth. When he didn't say anything, I eased out and closed the door. By the time I was on the steps, he was backing out of the driveway.

I threw down my case and went straight away to Momma and Daddy's bedroom to search through the closet and his dresser drawers. I slipped the shaving brush he left into my pocket. Momma came to the door holding Andy. She didn't say a word about my hair. I stared at her with my arms across my chest. She'd lied. Grown-up vacations didn't make everything magic-good.

She took me by the hand and led me into the living room where Micah sat on the couch drawing.

Andy asked, "Ginny Kate? You hurt?"

My eyes burned and itched. Momma pointed to the couch. I sat next to Micah, and she put Andy on the other side of me. She went into the kitchen and came back with big gooey brownies. We sat down on the floor and ate. Momma told us stories about when she was a kid, and I scooted up closer to hear every word. It was as if everything was a dream.

"Remember I told you about Petal Puss? That pig looked after me just like Bruiser watched over Ben. Too bad Bruiser died before Ben did or else maybe he'd a saved him from blowing his own . . ." Momma rubbed her eyes. "Oh, my baby brother."

"Petal Puss sounds good, Momma. I wish we had a pig," I said, so she wouldn't remember Uncle Ben under the willow tree, dead with a bullet hole in his brain. Gone dead on purpose.

Momma's smile came back. "Yes, and a dog. We could marry them and have digs or pogs. Baby poglets. A whole yard of Petal Pusses and Bruisers."

"I remember Bruiser," Micah said. "He had one ear and was old as my teacher—and she's real old. And I liked Uncle Ben. He was like he was my age even though he wasn't. He showed me how to write my name fancy."

"He was spoilt rotten," Momma said, but she smiled.

"So what about the pig?" I asked.

"I raised it up from a baby. Even let it come in the house when your grandpa wasn't around."

Micah said, "Grandpa was mean. I remember when he hit Grandma in the face, right in front of me!" He looked like Little Joe did before he took ahold of the bad guy. "Grandpa's like Aunt Ruby, even meaner."

"Let's don't talk about that, okay? Let's talk about Petal Puss the Pig." Momma looked far away, long enough for Andy to get bored. When she said the next part, she said it very quiet, and I knew Momma's happy left her. "I loved that pig and my daddy butchered it. Made bacon out of it. My daddy's a bastard." Her eyes had mad ray beams coming out. "I'll never have pork, ever. It's like eating a dog." She jumped up fast and turned on the television. Micah fiddled with the rabbit ears and we sat and watched *The Danny Thomas Show*, then we went to bed.

Later that night, I heard Momma crying. I went and peeked through the crack left in her door. She was sitting on her bed, holding one of Daddy's shirts against her face. She finally lay down, covering herself up with the shirt. When I didn't hear any more sounds, I sat outside her bedroom and leaned against the wall.

Next I knew, Micah was there to help me back to my room. I climbed under Grandma Faith's quilt. Micah sat in the chair by my bed and looked out my window. When I woke up later he was gone and the house was still. I waited to hear Daddy's shoes, but he never came home.

$$\bullet \quad \bullet \quad \bullet$$

A few weeks after we came back from Aunt Ruby's house, I was sprawled on the floor watching cartoons when Momma tore open a big envelope and spilled out what was inside. She hollered, "That bitch!", threw everything on the coffee table, and marched herself to the phone. I heard her yelling at Aunt Ruby.

I looked at what had Momma so riled. It was the pictures Aunt Ruby took of Micah and me after she beat us up. My stomach clenched up like a big fist, but I shoved one in my pocket.

She was on a tear. "I never want to see you again! Nobody hurts my sweet babies!" She hung up the phone with a bang.

Bugs Bunny was telling Elmer Fudd he wouldn't track him down til hunting season, and it made me think how everybody lied; they just don't always know they're lying when they say things. Or maybe they do. It was too hard to figure out.

Chapter 11
The party was over

Daddy came over for my seventh birthday and we had a party even though I thought nobody felt like it. Momma made my favorite, coconut cake with extra coconut. Daddy cranked and cranked the ice cream maker. We kids ate the salty ice that fell out while waiting for the cream to freeze. The radio blasted out of the window and we listened to it on a blanket under the tree. When *Hello Mary Lou* came on, Daddy and Momma danced. *The Purple People Eater* came next and Micah laughed all the cake right out of his mouth. Andy jumped up and down like a happy fool. I grinned at them all and waited to open my presents.

There were pick-up sticks and a Cootie game from Momma, Micah drew me a picture of Mrs. Mendel's cat, Andy colored a blue horse from his coloring book, and Mrs. Mendel gave me a Mr. Potato Head. The best present of all was from Daddy, even though I didn't let on it was the best to everyone else. He gave me an Instamatic camera just like his, with film already put in it. Mee Maw sent three more rolls and some money to develop them with. I snapped pictures right away. Everybody smiled like in toothpaste commercials.

I thought Daddy was coming back, seeing how Momma and Daddy danced, smiled, and struck poses for the camera with each other. Momma's cheeks were glowed up and she laughed like she had a long time before. But next thing I knew, someone honked a horn.

Daddy picked up his hat, said, "Katie, I'm leaving the Rambler for you."

"Well, how noble of you. How galoot."

"You mean gallant."

"No, I didn't." And Momma marched into the house.

"Well, children, I have to be going." Daddy tried to kiss all of us, but Micah turned his head.

I thought we'd all ask him to stay, but we stood there. Birds had pecked our talk boxes out. Daddy turned, loped around to the front of the house, and was gone. The party was over.

I started second grade even though my hair didn't have time to grow out right. Momma tried to fix it as best she could. She said, "Ruby did the same thing to me when I was a girl your age. She's got her nerve."

First grade had been easy, especially with Mrs. Lindy, even though I missed a lot of classes so I could help with Andy since Momma said he could get so tiresome with all his wants and needs. In my cigar box, I put in crayons, thick white paste in the little jar, scissors, pencils, and erasers. I opened the box and smelled it over and again. Momma bought me a plaid jumper, white shirt, white socks, and Mary Janes, and everything felt stiff and new.

The first week of school, Momma pulled my hair into two funny pigtails and put a rubber band on the ends. After that, I went around with wild hair instead of the pigtails. Momma was good with beginnings, but not so good with keeping up with stuff.

The weather turned cool again and the maple burned its color, along with most all the other trees. In school, I sopped up all the stuff I could learn.

Reading was my favorite thing. And Micah was right; my least favorite thing was my teacher. Mrs. Penderpast was meaner than a nest of wasps, and at least two-hundred-years old. She hollered at us, told us we were heathens, and made us stand by our desks for an hour if anyone talked in class out of turn. Right after Halloween, Mrs. Penderpast died. Just up and died right in the class.

There was a big boy named Edsel. The teacher was always making him bend over in front of the whole class while she paddled him. I squinched my eyes shut every time she swung.

Poor Edsel. The kids laughed at his big belly, his crooked teeth, and his goofy ways. He went around the playground by himself, picking his nose and scratching his butt. Most times he smelled like pee and that kept the other boys from beating him up, since they didn't want his pee and boogers on them. I felt sorry for him, but I wasn't stupid enough to try to make friends with him and get his cooties.

That morning before Mrs. Penderpast died, she had paddled poor Edsel because he forgot his homework. I heard him sniffling and right then I imagined what it was like to be Edsel. I wanted to grab that paddle and make Mrs. Penderpast bend over. My face was hot with the mad that took hold of me. She was three licks in, when I couldn't stand it anymore. I said, "Mrs. Penderpast, you best stop hitting Edsel."

She turned and stared at me. "What did you say?" She held the paddle in the air, ready to throw it at me. Edsel looked like a cross between in-love and grateful.

"He can't help how he is." My heart beat hard enough to make my shirt move.

A girl in the back row said, "Ohhhh."

"This class is punished. I'm sending a note home to all your parents, you hear me?" She sat at her desk and put her head in her hands, breathing hard for a bit before she rose up at me. "And you, Miss Smart Mouth, I'll be dealing with you."

My mouth had a mind of its own. "You're like my Aunt Ruby. You like to smite stuff like God does, just because you can."

Mrs. Penderpast was a Baptist, or maybe Catholic, or Presbyterian. Whatever she was, she didn't like that comment one speck. "You little heathen! Blasphemer!" She pointed to the door. "Get out, all of you. Out Out Out!" She pointed straight at me. "I'll get to you later, Virginia Kate. I don't like your kind."

The other kids looked at me as if I was a crazy girl while we walked in a line out of the room. Edsel was behind me; I felt his hot breath on my neck. I thought for sure I heard him say, "I love you, Virginia Kate," but I was hoping not.

I was scared out of my mind with wondering what Mrs. Penderpast would do to me. We lined up on the sidewalk outside of class and waited.

Afterwhile, Principal Tucker came by. He raised his eyebrows at us, went into the classroom, came right back out, and said, "Children, come with me." He took us to the cafeteria where the cafeteria ladies gave us milk. I liked the cafeteria ladies, they talked about interesting stuff. Like what teacher was acting up when they didn't know anyone was watching. Or how they saw the principal trying to pick up an Ohio girl in a bar.

The next week we had a new teacher, Miss Bowen. She was nice and friendly, and she never paddled Edsel. She gave me lots of silver stars. They stuck Mrs. Penderpast in the ground and forgot about her. Except me. I took home the picture of her poodle she kept on her desk. On the back was written, *Precious Piddles Penderpast. My best friend.* It made me feel sad.

It was strange knowing Daddy wasn't coming home so I could show him my stars. Micah stayed in his room drawing most times, or he'd run down to Buster's. Andy went around the house saying, "Daddy? Momma, where's Daddy?" until Momma screamed at him to stop. He'd cry, and Momma had to hug him.

Then Daddy called to say he had Important News and would be over. While waiting, I did my homework. I had a collection of silver-starred papers. I could never get enough of those stars.

Momma was cooking a big supper for Daddy. Chicken, potatoes, lima beans, and homemade yeast rolls. For dessert, Daddy's favorite apple pie with all the crumbly stuff on top. She wore one of her nice dresses, too. A light blue with a wide belt to show off her teeny waist. The top went up around her neck, leaving her back naked. Her hair was in a rolled twist and she smelled like a Shalimar explosion.

Daddy knocked on the door at six, stepped in, and Andy grabbed him around his legs screaming, "Daddy! Daddy! Daddy!" I stood holding out my schoolwork. Micah sat on the couch drawing. He didn't even look at Daddy when Daddy said, "Hi there, Micah Van Gogh. What's shakin'?" But I saw Micah's eyes when Daddy first came in. How his eyes looked like he missed Daddy and was secretly glad he was there.

Momma came in wiping her hands on a dishrag. "Hello, Frederick. Supper . . . I mean, dinner is almost done."

"You didn't have to go to any trouble."

"No trouble a'tall. I made you a drink, take a chair."

We kids stared at them as if they were from outer space.

Daddy sat on the couch next to Micah, who scooted away from him. I sat beside Daddy, leaned against him and put my nose into his shirt to take in his Daddy smells. Andy sat in Daddy's lap.

When Momma called us to eat, Andy and I grabbed Daddy by the hands and pulled him into the kitchen. The table was done up with the wedding-present dishes, at least the ones that weren't broken. In the middle of the table glowed two fancy candles. She'd spread a tablecloth and the food on it steamed good smells.

"My, this looks delicious, Katie." He dug in, eating like he hadn't for a week. The rest of us dug in, too, except for Momma.

"Oh, it's nothing." She sipped with her pinkie raised up. I copied her with my glass of milk, but it felt too strange not having all my fingers on the glass.

After we finished, Momma served the pie with vanilla ice cream. Micah ate the whole thing in two bites and held up his bowl for more before Momma hardly had a chance to sit back down. Andy tried to copy him, ending up with a big mess all over the place. But Momma didn't fuss at all. She laughed, and fetched Micah more pie.

After dessert, we all went into the living room to watch television like we used to. But Daddy ruined the warm goodies in my stomach. Ruined Micah finally grinning at Daddy. Ruined Momma's feeling happy. Ruined everything.

"I have some important news." He stood up and went to the kitchen. Momma straightened her dress around her knees and smoothed her hair. When he came back in the room, he poured his drink without ice down his throat in one gulp.

I was sure he was about to ask Momma to forgive

him for whatever, and then Momma would ask him to forgive her for whatever, and then they'd kiss.

He said, "I'm moving back to Texas." He cleared his throat. "To go to school, that is."

I heard Mrs. Mendel's cat meowing for me to come play with her. I heard the wind stir the redbud tree in her yard. I heard Grandma Faith sigh.

Momma stared at him, same as the rest of us. "What did you just say, Frederick Hale?"

"I said I'm going back to school." Daddy hurried back to the kitchen; I heard ice clink. He then stood in the doorway, looking at the bottom of the glass he'd emptied before he was back in the room.

Momma gave Daddy a stare that should have made him keel over dead. She stood up so fast the chair scraped hard across the floor. "And just like that you decide to leave your family? There's no schools in West Virginia? Or are our schools too full up with hicks for you?"

"It's not that way, Katie."

Micah jumped off the couch and ran out the front door.

"You see what you're doing to your family? You selfish bastard." Momma pushed Daddy aside and went into the kitchen. Ice pounded into her glass.

He smiled down at me. "Baby Bug, look at you how pretty. You're getting so grown up."

Before I could say anything, Momma came back with a glass full and said, "Like you care. You won't see your kids growing up." She gulped it down in three swallows, then asked, "Why, Frederick? Why so far away from me?"

Daddy looked down at his feet. "Mother said she'd pay for school if I moved back to Texas to help her since Runt's gone."

"Don't be such a coward. Tell your daughter and your son full face on."

I didn't want him to say it again. Andy didn't either, his bottom lip poked way out.

Daddy looked over my head. "I said, Mother is paying for school, but only if I move back to Texas."

Momma didn't take her eyes off Daddy. "Are you a wittle boy? Mommy's got to take care of yew?"

"I'm taking care of her."

"Ha!"

Andy looked from Momma to Daddy, and his face pinched up. If he took up to whining, Momma would make me take him out of the room and I'd miss what was going to happen to us. I sat still as I could, even though I had to pee.

"I can't pass up this opportunity."

"And your children? You'll pass them up? And me?"

"I'm bettering myself for them."

"They'd rather have their Daddy." She looked at Andy and me. "Wouldn't you, kids?"

Andy nodded, but I felt frozen up solid.

"It's not forever. And they can come visit anytime they want." He looked at me, then away real fast. "Mother said she'd send you money every month to help while I'm in school."

"Like hell my kids will visit you halfway across the world."

Andy ran over and grabbed Daddy by the legs. "Daddy, don't run off. I'll be good, I pwomise. Sister will too. And Micah. We pwomise." It was just like in the soap operas Momma watched, it was so pitiful.

Momma turned to me, her face a mask of mad. "Take Andy outside."

"But Momma . . ."

"Now!"

"Daddy?" I begged him in that one word.

He put his face in his hands.

Momma gave me her meanest I'm-not-telling-you-again look. I grabbed Andy's hand and he went limp as a dead dog. Momma had to pick him up, set him outside on the steps, then she pushed me out the door, and closed it behind us.

I ran down to the window where I could listen in, but Daddy came running out, slipped in a car I hadn't seen before, and drove off. I ran in the dust he left behind, screaming at him to come back. When I looked behind me, Micah was standing beside Andy with his arm around him. I went to stand by them and there we stayed. Soon after, Momma came to stand with us. We stared at the road. But it didn't make him turn around.

• • •

After he moved, Daddy wrote a letter to each of us. I read Andy's to him and it wasn't any bigger than an inchworm.

Dear Andy, I promise to see you soon. Be good and mind your momma. Love, Daddy.

I didn't know what Micah's said, since he tore it up without reading it and threw it in the garbage. I tried piecing it back together, but the bits were too small. I saw some words—you'll see, grown, angry, sorry, please—but that's all.

I waited until I was alone in my room to read mine.

Dear Bug, I'm in my own apartment. Can you believe it? Old man me with the young ones. I decided not to stay with Mee Maw, but I visit her every day. I'm catching up on everything I've forgotten. I don't know if I will get A's like you, but I'm trying to make everyone proud of me.

Here is a Shakespeare quote for you from the Merchant of Venice: 'The quality of mercy is not strain'd, it droppeth as the gentle rain from heaven, upon the place beneath. It is twice blest; It blessith him that gives and him that takes.' Do well in school, Bitty. I love and miss you, Daddy.

In the envelope was a photograph of him sitting in a leather chair. Books were piled up on the floor, on the coffee table, on the end tables, everywhere. He was grinning bigger than Mrs. Mendel's Cadillac. I put it in my new Special Things Box.

Mee Maw called once a week and I had to listen to her bellyache about how she missed her grandbabies. I said, "Then come live with us and bring Daddy back home."

"Me leave Texas? The greatest place in the Younited States of America?"

"West Virginia is the greatest place, Mee Maw. It's beautiful. We have mountains and the holler is quiet and the trees burn bright and we have lots of rivers like the Cranberry—"

"—I get the picture, Laudine Virginia Kate. But I'm too old." She told me she was lonely since Runt had passed, but he left her plenty of money and she sold his business for heaps of cash. "I can afford to help, so that's what I'm doing. Doing it for my grandbabies."

With the checks, Momma bought out the grocery store. She told us, "You never know when the well will run into the creek and leave us dry." She bought herself new dresses, stockings, and shoes with it, too. Momma's closet was near to bursting with beautiful clothes. Silks, cottons, linens in blue, green, red, and pale cream yellow. The nice clothes she bought my brothers and me were lost under the dirt and sweat of our playing. We liked our old clothes better anyway.

She said, "Your daddy will be back. Mark my words."

She was wrong. One day Momma opened a big envelope and without saying a word, marched into the kitchen for a bottle and her glass. Then she marched herself into her bedroom and slammed the door. I heard cussing, crashing, and bumping all the time I did my school letters. When it was quiet, I tiptoed into her room. She was laid out on her bed asleep, still dressed. The papers in the envelope were strewn all over the floor. I picked them up and took them outside to wait for Micah to get home.

An hour later, he came clunking down the road with crushed beer cans stuck under his shoes. Lately he'd taken to wearing shoes, even on the warm days, and said bare-footing it was too hick. I think he said that because Buster was from Massachusetts. He'd cut his hair in a crew cut like Buster, too, and it made him look taller.

I shoved the papers under his nose. "Momma got this and pulled a big doozy."

He stared at them a minute before he handed them back. He kicked off the beer cans, sending them flying across the road. "If I were you, I'd forget about having a Daddy anymore." He turned around and ran up the hill to the empty house.

I wanted to follow him, but was afraid Momma would wake up and see I had the papers. I took them back and laid them on the floor where I'd found them.

Momma never said anything to us kids. I heard her on the phone once with Daddy saying it was going to cost Mee Maw a lot more for her to sign those papers and for any other deals she had in mind.

• • •

With Mee Maw's money, we had plenty of Christmas presents that year. They were piled under the tinseled-up tree, wrapped in red, gold, and silver foil, with big green ribbons. Momma said, "Just the four of us, I reckon." She turned teary-eyed and decided to invite Aunt Ruby to have Christmas with us.

Micah was in the kitchen when Momma dialed her up and invited her. He winked big and silly at me. When Momma went out to get the clothes off the line, Micah called Aunt Ruby back.

"Aunt Ruby. Momma said to tell you she's changed her mind." He wiggled his eyebrows at me. "No, she said you aren't welcome anymore. You stink like a monkey's ass." I heard hollering on the line as Micah hung up. He laughed, slapping his knee.

The phone rang and Micah didn't answer it.

"You're going to be in so much trouble."

"No I won't. Just wait." He hummed along as he made himself some cinnamon toast.

Later, Momma hollered for Micah and me.

Micah came in with a smile, but I trudged in.

Momma said, "Why did you call my sister and tell her that? You answer me right now!"

"Momma, I don't know what you're talking about. Ask Vee."

I shook my head, pretending it was the silliest thing I ever heard.

Micah made sweet eyes. "I don't know what's wrong with her, Momma. Maybe she didn't really want to come and she's just trying to start something."

"You don't know that," Momma said.

"You know she hates us. Remember what she did to us, Momma?"

Momma blinked slow. "Well, maybe she's drinking too much again."

Micah left the room, first giving me a grin where Momma couldn't see.

The next day while Momma was having coffee with Mrs. Mendel, Micah called Aunt Ruby again. "Momma said you're a fat whore and she never wants to see you again."

Same as before, later Aunt Ruby called up Momma and Momma called Micah into the living room, her face as red as a fat baby's butt. "Micah Dean Carey, did you dial up Aunt Ruby and call her a fat whore?"

Micah's eyes went big and round. "I don't even know what that word means, Momma! Isn't that a nasty word?"

"Well, she used to torture the hell out of me when we were growing up. Come to think of it, she lied like a dog back then and she's probably lying like one now! I don't know why I invited her in the first place. I'm going to un-invite her right this minute!"

I drank my milk so I wouldn't say, "Yeehaww!"

"Whatever you think is best, Momma," Micah

said. "Hey, want me to draw your picture? You look pretty today."

Christmas day, and no Aunt Ruby, we jumped up early and opened our presents. My presents were puzzle books, *Tom Sawyer*, a Slinky, a hula hoop, clothes, and a new bike. Micah's were paints, three real canvases to paint on, clothes, Parcheesi, and a new bike. Andy got trucks, cars, and boats, Play Doh, clothes, and a new bike, too. Three bikes! We had surely died and gone to Rich People Land. Momma made a big Christmas feast of turkey, potatoes with gravy, stuffing, and pumpkin and cherry pie. We played with our toys and ate the nuts and chocolate Momma put into our Christmas sacks. I kept waiting for the door to open and Daddy to walk in, grinning his I'm full-of-Christmas-cheer grin. When it was time for lunch, Andy didn't want to eat. He sat at the table without picking up his fork.

Momma said, "Eat, Andy. Look at this feast!"

"Waitin' for Daddy." Andy stuck out his lower lip so far it covered his plate.

"Daddy's not coming, stupid." Micah tore into his food before it could get up and walk off.

"Micah, don't call your little brother stupid. I mean it."

"I want Daddy." Andy had on a pointy chin like Momma.

I said, "He's going to surprise us."

"He's not coming, Seestor. Geez, when are you

and Andy going to learn?" He ate a big scoop of mashed potatoes and let some ooze out of his teeth.

"He's going to surprise us." I took a bite of turkey, swallowing it before it was chewed enough.

Micah rolled his eyes and helped himself to more potatoes.

Andy picked up his fork. "Yaay, Daddy's coming!"

Momma pinched her nose. "Look, we'll call your daddy right now. Will that suit you?"

"Yes Ma'am," Andy and I said. Micah stabbed more turkey and said nothing.

Momma dialed Mee Maw's house, her mouth pulled tight with those lifted ends barely lifted. "Laudine, this is Katie." She twirled the phone cord. "Yeah, Merry kissmyass to you."

Micah laughed and I shushed him.

"I said, Merry Christmas to you, Laudine." She looked over at us and winked. "Look, is your pweshush son there? My babies think he's on the way here." She twisted the phone line around her hand. "Yes, that's what they think and no, no one is talking to nobody. We're eating our feast. So, is he there?"

All three of us stared, even Micah, waiting to see what Mee Maw would say.

"Uh huh. Okay, thanks." She hung up, said, "He's not coming kids. Andy, you'll have to deal with it, sweet pea. He's at your grandmother's eating 'so she won't be aw awone'. Boo hoo, poor old woman with all that money can't fly herself and her son here to see his family. A crock of it, I'll tell you."

The phone rang and Momma didn't answer it. It stopped after five rings and started up again. Momma sat at the table, cut her meat, and put it in her mouth, chewing, nothing mattered but the food in her mouth. I thought Andy would raise up a fit, but he ate same as Momma. Micah shrugged and reached for the gravy. I drank some milk to get the lump down.

When the phone stopped ringing, Momma took a deep breath and let it out slow. "Kids, I'm sorry, okay? There's nothing to do about it but enjoy all the good we got today. Sometimes people are just rotten in Denmark."

"Thanks for the food, Momma." Micah grinned at her, gravy around his mouth and on his shirt.

"You're welcome. Wipe your mouth."

And that was that, we finished eating and said nothing more about Daddy. But I was so mad I could've spit nails and made a house with them.

After we cleaned up everything (and the boys helped for once), we ran outside to ride our bikes in the cold. Momma sat on the steps and drank Christmas happy drinks with Mrs. Mendel. I pretended my bike was a trusty steed. I thought about how Daddy should be right beside Momma. I thought about what Micah said, about how I should forget we had a Daddy since he forgot about us.

I pretended that he tried to come but Mee Maw needed him. He couldn't get on a plane because they didn't have any seats left. The weather kept him home. He was too sick to drive. I pictured him going back to his poor lonely apartment with a teeny Christmas tree, not the big one like we bought with Mee Maw's money. He wouldn't have any presents, except for the things we sent him.

All alone. That's how I thought he was.

Chapter 12
Daddy got himself a slut
1965

In the spring, when the wind blew so gentle that nothing could go wrong, Daddy came to us in a blue Corvair convertible. We'd been doing just fine without him, at least that's what Momma said. I was swinging on the swing, trying to figure out what I wanted to take a picture of when I heard the car roaring down the long road. When he pulled up, I didn't know it was him at first. And he wasn't alone.

He jumped out of the car wearing a leather jacket, a cowboy hat, and a mustache. I ran up to give him a hug. His lips were cool when he kissed my cheek and his mustache tickled. He grinned like a monkey while looking around the yard asking, "Where's my little Andy? Where's Micah?" I didn't have time to answer before Daddy galloped up the steps and knocked at the door before going in. I forgot I was mad at him for not coming at Christmas.

The woman stayed in the car. When she pushed back her scarf, her red-blond hair caught up in a sudden wind. She turned to smile at me, and her front teeth had a little space between them. She took off her sunglasses and her eyes matched the green scarf. She looked as if she had no secrets, as if all her life was honest and good—but I knew we all have secrets, so she must have them, too.

She said, "You must be Virginia Kate."

I stared at her.

"I've heard all about you and your brothers." She looked in the backseat, then at me again. "I brought y'all gifts. Do you like books? I have an art book for Micah, *Black Beauty* for you, and a coloring book and colors for Andy."

I stepped closer, cut my eyes to the backseat.

She held out a pack of Juicy Fruit. Her hands were like mine, used to prying things open, digging in gardens, poking into tree holes, burying dead birds. I didn't take the gum, so she set it down. "Yes, well then. This is where y'all live."

I nodded, twisting up my feet in the grass.

"I'm Rebekha."

Micah came from behind the house, stood by me, looked at Rebekha, and said in a loud voice, "Momma said Daddy got himself a slut. Is that you?"

She pulled back her shoulders. "We'll wait for your daddy so he can answer that."

Micah leaned on the car. "What does slut mean?"

"What, Hon?"

"What's that mean?"

"I suppose it means your mother isn't happy with your father right now."

"Momma said you're a home-breaker-upper."

I pinched his arm so's he'd shut up.

"I see." Rebekha held out the pack of gum to Micah. He took three pieces, opening, then cramming, them all in his mouth.

Daddy stepped out the door and strode over like a rooster. "Rebekha, I see you've met Miss Virginia Kate and Mister Micah."

"Yes, we're having a nice chat."

"Baby Bug, Micah, this is your new step-momma." He put his hand on Rebekha's shoulder. "My new wife."

I felt like the time my old grass swing broke and I knocked all the air out of me when I landed on my backside. Micah turned to Daddy and spit out his gum by Daddy's feet.

Daddy was fast-tapping on Rebekha's shoulder.

I turned to Micah, but he ran away.

Daddy leaned over and whispered into Rebekha's ear, she whispered back into his. Daddy walked back into the house.

I left Rebekha, and sneaked around to listen at the window.

Momma was fussing up a storm. ". . . taking any crap off you and that slut you got there in your dandy little car. Mommy buy that for her wittle boy?"

"Don't talk about Rebekha like that. And it's none of your business what my mother does or does not do."

"I just bet it's not my business."

"I didn't come to argue. I came to see my children."

"Mr. High and Mighty. Who married some other woman without telling his kids, or me?"

"I wanted to tell them in person. You, too."

"Why Fred? *Why*? I loved you."

It was so quiet; I heard my breath come in and out. Was Daddy thinking things over? Was he going to tell her he loved her, too? I waited, hoping. Daddy would come home, he'd tell the woman in the car that he was sorry, but he had a family in West Virginia.

"You have a lot of nerve, Katie."

My heart sank down to my toes.

"I had our babies and I took care of this house. What do you think that is?"

"Might I remind you that you didn't have *all* of *our* babies."

"You *bastard*."

Someone took up to crying, and Daddy asked, "Andy, what are you doing under there?"

"Andy, to your room, right this minute," Momma said.

I heard Andy stomping off, cloggy voice saying, "I orter run away! I'm sadder than ever in my life."

Daddy was saying, ". . . came to see the children, not argue with you."

"Ha! After all this time—"

"—I needed to get settled first."

"Settled? What a shit you are."

"I had to do this, for the children's future."

"Okay, Mr. Shakeshit, prove what kind of daddy you are. Take Micah back with you."

Buzzing started up all around my head.

"Take Micah?"

"What I said."

"I have a new wife. She's still adjusting."

"You bake the cake, Fred."

"I need more time. Let me talk to Rebekha."

"They're your kids, too. Don't matter if you try to make a whole new family in place of this one."

"You're being unreasonable."

"You just talk like you want to be a good daddy. All talk. Blah blah blah."

"Okay, then. Fine. Micah will leave with us. Does that satisfy you?"

"Sure, I'm all happied up over you leaving, then Micah leaving. Just take bites out of me until I'm all eat up."

"Don't give me the martyr crap."

"That woman'll run screaming back to wherever she came from once you hold your kid in her face."

" 'Asses are made to bear.' "

"Screw you and your Shakesweird."

Daddy's shoes stomped hard across the floor.

Momma hollered for Micah, then opened the back door and hollered for him again. My head was tight around my brain. I ran inside. Micah wasn't in his room. I threw myself into his closet and the light from the keyhole was bright. I closed my eyes. I was riding up my sweet mountain on Fionadala. I heard my name called. I rode harder, her hooves making thunder. My name again. I put my face in her sweaty neck. I fell right back down to earth when I heard the screen door make its *scrang* sound and Micah hollered, "Vee! Vee! Hurry!"

When I ran to the back, Micah stood holding a big green suitcase. He went over to the maple, broke a piece of limb, and put it his pocket. He wore clean jeans and a checkered shirt buttoned all the way to his chin. His eyes were dark and hard as he looked back at me. I saw how handsome he would be one day. We walked together to the front yard. Andy came outside and stood beside us. I had a clog of frogs in my throat.

Andy said, "Why're you going?"

"Have to." That's all Micah answered.

I grabbed Micah and held on. He didn't push me away and call me a pest. I looked over at Rebekha and decided I had to hate her. She was watching us while Daddy leaned in talking to her. She never looked at Daddy while he talked, just kept her eyes on us. She looked sad, but I didn't care. Daddy walked over and took Micah's suitcase. Andy wrapped himself around Daddy's legs and said, "Daddy, you don't got to go run off."

I held on tighter to Micah. I imagined Mrs. Mendel at her window, getting her heart broken in ten pieces by what she saw going on.

Micah showed the first scared look I'd ever seen. His hands were sweaty when he grabbed onto my arm. Daddy set down the suitcase, pried Andy off his leg, saying, "Son, I'm sorry, Daddy has to. I'm sorry." Andy ran off as fast as he could, his feet kicking up leaves. Daddy pulled Micah and me apart, and took Micah's arm. Micah stiffed up, and even though he was getting tall and strong, Daddy was taller and stronger as he made him go to the car.

Daddy came back for Micah's suitcase. He put his finger under my chin. "I'm sorry, Baby Bug. I'm so sorry." I hit him in the stomach as hard as I could. He grabbed his belly and said, "Oh no, my Bug."

I ignored him and ran to Micah.

But Micah held up his hand while shaking his head at me. I felt young and silly and scared. He said, "Tell Buster I had to go." He climbed into the backseat and looked straight ahead. I stared hard at my brother, sending him mind messages that I thought he was giving up too easy. That he was leaving Andy and me alone with Momma. Daddy put the suitcase in the backseat with my brother and turned to me again. I pretended I didn't notice his wet eyes. Momma didn't come out of the house. I wanted to hate her, too.

Daddy got in the car, turned on the engine, and backed up. Micah gave me a thumbs up. I saw his eyes, how they were already far away. I waved at him, but my arm belonged to someone else. My feet in the grass belonged to someone else. Everything belonged to someone else. As Daddy drove off, I thought how that woman hadn't remembered to give me my book. I thought of that day I told Micah he could never go away.

After Micah left, I took a drawing pad he left behind to my room and kept it under the Easter picture. Momma told me to stop my moping since it didn't do a person a bit of good.

Later, I heard her on the phone with Mee Maw. She said, "One gone and you must be gloating." She tapped with her nails. "Yes, a deal's a goddamn deal. I can't hardly make it on what I got and you prey on me like a vulture to dead meat." Tap tap tap. "Well, I hope you're happy, you cold-hearted bitch. You just wait, I'll get them back. You wait." Tap tap tap. "You do that." The slamming of the phone.

That night, I heard her crying in her room and Andy crying in his. I had a mess of hornets flying around in my head, their buzzing covering up the sound of all that crying.

Chapter 13
What's missing from this picture? You!

Micah's ghost showed as if he'd died. I'd turn the corner and see him, but it turned out to be the sun spilling in the window, or a shadow falling on the floor.

After a time, Andy quit asking when Daddy and Micah were coming back and that seemed as sad as when he asked it. He'd come into my room nights when he was lonely or scared and stand by my bed until I woke up. Sometimes, I'd go sleep in Micah's bed so he'd feel better. One night I heard him sniffling in his pillow, so I lay beside him and patted his back until I thought he fell asleep.

"Sister?"

"Yeah?"

"Can I call you Seestor like Micah did?"

"I dunno. It's kind of stupid."

"Nuh uh." He let out a big sigh, then, "Seestor?"

I sighed, too, then, "Yeah, Andy?"

"Somebody's in the room with us sometimes."

I sat up and stared down at him. "Who?"

"I dunno. Just sometimes I think someone's here."

"Maybe it's just me when I come check on you."

"No." He sat up and copied me cross-legged on his bed. "It's kinda scary."

"Maybe it's Grandma Faith. She isn't scary. She talks to me and I see her lots."

"I don't want no ghosts around me."

"I bet it's just the wind. Look, see how your curtains blow around?"

He watched the curtains for a bit then lay back down and was soon asleep. I eased back in Micah's bed, but I couldn't go to sleep for a long time. The next day in school, I was tired all day from not sleeping. I made my first B ever on my spelling report.

The last day of class, poor Edsel handed me a flower and a box of chocolates, carrying on about going away to Tennessee until I thought I'd die from everybody giggling. Finally, he left off, big-tooth grinning because I said, "Why thank you, Edsel. Have a grand time in Tennessee."

The box was opened and some of the candies were missing, and the flower was made from a dirty pipe cleaner. I threw it all away when I got home. I was the only girl Edsel bothered. I was the only one in my class whose parents had a divorce. I was the only one whose brother had moved away. I was the only one with a momma like Momma.

Momma had dates, but they didn't come calling for her at the door. She'd tell them over the phone that she'd meet them on the long road. She'd wait at the end of the road in her high-heels and pretty dress. Momma let Aunt Ruby find her dates at the grocery, at the hair salon next to the barber, and at the butcher's shop. But, Momma met Timothy on her own, at the five and dime.

It was the day we went to the library to get her more romance books. She'd go through two a week sometimes. I was happy since it meant I got to go to the library and get books. We would pile into the pink Rambler and tear off leaving clouds of dust. Her hair flew out of the window, and I let my hair do that too, where it tangled all in a mess. Momma threw her hand out and hollered, "Wheeeeeee!" while Andy and I laughed. We liked her best on library days.

That Thursday, she pulled into the five and dime first. She said, "I want to see that Kimberly. I got something to say."

We marched in with Momma in the lead. Andy ran straight for the candy aisle, but I stayed by Momma to see what she'd do. She wore her favorite red dress, red lipstick, and her hair was wild over her shoulders from the wind. She was more beautiful than any movie star. Through the store we went, Momma sashaying, her head tilted up same as she used to do, her eyes so dark I couldn't read a thing in them.

By the aspirin, there stood a yellow-haired thing just turning to chubby. Her nametag read, "Kimberly," and her whiteness made her disappear next to Momma. Momma tossed her tangled up hair. "You couldn't keep my husband here either, could you, you little twit?"

"I don't know *what* you're carrying on about." Kimberly's voice was prissy whiney.

Momma up and sniffed Kimberly. "My husband came home smelling like you more times than not."

"I think you need to leave." Kimberly stuck her nose in the air, but her hands were shaking.

"I 'tink yew need to weave." Momma pulled her lips in a snarling dog look. "What my Frederick saw in a sniplet of nothing like you, I'll never know. Maybe he thought you were that Juliet in his Flakespeare books." She did a coochy jig and made kissy smack noises, then said, "Oh Romeo, Romeo, where the fuck are you Romeo? Why it's Juliet, little whore from the five and dime."

My mouth dropped open big enough for a cow to walk in.

Kimberly tossed her hair. "You're a fruity fruit-cake."

Momma flew at Kimberly and knocked her into the cold medicines, sending bottles rolling and flying everywhere.

I laughed with my hand over my mouth. I couldn't help it, it was funny.

Kimberly's tears sprung out, and snot came running from her nose while she boo hoo'd. Andy had come to watch, pointing and laughing. There were also three men and a curler-haired lady.

Momma said, calm as a kitten, "You couldn't keep him happy. No woman but me ever will."

"I wasn't with him!" Kimberly wiped her nose with her hand.

A man with a glob of mayonnaise on his cheek rushed over to Kimberly and patted her on the back, "What's going on around here?"

Kimberly turned her face into his white jacket. "She's crazy, John."

"I'd watch that. She's been had more'n my neighbor's cat." Momma turned her back on Kimberly, took Andy's hand and mine, and walked down the aisle with her head held high, the Queen of West Virginia.

The curler woman turned her back, and the men parted for her to pass. But one of them whistled low, stepped in front of Momma and said, "Woman, your husband's an idiot." He stuck out his hand. "I'm Timothy."

She grabbed his hand, reached into her purse for a pen, and wrote our phone number on his palm. "Well, Timothy, I reckon he isn't around to answer the phone now." She dropped his hand, grabbed ours again, and we headed on to the library.

The next day Timothy called and they talked for an hour. They did that four times, and when they had their first date, Momma let him come to the door to fetch her. He tipped his hat to us, but I didn't think he looked too friendly. He ate supper with us on the second date. He hardly paid any mind to Andy and me.

On their third date, Momma dressed in a swirly

154

black dress. Her hair was pulled up and she had on new earrings. Timothy grabbed her and kissed her and it made me want to vomit. She turned to me. "Virginia Kate, me and Timothy are going to Charleston to go dancing. I need you to watch Andy, hear? Mrs. Mendel's right next door."

"Yes Ma'am." I slid my eyes to Timothy; he slid his eyes to me. I knew right then he was No Good, but I didn't say a word.

I fixed Andy and me peanut butter and jelly sandwiches for supper, and we watched television until we were sleepy. I tucked Andy into bed, even though he said he was too big to be tucked. It turned later and later. I was worried.

Mrs. Mendel called. "You chil'ren need anything, you just holler. You hear? I'm right acrost the way."

I said, okay, then hung up, snuggled under Grandma's quilt, and even though I didn't think I could, I fell right off into sleep. When I woke up, Momma was by the side of my bed. "Good Morning, daughter."

"Morning, Momma." I stared at her face. She had a fat black eye and a split lip. "Momma?"

She put her finger on my lips to shush me. "I've made breakfast. Blackberry pancakes."

That was all she said. We never laid eyes on that Timothy again.

I daydreamed that I'd get to visit Daddy and Micah for the summer. Daddy sent pictures and letters about Shakespeare, school, and Mee Maw's driving Rebekha insane. I tried to put myself in the pictures with them where they grinned out at me. Mee Maw sent one of Micah and Daddy and Rebekha in front of Mee Maw's house. The house was long and brick with an iron fence around it. I couldn't imagine being behind big black bars like that. Little squatty-man trees stood willy-nilly in the yard. Daddy had his arm thrown across Micah's shoulders, and Rebekha was on the other side of Micah looking down at him. Micah was squeezed like the insides of a sandwich.

Mee Maw wrote on the back "What's missing from this picture? You!"

I felt sad looking at them. I wanted to holler my mad, but couldn't.

Momma came in while I was all hangdog and said, "You better get that picture out of here before I tear it to pieces and flush it! I'm so mad I could spit nails!"

I put it in my Special Things Box even though I wanted to tear it into a bazillion pieces myself.

Then Momma got a letter from Daddy that said his family (that's what he said, his family) was moving to Louisiana so Daddy could finish school there.

Momma said, "I don't think that snip will put up with him for long with his moving to Loo-see-aner, and taking on another woman's kid to boot." She did a jig, shaking the letter around, and then flopped on the couch to read the rest. Her smile turned upside down. "Well, that woman is *from* Louisiana. Says right here." She showed me, pointing at the words "born in Louisiana." She smoothed the letter on her lap, tore it in three pieces, wadded it up, and threw it in the trash, for me to secretly fish out later. "Well, still. I expect she'll get to hating things enough to leave him."

"What'll she hate, Momma?"

"I wouldn't want to take on another woman's kids. Your daddy having fun in school while she cooks, cleans, takes care of Micah." She was counting off on her fingers again. "What you want to bet?"

"They look happy."

"Go on to your room, Virginia Kate. My head's pounding."

I looked up Louisiana in the encyclopedia Daddy sent. It was right next to Texas.

Momma asked Daddy to send Micah back for a visit but he wouldn't do it.

She screamed, "Frederick, you're a Fucklehead!" slammed the phone down, fixed herself a bamboozeler with a cherry, and told me, "Your daddy won't let Micah visit out of spite. He said to send you and Andy to him. I won't. I won't! He said Mee Maw would . . ." She stopped, shook her head.

She called Daddy back with her cat's purr voice. "My family's all torn up, Frederick. I can't stand looking at Virginia Kate's face every time you send pictures of your new life. Don't you want to come home?" She slammed the phone again and the kitty's purr was a bobcat's scream. "Selfish Bastard!"

I went to my room and pulled my Special Things Box from under my bed. I took out the picture of Daddy and Micah before they left, when they went fishing in the Greenbrier River. They held fishing poles in their left hands. Daddy wore rubber boots and Micah had some to match, but his were too big for his skinny legs. Micah held a trout like it was a whale. Later that day, Momma and Daddy kissed and she wrinkled her nose to the fishy smell, but she didn't pull away from him. We ate the trout, fried potatoes, bread with butter, and for dessert, Daddy had chocolates from the five and dime. We stuffed the candy in our mouths, laughing at the good luck of it all.

I stared at the photo until their faces came clear to me again, then I put them back in the box. I went into the kitchen for two aspirin and went straight away to bed, even though it was hardly dark and I didn't even hear frogs or night bugs singing. The aspirin pushed up from my belly and tried to spill out. My throat burned and my head pounded. I rode Fionadala up, up, up where we rested together until I fell asleep.

I woke up to someone in my room. I opened my eyes, but no one was there even though I knew I felt the bed sink. I heard breathing, soft and gentle like a summer wind. I said, "Grandma?" The curtains blew to me and I smelled good smells. I snuggled in, and next I knew, it was morning. On the windowsill sat a cardinal, peering in with its bright black eyes. When I sat up to get a better look, it flew off. I went to the bathroom to wash my face and the whole house was quiet. Into the kitchen I tiptoed to put the pot on to boil for Momma's coffee. I knew she was going to need it since the bottle on the coffee table was almost empty.

When Momma woke, we sat at the table across from each other and sipped our coffees. I loved looking at her through the steam, how she looked like an angel in a cloud.

She eyed me over her cup. "I never meant for him to stay gone. You believe me, don't you, Virginia Kate?" I didn't know if she meant Micah or Daddy, or both. She pushed back her hair. "My family is torn right up. How'd it happen so fast?" After her second coffee, she dialed up Daddy and called him bastard and fucklehead until I thought I'd go crazy.

Andy came in and ate his toast, kicking at the table leg over and over, harder and harder.

To get some peace, I went outside with my camera. Daddy'd sent me a photography book and I'd read it cover to cover. I saved the money Mee Maw gave me and used it to buy more film. When I developed the pictures, I'd study them to figure out how to make my photos better. I took pictures of our house, of my bedroom, of Mrs. Mendel's garden, the maple, the mountains, anything I could.

One special picture stayed wrapped in tissue. I was swinging on the swing in my favorite blue shorts and striped t-shirt. My mountain stood behind me and the wind blew in front of me. I grinned and preened, and Andy snapped the picture. After it was developed, Momma said she thought there was something wrong with the film. But I knew. A soft light glowed all behind me and around me. I knew it was Grandma Faith with me.

The next roll of film I started on, but it didn't get used up before things changed again. I took a picture of the mountains shadowy in the sky during a big storm full of lightning and mists, Momma reading her romance books while pinkie-raised-sipping from her circle glass, Mrs. Mendel in her garden with her kitty, and of Andy acting silly. I didn't see any of those pictures until I was away from everything my camera held inside it. When that June became the last Junetime in the holler.

Chapter 14
Life is too hard sometimes, daughter

The three of us were outside and I decided we didn't have a care in the world just because I felt like it. It was warm and the sky matched Momma's dress. I had my camera beside me, with six more pictures to take before the roll was gone. I leaned up against the old rough bark of the tree, while Andy rolled around in the grass.

"Want to play a game, Andy?"

" 'Kay." He flopped beside me.

"Guess what I see?"

"A flying butt?" Andy pointed to the sky, snickering.

"No, it's blue."

"Oh, that there's my butt." He rolled up and did cartwheels.

"No. It's blue with white dots."

"Your butt." Andy fell backward on the ground, kicking up his feet and laughing.

"It's Momma's dress, dummy."

"I'm bored." He dug around in the grass for bugs.

"What do you want to do then?"

"Nothing. Nothing. Nothing. Nothing." He jumped up and ran about the yard, waving his arms around.

"Stop acting stooopid, Andy."

"Nanner Nanner Nanner, sister can't catch me." He ran around the tree, but I stayed right where I was.

"You two stop all that racket." Momma finished hanging out the clothes on the old rusty clothesline and looked at us with her hands on her hips. Her hair was up in a ponytail and the end of it was over her right shoulder, curling up in a C. The way she watched us, I knew something was swirling around in her head. She went into the house, and came back with a full glass in one hand, the blue blanket in the other. After spreading the blanket under the tree, she settled on it with her legs tucked under her. Andy and I ran to sit on either side of her. Momma slupped up her Coke-a-Whoopsie, and said, "Ahhhh. How relaxing."

"Can we have a picnic, Momma?" I asked.

"I want a worm sandwich," Andy sometimes said want like *ownt*. "And dirt brownies."

"That's nasty, Andy." But I laughed.

Momma took another sip and her eyes went soft. "It's so pretty here. I could never leave West Virginia."

"Me either." I almost leaned my head on her shoulder.

"Me either!" Andy jumped up and tried to grab leaves from the tree.

"What can we have for a picnic, kids? Besides worms and dirt."

"Hamburgers and french fries?" I asked.

"Or hot digity dawgs." Andy flopped back down.

I didn't want even a wind to come and bother us, right then things felt so happy. I knew Momma wasn't feeling the same thing when she said, "How could I of sent Micah away?" She brushed her ponytail back and took three swallows from her glass. She said, "Groceries have got so expensive."

"I won't eat much, Momma. I can skip break-fast."

"Me, too," Andy said.

"I'm losing everything. It's all falling apart." Momma stared at the bottom of the glass for magic answers.

"No it's not, Momma, it's not." But my stomach did a double ferris wheel.

I knew Momma missed shopping at the big fancy store in Charleston where she'd come home and press cotton balls full of spicy perfumes onto my wrists. I'd kept my arm held out of the bathtub so the smell would stay put all night. She'd tease up her hair big and high, put on a nice dress, and color in her lips, smacking them together to even them out, but even then she said sometimes the other women gave her mean looks like she didn't belong there.

Momma stuck her legs out in front of her on the blanket and wiggled her red-painted toes. "Look at these toesies, you two. How do you think plain old toes'll look on me?" She held her hands out for us. "And plain fingernails. I can't imagine."

"You'll be pretty forever, Momma," Andy said. "Are we still gonna have the pic-a-nic basket, Boo-Boo?"

I didn't say anything.

Momma had on a spooked look. Getting up as ladylike as she could, she rattled the ice in her glass. "I need another one of these." She put the clothesbasket on her hip, went into the house, and came back out with an empty cup instead of her glass. Handing it to me, she said, "Go over to Mrs. Mendel's and borrow a cup of flour."

"For what?" I asked.

"I need to bake some bread. Andy, you go with her."

I walked with my head down, thinking about Momma's eyes, watching my dirty feet slap on the ground. I knocked on Mrs. Mendel's door, and when she answered, Andy and I went into her little house. She had doilies everywhere and she even had pictures of us kids setting around. Mrs. Mendel gave me the flour and Andy a plate of cookies to take back. Andy took up to eating them as soon as she closed the door behind us. I walked slow as I could trying to figure stuff out.

When I went inside to give Momma the flour, she was hanging up the phone. She grabbed a bottle and a glass, then turned to me. "I'm going to my room awhile. I'm not feeling so good."

"Momma?"

She went into her room, locked her door, and didn't come out for supper. Andy and I ate tomato soup and watched television until late, but she still didn't come out.

Next morning, Momma made a breakfast of toast and peanut butter, with eggs on the side. The phone rang. Momma answered it, then said, "What else do you want from me, Laudine? My blood?"

At lunch, she made grilled cheese sandwiches,

with chocolate chip cookies for dessert. We never had dessert at lunch. Momma ate crackers and milk, dipping each cracker into her cup of milk, then chewing while she stared at a spot on the wall. She acted strange the whole day. To stay out of her way, Andy and I went down to the creek and looked for special stones.

That night, I woke up smelling smoke. When I opened my eyes, Momma stood at the foot of my bed. She sipped her drink and then took a big puff of her cigarette. I didn't even know she smoked until then.

"Momma? What's wrong?"

"Virginia Kate, do you remember that birthday picnic we had when you turned four years old?"

"I don't know, Momma."

"You wore a flowered dress without even fussing, and I brushed out your hair until it shined." She sipped, swallowed, took another pull, let the smoke come out slow, and said, "Your shoulders got sunburned, so I put salve on them."

"I think I remember."

"Your toes were like corn niblets." Another sip, another pull and blow. "You jumped right in my lap and your hair smelled like warm vanilla."

I was hypnotized by her voice. The moon through the window lit her up. Her white cotton gown glowing. The lit cigarette glowing. Her teeth glowing.

She stabbed the cigarette on the windowsill, and

with her thumb and forefinger, flicked it into the yard. "You had ribbons in your hair." She leaned, kissed me, her hair tickled my face, and she said, "Life is too hard sometimes, daughter." She turned and left my room.

I lay awake a long time.

Next day was the same strange momma. She made pancakes and chocolate milk for breakfast. She smoked, drank her coffee, looked out the window towards the road.

When Andy finished eating, she took him by the hand. "Come on Andy, time to go to Mrs. Mendel's for a spell."

Andy had chocolate milk spilled on his shirt and his hair stuck up from sleeping.

When she came back, she went straight to the cedar robe and pulled out my yellow suitcase. She next went into her room and got Daddy's old burlap bag with the drawstring at the top.

"Pack your clothes. You can take this bag and put whatever toys and books you want."

"Why?"

"Don't ask me questions right now. My head's about to bust open."

"But Momma . . ."

She grabbed my shirtsleeve and pulled me to my room. Pointing, she said, "Pack, Virginia Kate Carey."

I stuffed clothes into the suitcase, wrapped my camera in a t-shirt to protect it, and put it on top of the clothes. I turned in a circle, and then went back to see what Momma was doing.

She was on the couch, smoking, a washrag on her head, a full glass on the coffee table. Her eyes were puffy, but there was fire in them. "Did you pack?"

"Am I going back to Aunt Ruby's?"

"No."

"Then where?" I shot a fiery look right back at her.

She blew smoke in a long puff, then said, "Your daddy's coming to get you."

"I'm visiting Daddy and Micah!" I almost danced. "Is Andy coming, too?"

She stood, and picked up her drink. "Not visiting. He's coming to get you to live with him and that woman."

I stared at her. "Live with them? You mean forever?"

"I don't know." She rubbed her neck, sighed. "I just don't know, Virginia Kate."

"What about Andy?"

"What about him? He's staying with me." Momma looked at me then, full in my face with that pointy chin.

"I don't want to leave Andy."

"Your daddy will be here soon and you're getting in that car without a fuss, you hear?"

"I can't leave Andy." The buzzing came loud and mean.

"I thought you wanted to be with Micah? I thought you missed your daddy, too."

"I do! But why can't we all be together like it was?" I sat on the couch and pressed my arms over my chest. "Andy gets scared at night, he needs me."

"You don't know nothing about nothing." Momma tipped her glass and gulped it all.

"Did Andy cry when you told him?"

"I didn't tell him yet." Momma crossed her arms over her chest, too.

"He'll think I don't love him."

"I expect he'll get over it after things settle down."

"Please, Momma, please." I didn't care if I was begging. I ran and grabbed her, pushing my face into her dress.

She pushed me away. "All you're doing is upsetting me. You think it's easy handing over your kids one by one? I don't have any choice." She went into the kitchen and I heard the ice noises. When she came back, her face was set hard. "I'll keep Andy and at least I'll have that." She went to my bedroom and I followed her. She grabbed the suitcase and walked out, saying over her shoulder, "Your daddy's got that silly toy car. I reckon I'll have to send your other things."

When I didn't leave my room, Momma came back in, took my hand, led me to the front door, held the screen door open for me to go through, and then stepped out after me. I stared at her, but she looked away, running her hand through her hair.

"You stay right there and watch for your daddy. I'm going to talk to Mrs. Mendel." She eyed me and I thought she was ugly, even though I knew she wasn't really.

I sat on the steps while she walked to Mrs. Mendel's house with her back like a broomstick. Mrs. Mendel's curtains opened and Momma's face poked out to look at me. When she closed the curtains, I went back into the house and into Momma's room. I grabbed her silver-handled brush, her Shalimar powder, and her red lipstick. I stole a picture of Momma and Daddy she kept hidden under her dresser scarf. On the way out, I took Momma's shirt hanging on the door and put it over my t-shirt, buttoning it up to the neck. I pushed her other things down into the bottom of Daddy's bag. I next went into Andy's room and took Fiddledeedee the Tiger.

Holding on to Fiddledeedee, I decided I'd go see Andy even if it did rile up Momma. I ran outside; that's when I saw Momma, Andy, and Mrs. Mendel driving away in Mrs. Mendel's Cadillac. Momma looked straight ahead. Andy's head popped up and down, happy, happy.

I stood in the hot road. When I couldn't stand the fire in my feet anymore, I went back to the steps to wait for Daddy. I did my multiplication tables and I was up to the fours when Daddy drove down the road and into the driveway. Without opening the door, he jumped out, wearing a black shirt and black britches with black boots. His hair was longer than before and he had sideburns that went halfway down his cheeks, but no mustache. He looked like Elvis's lost cousin.

"Bug! Look how big you've grown." He grabbed my suitcase and put it in the back, yappering on about how the drive back would be fun, and how he missed his little girl, and how pretty I was (he lied, for I had on the ugliest pair of checkered pedal pushers ever made in the whole world). When I didn't answer, his grin was less big. He said, "Is there anything else, Bug?"

I walked up the steps to go back inside. He followed me into my room and I pointed to the bag. He picked it up. "That it?"

I nodded, tensed my stomach and clenched my fists to hold myself tight. Sometimes it was hard not to cry.

He tried to hug me, but I ran out of the bedroom and out the front door, even though there was nowhere I could go. I thought maybe Momma might come back, see me there pitiful and change her mind. Daddy put the bag in his car and came over to grab me in a hug. I didn't hug him back, but I took in the smells of him. The Old Spice was gone. Not a speck of it was to be found no matter how deep I breathed in. He patted me on the back, saying, "It's okay, Baby Bug. I'm sorry."

I thought how Daddy sure said I'm sorry a lot but

he didn't do much about making the sorrys not happen in the first place. I climbed into his stupid car. He jumped in, gunned the engine, and when we drove away, I didn't want to look back. But I had to. I just had to tell my mountain goodbye. And the maple—its leaves waving at me, telling me goodbye with a zillion little hands. And my swing, telling me good-bye, good-bye, good-bye in the wind.

I felt the doors to my inside house closing. I pictured them shutting, the locks turning with a loud clackityclack. I saw how things worked. How people you love could hurt you and still go around grinning and looking like Elvis's cousin. Or drive away so they wouldn't have to tell the truth. I figured out all my multiplication tables, so I could figure out all that.

I tried to force my heart to thump regular and smooth, but it wouldn't listen. As we drove away, sister mountain called to me. I heard it on the wind as we drove down the long road out of the holler. I watched it one last time as it rose up behind me, dark and sad.

As we drove down the highway, I imagined Grandma's ghost might be flying around the trees and she could take me by the hand and we'd fly, looking down over West Virginia. I'd see Daddy driving in his car, wondering where I went off to. And Momma, she'd be sad because she let me go. Just when I was almost smiling, Daddy took to whistling and ruined it. I hated whistling more than liver.

He said, "We'll be in Kentucky soon. You'll see blue grass. It really does look blue. And horses, thoroughbreds. You'll like Kentucky."

I answered him inside my head, "I like West Virginia so you can put that in your stupid pipe and smoke it until you're green."

"Then Tennessee comes next and that's where we're staying the night."

I pressed my lips together. "So what? I don't care."

"It's going to work out great, you'll see. Louisiana is interesting. It's eerie—a mysterious beauty, like seeing things in a fog that aren't there."

I turned my head away from him. "Louisiana is full of swamp rats."

"Well, since you aren't talking to me, I'll just have to keep whistling." And it was inside my head like biting on foil, but I didn't say a thing. He finally gave up and drove quiet. I felt like I won something.

Kentucky was pretty. There were horses just as he said. The most beautiful ones I'd ever seen. I watched one gallop along with us, tossing its head about. I had a want then to have one of my own. I could ride it up, up, just as I did with Fionadala, but for real, not just pretend.

Tennessee was a pretty place, too. We pulled up to a little hotel with a flashing sign and Daddy went in to pay for our room. From the car, I watched a little boy and girl walk with their parents. The momma was laughing at something the daddy said. The little boy jumped up and down, holding on to his daddy's hand. His jumping was so happy I had to smile. The little girl stepped as if she was a princess. Tossing her short brown curls, she grinned up at her daddy. When they passed the car, Miss Priss looked right at me and stuck out her tongue. She skipped away, grabbing her momma's hand and I decided I hated her.

When Daddy returned, he put up the top and drove around to park. He jumped out and grabbed our suitcases. He was always moving, drive, park, jump, pull, talk, whistle. Inside our room, there were two plumped-up beds, a dresser, and a desk. I pulled back the bedspread like Mee Maw said she did and looked at the sheets. They were white enough to glow in the almost dark room.

"Want something to eat? I saw a diner just down the road. How about it?" One side of his mouth turned up a little higher than the other while he pushed his hand through his hair, messing up the combing he'd done before he went in to get our room key.

I gave him a nod, which was the least I could do. At the diner, I ordered fried chicken and corn on the cob, with a big glass of milk. Daddy had the same thing, except he asked for beer with his. For dessert, we asked for ice cream—I wanted strawberry and Daddy wanted chocolate. The waitress, who said her name was Shaline, put a cherry and some whipped cream on top, giving Daddy a wink when she set the bowls in front of us. She licked her lips like Momma did. We finished up our dessert and Daddy paid our bill, leaving Shaline a big tip. He said something to her when he handed her the money and she laughed and nodded her head, touching his right arm.

Back to our room, I pulled out my book and leaned back against the pillows to read.

"I'm going to make a phone call, Bug." Daddy took the phone into the bathroom. After he shut the door, I waited for a bit, and then sneaked up to listen.

". . . left Andy there with her." Daddy's shoe shadow passed in the door crack. He was walking the bathroom, back and forth. Enough to take a step, turn, take a step. "Now, hold on, that's not fair. I do what I can." Shower curtain sounds—I knew he looked at the tub, more Mee Maw ideas. "That's your opinion, Jonah." Jiggling the toilet handle. "No, she agreed to this deal." The faucet squeaking on then off. "When did your daddy get out of prison?" The toilet seat banged. "Oh. I guess the cancer will finish what prison didn't. Well, I just wanted to let you know what was happening." Paper crinkling. "I know, I hate splitting them up, too, but . . ." More squeaky faucet and the water running. ". . . give Billie . . . best . . . keep . . .

touch." Water off. "I always liked you, Jonah . . . okay, yeah, bye." Phone in cradle.

I jumped in bed and pretended to read my book. Daddy came out, set the phone back on the nightstand, and stood jingling his keys in his pocket. He wandered around the room, studying the lamp, his bed, the pictures on the walls, the curtains. Checked his watch three times.

He tapped his right foot, heel to toe. "Is that a good book, Bug?"

I shrugged.

"What are you reading?"

I showed him the book.

"What? No Shakespeare?" He smiled halfway, then tapped his fingers on his leg. "I'm going to grab a beer. Keep the door locked, okay? I mean it, don't come out." Daddy kissed my cheek, then said, "And don't stay up too late. We still have a ways to go."

I opened *Tom Sawyer* to page 109 where the gum wrapper held my place. I read, " 'One of the reasons why Tom's mind had drifted away from its secret troubles was that it had found a new and weighty matter to interest itself about.' " Our room door clicked. I read that sentence again, and then again before I finally forced myself to read on. I woke up to the door opening and Daddy coming in the room. Without saying goodnight, he fell onto his bed and let out a beer-stinky sigh.

I lay awake until I heard his snoring. Then I

remembered I left my Special Things Box under my bed. And Grandma Faith's quilt. I'd been so busy being a big baby that I forgot my important things. Later, I dreamed I was holding Momma's hand as she pulled me away from Andy. He grew smaller and smaller, but we didn't care. Both of us were laughing and swinging our arms higher and higher. I looked up at Momma and she was grinning big, then she turned into Shaline. When I woke up, Daddy was already shaving.

For breakfast, we ate biscuits and white gravy at the diner. Daddy drank three cups of coffee, and kept rubbing his face and eyes. Shaline wasn't anywhere around, and instead, there was a gray-haired woman with a name tag that read *Doris*. I liked her laugh and she didn't lick her lips or wink.

Back in the car, Daddy didn't put the top down. He said it would get mighty hot soon. I looked for interesting things, even though I wasn't very interested in anything. There were no more mountains to be seen. No more horses running. It was all wrong. I pretended to sleep until Daddy stopped for lunch.

We ate in the car, the grease from the hamburger dripping down my arm. I didn't worry about greasy arms, or my tangled up hair, and I wore the same clothes I left home in, the same clothes I slept in. I wished Momma knew how I looked so I could be spiteful about it.

I fell asleep after lunch and when I woke, Daddy

grinned over at me. "Good, you're awake. Look at the Spanish moss hanging off those cypress trees. It's good to be home."

I mind-thought, "Whose home?" Everything looked secret and mysterious.

Daddy pointed to the biggest oak trees I'd ever seen, like big strong old men standing guard over all the other trees. Everything was green and mossy and moldy. We stopped to get a pop at a filling station and it was hot as the exhaust pipe's smoke. My clothes stuck to me and I couldn't breathe right, all that thick wet air cramming down my lungs. Daddy laughed when I said, "Whew."

"You'll get used to it, Bug."

I was pretty sure I never would.

Chapter 15
Well, isn't this a pretty picture

Daddy said, "We're home!" The house was tan with dark-green shutters and had a tall roof. There was a giant oak in his yard that shaded most of the house and the neighbor's, too. As I spilled out of the car, I looked way up at it and around it. It would take at least four of me to circle its trunk, hand to hand. I thought it could give my maple a good run in the beautiful department. There were more oak trees leaning across and over the street, touching branches as if they were sweethearts.

Daddy grasshoppered around, pointing. "Those

are our camellias, and the mimosa that'll be by your window, and look at the crepe myrtles. Isn't it something?" He hopped back to the car and began pulling out our things.

I stood still while he swirly-whorled. He held the suitcase and my bag and smiled at me. I took the bag from him and held tight to it. It was so hot I thought my brains would cook and I'd lose all my thoughts.

We went through the front door into the living room. But nothing was like home. Daddy's Louisiana house had shiny red-colored wood floors, and there was a rug in front of a black leather couch that was up against the wall. A marble-topped coffee table was on top of the rug. Two big chairs were around the table, with another smaller chair up against the side wall. Framed pictures were hung on every wall.

At home, Momma liked to hang different things on different days. Sometimes pictures of us, sometimes Micah's drawings, and the pictures from magazines she liked.

Daddy dropped our things on the floor and pointed around again. His mouth moved fast.

My feelings were in a bad hurt. I thought Micah would be waiting for me. Rebekha wasn't around either, but I didn't care one speck. I wondered if Daddy was rid of her. But the door opened and Rebekha walked in with two bags of groceries. She looked right into my eyes for signs of a baby who missed her momma. I'd show her I was no crybaby.

"Hello, Virginia Kate. I hoped to be back by the time you arrived, but the Bet R was busy today." She smiled her gap-toothy grin and left the room with her groceries.

I felt itchy, thinking that maybe I'd been tricked. That maybe Micah was on his way back to West Virginia and we'd been traded.

Daddy turned to me. "Go help Rebekha with the groceries and I'll put your stuff in your room. Go through that door, it's just past the dining room."

I knew what he was doing. Five times five equals twenty-five. Five times six equals thirty.

I went to the kitchen. Rebekha came over and hugged me. I pulled away from her. I didn't need her to go hugging on me none.

She took a step back. "Well, let's see, okay. I better get all this put away."

I stood in the middle of the kitchen and watched her.

"How was your trip? Did you see lots of things?"

My tongue was stuck to the roof of my mouth. My feet were stuck to the floor. My brain was cooked. And Micah was on his way to West Virginia.

She poured a glass of milk, then held it out toward me before she asked, "Would you like a glass of milk?" I didn't take it, so she set it on the counter. "Well, yes. Let's see." She put up the last of the groceries. After she folded the empty bags, she dusted her hands together and asked, "Well, would you like to see your room now, Hon?"

I shrugged, but followed her.

My room was just off the living room. It was done in pink and white with girlyfied lace stuff on the bed and curtains. The walls were pink with white trim. The paint smelled fresh and everything looked new, except the furniture. The furniture was an old dark color, like coffee. I thought if I touched it, it would feel as warm and smooth as it looked.

The bed had a tall headboard, the footboard curved around the sides of the bed. On it lay a pink and white bedspread with two pink pillows. There was a big soft chair by the bed and a table with a lamp on it. Pictures of baby animals were on the walls. On top of the dresser were two glass lamps, a comb and brush, and a jewelry box. I had no idea what I'd put in the jewelry box. I walked over and opened the top and a ballerina with a pink tutu turned around and around while soft music played. I closed the box to shut it up.

"I didn't know what colors you like. I thought little girls like pink. The jewelry box came from Penney's." She touched the top of it and then her shoulders fell forward.

I thought all the pink would make me go insane. Not like my room at home with its yellow walls, white lamp, and Micah's pictures. And not like my iron bed and feather mattress. Or my dresser that Uncle Jonah made when I was born, or my cedar robe. And not like my scatter rug. And most especially, not Grandma Faith's quilt, or my window with my mountain smiling down. I looked out my Louisiana window and saw the mimosa waving at me. I didn't wave back.

Rebekha stepped towards me with her hand held out. "Everything will be okay. I know this must be traumatic for you."

I stepped back.

Her hand fell away. "Why don't I start dinner?" She went back into the kitchen, and I trailed behind her to get away from the pink. She wore brown britches, one of Daddy's white shirts, and flat-soled shoes, and was as tall as Momma was, but that's all that was like Momma. A headband that matched her green eyes pulled her light red hair back. Her veins showed all blue under that so-white skin.

I leaned against the icebox while she chopped onions. I wanted to ask if I could help but I didn't want to talk to her. The back door smacked and Micah came into the kitchen. He stood blinking, as if he didn't know I was coming. After a minute of us eyeing each other like fools, he hooked his hands in his jeans pockets and grinned. He was a little taller and his hair was curling around his head dark and messy. He had on a black t-shirt, jeans with holes in the knees, and tenny shoes without any socks. I put my face in my hands, pressing my palms to my eyes to stop the hot itchy feeling.

He asked, "Squirk-brain's here?"

"I told you she was coming today," Rebekha said.

"Vee, look! I'm Elvis."

I peeked between my fingers and smiled when he swung his hips with his lip curled.

"Come see my room." He grabbed my arm and pulled me down the hall to his room. His walls were white with no paint smells. Just like at home, his drawings were all over. His bedspread was blue, green, and white checked, all the rootin' tootin' cowboy gone. He pulled a pad from under his bed. "Want to see?"

I nodded and we plopped on his bed. As he turned the pages, I knew they were better than anything he'd done at home. It made me feel as if my brother was not like other brothers even more.

"These are the dogs from next door. One's named Pebbles and the other Otis."

"That's funny names." I always liked a good name. "Can I pet them?"

"They moved off. Some old lady's there now."

I grabbed one of the loose drawings he set face down on the bedspread. It was a screaming-faced man with holes all over him, blood running out of the holes.

"Give me that!" Micah grabbed it and tore it in half, his face scrunched up like a mad dog. I stood up and backed away. The closed doors to my rooms banged open, shut, then open again, wind blowing in and out. I pressed my hands to my eyes again.

"Geez, Seestor. I'm sorry." He touched my arm. "Come on. It's okay."

I sat back down.

He picked up a drawing of a woman reading in a chair, smoothed out a wrinkle, then held it up. "Look."

"Is that her in there?" I pointed towards the kitchen.

"Yep."

"Does she yell a lot?"

"Nope. She's not like Momma."

My hands twisted in my lap. "Momma didn't yell a lot."

"She did when she felt like it. Rebekha is kinda quiet."

"Does she like the booze, too?"

"She doesn't guzzle stuff like that." He turned to a picture of a pretty white bird taped to the blank page. "This is an egret. Did you see them? I'm going to draw it from this photo." He touched the egret picture. "I don't know if she likes me."

"Who?"

"Rebekha."

"How come?"

"Don't know." He turned the page and pointed to an alligator. "I saw this huge, fat, scaly alligator at the lake, so I drew it."

I stared at the teeth ready to chomp me into eighty pieces. "Are there alligators in the yard here?"

"No, not usually. But I saw a giant, tremendous, horrendous snake under the porch two weeks ago."

"A big snake under the porch?"

"Don't worry, they don't bother anybody." Micah laughed, then said, "My friend saw one in his bathroom."

"You have a friend?"

"More than one." Micah turned to a drawing of Andy. "I did this by a picture you sent."

"You did it good." We both stared at Andy holding on to his stuffed tiger. "I didn't get to tell him goodbye."

"How come?"

"Momma wouldn't let me," I said.

"That's cause she didn't want you telling him she stinks."

"She does not!"

"Yes she does! She doesn't care about me and now she doesn't care about you."

"That's not true."

"Then how come you and me are here and she's there?"

I shrugged. "I just miss Andy."

"Yeah, me too." Micah stood up, walked around the room. I was afraid there were other things he wanted to do instead of being stuck with his little sister. He didn't look at me when he said, "Momma should let Andy come here, too. It's not so bad."

"She said she wouldn't."

"Well, she should so we can all be together again."

"Or we could go back there." I wanted to day-dream under the maple, feel the cool wind.

Micah shook his head because I was as dumb as a worm.

I was tired of talking about Momma. "Can I come with you and your friends sometimes?"

"Girls aren't allowed." He cracked his knuckles then picked up loose drawings that were on the floor.

"Why not?"

"Look, you'll make your own friends."

"I guess."

"Aw, you will." He put the loose drawings, even the one he tore in half, inside the pad.

Rebekha called us, and Micah said, "Time to eat!"

I didn't ask him again why he thought Rebekha didn't like him. I wanted to study them awhile, see what they were all up to.

On the table in big plates and bowls, Rebekha had chicken, round potatoes with butter sliding around, green beans, cornbread, and fruit salad. The fruit bowl sparkled all pretty under the light. Nothing like the carnival glass Momma threw at Daddy. All of Rebekha's dishes matched and we had cloth napkins by our plates. Momma liked to mix things up where nothing matched. She said it was more fun.

Daddy wasn't at the table. Rebekha ate her food

and didn't look at us much. I wondered if maybe Micah was right, that she didn't like him, or me. I remembered what Momma said about a woman raising up another woman's kids. While she ate, she kept one hand in her lap where her napkin was. I looked at Micah to see if he was copying Rebekha, but he had his elbows all over the table and his napkin was tucked in his shirt collar. He let out a burp and laughed.

"What have I told you? We don't do that at the dinner table."

"Sorry. I forgot." Micah's mouth was full of cornbread dripping with ten pounds of butter.

Rebekha picked up the bowl and asked, "Virginia Kate, would you like some fruit? It's all fresh."

I held up my plate, wishing I'd sopped juice up with my cornbread so my fruit wouldn't get regular food on it.

"No, Hon, use the little bowl there. And your spoon is at the top of your plate."

I wondered what the extra stuff was for. I held out my bowl to let her scoop in the strawberries, blueberries, cantaloupe, watermelon, bananas, and grapes. She filled Micah's bowl and her own. Then she put the napkin back in her lap. I copied her and poked Micah so he'd do the same. He made a face, but did it.

I was about to dig in when Rebekha said, "Hey, why don't we put some whipped cream on that? Would you children like some?"

Micah said, "I would!" And gave her his biggest grin.

"And you, Virginia Kate?"

I smiled, but only a bit, so she wouldn't look so jittery at me.

She went into the kitchen, and while she was gone, Micah wiggled his nostrils. She came back with the bowl of whipped cream, said, "I made this myself." She scooped out big fluffy clouds on each of our fruit salads.

"This is very tasty, Rebekha," Micah said. He turned around and showed me the fruit in his mouth. He then spooned out another helping before Rebekha and I finished our first. Where it went I never knew, he was as skinny as he'd always been. I think it went to his brain because my brother was too smart for his own good.

Daddy came back right when we were licking the last of the whipped cream off our spoons. We were laughing because Micah had a spot of it on his nose. Daddy walked in and laughed, too, even though he didn't know what we were laughing about, he just wanted to belong. Spreading his arms wide, hugging us all at the table from the air, he said, "Well, isn't this a pretty picture." He sat down and I smelled sweet booze and salty sweat. "Sorry I'm late. I ran into Professor Rosso and we had a lively discussion about whether the Trojan War actually happened and then . . . well, it doesn't matter." He filled his plate. "It's hot as Hades out there." The food was cold, but Daddy didn't seem to notice.

"I'm glad you could join us." Rebekha stood up and kissed Daddy on the cheek. It was strange seeing another woman kiss Daddy. "I'd be interested in hearing about that. I love ancient history." She sat across from him.

"Oh, it's boring school stuff."

"Not at all, Frederick. I minored in history and I miss all that." Rebekha was sparkly-eyed as she leaned towards Daddy.

"I can't recreate the entire argument. You had to be there."

All the sparkle glugged right out of Rebekha. "But, I *wasn't* there."

Micah stood up, said, "Well, I'm finished," and left the table.

I burned my eyes into his back, but he didn't turn.

Daddy talked about the new neighbors down the street, the McGrander's. "We should invite them over sometime, seem like a nice couple."

"Yes, and Mrs. McGrander is quite attractive, isn't she?"

"I haven't really noticed."

Rebekha poked at a strawberry. "She's hard not to notice."

Their voices faded on away while I daydreamed about what Momma and Andy were doing. I pictured Andy asking for me. Momma telling him I was gone to Louisiana. Then they set themselves on the brown couch and cried and cried. Momma saying, "Oh, Andy. Why oh why did I send my Virginia Kate away?" And Andy saying, "Oh, Momma. You're mean." I thought maybe the phone would ring, since they'd have been blubbering for near-about two days already.

I asked, "Daddy, can we call Momma and Andy?"

"I called her, Bug."

"But I didn't get to talk to Andy." I wondered who would take care of Andy when Momma drank herself into stupidity? My head tightened and I felt a little sick.

"It might upset him."

I pressed my lips together tight before something mean and hateful came out.

He reached over and patted my head, but I wasn't in the mood. He said, "Rebekha works at the hospital. In the lab. Isn't that exciting?"

I looked over at her but she was staring down at her plate.

Daddy pushed away from the table. "That was good, Rebekha." He looked at me. "Bitty Bug, why don't you help her clean up?"

Daddy went to watch *Dr. Kildare*. I didn't think it was fair that since we were girls we had to do the cleaning and the cooking while the boys did what they pleased. I helped take dishes to the kitchen, waited for her to tell me what to do next.

She said, "Wash or dry?"

"Wash?"

She filled up the sink with soapy water. We didn't say another word. When the dishes were done, she thanked me, said she had a headache, then went to her room and shut the door. I wandered into the living room, but Daddy was asleep on the couch. I went to my new paint-smell room and looked around. I opened the window, reached out and touched the mimosa. The night smelled strange, thick, and was alive with sounds.

I put Fionadala and Fiddledeedee on the bed next to the pink pillows, climbed in with the same clothes I left West Virginia in, and lay stiff. I missed having Grandma Faith's quilt to snuggle under. I wondered if she could see me all the way from West Virginia to Louisiana.

I dreamed about Grandma. She was giving Petal Puss an apple, laughing when the pig ate it with its eyes closed in pure pig happy. Grandpa Luke sneaked up behind them with a hatchet. I hollered at her to run and take Petal Puss away. My feet were moving but I wasn't going anywhere. Grandpa drew closer and closer, while Grandma petted and hugged on Petal Puss. Just when Grandpa raised up the hatchet, I woke up. A hot wind blew through my window and the mimosa scratched against the top part of the pane. I heard the front door open and close. Next came the sound of Daddy's shoes hitting the floor. If I pretended hard enough, I could almost imagine I was in my West Virginia bed.

Chapter 16
West Virginia Kate wasn't good enough

I woke the next morning and didn't remember where I was until I saw all that pink. I stretched, got out of bed, and tried to make the bed like it was before. I eased from my room, then went quietly outside to rock on the porch. It was only six o'clock and already hot as a griddle.

In a little while, Micah came outside. "Hey."

"Hi." I pushed with my feet to make the rocker go faster.

"No, it's 'Hey'. That's what we say here, 'Hey.'" He sat in the other rocker and kicked off with his foot, making the chair go back and forth harder and faster. He made a scared-face. "Help! Help! My rocker's gone mad as a farting bull!"

I laughed.

"What're you doing in your same clothes?"

I looked down at Momma's top and those ugly plaid pedal pushers. Both were wrinkled to an inch of their cotton, plus they had food stains. I said, "It's sure hot here."

"Yep." Micah jumped up out of the rocker and tried to touch the ceiling. "Hotter than an elephant's ass." He slapped his thigh and laughed one of those loud half-fake laughs.

"Hush! You'll wake up people in five counties."

"No I won't, guess why?"

I shrugged.

"Because they don't have counties. They have parishes."

"Par-what?"

"Like a county, but it's a parish."

"Huh?"

He jumped off the porch, then ran back up the steps. His hair was already getting soppy. "Okay, you got to learn some stuff about living here if you're going to survive."

I was kind of scared then. Maybe there were alligators under the houses with the snakes. And the encyclopedia said they had hurricanes blowing everybody to Kingdom Come. And lots of weird bugs crawling around.

"First, you have to say *yawl*. It's spelled y-a-l-l."

"I know what yawl is. Mee Maw says it all the time. I heard it at school, too." I gave him my you-don't-know-everything-smarty-britches look.

"Yeah, but you have to say it like yaawwwlll, like that—if you want to fit in."

"Well, maybe I will and maybe I won't." I kicked my feet against the porch floorboards.

"Don't matter to me none." His eyes said I hurt his feelings, like he was about to run off.

"Tell me more stuff."

He grinned and punched the air around him. "Okay, y'all means one person, and y'all means more than one person, but sometimes they say all y'allses. But y'all could mean animals, too."

"It's like you and all together."

"Yeah, like, 'All y'allses come here,' or 'Y'all look like a monkey' and 'Y'all dogs get from out that garbage.'" He sat and rocked in time with me while I sat quiet.

He picked at a scab on his knee until blood trickled down his leg and then wiped it with his white t-shirt. "And nobody drinks pop."

"But I had one at the filling station."

"They just don't call it 'pop'."

I was getting dizzy-headed. I didn't know I'd have to learn a foreign language. "What do they call it?"

"It's called coke. So, don't go asking for pop or they'll look at you like you're stupid or something."

"So, the only pop they have is Co-Cola?"

"No, Worm-brain. Orange drink is coke, grape drink is coke, and Co-*ca*-Cola is coke. It's easy once you get used to it."

I didn't think so.

"Rebekha calls them soft drinks."

"Well, which one do I call it then?"

"Just don't say *pop* and you'll be fine." He looked down at my dirty feet. "You should wear shoes."

I thought how I surely dirtied up Rebekha's sheets.

He came over and flopped his arm over my shoulder, just like at home. "You'll get used to stuff. I did, I guess."

"Yawwwl did, Booger-face?"

He punched me in the arm and pulled my hair until I said Uncle. The front door opened and Rebekha came out wearing a green and white polka dot robe and fuzzy white slippers. "Hey. Y'all's breakfast is ready." Micah and I laughed. She said, "What?"

He said, "Yawwwl got any coke in this here parish?"

"I want a soft drink, yawwwl. In this parish county," I said.

My brother and I laughed some more.

Rebekha shook her head. "Y'all come eat. We have orange juice."

For breakfast, Rebekha made waffles and eggs. Daddy came in with his hair stuck up like a porcupine. "Hey Bug, how'd you sleep?"

I scrunched down at the table so he couldn't see what I was still wearing.

When we finished, Daddy said he'd clean up the kitchen after he drank one more cup of coffee. I didn't remember him doing dishes at home. When he waved his hand at us, I noticed the ring he wore was silver instead of the gold one that matched Momma's. "Go on now, all of you. Daddy's cleaning up today." He kissed Rebekha on the mouth, putting his hand on her rear. She pulled away and laughed.

Micah whispered in my ear, "I think I gotta vomit." He made gagging noises.

Daddy said, "If you want to do that, you can help me with the dishes."

Micah and I hightailed it out the front door. He showed me around the neighborhood, pointing out the nice people, the meanies and the snooty-think-their-poop-don't-stink people. On the next street over, a girl who looked my age sat on her front step playing with a doll. I smiled at her, but she frowned back. I looked away but not before I took in how she wore a dress, lacy bobby socks, patent leather shoes, and had her hair pulled back with a big black bow on top. It looked like she had a bat setting on top of her head. She was so pale I thought she might be a ghost.

I felt like I was ten feet tall with a light shining on me that showed all my dirty.

Back at Daddy's house, Micah said, "See ya! I'm off to the wild blue yonder." He tore around the house, came back on a bike, and raced off. That was when I remembered I hadn't brought my bike, either. I had left too much behind.

I went back inside to my room and saw *Black Beauty* propped on the pillows. I sat in the chair next to my bed, opened it, and read, *My Early Home—The first place that I can well remember was a large, pleasant meadow with a pond of clear water in it.* I read on, smiling because it was the horse doing the talking. By the time I was to *My Breaking In*, someone knocked at my door. I didn't know what to do since nobody knocked on doors at home. If you didn't want someone coming in, you locked the door. So I said, "Hey!"

Rebekha came in. "Hey. I see you found the book. I forgot to give it to you that day."

I closed the book, using my thumb to keep my place.

"I loved reading it when I was a girl." She looked down at my feet, then up to my face. "I drew you a nice bubble bath."

"Thank you, Ma'am."

"You can call me Rebekha instead of Ma'am." She crossed the room and sat on the bed facing me. "I thought I'd see what you brought with you, your clothes I mean. School starts soon."

I didn't want to think about school in a different world, with new ways of talking.

She smoothed the bedspread and looked around the room "So, do you mind if I take a look?"

"No, Ma'am."

In the dresser, she found three pair of white cotton underwear, Micah's old britches he'd left behind and I'd took up to wearing, a pair of grass-stain-on-the-seat blue shorts, two shirts—the white one had a hole under the arm, a nightgown, and one pair of flip flops. Everything was just crammed in the dresser drawers, even the shoes.

She laughed and said, "You must have packed, Virginia Kate." She turned to me with one eyebrow cocked up. "Hon, we need to go shopping. You'll need dresses, and more shoes." She looked down at my feet again as I tried to tuck them under me. "Well, don't you think a bath would make you feel better?"

All I thought was then I'd have to take off Momma's shirt with her smells on it, and I'd have to wash off the rest of the West Virginia dirt that was getting mixed up with the Louisiana dirt. Momma's shirt would be washed where it'd smell like soap instead of her powder. I thought how I was dirty and didn't have proper manners. How everybody wanted to make me into someone else since the West Virginia Kate wasn't good enough. But all I said was, "Yes Ma'am."

"Just leave your dirty clothes on the bathroom floor and I'll wash them for you. You can use the vinegar to rinse your hair with, it really does work. Just put a little in the plastic cup by the tub and pour it over your head. It makes your hair all shiny and soft. My mother had me use it all the time." She hardly took a breath until she got all that out.

While I marked my place in *Black Beauty* with a rubber band I kept on my wrist, she took the bedspread and sheets off the bed. She said, "We'll get these freshened for you, too." With my face as hot as the Louisiana wind, I helped her with the sheets. She carried them with her to the washroom.

I shut myself in the bathroom, sat on the toilet, and looked around. There was a pedestal sink, and a claw foot tub just like Grandma Faith bathed me in, except Grandma's was old and beat up instead of white and gleaming with all those bubbles making rainbows. I stood, opened the bath closet. There was a hundred and two blue and white fluffy towels, even the washrags matched each other. They all faced with the folded side to me, not a one out of place. I sniffed and they smelled like soap. Momma had different colored towels facing any way we put them, and they smelled like fresh mountain air from drying on the line.

I eased shut the closet door, and then took off my clothes, dropping everything on the floor but Momma's shirt, which I hung on the door. I slipped into the bubbles and scrubbed with the washrag full of almond-smelling soap. I washed my hair with the soap, rinsed it in the dirty water, and then poured some of the vinegar over it, wrinkling my nose at the smell. I rinsed again under the faucet extra long to get the stink out. Finally, I stepped out, dried off, put on the clean clothes. I was almost brand sparkly new.

Daddy took me for a ride with the top down so all the hot could blow around our faces. I snapped pictures whenever we stopped at red lights or stop signs. I liked how some of the granddaddy oak branches came down to the ground and rested, too heavy for the old tree to hold them up anymore. Crepe myrtle bloomed white, pink, red, and purple. Those Louisiana people walked around as if it wasn't hot at all, talking loud and all wearing shoes.

We drove around the little lake (it was nothing like my creeks) and I took pictures of ducks, egrets white as the moonshine, cypress trees and cypress knees, and lots of Spanish moss hanging. Daddy said the moss was full of bugs and that's where the saying don't let the bed bugs bite came from. He said because people used to make their beds with moss and then got all itchy. When I took enough pictures to share with Momma and Andy, Daddy took me to a diner for lunch. It was old and a bit dirty, but smelled like good food.

We sat down and a girl came over to the table. Her hair was long down her back and it was almost as dark as mine. Her name tag read, *Soot*. Her eyes were dark and sparkly, and she grinned at me with big orange-lipstick lips. She asked, "Whatchoo two hungry for?" She set glasses of ice water on the table.

"Are *you* on the menu?" Daddy grinned like that *Alice in Wonderland* cat.

"Why dontchoo ask my boyfriend. He's right over there—the big fella fixin' to bust you one."

I looked at her big ole boyfriend and figured Daddy better keep his mouth shut. He cleared the donkey out of his throat and said, "We'll have two shrimp po-boy's with extra tartar sauce. My daughter hasn't ever had a po-boy." He winked at me. "And a big order of fries, Soot."

"Whatchoo want to drink, Boo?"

I didn't know what a *boo* was, but she was looking at me. "I'll have a pop . . . I mean, a coke. An orange coke soft drink."

She laughed, showing her strong white teeth— just like mine—and then touched my nose. "An orange coke soft drink it is. Boy, you're the cutest. I could carry you home with me."

I felt warm inside.

Soot turned to Daddy. "Whatchoo drinking, Don Juan?"

Daddy laughed, then said, "Whatever beer you have that's good and cold."

"It's all good and cold." She tossed back her hair and walked away with her hips rolling.

Daddy watched her for a bit, then said, "Well, Bug, you're in for a treat."

Out the window, an old man picked up used cig-arettes off the sidewalk and put them in his pocket. He saw me looking and waved. I waved back.

Soot brought our drinks with a big plate of fried potatoes. "Get started on these while they're hot."

She waited, so I took one and bit into it. I chewed, said, "Mmmm."

"Good, huh? Marco fried extra just for you 'cause you're so pretty."

I felt prissy, because she paid so much attention to me. I thought I might love her.

"So, you hadn't ever had a po-boy, huh?"

"No Ma'am."

"Where you from? I hear an accent."

I thought it was Soot had the accent. "I'm from West-By-God-Virginia."

She laughed beautiful, then asked, "You're a long way from home, arentchoo?"

I nodded, ate another fry.

"You poor thing."

Marco hollered out, "Come get this here food, Soot. You just love them kids too much." He said kids like kee-yuds.

Soot winked at me, then turned to get our sandwiches. "Oh, put a sock in it, Marco." She snapped a towel at him and he laughed. I thought it would be grand to go home with Soot. Pretend she was my sister, or my momma.

She soon carried us sandwiches as long as my arm. "Y'all enjoy. Call me if you need something."

Daddy took a hippopotamus bite and I did the same. The bread was crunchy on the outside and soft on the inside. The fried shrimp were stuffed full inside the bread and had a spicy taste. Even though I tried, I couldn't finish mine. Soot wrapped it up for me to take. I felt sad when it was time to go.

Soot said, "Y'all come on back so I can see that pretty smiling face again."

I carried my po-boy out, my stomach full of food and my heart full up with Soot. I was getting in the car when I had a thought. "Wait, Daddy."

"What is it?"

I took my camera and ran back in the diner.

Soot turned around and put her hands on her hips, "You still hungry, Boo?"

I felt shy, but I wanted that picture. "Can I take a picture of you?" Then to be nice I said, "And Marco, too."

She grabbed Marco by the sleeve and they stood together, grinning big and happy. I snapped two pictures, one for me and one for Andy. "Thank you, Soot." She came over, hugged me, and underneath the fried food, I smelled clove in her hair.

She said, "Come again soon, Sweets."

When I climbed back in the car, Daddy roared away, both of us grinning because of Soot.

Back at the house Daddy made himself a big fat drink, and then flopped on the couch to sip and read. I sat beside him, leaned into him, closed my eyes, and pretended we were home.

Rebekha brought the surprise on a day that melted my ice cubes before I took the second sip. I was finishing *Black Beauty*, sipping down a glass of Amy Campinelle's tea that was so sweet it curled my tongue up in a knot. Amy Campinelle liked to feed and drink us all to death. She walked across the street with all her body jiggling to beat the band, holding things in her big hands like sweet tea, lemonade, gumbo, bisque, and shrimp salad sandwiches. She had a nest of frizzy Louisiana-egret-white hair that puffed around her head like a

Q-tip. Sometimes her friend Mrs. Portier came with her and they both clucked over me and Micah like funny chickens.

I was just to the sad part about poor Ginger when Rebekha pulled up in her serious Oldsmobile, black with a white stripe down the sides. Different from Momma, Andy, and me flying down the road in our pink Rambler, Momma's hand stuck out the window, our hair in tangles.

Rebekha stepped out grinning, ran around to the back of the car, calling out, "Virginia Kate, come see!"

I put down my book, jumped off the porch, and stood in the middle of the yard while she untied a rope from the trunk.

She said, "It's almost brand new."

I eased over, peeped in the trunk. And there it was.

"It was my boss's daughter's. She didn't want it, can you imagine? Never even rode it."

I couldn't imagine. It was beautiful.

"I was going to wait for your birthday, but, well, I couldn't stand it."

It was fire-engine-red with happy-colored streamers hanging from the handlebars and a white basket on the front just perfect for books. I asked, "For me?"

"Yes, for you."

I helped her pull it out of the trunk, my heart thumping with all the happy I felt. I hopped on it, rode it down the driveway and back. I couldn't help it; I had to smile at her since she bought me a bike. "Thank you, Ma'am."

"You're welcome. And remember, you can call me Rebekha."

"Yes Ma'am."

"I have to run. Can you tell Miss Amy I have a doctor's appointment?"

I nodded, and then rode back down the driveway and part ways down the sidewalk, until she ran to the end of the driveway, shouting at me to, "Wait! Virginia Kate!"

I pedaled back to her, hoping she hadn't changed her mind. Sometimes those things happened.

"Solemn swear you'll be careful."

"I swear, Ma'am."

"Don't talk to strangers. And, don't go far. And tell Miss Amy where you're going."

I nodded.

"Where are you going?"

"To the library." I smelled the books already.

"Straight to the library and back and nowhere else."

"Yes, Ma'am."

I watched her climb back into her car, wave, and drive away. I rode across the street and yelled in Amy Campinelle's back door that Rebekha was off to the doctor and I was off to the library. I tore off, my empty basket ready to fill up with books. At the library, I parked and went into the cool and book smell. After I got a library card, I picked out five books, checked out, and put the books in my basket. The wind felt good blowing my hair back as I rode. I wished that Micah would happen by so he could see me.

Back at the house, I corralled my bike in the back yard. Rebekha's car was already back in the driveway. I went through the kitchen and saw a plate of cookies with a note, "Help yourself. Three for Virginia Kate and three for Micah." I took four cookies and went into the living room. Rebekha lay on the couch with her right hand slung on the floor and the other over her stomach. I sneaked over to see if she was still alive. She was hard asleep, with wet on her cheeks and on the pillow.

I put my hand on her forehead to see if she was sick and she opened her eyes. I jumped back, hoping she didn't know I'd touched her. "Thank you for the bike, Ma'am."

"You're welcome, Hon."

I left her there and went to my room.

Chapter 17
She's in her whirly-world again

For my eighth birthday, there was white cake with pink frosting, crab cakes, and potato salad. Rebecca decorated the dining room (in pink and white) and used her pink dishes to serve the cake and Neapolitan ice cream. On the white tablecloth were two presents from Rebekha and Daddy; a card from Mee Maw, who was in Colorado with her new boyfriend; and presents from Amy Campinelle and Mrs. Portier.

I was bug-eyed. I thought the bike was my only gift. Everyone sang *Happy Birthday* all silly. Daddy and Micah ended with, "You look like a monkey and you smell like one too!" I blew out the candles and wished for Andy, even though I knew wishes didn't come true.

Rebekha cut huge slices of cake; Daddy scooped big scoops of ice cream.

Micah stuffed half of his in his mouth, said, "Hurry and open the presents, Monkey-face."

"Do you have to call your sister names, Micah?" Rebekha asked. "And no talking with your mouth full."

"She likes it, don't you, Worm-brain?"

I smacked him on the arm.

"Okay, you two, cut it out." Daddy held his sparkly crystal glass in one hand and my camera in the other, snapping pictures in between swallows. "They're just playing around, Rebekha. That's what kids do."

She smiled small at Daddy.

After we ate, I unwrapped my presents nice and slow, so they wouldn't think I was excited. Amy Campinelle gave me a sweater she knitted out of red yarn, and Mrs. Portier gave me a Barbie doll with a shiny silver evening dress.

Rebekha said, "Oh, that red will look good with your coloring. Be sure and go thank them both tomorrow."

"Yes Ma'am." I opened Mee Maw's card. She'd given me a ten-dollar bill, with two quarters and five dimes taped on the inside.

She wrote, *To my Laudine Virginia Kate, may you have the happiest of birthdays. I knew some day you'd be where you belong. Two down, one to go!*

I decided Mee Maw was No Good even if she did send me money. I wanted to put her money right in the garbage, but I didn't. Next, I unwrapped the pink-and-white-papered boxes. I was getting right tired of pink and white, but I didn't say a thing. The first box held a baby blue diary and fancy pen. I turned the diary over in my hands, liking the little lock and key to hide my secrets in. I thumbed through the blank pages, thinking about what I'd write.

Micah hummed, which meant, "Hurry up, Stupid-head."

In the last box lay hair ribbons in blue, red, green, and—pink. Underneath the ribbons was a bookmark with a horse like Black Beauty, running in a meadow. I said to Daddy. "I like my presents a lot."

"Glad you like them, Baby Bug." Daddy went to the kitchen. Ice dropped into the glass. All the thoughts of home were in that sound. Times Momma turned on her radio to dance, and didn't matter whose birthday it was. Times Momma wrapped the presents in foil then put a ribbon over it, Momma liked shiny things. I decided that the first thing I'd write in my diary would be about birthdays. I'd write about all that dancing and smiling and eating cake.

"Virginia Kate? I asked if you'd like more cake." Rebekha held out a slice.

"Oh. No, Ma'am."

Micah said, "She's in her whirly-world again, aren't you, Vee?"

"Am not."

"Are to. This is you." Micah stared off with his mouth open just a little, his body still as dead.

Daddy laughed, said, "That does look like her."

I mean-stared x-ray beams at my brother, but he didn't care, he was too busy pretending he was me.

"Well, girls have all kinds of secret things they think about," Rebekha said.

Daddy sipped, wet his mustache that sprung out from his lip like Rebekha's bottlebrush plant.

Micah finished up a third piece of cake. "Can I go to my room now?"

"*May* you. And yes, you may be excused," Rebekha said.

Micah pretended he was Elvis, singing about a jailhouse rock, swinging his hips as he left the room.

I went around the table to hug Daddy, then turned to Rebekha. She *had* bought me the bike. "Thank you, Ma'am."

"You're welcome, Virginia Kate." She leaned towards me.

I stepped back. I still hated her some, but I wasn't sure. I was all mixed up since she was good to us, and to Daddy. My head hurt, thinking about things that were too hard to figure out. Like maybe Micah was wrong about her not liking him. Seemed she smiled at him a lot with kind eyes.

The phone rang and Rebekha left to answer it. Daddy tried to snake-charm me again. "You look so much like your mother and grandmother." He sipped from his glass, swallowed. "But you have your grandma's spirit."

I was getting ready to ask him what he meant when Rebekha came back into the room and whispered to Daddy. He said, "I'll handle it."

"Are you sure, Frederick?"

"I know what's best for my children."

"I see." Rebekha picked up dishes real fast.

Daddy went to the phone and soon his voice rose up louder, "Katie, this isn't the right time and you know it."

I hollered out, "Momma?" and ran into the living room, but Daddy hung up just as I got there. "That was Momma! She called for my birthday. She remembered it." I gave Daddy a look worse than cats give dogs.

"Bug, I'm sorry. She was drunk."

"I don't believe you." But I did.

He came over and sat on his heels so he could look straight at me. "I'm doing the right thing."

"What about Andy?"

"He wasn't there. He's at your Uncle Jonah's for a few days."

I ran to my room, slammed the door a good one, and lay in bed with all that pink tickling my nose. Through my door, I heard them.

"When Katie grows up maybe I'll change my mind," Daddy said.

"I'm worried about what this does to the children. They need their mother, don't you think? I mean, some kind of contact?"

"Let me worry about my own, Rebekha."

"Oh, I see how you do that."

Another door whammed. Then the front door ker-blammed. The whole house rattled with doors hitting the frames hard. I got up, dug in my dresser drawers, and pulled out Momma's shirt with all her smells washed away. I lay on it, closed my eyes, and tried to pretend I was home again. But it didn't work.

Rebekha knocked on the door and walked in before I could say anything. "Hon, here's your birthday presents. Thought you might need them about now." I listened to her breathing, but I wouldn't look up at her. She laid my things on the bed beside me and left, closing the door soft behind her.

Propped against the presents was an envelope. I

recognized Momma's scrawly writing on the outside. My heart beat like a baby bird. I picked it up, sniffed it, and smelled Shalimar. I sat up and opened it. A birthday card with a blue bird sitting on a branch and a note inside from Momma, three dollars, and a folded piece of paper.

I read, *Virginia Kate, please don't hate me. You're my daughter. One day you'll understand. One day we'll be together again if I can work things out. I'm sorry I couldn't send more. Love, Momma.*

The folded paper was Andy's school letters written between the wide-lines, the same ones he used to watch me work on. There was an A and a silver star from his teacher, my own Miss Bowen.

My eyes burned, and I lay back, holding onto the paper. I fell asleep and dreamed I was driving the Rambler, the wind blowing my hair out the window. Andy and Momma were in the back seat, jumping up and down. I hit a bump and we all laughed when the car flew up into the air. I woke when my leg jerked, got up and put away all my presents, except the diary.

On the first page, I wrote, *I miss Andy. I miss Momma. I miss my good old mountain and the maple and Grandma's quilt! Everything is stupid here. Everything is hot and pink and neat and clean.* I wrote about Daddy not letting me talk to Momma or Andy. I wrote about Micah making fun of me. About all the neighborhood kids who acted as if I was see-through. When I was tired of writing, I closed up the diary, locked it with the little key, and hid it in my underwear drawer along with Momma's card and Andy's school paper.

I left my room and wandered around. Daddy's keys were off the hook and his hat was gone. Micah was in his room with his *Keep Out and That Means You* sign on the door. I peeked into the living room. Rebekha sat reading in her big chair. I studied her where she couldn't see me. Her hair was combed neat to her chin and she wore a green blouse and tan skirt. I thought how Momma fidgeted. Even when she slept, her face moved and her feet twitched. Everything about Momma was itchy. Everything about Rebekha was still.

I went in, sat on the couch, and waited to see what Rebekha would do next.

She put down her book. "I think I'd like another piece of cake. You?"

I didn't say anything.

She went to the kitchen, and came back with two pieces as big as my head. "How about we sit on the porch and eat?"

It was still steam-hot outside, even at full dark. I heard mommas calling their kids inside. Their voices carried across the breeze that rustled the oak trees. Raindrops hit the banana plants against the house. Rebekha and I ate without talking. The night bugs and frogs started up a racket. We rocked on the porch, watching lightning bugs light.

Micah came out with a rolled up piece of paper. "Happy Birthday, Squirk-brain."

Rebekha turned on the porch light. Micah had drawn me a swirly color painting. In the middle was an outline of a horse, its mane and tail flying out behind him as he ran through all the color.

Rebekha said, "Oh, Micah! How beautiful." She smoothed his hair. "You are such a talented boy."

Micah smiled and didn't step back.

I said, "Thanks, Micah. It's the best one yet."

He sat on the top step and leaned against the post while Rebekha and I rocked. Somewhere way off I thought I heard my name called, but I wasn't sure. All a sudden, everything felt straight and even. I rocked, closed up Momma behind one of my doors, and locked the key. That's what I pretended.

Chapter 18
My name is Virginia Kate Carey

I waited for the leaves to start turning gold, red, and yellow like home, but most everything stayed green. Micah said it never snowed either, unless hell snowed, too. He said we had to worry about Hurricane Betsy. We had lots of hard wind and rain when she came howling up the Mississippi, but that's all. She tore up New Orleans instead.

My teacher's name was Miss Sherry Melon. She had clear blue eyes and thick brown hair. She *clomped* crooked in front of the class, since one shoe was bigger, the sole of it thick and black. The others made fun of her. Maybe that's why I liked her. In the school library, I looked up West Virginia in the encyclopedia and studied it, pretending I didn't know anything about it at all.

I read about how in 1926 almost all the chestnut trees died, how a famous writer named Pearl Buck was born there—and so was Barney Fife of *Mayberry*, and how Spruce Knob is the highest place and the Potomac River is the lowest. I read about all the things I already knew so I wouldn't forget.

Football time came around and for two dollars, Daddy let people park in our driveway and in the front at the curb, even though we were a fair piece away from the stadium. He said the money he made would go into Mr. Campinelle's need-more-beer bucket. Some people came just for the party and they helped fill the bucket, too. Amy Campinelle served up jambalaya on paper plates, with butter and garlic French bread on the side. Some called it *jam*-bah-lie-ya, and some called it *jum*-bah-lie-ya. I called it rice with stuff in it.

Mr. Campinelle liked to be called Mister Husband. He was as big as a gorilla who ate lots of fried chicken and gravy. When I took Mister Husband and Amy Campinelle's picture, I had to stand across the street to get them both in it. I loved them more than coconut cake.

Mister Husband stirred up the rice, sausage, and

chicken in an iron pot as big as a rhinoceros' rear. He held a beer in one hand and a big boat paddle he used as a stirring spoon in the other.

Amy Campinelle called out, "Come here, sweet girl. You're way too skinny, yeah, come get a plate."

I liked being called skinny.

Mister Husband wrote with shaving cream onto the grass, "Geaux Tigers," and Amy Campinelle sprinkled confetti and glitter over it.

I asked, "Gee-a-ux? What's that?"

Mister Husband answered, "It's *Go*, Little Bit. Can't you speak Looseeana yet?"

I took my plate back across, sat on the steps, picked out the sausage to save for stray dogs, and ate the rest. I wore Micah's old britches and in the pocket I had candy cigarettes, so I could pretend to smoke.

A bald man in tiger-striped pj's going to the game teetered over and handed me a beer. "Here, little girlie. Have a coke."

His friend grabbed it back. "That ain't no coke, you drunken idiot." I took a picture of them while they stumbled off down the street, yelling, "Aiyeeeeee!" Micah told me it was a Cajun's way of hollering yeehaa.

Sort of cute boys passed by punching the air, or each other, hollering louder than they needed to. I held up my head like Momma, pretend-smoking, and hoped I looked like I had lots of mysterious ways.

Daddy came out with his new mustache trimmed, but his hair still long on his ears. He held a thermos in his left hand and a jacket slung over his right arm. "Young Princess, as soon as my chariot arrives, I'm off to watch our team slay the Dragon!" He took a gulp from the thermos, said, "Ahhh! The elixir of strength." When he leaned over to kiss the top of my head, I smelled sweet mixed with his usual, and wrinkled my nose to it. He said, "I'm going with a wild herd of students. And, forsooth, there they are now."

The driver honked his horn like a fool. The car was full and I didn't see where Daddy would sit. A girl with stringy brown hair stuck her head out of the window. "Hey man, let's go."

Someone else shouted, "Hurry up, old man!"

Daddy cupped his hands and shouted back, "Keep your shirts on. Except you, Janet." He laughed and winked at me, "Just kidding there, Bug." He threw the thermos in the air, couldn't catch it, and when it rolled away, had to chase it across the porch. When he got it, he said, "Well, I'm off. Don't forget to leave the light on. 'Light, seeking light, doth light of light beguile!'" He jumped from the porch, ran to pile in the car. The girl sat on his lap. Before they sped away Daddy hollered, "Check on Rebekha for me, will you? She's not feeling well."

The fools honked while leaving, too, and I was glad when they turned the corner out of sight.

Daddy never even noticed I hadn't said hello or goodbye.

I forgot Daddy, since there was a ruckus going on across the street. Mrs. McGrander, in a sweater and skirt tight enough to cut off her blood flows, danced over to Mr. Portier, and fell right into his lap. Mr. Portier wrapped his arms around her while Mrs. McGrander laughed and kicked up her legs. One of her high-heels flew into the air and landed in the jambalaya.

Mister Husband shook his head and threw the shoe in the bushes.

Mrs. Portier ran over and splashed her drink on the both of them. She yelled, "Maybe this will cool you two off! I'm sick of it!" They jumped up sputtering. I thought she should have smacked them both upside the head, and hard.

Mrs. McGrander looked in the bushes for her shoe, her rear end stuck out for anyone to see. I sent a mind message to Mrs. Portier to go over there and kick her right in the hiney.

Mrs. Portier must have read my mind message. She did just that, kicked Mrs. McGrander right into the azalea bushes.

Mrs. McGrander jumped up screaming, "You red-headed Bitch!" She pushed Mrs. Portier, and then they lit into each other. I sat on the edge of the step and rooted for Mrs. Portier. I wished Micah were there to see them. Rebekha missed it, too, since she'd stayed in bed most of the day. (I tried to be quiet and make sure my chores were done just right, just in case Micah and I were what she was sick about.)

Mister Husband finally made them stop. Mrs. McGrander's stupid bleached up hair stood wacky all over her head, but Mrs. Portier wasn't hardly messed up one bit. Everybody went into the house talking at once.

It was so quiet, I thought the world was ending, not even a dog barked. I hummed while I explored, seeing how many things I could name. Naming things made them solid and real.

I said, "That's an iris, this is a caladium, and that's monkey grass, begonia, impatiens, and in the neighbor's yard a dogwood tree." I wondered if Grandma Faith heard me and felt proud. Maybe this was my prodigy, knowing the names of things. I dug in the garden until my hands and knees were extra dirty. Then a roar went up in the sky, like forty million voices, all coming from the football stadium.

I went inside and put my ear to Rebekha's door. I didn't hear a thing. I took a sort of bath at the sink with a washrag full of soap, and went on to my room to read *The Incredible Journey*. I loved the story of the two dogs and cat trying to get back home. I was at page fifty-two, reading *Nomadic life seemed to agree with the cat,* when my door opened and Micah came in.

He said, "Hey."

"Hey."

"Guess what me and Denny did?"

"I don't know."

"Guess."

"Ate a frog?"

"No, Fart-brain." He sat on the bed and grabbed my book. "You're always reading."

"You're always drawing. Or at least you used to."

"I still do."

"Not as much."

He picked up Fiddledeedee and socked it in the face. "Isn't this Andy's?"

I shrugged.

"Well, if you aren't going to ask, I'll tell you anyway." He went to peek out the door and all a sudden I saw him like he was back at Momma's. He shut the door and sat on the side of my bed. "You better not tell."

I shook my head. I never told on Micah.

"I puffed on a cigarette, and not that candy stuff you have. The real kind."

I picked up my book and pictured all the words telling a story.

"Don't worry. I won't do it again, it was gross."

"I'm not worried."

"Yes you are." He stood up and walked around my room, picking up things and putting them back down. "What's with all this pink stuff?"

"I don't know. She likes it."

"Did you tell her it's ugly as a worm's butt?"

"No."

"Well, she doesn't bite, you know. Just tell her you don't like pink."

I looked at him as if he was dipped in stupid sauce.

"Guess what else we did?"

"I don't want to."

"We threw eggs at old Mrs. Hodges house." He slapped his knee and laughed.

"Why'd you do that?"

"Because it's funny. Geez, you're like an old woman." He stomped for the door.

I threw a horrid pink pillow at him. I threw the other one, and then Fiddledeedee. Micah laughed like "Muwahahahaha" and threw everything back hard and fast as he could. I yelled, "Stop it!" but I didn't really want him to.

"You asked for it, leetle seestor!"

I had to go ruin it. "Don't you want to go home sometimes?"

"No." He stuck out his tongue, knocked his knees together, and opened the door. "See ya later, smashed potater!" Then he was gone.

I sat in the middle of my bed, liking how messy it looked. Down the hall, Micah's door shut with a blam. I went to get some milk and heard water running in the bathroom. The water sounds didn't stop me from hearing Rebekha throwing up. I went quiet to the bathroom door and listened, feeling scared and fidgety. When the toilet flushed, I went back to my room.

I sat in the chair, looked out at the mimosa

branches blowing in the wind, and waited to hear Rebekha stirring around. I got up and touched things in my room, like Micah had. From the burlap bag, I pulled out Momma's brush, her red lipstick, the Shalimar powder, and put it all on the dresser. I stared in the mirror. My hair was tangled and a piece of leaf was stuck in it. There was dirt on my face, and more under my fingernails where I dug around in the yard. Inside my pocket were leaves and seeds I found in the flower garden. I wanted to look things up in my nature book. I wanted to know what everything was, put a name to it, and make it real.

I leaned in until my nose almost touched the mirror. "My name is Virginia Kate Carey." I watched my mouth say my name and it almost didn't feel like I really said it.

I opened the lipstick and twisted the bottom until a little bit of the color poked out. I touched it to my top lip, sliding it first to the left side, then the right side. I pressed my lips to bleed the color onto the bottom lip. It was sticky and warm. I waited to feel different. I said, "I am Virginia Kate Carey." I heard Rebekha, so I went to the kitchen.

She stood at the sink, her hair all stuck to her head. "Virginia Kate, what in the world is that on your mouth?"

"Nothing." I stepped back. "I was just going to get some milk."

"I see. Well, that nothing looks a little too old for

you, but I like the color." She smiled, just a little, said, "Maybe you can borrow my light pink, I mean, just around the house."

"Yes, Ma'am."

She sighed, said, "I was so tired today. Did I miss anything at the Campinelle's?"

"Mrs. Portier beat up Mrs. McGrander."

"You're kidding!" Rebekha's tired went out the window when she laughed with her head thrown back. "Why-oh-why did I have to miss that?"

"Mrs. McGrander got on Mr. Portier's lap. He didn't even push her off."

"Mrs. McGrander should sit in her own husband's lap for a change." She ran her hands through her hair, frowned, and then turned it up into a smile. "I bet that was hilarious."

"Yes, Ma'am."

Rebekha took the milk from the icebox and set it on the counter. I opened the cabinet to get a glass. "Want some, Ma'am?"

"Yes, please. I'd love some."

I got down another glass and poured hers first. When I handed it to her, her hands were cold. I said, with my back to her as I poured my milk. "I'm sorry you got sick."

"Thank you. I'm feeling better now." She sipped her milk, then said, "Want to watch television? I could make us some popcorn. I mean, if you'd like to?" When she smiled, I noticed a dimple in her left cheek for the first time.

"Can we put butter, salt, and sugar on it?"

"I don't see why not." She took out the oil, some butter, her big heavy pot, and a smaller one. She melted the butter in the small one first, and then put oil in the bigger one. The pots were heavy and shiny, with handles that weren't burnt and melted. "Can you get one of those brown paper bags over there?" I did that while she put popcorn in the oil. She stood over it, waiting for the first kernel to explode. Then, she put the lid on and shook the pot to get them moving around. They popped slowly at first, then faster. It was a happy, fun sound.

With her back to me this time, she said, "I have some gossip about Mrs. McGrander, but you're probably too young to hear it." She cleared her throat, said, "Well, anyway, gossip isn't nice. I don't know why I said anything."

I stood up straight to make myself look taller.

When the popping slowed up, she turned off the burner, gave the pot one more shake, and then poured the popcorn into the paper bag. She drizzled the butter in and shook it, then sprinkled in salt and shook it again. "How much sugar?"

"Can I do it?"

"Sure."

I scooped sugar and slowly sprinkled it in, and then gave the bag another shake. I dumped the popcorn in the bowl.

"I've never had it this way," she said.

I handed her three pieces to taste.

She chewed and swallowed. "Mmmm. Best popcorn I've ever had." She took two Orange Crush from the icebox. "Let's go sit in the living room."

"What about the No Eating In The Living Room Rule?"

"I changed my mind, at least for tonight. That'll be our secret, okay?"

"Okay."

We settled ourselves on the couch; I put the bowl between us. She studied me and I remembered I still wore the lipstick. I wondered if it made me look old enough for gossip secrets. She looked around the room, even though nobody else was there and said almost in a whisper, "I heard this from Miss Amy, who knows everything about everyone." She ate a handful of popcorn, said, "This is so delicious."

I waited for secrets to be told, eating my popcorn like watching television.

"Oh dear. I can't believe I'm telling you this." She swallowed some Crush and made a face. "This stuff is so tangy. Well, then, okay." She looked around again. "Mrs. McGrander used to work as a dancer girl. She called herself 'Miss Double-Dee-Light-Full the Reversible Stripper'." Rebekha turned pinky-red, tucked her hair behind her ear.

"What's a stripper?"

"Oh, I knew you were too young. I shouldn't have said."

I puffed my lips with the red lipstick.

She chewed and swallowed. "Okay, well, it's when women take their clothes off and dance around in a room full of men."

"Mrs. McGrander did that?" I remembered her dancing out in the yard. "She's not a very good dancer."

Rebekha put her hand over her mouth and laughed, then said, "Well, I suppose that doesn't matter to the men."

When I took a gulp of Orange Crush to wash down my popcorn, I noticed the bottle had a red stain from my lips.

Rebekha went on, "She did it differently than usual. She came out on the stage with no clothes on, danced around, and then put her clothes back on a little at a time. First her stockings, then comes the shoes, and so on. Oh, it was all the rage for a while at this little club across the river." She cleared her throat again, said, "It was a long time ago, I'm sure." She handed me a napkin. "Wipe that lipstick."

I wiped it gone.

"I shouldn't have told you, but I did. Miss Amy made me pinkie swear about it. So, now we have to pinkie swear."

"What's that?"

Rebekha looked at me as if I was behind the bars at a zoo. "You've never had a pinkie swear?"

"No, Ma'am."

She stuck out her pinkie. "Stick out your pinkie."

I stuck it out and she hooked hers around mine. "Pinkie swear you won't tell a soul that I told you something I shouldn't have in a weak moment of silliness and popcorn."

"Yes, Ma'am."

"No, you have to say 'pinkie swear' back to me."

"Pinkie swear."

We shook pinkies.

"Now it's sealed." She got up to turn on the television. When she sat back down, she let out an old dog sigh. In Louisiana, there was color television, but some shows were still in black and white. *Flipper* was on—he was like a fish Lassie. Rebekha was asleep by the time *I Dream of Jeannie* came on. Jeannie crossed her arms and nodded her head whenever she wanted something. I daydreamed I could do that, and that I had a room like hers. Next came that *Get Smart* guy. I turned off the television the first time he answered his shoe. I left Rebekha sleeping on the couch and went to bed. I didn't tell Rebekha why I wanted to know about Mrs. McGrander. I didn't tell her about the time I saw Daddy giving her a ride in his silly car.

The next morning, I woke up to a thunderstorm and smelled bacon. I wrinkled my nose as I went down the hall and eased open Micah's door. He was still asleep. I was going to throw something at him, when I heard Daddy and Rebekha in the kitchen talking in those loud-whisper voices, so I sneaked to listen.

". . . a little old to be acting that way," she said.

"You were born old, that's your problem. The bacon's getting too crisp."

"Thank you for that assessment of me. And the bacon is fine."

"You're two years older than me, don't forget."

"You didn't get home until daylight. I was worried."

The icebox opened and things rattled around. "What's the harm?"

"You have children and they need you—that's the harm. If you're looking for the orange juice, we're out."

"Does that mean I have to sit around in a rocker and be wise?" The icebox closed. "Shoot, no orange juice?"

"It means you could stay around here more and help me with *your* children." Something hit the counter hard.

I stared at my feet.

"If you don't want my kids, just say so."

"I didn't say I didn't want them. I just don't know what I'm doing."

"They're just miniature adults with big eyes and funny ideas." I heard ice falling into a glass. "What's to do?"

"Are you doing that again already? My god, it's eight in the morning."

"Morning for you, I just got home a few hours ago. I'm still in yesterday." Daddy laughed. Only *he* thought it was funny. The cabinet opened and shut, then another one. "Ah, there it is."

"What's happening to us, Frederick?"

"Nothing. You're imagining things."

Micah came out of his room. "Are you listening to people's stuff again?" I gave him the hush-up look. He blew morning breath on me, then went into the bathroom, laughing as he shut the door.

A big thunderclap came and I didn't hear what Rebekha said, but Daddy answered, "I thought this is what you wanted. To have a family. You said that's all you ever wanted. Now you have one."

"Yes. Well. I'm pregnant."

For five blinks, all I heard was bacon crackling and rain hitting the roof. Then the sound of a glass hitting the counter. Daddy said, "You're pregnant?"

"Yes, and I'm scared. I didn't plan for this."

"We're having a baby! How wonderful!"

"How could you brush off the possibility of—"

Daddy didn't let her finish, he was talking away, his voice all jittered up with happy. "Let's tell the children. They'll be excited. I'll go get them." I pushed myself from the wall and tiptoed towards my room.

Rebekha said, "Stop right where you are! I want to discuss this . . . this baby thing. It's important."

"What's to discuss?"

"After breakfast we're going to talk."

Micah came out of the bathroom and hollered

out, "Hey, what're you doing in the hall? Huh? Huh?" He tore off to his room before I could clobber him one.

I went into the bathroom, shut the door, and waited a minute before I flushed the toilet. Then I went to the kitchen pretending I just woke up. Rebekha was pouring milk for everyone. She turned to me with her eyes red and puffed. I wanted to hug on her to make her feel better. I even felt my foot ready to step, but I didn't do it.

"Good Morning, Virginia Kate."

"Morning, Ma'am." I thought about last night and how she was like a happy little girl, and now she wasn't. "Can I help with stuff?"

"Yes, that would be nice. Thank you."

I helped her fix the plates, not touching the bacon, and took them to the table. Daddy drank his coffee with the newspaper in front of his face. Micah walked in scratching his head and yawning. When he saw me, he made a you-are-stooopid face. Both he and Daddy had messy hair and sleepy eyes. During breakfast, no one said three words, but a billion words were hanging right in the air all thick and dark. When we finished eating, Micah and Daddy scattered to the ends of the earth. Rebekha and I had to clean up all that mess they left behind.

I carried plates to the sink, poured in Joy dish-washing soap, let the sink fill up with hot bubbly water.

Rebekha brought in the rest. "Virginia Kate, you can go play."

I shook my head.

"You wash, I dry?"

I stuck my hands in the soapy water and washed. The window in front of me faced the next-door neighbor's house. An old woman stood in the rain with a dog. I wondered why I never saw her before. I liked how her hair was still long, even though it was Crayon gray and sopping. She looked like she was singing. I couldn't hear her, but her mouth made Oh's and Ah's. Beside her, the little dog with a smushed-in face looked unhappy and wet. I'd look up that dog in my Dog Breeds of the World book later. I let myself pretend she was my grandma down to visit and that dog was mine.

Rebekha rinsed and dried the dishes I handed her. She said, "After this, I think I'll go lie down." She looked out the window at the neighbor. "That's Miss Darla. She just got back from Egypt. She's never been married. Maybe that's why she's so happy and singing out in the rain."

After that, we finished the dishes without talking and Rebekha went to her room. I opened the cabinets and found two bottles. I poured them down the sink, every last stinky drop, and the smell stayed in the air, even after rinsing twice. I looked out the window again and stared at Miss Darla until she turned around and waved.

I waved back, then went into Micah's room to

snoop. There were lumps underneath his bedspread where he didn't pull the sheets and blanket up all the way. His room was full of drawings, and model cars glued together that were painted colors cars never were, like a purple Ford, a polka dot Chevrolet. There were Superman and Spiderman comic books on the floor by his bed.

On his desk was an upside down piece of drawing paper. I flipped it over. Micah had erased and drawn Momma's face enough times to thin the paper out. I turned it back over. Touching the top drawer to his desk, I sort of accidentally pulled on it too hard and it sort of accidentally slid open. There were paints, brushes, and charcoals inside. I peered to the back and saw a tin box. Inside were a lighter, a cigarette, a label off of a bottle of beer, and a stick of Juicy Fruit. I put the cigarette to my lips and pulled on it, but it was so nasty I wanted to vomit. I put everything back just as I found it.

Seems Daddy and Rebekha weren't the only ones with secrets.

Chapter 19
Today

The storm is really blowing now. But I like it, like how the wind howls down from the mountain. I have to shut the window a little, but only to keep the rain from wetting everything up. I listen to the moans and groans the house makes, listen for secrets. The house is living, breathing as it sighs in and out. I look at the mess around me. I made a promise. I said I'd tell our story. That's what I'm doing. Making it all real in the telling, just as Grandma said.

I say to the urn, "Momma, did you ever take out my things and look at them?" I'm trying to picture Momma coming in my room to sweep the floor and bumping the box under my bed. Pulling it out and going through the drawings, photos, and other mementos her little girl thought special. Maybe she'd wailed and bawled as she climbed up the attic steps to put my things out of her sight.

The wind rushes through the window and knocks photos and notes to the floor. I say, "Did you do that, Momma? You were always ornery, you know." She won't say a thing.

I look out the window and watch the rain, leaving the stuff on the floor right where it landed. I've spent hours upon hours drinking coffee and remembering, writing notes down, going back and forth between crazy, mad, and sad. I'm not finished yet.

I say to the room-spirits, "I'm tired. I need to rest a little while."

I hear on the wind, "Rest, rest, rest, Virginia Kate."

I begin to clear everything else off the bed. When I pick up the bit of Spanish moss, it's like old witches hair, thick and wiry-soft. I think about Louisiana. The big daddy oaks, and the cypress with moss hanging down so mysterious. The egret, winter's white pelican, and all the eerie strangeness. Micah always said I'd be trapped there if I didn't watch it. My mountains had been calling me and I hadn't been listening. Things had held me in Louisiana, but would they keep me there now? Where would I end if not at my beginning? Maybe somewhere new?

I pull back Grandma's quilt, and the white sheets with yellow flowers. When I lie down, I release a sigh like an old dog on a porch. The sheets smell as if they've just been tugged off the line. Still holding the moss, I whisper, "Sleep tight, don't let the bedbugs bite." How many times did Daddy say that to me? And then I said it to Adin. I'm drifting off. I all a sudden think about little brother Bobby, and how I held him in my lap. That was after I fell into a waking sleep.

That day comes back clear. I can see the day behind my eyelids, like a movie. It was a good day. Andy wasn't in Louisiana yet, that was the only sad part. I remember Rebekha standing in front of me, her face flushed from cooking and loving Thanksgiving. She took the picture of Bobby and me and I felt happy. I remember I hardly thought about Momma at all that day. Hardly at all.

I'm near asleep when I hear, "Virginia Kate,

when're you going to my room? What're you a scaredy-cat about?"

I turn into my pillow and answer, "Momma, I'm afraid you'll be just who everyone says you are instead of who I hope you are."

She doesn't say anything to this, shuts right up.

Chapter 20
Something sure is on the wind today, Girl 1966-67

Nobody talked about the baby Rebekha carried around inside her. Daddy went around grinning stupid. Micah just shrugged when I asked him about it. Rebekha acted as if she walked in a room of eggs, holding on to her stomach. We didn't have popcorn, watch television, and talk about stuff. I didn't care one speck. All I did was try to help her since she was so tired all the time, but I didn't ask her one question about that big stomach. Not one bit did I care.

I was in the kitchen cooking pinto beans and had just thrown a whole raw onion in when she came into the kitchen holding onto a yellow baby bathtub.

"Well, Virginia Kate, I'm going to have a baby." She looked at me like a dog that just chewed up my shoes.

I stirred the beans, feeling older than the grown-ups.

"Look at all the gifts from my shower today." She picked up a tiny pair of booties and held them out to me.

They were as light as a butterfly. I thought about Momma and how she went to the hospital that day and when she came back, there was no little baby. It had disappeared.

"I should have talked to you long ago. I was scared I'd jinx it." She rubbed her face on a fuzzy rabbit. "Oh, this is so soft." She held it out. "Here, feel it."

I rubbed my face against its back.

Picking through all her baby gifts, she held up each one to show me, including a box with a silver rattle nesting in a bed of cotton. She put her hand on my shoulder. "From now on, I'll not keep important things from you. Okay?"

I hated to move away. Her hand felt like belonging. But I did move. I was full to the top at how everybody had been acting stupid.

She picked up a tiny t-shirt and held it in the air, frowned, then said, "So, I'll tell you that there are letters from your mother that you should have."

I stared at her.

"She wrote you and Micah several times. Your father thought it best to wait until you were older and until Micah was, well, less angry." She looked down at her stomach, rubbing it. "I've been trying to stay out of it. I mean, I'm not your mother and

235

it's hard to know what's the right thing to do. Do you see?"

My head felt tight and my stomach did the twist.

"Your father hid them, but I know where they are." She went into her room. I waited, turned into a cement pole. When she got back, she held a brown envelope in her hand. "I'm so sorry, Virginia Kate. But sorry isn't good enough, is it?"

I grabbed the envelope from her. Inside, there were a few letters tied with a red ribbon. "He shouldn't have kept them. They're mine!"

"Hon, your father . . ." She stopped and sighed. "You're right. They *are* yours and he had no right keeping them from you."

"I hate him! He's not the same Daddy. All he does is act stupid and drink his stinky stuff! And nobody talked to me about the baby. I'm not a stupid kid! Everybody thinks I'm see-through and I'm not!" I tore off to my room, jumping face first into the bed. I lay there half-smothered in the pink with my head pounding. When I found my breath, I sat up, opened the letters one by one and read them.

Momma saying she had a new boyfriend named Harold. Momma saying she sold the Rambler and bought a Chevrolet. Momma saying Mrs. Mendel wished me a Merry Christmas and a Happy New Year. Momma saying did you take my powder and lipstick, and what about my brush? Momma saying

Aunt Ruby says hi. Momma saying ask Daddy for more money.

Then, I read the last letter from her.

Dear Virginia Kate, How is my baby? I'm fine. Andy's fine. He's getting big. I bet you're getting big. How's Micah? I bet he's big, too. I would like you to visit me sometime. But, I don't reckon that'll ever happen, unless your Daddy brings you all back home for good. He should come home and he should bring my babies home where you kids belong. I expect he's just selfish! It's his fault we'll never be a family again. His fault I'll never see you or Micah ever again, ever. And you won't ever see little Andy again. All because of your Daddy won't come to his sensables. It's all his fault, you remember that Virginia Kate. I'd call, but my phone got cut off (tell your daddy I said that, you can show him this letter). I bet you have all kinds of pretty things now. I bet you even have more toys than Andy does. And maybe even more clothes than me. I bet that woman buys you stuff and thinks she's something she isn't. I bet she has good perfumes, too. I think I'll marry Harold and move to Paris. Don't forget me, Momma.

I read it four times and it still said the same thing.

Andy's letters were all papers from school and pages out of coloring books, except one. It read, *Dear Seestor, I misses you. When you coming home? When is Micah? Why haven't not you wrote me? I hurt a lot because you forget me. The moun-*

tain cries loud noicses. Momma quit crying lots of days ago. I'm getting big so I'm not soposed to cry. But I misses you too much. Why don't you love me? Momma said you won't ever come back. Why not? Love, Andy.

Inside was a school picture of him. His face was a full moon of sorrows.

I clenched up my fists until it hurt. I gritted my teeth. I wanted to scream at someone but there was no one to listen. I wanted to jump in the closet and ride Fionadala. My stomach turned, twisted, and flopped. The hornets buzzed loud and louder—and then my head exploded. I lay back on the pink and white, holding my head while the hornets flew and stung and the drums banged.

When I couldn't stand the hurt anymore, I fell away into sleep. I saw Grandma Faith crying and crying, getting smaller and smaller. I fell until she was too small to see, and I didn't hear her, or Andy, crying anymore. I slept for hours, for days, for months. While I was sleeping, I didn't write Momma or Andy, didn't make A's; didn't take any pictures, my camera getting dusty on my dresser; didn't write in my diary, all the blank pages stayed blank. Slept when Rebekha had Robert Laurence Carey, and I didn't play with baby Bobby; didn't read; didn't eat sugar popcorn that Rebekha made.

I slept right on through Mee Maw's visit where in one day she started a fire in the kitchen, spilled bleach all over Rebekha's new suit hanging in the washroom to dry, and told Rebekha she looked like death warmed over on a Saltine. The whole world went on about its business without noticing I was asleep. I slept and slept and slept until Miss Darla talked inside my head, and then little Baby Bobby looked at me and smiled.

It was on Thanksgiving Day, when the wind was cool and sharp and crepe myrtles had no blooms. Inside, the house smelled like turkey, dressing, pecan pie, and bourbon. Daddy and Micah were watching football games. The Campinelle's were off to Okalahoma to visit Amy Campinelle's momma, and took Mrs. Portier with them. Mee Maw's broken arm (broken by Mack—who Daddy said she kicked out, right after she had a lawyer kick the dog spit out of him where it hurt in his wallet) kept her in Texas.

Miss Darla ate Thanksgiving with us, her hair pulled up in a big braid on top of her head. She asked me, "Girl, aren't you tired of sleeping yet?"

I hitched a sigh.

"Your Grandma Faith's been worried about you, don't you know."

And I said, "Did she quit crying? Will I see Andy again?"

"All will be well." Miss Darla smiled. And nobody heard us. Our mouths were closed and we talked in our heads, just like Grandma and me. I pinkie swear.

After Miss Darla tottered on home, I sat on the

porch rocker and let the cool air clear the sleepy feelings away. Rebekha came out with Bobby and he was cute and chubby. He held out his arms to me. When I rocked him, he looked up at me and grinned, and right then, I burst wide open awake.

Rebekha smiled at Bobby and me and took our picture. She said, "Virginia Kate, you look happy. I'm so glad. You've been really sad."

"Well, I'm awake now." But I don't know if I said it aloud. I don't know if my lips moved, because they were stretched out in a smile.

I sent Andy pictures of Micah, Bobby and me, of Soot, of Amy Campinelle and Mister Husband and Mrs. Portier, the oak and mimosa. I sent a handful of Spanish moss to him, and I asked Andy for the umpteenth time to get Momma to send Grandma's quilt to me. I wanted to ask for my Special Things Box, but I was afraid she'd look in it, or throw it away like trash. She didn't send anything. The azaleas had already dropped their petals. My mimosa sprouted blooms. It wasn't real hot yet and I could ride my bike to the library without hardly sweating.

Micah was as tall as Rebekha and more mysterious than ever. I hardly saw him, except for supper and *Mission Impossible*, his favorite show. He liked *Batman*, too, and would stand up and pound the air with his fists, saying, "Biff, Bow, Bam!" I liked *The Monkees*, even though Micah made fun of them. I thought Mickey was cute, Peter was silly, Mike was serious, and Davy was a dream-boat—even if he was short.

I came back from school that day, kicked off my shoes, and put on my red shorts and striped t-shirt. I peeped in on Bobby, asleep with his thumb in his mouth. His room used to be the study, but Rebekha re-did it in bright happy-go-yippee colors. Micah's painting of purple teddy bears dancing around was over his bed. I peeped in Micah's room, but he wasn't there. His room smelled like model glue and oil paint.

I wandered into the kitchen where Amy Campinelle made ready to cook shrimp Creole. She watched over Bobby while Rebekha worked, which was only two or three times a week, since Bobby kept getting sick. Most times, Mrs. Portier and Amy Campinelle watched soap operas when they weren't playing with Bobby. Mrs. Portier had lots more time on her hands since Mr. Portier ran off with Mrs. McGrander right after Christmas. That didn't last but two months, then Mrs. McGrander took up with a dentist and left Mr. Portier whining boo hoo hoo in his beer. Mrs. McGrander became Mrs. Baycowitz. Little red-headed Mrs. Portier got her a lawyer and socked it to Mr. Portier. Then she headed over to Mrs. McGrander-Baycowitz and socked her in the nose.

That's what Amy Campinelle blabbered to me while she peeled the shrimp, shaking her Q-tip head. "That Mrs. McGrander-Baconbits has caused lots of grief around here. Hope she stays herself away." Amy Campinelle went Humph and Tsk-Tsk and Some-People-Have-Nerve all the while she talked about Mrs. McGrander-Baycowitz. "For sure, she tried to mess with my Mister only onest. He cut that off quicker'n a blink." She turned and pointed a shrimp at me, "He don't love no one but him some Amy, yeah." She laughed, and I did, too.

The phone rang and she ran to answer. "Hall-oooooo Carey residential." I heard her cackling laugh, then, "Jiminy Christmas, I was just talking about that hussy. Lawd, she's a mess that makes a bigger pile than the rest."

I thought about listening in, but needed to do my homework. I went outside, leaned against the mimosa, and opened my math book. I picked a mimosa bloom and pretended it was a ballerina, spinning it around and around like the one in the jewelry box Rebekha gave me. Miss Darla's dog was in her back yard, sniffing the grass. The dog's name was Sophia, after Sophia Loren.

I called to it, "Here Sophia. Here, girl." But Sophia was too prissy to pay me any mind. I didn't think the name fit one bit. I said, "The real Sophia Loren would come over and say hello. The real Sophia Loren would be nice to me and she's lots prettier than you."

Sophia showed me her furry rear end, squatted, and peed.

Miss Darla came out and the prissy dog jumped around her ankles. "Sophia, you little rascal." She picked her up and snuggled her. Looking over at me she said, "Something sure is on the wind today, Girl."

I loved hearing Miss Darla's stories.

"My index finger's been aching, and when I woke up this morning there was a dragonfly on my headboard." She stood still, holding on to Sophia, her feet planted wide as if she was steadying herself. "I smell sweet olive, don't you?"

"Yes, Ma'am."

"Don't you be calling *me* Ma'am, don't you know." She eyed me good, then put Sophia down and came through her gate to stand in front of me. "I know about things. I know you're a sad, sweet, lost girl." She had on frosted pale lipstick, her hair was loose and fell past her waist, she wore blue jeans rolled up at the ends, and a man's shirt. She looked like she wasn't afraid of anything. Her gray eyes went right through me until I went to fidgeting. "All the signs are saying change is on the way."

First, I thought, *No. No more changes*. Then, "I wish you were my grandmother instead of Mee Maw Laudine."

Miss Darla laughed. She looked at my math book on the ground. "It's too pretty to do division, isn't it?"

"Yes Ma'am, I mean, yes, Miss Darla."

"Well, I'm off to Calandro's. I'll bring you back a treat." She slipped into her car and drove away. I sent her a mental message to bring me back a Zero bar, Tootsie Rolls, wax lips, or maybe candy bracelets.

I heard the car before I saw it.

The yellow car rounded the corner and stopped at the curb in front. I stood up and shaded my eyes. Andy climbed out and Momma handed him a tan suitcase. I reached out a hand and began walking towards the car.

The top was down and Momma's hair was very long again, tangled like blown branches after a storm. She was more beautiful than I ever remembered. She wore a dress like Marilyn Monroe—that white one that blew up around her—and lipstick the color of crushed plums. The man stared straight ahead, both hands holding the steering wheel.

Momma said something to Andy and he dropped the suitcase on the ground. I heard him holler out, "No, Momma! Wait!" The man said something to Andy. Andy shouted, "You shut up, you big fat idiot!" The man's eyebrows shot together like two fighting caterpillars.

I screamed, "Andy! Andy!" and tore across the yard to him. He might have climbed back in that car and stayed there if I hadn't of hollered his name.

When Andy turned to me, he looked as if he'd seen the headless horseman ride up and hand him his pumpkin head. "They's leaving me, Sister!"

I ran into him hard and hugged on him so tight, it made his breath grunt out.

The man began to drive away, but Momma hit him on the arm with her fist and he stopped. Her plum mouth opened and closed, those turned up corners working. He said something back to her, stroking her hair, and then he put his arms around her. And stupid Andy and stupid me stood like rooted trees when we should have done something, anything. When he let her go, she turned to wave at us, her hand going back and forth real slow, then she turned her back and they flew off.

I pulled my roots out of the ground then and raced off after them. I hollered, "Momma! Wait! Come back so I can talk to you." I ran, but the car was soon out of sight. I stood in the middle of the street until I heard the car coming back. I waved my arms and yelled loud so Andy could hear me, "She's coming back, Andy!" And around the corner came an old Ford with a whole family inside, grinning and laughing as they headed on down the road. I turned and trudged back to the house.

Andy sat on his suitcase, looking down at his feet. I saw a tear fall on the grass.

"Don't cry, Andy."

"She told me I'm living here now." He dried his face with the bottom of his shirt. "She lied. She's a liar."

"It's not so bad when you get sorter used to it."

"She's a big fat liar."

"Maybe she'll change her mind."

"She's not. She won't." He had mad-crabby eyes. "I don't care. She can rot!"

Rebekha pulled up, slipped out of the car with a look that would've been funny if it had all been something to laugh over. I figured she'd be really mad with another one of us in the way. She stood by her car, shading her eyes. "What's going on here?"

"Momma left off Andy for good." I grabbed Andy's hand and pulled him up.

Rebekha walked over, her high-heels sinking in the grass. She bent over to Andy. "What's going on, Andy?" He wouldn't look at her.

"Momma told him he's got to live here, Ma'am."

"She did what? Just now?"

"Yes Ma'am. Just now. She didn't even stop so I could talk to her, or hug her or nothing." I took breaths to dry up anything that wanted to come out of my eyes.

"I'm amazed, simply amazed." And she looked amazed, too. Standing in her pretty black and white suit, her hair neat and shiny, her purse over her shoulder with a paisley scarf sticking out. "She just dropped him off?" She looked down the street as if she thought Momma might come back, too.

"Yes Ma'am."

Andy squeezed my hand tighter, still looking down at the ground.

"Well I'll be."

We stood there for a spell. Rebekha looked down the street. Andy looked at his tenny shoes. I looked at Andy. Amy Campinelle came out the door looking at all of us looking. We didn't know what else to do but stand around like looking-fools.

Rebekha smoothed Andy's hair. "Come in the house. Let's get you something to drink, poor little boy."

He let go of my hand and walked with her up the stairs and into the house. Amy Campinelle went in with them.

I picked up his suitcase, and put on a hound dog face in case they came back by, so Momma would see me looking pitiful. When nothing happened, I went on into the house. Andy sat at the table between Rebekha and Amy Campinelle with a plate of cookies and a glass of chocolate milk. I noticed that with Rebekha there to help me know what to do, my head didn't hurt so bad. I thought about that, and wondered on it, and decided to think about it later.

"Where should I put the suitcase?" I asked her.

"Let's see. Put it in Bobby's room, will you, please?"

Amy Campinelle said, "I got to stir my pots at home. If you need me, Rebekha dear, just holler."

"Thanks, Miss Amy. For dinner, too. I'll walk you to the door." I heard them talking low. I figured Rebekha was telling Amy Campinelle what a bad momma we had and how she was stuck with all these kids that weren't hers.

Andy started up again. "Momma didn't tell me nothing. I didn't get to tell Mrs. Mendel goodbye or nothing. I hate Momma's stupid guts!"

"I didn't get to tell her goodbye either. And I didn't get to tell you goodbye." I took one of his cookies so he wouldn't feel so lonesome eating them.

Rebekha came back in and looked at me. "She didn't stop and say anything to you?"

"No, Ma'am."

"I see. Well, we'll work all this out." She stared out of the window, talking to the squirrel in the tree next door, instead of us. "Bobby's room is plenty big enough. Oh, and there's school to register and clothes and, well, so much to do."

All this time I hadn't seen my little brother and we were too sad to be happy. "Want to look around, Andy?"

He nodded his head. I showed him around the house, and then the yard and neighborhood, just as Micah had shown me. I told him about alligators, yawl, coke, parishes, po-boys, and Hey! He stopped carrying on, but he had far and away eyes. When we got back to the house, he laid down on the couch. I sat with him until he fell asleep, then I went to get my math book, still under the mimosa. The pages were flapping open like a bird too heavy to lift off.

Miss Darla came out swinging a bag in her hand. "Here, Girl, some candy for you and your brothers."

"Thank you, Miss Darla." I dug into the bag. There were three Zero's, three bubble gum cigars, six fire balls, a Chick-o-Stick (which became my new favorite candy after Zeros), Micah's favorite candy corn, and Andy's favorite peanut bar. I looked up at her grinning at me and thought, *How'd you know? You're weird, Miss Darla.* She just grinned bigger. When she went back inside, I took the candy to my room and sucked on a fire ball, letting it burn my tongue so things I didn't want to say about Momma would burn right off.

Micah came into my room. "What's Andy doing on our couch?"

I gave him his candy, told him the story, and we went to stare at Andy sleeping.

Micah opened his candy corn and popped a giant handful. I put Andy's on the coffee table for him, whenever he woke up. With his mouth full up to the brim, Micah said, "Momma'sh losht her mind."

I wanted to say, "Nuh uh." But I didn't.

Later, after we ate the shrimp Creole supper, Andy had two helpings and Micah had three, we sat in the living room to watch Red Skelton.

The phone rang and when Daddy answered and listened a bit, his mouth went into a straight line. He said, "Don't give me that. You should have told him." He jingled the change in his pocket. "Harold? Give me a break. You could've come in and talked to us about that." He tapped his left foot on the floor. "He's been crying since you left." His mouth turned down. "I hope you and Harold will be happy." Gulped down all his drink, said, "Ha. Well, did you get Mee Maw's check?" When he said, "check" he had a smart-aleck look and his voice was even more smart-alecky. "What? Forget it. You're too drunk to talk to. Goodbye." He put down the phone, looked over at Rebekha, and shrugged.

I asked, "She didn't want to talk to me, to us?"

Micah said, "Get in the real world, Vee. Geez."

"She didn't want to talk to me?" Andy looked like he might start up again.

Rebekha rubbed and patted him on the back.

"No, she didn't want to talk. She and Harold are off to France for a month. She had to pack."

I hated her. And I never wanted to see her again.

Before bedtime, I went to Andy and Bobby's room to read *Tom Sawyer*. Rebekha had made Andy a pallet on the floor until she could buy him a bed. He was with Bobby on the piled up blankets, bedspreads, and sheets. I said, "Hey."

"Is Bobby my brother?" Andy asked. Bobby giggled when Andy poked his stomach.

"I guess so. He's like half of a brother."

"What half's our brother? I don't want no poopy half." He laughed and I liked how it sounded.

Bobby laughed, too, pulling at Andy's hair. "Ouch, he's strong."

"Yeah, he gets sick lots though."

"How come he gets sick lots?"

"Daddy said it was funny molecules or something. Want me to read to yaawwlll?"

"Naw. I don't feel like it."

I sat on the pallet with them. "I don't want you to be sad."

"Not sad. Mad at Momma. She's a goddammer." Andy stood up and stomped his foot. "Stupid. Stupid. *Stupid goddammer!*"

Bobby giggled.

"I'm reading to Bobby, you can listen if you want to." I opened the book and read, "Chapter one, A Young Battler. ' Tom!' No answer, 'Tom!' No Answer. 'What's gone with that boy, I wonder?' " I looked up as Andy lay back on the pallet with Bobby, smiling just a little bit. So I read until I was sleepy.

I might have quit hating Momma if I hadn't overheard Daddy talking to Rebekha the last day of fifth grade. I stood outside of the dining room in my blue dress with the white collar.

"I can't believe she's pregnant with Harold's child," Daddy said. "She gives up her children and then gets pregnant with a man who hates children."

"She's confused, Frederick. I feel sorry for her."

I heard a cup hitting a saucer. "Harold won't stick around. He'll run off and find another easy target."

"It's a shame these children are in the middle of this."

"I'm doing the best I can."

"I'm not pointing a finger at you."

"Yes you are." A chair scraped against the floor. "This is all my fault, isn't it Rebekha? You're the saint and I'm the sinner. That it?"

"Don't talk to me that way. I'm not some girl you can pull things over on and talk to as you please."

Daddy sighed, said, "I'm trying, Bekha, really I am."

"All I ask is that you pay attention to what's happening around here."

"What do you mean 'what's happening around here'?"

"Micah runs around like a wild boy. Andy needs us both to be strong. And I can't reach Virginia Kate because she's afraid she'll get hurt. She walks around in her own world with her head in books or the clouds. I can't hug her without her backing away. She's hurting, they're all hurting and I can't stand it. I know about being a hurt child, I understand the pain. And, Bobby, what if Bobby has what my . . . god, I couldn't."

I backed up a step, feeling as if I was under Micah's scientific microscope.

"Why are you so worried? You've cut back your

hours and the children seem to be thriving. Why are you so damned negative?"

"Can't you see, Frederick? If you'd just stop drinking so much, like when we were first together, remember how it was?"

"I'm going to campus. I'll be late." Daddy's voice was chewing up nails.

"What else is new? How can you ignore me when I need your help? You live in some fantasy-land—or maybe it's Bourbon World. Do you have a Shakespeare quote for me? One that will make it all okay?"

I didn't bother to hide myself when Daddy tore off by me. He saw me there and I sent him my most hateful ray beams out of my eyes. I felt bad when Daddy's face turned inside out and he said, "I'm sorry. So sorry." Then he was gone, out the door.

Rebekha went to Andy and Bobby's room and shut the door.

Micah came to stand by me. "Hey, Veestor. What's going on now?"

"I don't know why grown-ups always fight. Why can't things be good all the time?" I kicked the baseboard with the toe of my saddle oxford.

"You worry about stuff too much." His satchel was over his shoulder and his hair was combed shiny. He looked too much like Daddy. "Just be a kid. Kids don't have to worry about stuff. I don't think you should get like you were before."

"Before what?"

"When you walked around worse than whirly-brained. It was weird."

I picked at my nails where dirt stayed packed away from my digging. "Don't you wish about stuff sometimes?"

"Nope. I know what I want. I'm going to be famous and when I am, I'll do whatever I want when I want."

"You almost do that now." I smiled a little.

"Ha! You wait, I have it planned out."

"Like what?"

"Moving to New York and living in a building in the middle of the city. Lights will be spread out everywhere and I'll look out of my big window and paint everything I see. The moon and stars if I want to." His eyes shined like his lights and moon and stars. He grinned at me, said, "I got to flee, Vee. See?" And he was off, down the hall, and out the door.

I went to the kitchen for my lunchbox. Rebekha packed our lunches full of good stuff. Thermoses with soup when it was cold and ice tea when it was hot, fruit, a sandwich, and notes that read things like, *Have a good day,* or, *Learn well*!

I opened the cabinets and looked for the bottles. He'd hidden them good this time. I gave up, grabbed my lunch, and left to catch my bus, shutting the door behind me like everyone else had.

Chapter 21
Crazy, silly little boy
1968

I thought Andy would be sad forever, but he wasn't. He liked the way Louisiana was sloshy with water and how there were all kinds of crawlies: bugs, reptiles, amphibians, crustaceans, and weird things that nobody knew what they were—but people in Louisiana ate them anyway. He shucked off Momma and home like a rotten ear of corn and took to being a Louisiana fellow as if he needed to do that real bad.

Rebekha stayed after Andy all the time, fussing at him to get cleaned up, to stop riding his bike in daredevil stunts, to get out of the tree, off the roof of the house. She hollered almost every day, "Watch out Andy before you get hurt! Andy, get down from there!"

It rained hard and mean for weeks that summer. Poor little Bobby was real sick. He coughed and coughed and Rebekha kept pounding on his back, putting Vicks VapoRub on his chest, taking him to the doctor, staying up with him all night. He kept saying, "I hurt Mommy. I hot."

And Rebekha rocked him back and forth, saying, "It's okay, sweet one, it's okay."

Andy was about to go slap dab insane with the rainy days, in a room with a sick brother he couldn't play with, or lord it over with. He ran through the house breaking things. Not on purpose, he just had all that energy with nowhere to put it. Finally, after it rained so much Rebekha said we'd better grow webfeet, it stopped, just like that.

Micah tore out the door.

Daddy said he'd take Bobby to the doctor to get a shot so Rebekha could rest. He told her, "You've been up all night. Let me do this, okay?"

"I can take him, Frederick."

"But I need to do this and you don't need to, do you see?" He picked up Bobby and smoothed back his hair. "Ready, little big man?"

Bobby hugged onto Daddy. It sure was sweet.

Andy jumped up and down yelling, "Freedom! Freedom! Whoopie whoopie!"

"Thank god," Rebekha said. "Go play, for heaven's sake. But be careful. Andy, do you understand? Andy?"

He just grinned and said, "Whoopie," again.

She cornered me. "I know he's your younger brother and y'all have territorial sibling rules, but can you keep an eye on him, just this once? Could be some flooded areas and he's such a daring boy."

I rolled my eyes, but secretly I didn't mind. Andy had been plotting adventures the whole time he was locked up and I wanted to see what he'd get into.

The world was wet and mushy. The sun steamed everything right up.

Andy ran out of the front door, raising his arms up with one more "Whoopie!"

I followed him. "Where you going, Andy?"

"You can come if you want, Seestor."

"I don't have anything else to do." I pretend-yawned.

We rode off on our bikes. Andy had playing cards clothes-pinned to his tires and when he went fast, it usually sounded like a motorcycle, but the cards were soggy. The wind in my face felt wet and heavy. We rode around the block, talking about how we hated math. Andy pointed to trees, plants, and birds and asked me to name them, and I told him. That's what I did best.

A few streets over, Andy's friends, Dan and Neil, were having a race, with Neil in the lead. Andy called to them and we all raced off on our bikes, riding through the puddles. The dirty water shot up behind us and wet our legs and backs.

Neil splashed me with dirty water on purpose, getting some on my nature book in my basket.

Dan slowed his bike up to ride beside me. I tried to speed up, but he kept up. I was almost eleven and he was only nine, it was too weird.

Andy said, "She gots a nature book she studies lots. She knows about all kinds of stuff." Andy glanced back at me. "She knows about worms and centalpeeds. And she can help us find moccasins and stuff."

"Oh yeah?" Neil said. He never believed anything or anybody. He had yellow hair and nasty yellow teeth.

Dan google-eyed me. "I think that's innerresting." He had curly brown hair and lots of freckles, but at least his teeth were white, even if they were a bit bucked.

Neil weaved his bike over to Dan. "You idiot. Girls is stupid, my dad says so."

"Your daddy is stupid." I gave him the evil eye.

"Take it back, stooopid hick girl. Hick-hick-hick."

I pedaled fast until I was ahead of him and pushed off hard as I could in a puddle, sending a big wave of brown water all over the front of him. Andy and Dan laughed, pointing at him while Neil sputtered and spit.

"Sister's coming with us, Neil." Andy tore off faster on his bike, skimming up more muddy water. Andy bossed the other two because he was smarter, even if he was foreign and strange to them.

We parked our bikes by the canal and walked around to see what the high water had brought out. I didn't care that my bare feet were soaking up germs. I figured they were used to it.

Neil took up to bragging about how they walked the whole way through the inside of the canal, in the cement tunnel. He said they ended up clear across town.

Andy said, "That there water's too high to go today. We can look for snakes and stuff."

They hooped and hollered and tore off down the side of the canal calling out, "Here snaky snaky! Oh Mr. and Mrs. Moccasin! Come out come out wherever you are."

I studied the plants and bugs, looked them up in the nature book I'd tucked in the waistband of my pants. I wanted to find something really weird to show off to smart aleck Neil. The canal was near a small woods that had been part way cleared, and there were big clumps of weeds, bushes, some trees, fallen branches, and logs from oak trees lying around.

Behind the bushes, I heard an animal sound. I sneaked on my hands and knees and parted the bushes to peer through. On a log sat a blonde-haired girl with long skinny legs. Two plaits came to her shoulders, the ends tied up with bands that had two big orange balls on the ends. She was bawling and didn't even bother to hide her face or wipe the tears.

I turned to leave.

She saw me before I could escape. "Hey!"

I stopped, looked back.

"Where're you going?"

"My brother's hunting snakes, I'm going to watch."

She smiled crooked, still sniffling and hitching. "Can I come?"

I smiled big-toothed with stupid. "Huh?"

"Can I come with y'all?" She swiped her face,

leaving a dirty streak across her cheek. Her feet and hands were dirty and so were her flowered shorts and shirt.

"I guess so."

Her face lit up like a full moon. She stood up. "I'm Jade. It's short for Jadesta."

I felt shy as a stray dog. When she walked over and stood close by me, I backed away. She stepped close again, and I let it be.

"What's your name?"

"Virginia Kate." I picked up a piece of grass and tried to blow through it to make it screech. I'd seen Andy do it a bunch of times, but hadn't figured it out yet.

"That's a nice name." She picked up a blade and screeched it easy.

I jumped over a stump. She copied me. I bent over and studied a rock. She studied it, too. I'd never been copied before.

She sighed. "My dog died. She was my best friend and I'll miss her forever and ever and ever."

I stared off towards the boys' hoops and hollers. When I turned back to Jade, she was studying me like I did the plants and bugs. Her eyes were like the marble I found in Rebekha's garden that I'd washed off and kept on my dresser. I turned away from her and fidgeted around. Andy and his friends' heads bobbed as they ran up the sides of the canal, then down again.

She asked, "Do you have a dog?"

"No."

"Well, I don't know if I can ever ever have another one. Sasha was the best dog ever. But if I do get another one, you can come play with it until you get your own."

I heard Andy shouting, "There's a big one, look! Hey, Virginia Kate! Come see!"

I pushed in my nature book nice and tight and off I ran, Jade right beside me.

The boys were looking at something on a piece of concrete in the grass.

"Is that a moccasin, Sister?"

I stared at the fat greenish-black snake. "Yep, that's a moccasin. Unless it's a water snake, they look kind of alike."

Neil looked at me as if I was stupider than stupid.

"Let me check, but I'm pretty sure it's a moccasin." I pulled out the book and flipped the pages.

"Hurry up, we ain't got all day. And who's that? Another stupid girl?" Neil curled his lip.

Jade kicked the ground and sent mud spattering on his already filthy legs. "Shut up."

Dan stood close to me. Jade stood on the other side. I felt like the insides of a sandwich.

I found the pictures, decided Andy's snake had to be a moccasin, and if it wasn't, nobody would know anyway. "Yep, that's a moccasin. And it's very poisonous."

"We ain't a-scared. You girlies can be a-scared if

261

you want to." Neil put his hands on his hips and bared his ugly golden teeth. "Ain't that right, hick girl?"

"You call Sister a hick again and I'm bustin' you a good one." Andy took two steps towards Neil, who jerked back, tripped over a branch, and fell on his backside. We all laughed, pointing at him.

"I'm not scared one bit, Neil." I looked at the snake, how its thick body flopped on the concrete. Another one shimmied into the water, swimming towards us. My stomach did a slow roll around.

"I'm scared." Jade grabbed my hand.

I had to drop the book on purpose so I could get my hand away from hers. I stuck the book back in my pants.

The boys got in a huddle. Andy said, "Snake polo! You coming, Sister?"

I tried to swallow the big fat scared frog in my throat.

Jade pulled my arm. "Don't. Come with me. We'll watch from over there."

"I'm not scared."

"I know." She sat on a log, patting the space beside her. "Keep me company, Virginia Kate."

"Okay." I acted all down and out that I couldn't snake polo.

The boys picked up oak limbs for polo sticks and climbed back on their Huffy bikes. Andy raced in the slime towards a snake, his tires slipping back and forth as he pedaled with his dirty feet, rode next to it and hit it with his stick. "I got it!" He laughed and whooped.

The snake flew twisting into the air towards Neil and landed a foot from his tire. Neil screech-laughed and gave it a fat whack. The snake headed towards Jade and me. We both screamed and scrambled away from it. When it landed, its mouth was open and I thought I saw blood on it. The snake slithered in the other direction, back towards the boys. Jade covered her eyes, opening her fingers a crack to peep.

I kind of felt sorry for the snakes. I stood up and hollered, "Andy! Let's stop." But he didn't hear me.

Jade looked down at her feet. "Poor snakes."

I looked at my feet, too, but just for one blink in case I missed something.

Neil yelled, "*Aiiiyeeeeee!*" He hit the bigger, uglier brother of the first snake. It landed on Dan's front tire and he pedaled hard to get away. Both snakes were ready for a fight by then.

Jade's eyes were open wide.

I was afraid they really were moccasins. I was afraid all the nature world was mad at us for hurting its creatures and would send more snakes, and alligators, and nutria rat with big yellow teeth. I said, "Let's go *now* or I'm going to tell."

"I told you she's a-scared." Neil looked for the other snake in the tall part of the grass. "Here snaky."

"Andy, come on, let's go."

Andy had his pointy chin on and ignored me.

Dan rode over to me, looking worried. "Don't worry." He stayed by us, legs on either side of his bike. He said, "Hey, Andy, this is boring, let's go." He looked ready to throw up.

Neil turned on him. "Bawk bawk bawk. Titty baby! Titty Baaaabbeeeee!"

Dan's face turned red. He jumped back on his bike and rode to look for the snakes, because he had to.

"Jade, I better get Ma'am."

"Ma'am? Who's Ma'am?"

All a sudden I felt silly for calling Rebekha Ma'am all this time. "She's my . . ." I shrugged. "Just wait here, okay?" I figured she'd hightail it home soon as I turned my back.

I jumped on my bike and pedaled hard as I could, but my bike slipped and I fell into the mud. My nature book landed on the ground and I left it there when I heard Neil, "Here it is! Gawd he's huge and he's mad!" I got back on and raced to get Rebekha. When I burst through the front door, she was reading a book.

Looking at me as if I was a crazy girl, she said. "What in the world happened to you?"

"Andy's at the canal playing with the moccasins!"

She lit out to her car in her house slippers. I left my bike and rode in the car with her, telling her about it on the way. She said, "Oh my god, that crazy silly little boy!" We were there quick as a bird flies. I was surprised that Jade was still there, waving her right hand at us, my nature book in her left hand.

Rebekha flung herself out of the car hollering, "Andy! Andy!"

Andy didn't hear, he was shouting, "Hurry up, Dan. Hurry!"

Dan was half in the water scrambling up on his hands and knees. I bet he didn't care about being a chicken titty baby anymore as he slipped around in the mud, ripping out of the canal wailing and crying.

Rebekha ran towards the boys, slipping in her slippers. Neil looked over at Rebekha, and then out of slap pure meanness, rode his Huffy to the snake slithering towards the canal water, and hit it hard as he could towards Andy, laughing his stupid high screech laugh. The snake flew arching and wiggling into the air.

Rebekha screamed, "Watch out, Andy!" It looked as if the snake fell in slow motion, falling, falling down to Andy. He turned, but it was too late.

Rebekha flew down the slope of the canal in two gigantic slip-slidey steps, losing her slippers on the way. She was almost to him when the snake hit Andy in the back. He let out a banshee holler, twisting around with a fit. He fell off his bike right in front of the snake—its mouth was open and it looked madder than a gone-bad bull. All that hitting hadn't hurt those snakes much, it seemed to me.

Rebekha grabbed up Andy's stick and beat the snake to a pulp while its body wiggled around, its mouth opening wide. Even after it was mangled up and bloody and dead she kept pounding it. We kids had our mouths open wide enough to catch a pound of flies. Rebekha had mud from tip to toe, blood splattered on her legs, and her hair was wet up with sweat, mud, and spit.

We oohed and aahed over the guts as she picked up what was left of the snake and hurled it hard as she could into the water. "I hate snakes! Nasty shitting bastards!"

I hadn't ever heard her cuss before. It was as if she was taken over by aliens from outer space. She held the stick like a bat, and when the coast was clear, she threw it down, dusted off her hands, said real slow, "Get—away from—this—canal—*now*." We were already scrambling up before she could finish. She followed behind, looking backwards to make sure the brother of big fat snake wasn't following.

"Wow, Rebekha!" Andy stared at her like he did puppies. "You could join our club if you want."

Rebekha shook her head. "No. No. And a thousand times no. Stay away from this canal, you hear me?" She stared down Neil. "And you!" He turned and ran off to his bike before she could wallop him with words. She turned back to Andy. "Andy, I mean it."

He laughed, then he and Dan hooted off for their bikes, talking both at once about the snake.

Rebekha limped to her car. "You and your friend want a ride, Virginia Kate?"

"Yes, Ma'am." I tried to look like I was sorry, but since everything worked out okay, I was feeling excited about it all. And Rebekha had said *friend*. I asked Jade, "Do you need a ride?"

She grinned big as a truck, handed me my book, and asked, "Do y'all always have this much fun?"

I nodded my head even though I never had. I wiped the book on my shirt, put it back in my waistband, and we piled into Rebekha's Oldsmobile. She was leaning over the steering wheel saying, "Oh my god. That silly crazy boy."

Jadesta asked where we lived and Rebekha told her. She showed us where she lived. Her house was on the university lake, had big wide columns, lots of windows, and in her front yard, four big oak trees with moss hanging down.

Rebekha stopped the car. "Your mother will have a fit."

"Yep." She laughed, said, "Bye Virginia Kate. See you tomorrow."

I said, "Tomorrow?"

But she had already taken off running to her house.

Rebekha gunned the car. From the corner of my

eye, I watched her as she drove. She was almost always the same and it made me feel heavy in my seat, but a good heavy, the kind where I wouldn't go drifting off and away like a lost balloon. After she pulled into our driveway and stopped, I said, "Thanks for saving my brother's life, Ma'am . . . I mean, Rebekha." The name tumbled from my tongue, but it didn't feel bad at all, it felt like a good name to say.

She turned to me with a glowy smile, said real quiet, "You're welcome, Virginia Kate," then looked down at her feet. "I lost my slippers."

We both laughed.

"I think I should get some of those floppies like you girls wear."

"Floppies?" I thought a minute. "Oh, you mean flip flops?"

She nodded, then said, "Well, now. Let's get cleaned up and you can help me cook dinner."

I sat in the tub of bubbles thinking about when I first came to Louisiana. How I washed off the West Virginia dirt and let it go down the drain. How Momma's shirt was washed and it took away her smells. It felt like it happened a hundred and one years ago. My mountain floated in my head, losing its shape. Momma's face was doing that, too. The house, the maple, the swing, my room with the iron bed and yellow walls—all fading away.

After soaping my hair, I pulled the plug, and then rinsed under the faucet, letting the Louisiana dirt gurgle down the drain. I felt the suction pulling my hair down with it. I'd be sucked right down, too, right out into the Mississippi, except I was heavy enough to stay where I was. The water fell over my face and I opened my eyes, and then closed them.

Chapter 22
So quick bright things come to confusion

After the snake kill, Rebekha cooked hamburgers, fried potatoes, and pralines for dessert. Daddy moved the coffee table. Rebekha spread a blanket on the floor of the living room for us to eat on. Andy told about the day with his hands going ever which a way and his eyes big and round.

Daddy looked at Rebekha. "You killed the snake?"

"Uh huh." She took a big bite of hamburger. Mustard caught on the side of her mouth.

Bobby, Andy, and I had our rears propped up by pillows. Elvis was on the record player. Daddy held a tall glass, two ice cubes. We kids drank grape Kool-Aid; Rebekha had sweet tea.

We were eating from paper plates; my idea. But Rebekha served the food on nice platters and we used the fancy glasses. Micah and Andy made their hamburgers double-decker so that they had to open their mouths big and wide. Bobby's was cut up and he opened his mouth like his brothers, even though he didn't really need to.

I thought maybe everything would be okay since we were all there and everybody was smiling.

Daddy wiped his mouth, said, "I have a meeting with the Chancellor."

Rebekha ate a potato and swallowed. "Why didn't you mention it earlier?"

"I thought sure I did." Daddy had eaten only half his hamburger.

Rebekha crammed a whole handful of fried potatoes in her mouth and chewed fast. The mustard was still there on her face and there was salt added to it from the potatoes. When she talked with her mouth full, we kids stared at her like it was an episode of *The Twilight Zone*. "I killed a snake today. I saved a daredevil boy's life." She reached over and rubbed Andy's hair. He looked at her the same way he used to look at Momma. "So, I'm not going to worry about you tonight."

"My, aren't we the feisty one." Daddy took a long swallow, his Adam's apple going up and down up and down. I noticed a cut on his neck where he shaved that morning. When he lowered the glass, it was almost empty. He saw me staring at him and his face turned soft. "Hey, Bug. You're getting prettier every day. How'd you get so big just like that when I wasn't watching?" His voice sounded thick and funny.

"I don't know, Daddy."

"Rebekha, tell us about the snake guts again." Micah was thirteen, but he still liked a good gut story. He slid his eyes over to Daddy. "Tell us about snakes in the grass."

Daddy stood. He looked as if he wanted to go, but he didn't want to go, all at the same time.

Bobby said, "Guts-guts-guts." Then giggled and rolled around, knocking his potatoes all over the blanket.

"I hate snakes." Rebekha swallowed a sip of tea, said, "I had a cousin who nearly died when he was bit by one. I was there and didn't do anything but scream. Luckily, my father heard me and came to the rescue. I was only five, but I felt bad about being scared."

Daddy bent down and touched a napkin to Rebekha's face, wiping off the mustard and salt. He still had soft eyes. Rebekha looked up at him and her lips opened a little, letting him wipe her mouth. He said, "You hate snakes, but you killed it for Andy. 'Screw your courage to the sticking place, and we'll not fail.'"

Everyone was quiet and still, seeing how Daddy wiped Rebekha's mouth like she was a little girl.

Rebekha touched where he dabbed the napkin. She reached for his hand and held on. Looking him eye to eye, she said, "So, still going to your meeting?"

Daddy straightened up, and Rebekha's hand fell to her lap. We waited to see what he'd do.

"Frederick?"

Daddy drank the rest from his glass, making a sour face at the taste. He said, "Yes, I have to."

271

Rebekha's eyes slammed shut to Daddy. "I see. Well, then, we'll have our pralines and Elvis without you." She went back to eating, not looking back at Daddy.

"Daddy, can't you call the Chancelet guy and tell him you'll see him later alligator?" Andy had a wad of hamburger in his mouth and a piece of half-chewed bread flew into the air and landed on the blanket.

Micah rolled his eyes. "Geez, Andy-Bo-Bandy."

"Yeah, why not?" But I knew Daddy would go by the way his fingers were tapping against his leg, pinkie to thumb, thumb to pinkie.

"You all enjoy this wonderful picnic. I won't be long." He jingled his keys in his pocket, then turned and was out the door.

We finished eating, mostly not talking. While Rebekha went to the kitchen for the pralines, Micah turned the record over. Andy and I did the twist. Rebekha came in, set down the tray of pralines and clapped. I caught Micah looking proud at Rebekha a couple of times. He couldn't get over the idea of the snake story, or Rebekha saying *shitting bastards* (I told him about that before supper).

I thought he'd go to his room as soon as he tossed about fifty pralines in his mouth, but he stuck around. When the song about blue shoes came on, he jumped up and sang, swinging his hips. He pretended a potato was his microphone, and he sounded pretty good for a brother. Under the ceiling light, his dark hair shined. He wore a tan shirt tucked into dark brown corduroys. He was getting a bit of a mustache, and I wondered when that happened the same as Daddy asking when had I gotten so big. We were all changing.

The windows were open and the attic fan was on, stirring around the air, sucking it in and then out, sending little dusties dancing around with us. I smelled sweet olive and the dark dirt that Rebekha planted her flowers in.

Andy's hair stuck straight up in the back where he hadn't combed it down after his bath. He wore ragged-up cut-offs and a torn t-shirt, like usual. He picked at a scratch on his arm, laughing at Micah. He stood up, peeked at Rebekha out of the corner of his eye to see if she was watching him while he copied his older brother playing pretend guitar and drums. His feet were still a little dirty and he stomped them in time to the music.

Bobby copied Andy stomping. He twirled around in circles until he was dizzy and fell on his rear. His hair was still soft and wispy and it was turning a dark reddish-brown. His eyes lit up as he turned to me and said, " 'Ginia Kay! 'Ginia Kay!" He hugged my neck and then ran back to be with his brothers.

I turned to study Rebekha, but she was smiling at me. I felt different inside, different about her and about me. She stood and picked up Bobby, dancing him around the room. I thought about Momma dancing with us, when we all smelled like Dove soap. I missed her, but I missed this kind of momma, not the other kind of her.

Rebekha's single-pearl necklace bounced on her long neck as she danced. I'd never seen her look as she did then. When Bobby squirmed to get down, then swung his hips from side to side, she threw back her head and laughed. She took to doing some kind of weird tappity dance across the floor.

We kids stared at her. I leaned over and sniffed her glass, but it was only tea. Micah grinned at me, still holding the mushed-up tater-phone. He shrugged and ate it. Andy stared up at Rebekha as if she had the moon right on her head.

I skipped to my room to get my camera. In the mirror, my face was glowy; my hair springing out of the pigtails, and my eyes had a star sparkly look. I didn't know who I was right then. My white shirt had a ketchup stain on the front, spreading like the snake's blood. I ran back to the party and snapped pictures. Micah and Rebekha doing the twist. Andy holding Bobby in his lap, both of them clapping. The way the room spun around when I danced.

Micah grabbed the camera from me and took more pictures. Everybody had their turn. The whole night felt like those kaleidoscope toys where you look through the peephole and see all the colors changing and turning and running in and out of each other.

We used the whole roll—all of us caught in the camera, except Daddy.

When the record stopped, we flopped on the blanket to eat the rest of the pralines. Rebekha turned on the radio right when Herman's Hermits was finishing a song about somebody's daughter. Micah sang in a funny West Virginia-Louisiana-Herman's Hermits kind of voice that made us all fall out laughing.

Daddy walked in right then and stared around the room. "Well! What have we here?" He grinned big at everyone. Micah stuffed a praline in his mouth, chewed a little, then opened his mouth to show me the chewed candy, flaring his nostrils at the same time. He left the room, his shoes clomping down the hall to his room.

"Daddy, just like you said, you wasn't gone long at all," Andy said.

"You *weren't* gone," Daddy said.

Bobby ran over and pulled on Daddy's britches leg, grinning lopsided. Daddy reached down and patted his head, but he was looking at Rebekha.

"I didn't expect you back so soon." Rebekha pushed her hair behind her ears.

I handed Daddy a praline. "Take it, Daddy. They're yummy."

"Why, thank you my dainty Ariel." He sat on the couch, took a bite, and then put the rest on a plate.

Rebekha leaned over to kiss Daddy. When she was just to his lips, she jerked up, giving him a look you give someone you want to punch in the nose. "Nice cologne you have there, mister."

Daddy looked at Rebekha, in her white pedal pushers and yellow top. He traveled up the whole of her until he got to her eyes. They stared each other down like two stray dogs until she turned away to clean up the mess.

Daddy said, "What's wrong?"

Rebekha went into the kitchen and I heard water running.

Daddy's eyebrows came together, then he clapped his hands on his knees. "Well, you all, 'To sleep, perchance to dream' . . ."

"Tuck me ina bed, Daddy." Bobby held up his arms. Daddy picked him up and left the room. Andy followed them, looking over his shoulder at me with a what-happened-here look.

I shrugged, straightened all the records and turned off the radio.

Daddy came back in and sat on the couch, his hands on his knees, staring at his fingers. I didn't know what he needed. He looked up at me. "Well, what a night." His smile hurt my insides; it was almost like Bobby smiling at me.

I couldn't help it; I went over and hugged his neck. I leaned into him and he patted me on the back. Nobody said anything to ruin that bit of time I took from him. "Can you read me some Shakespeare, Daddy?"

"What would you like?"

"I don't care."

He went to the bookshelf to get his book of plays.

I heard Rebekha washing dishes, Andy talking to Bobby, music from Micah's room, and the air crackling with things nobody was saying.

Daddy opened the book. "I'm pretty tired, Bitty Bug, how about I just read a passage?"

"Okay, I guess."

"Here, from 'A Midsummer Night's Dream'." He cleared his throat. " 'Or, if there were a sympathy in choice, war, death, or sickness did lay siege to it, making it momentary as a sound, swift as a shadow, short as any dream, brief as the lightening in the collied night, that, in a spleen, unfolds both heaven and earth; and ere a man hath power to say 'Behold!' The jaws of darkness do devour it up: So quick bright things come to confusion.' " He closed the book and sighed.

I kissed his cheek, went to my room, and shut the door. I changed into a nightgown Rebekha bought for me. It had tiny roses all over it and a ruffle at the bottom. It was girly, but I didn't mind too much. At least it wasn't pink. I climbed into bed without brushing my teeth. I heard Rebekha still rattling around in the kitchen, and then the sound of a broom across the floor. I fell asleep and dreamed about Fionadala, Miss Darla, and Grandma Faith. The two women were talking to each other while I stood off to the side, still in my gown. Fionadala was a real live horse and she pawed the ground, nodding her head up and down, snorting. I wanted to ride her, but she ran into the mists. Miss Darla and Grandma turned to me. Behind them, my mountain rose up higher than ever, making a shadow across them. Fionadala was all the way at the top, stamping her foot.

I woke up to a noise in the living room. My glow in the dark clock showed two in the morning. I got out of bed and peeked out my door. Daddy was just then getting off the couch, heading towards his bedroom, walking as if he was a hundred and eight years old. I wanted to call out to him, but my lips glued together and a lump of coal stuck in my throat. Getting back into bed, I lay face up. I didn't know I had any tears, until I felt just a bit of wet trickle in my ear.

Chapter 23
So, these are his children

In the developed Elvis-and-hamburger-night pictures, we were all grinning like a big sack full of happy. Rebekha looked like one of us kids. I imagined what she was like at my age, in a room with Barbie dolls and hula hoops, at her dresser brushing her hair.

I put the pictures away in a shoebox, and hid them under my bed. When I wandered into the kitchen, Rebekha was cleaning the icebox, wearing Daddy's old brown sweatshirt and a pair of blue jean britches with a hole in the knee.

"Rebekha?"

"Yes?" She stopped swishing the sponge around and waited. Her eyes were droopy, as if she hadn't drank enough coffee.

"Do you have pictures of you when you were my age?"

"Why do you ask?"

"I don't know. I just can't picture you young." But I could.

She laughed, said, "Thanks a lot," then stood up and threw the sponge in the sink. "Come on. I have some old photographs stuck in my closet. I'm sick of cleaning anyway."

I followed her to her room and stood in the doorway after she went in.

"You can come in, Hon."

I thought how I'd never sat on her floor and watched her dress, put on lipstick, or powder, or Pond's cold cream.

"You're welcome in here anytime, unless I have the door closed, then I'd appreciate a knock." She opened her closet, reached up to push things aside on the shelf.

I looked around. A white bedspread was smoothed without a wrinkle, with a dark green blanket folded at the bottom; the walls were white, with a green and white shag rug on either side of the bed. The bed, chest of drawers, and dresser were dark wood like mine. On the left side of the bed, over a small table with a lamp and a stack of books, was a wedding picture of a happy-gap-toothed-grinned Rebekha and a silly-lopsided-smiling Daddy. There were more books on a bookshelf across the room, and another stack on the floor by the dresser. I never thought before how much Rebekha liked books, just like me.

"You can sit on the bed, if you like."

I was afraid I'd leave a dent, so I kept standing.

The suits, shirts, and britches were together by color. It made me feel ashamed of the way I threw and stuffed things in my room.

"Aha. Got it." She placed a wooden box on the bed, smoothing back her hair before opening it. I was excited to see something secret. Something hidden away. Inside, there was a stack of letters with a rubber band around them. Looking at one of the envelopes, I saw Rebekha's name written in Daddy's handwriting. She picked up the bundle and held it with two hands, as if she thought the words inside were heavy. "Love letters from your father." She put those aside, and pulled out a photo album with *My Life* written in dark-blue ink. At the bottom of the box, I saw a framed picture of her parents.

"That's my parents' tenth wedding anniversary photograph." She frowned down at them in all their fancy. Her daddy was smiling without showing any teeth; her momma had a sucked–on-a-lemon look. Earl and Victoria Patterson. We'd visited them only once, before Bobby was born. Earl joked around a lot, but Victoria thought her poop didn't stink.

Rebekha didn't have many pictures of her parents around. She had pictures of us in her room, though—all us kids, not just Bobby. We grinned out on her dresser and on the wall. I liked seeing us there, it made me feel as if I belonged. Rebekha put the letters back on top of her parents and closed the box. Picking up the picture album, she said, "Well, let's go look at these old things over a snack."

We sat at the table, our shoulders touching as we leaned over the album, with a plate of chocolate chip cookies, and two glasses of ice-cold milk.

She rubbed her hand over the leather. "Well, let's see here." She opened the album.

Rebekha and her momma stared out with their pale skin and that reddish-blond hair. But, Victoria was slitty-eyed and had a poochy pout mouth. As Rebekha turned pages, Victoria's hair was always the same, whether young or old, it was stiff and flipped up at the ends. She dressed up in almost every picture, never in britches.

Earl was near-bald, even in the wedding pictures, and he was smiling all the time. Most times, his smiles were so big, they didn't look real. Seemed to me Mr. Patterson didn't care about dressing, but Mrs. Patterson dressed like it mattered a lot.

Rebekha flipped fast through her life.

"You don't have to hurry up. I like looking at them."

"Oh. Well. They're just old pictures, boring stuff."

"Did you like being an only child?"

Rebekha put her finger on her chin, staring down at the faces staring back. "It was lonely."

"Sometimes I want to be an only child when my brothers bug me."

"We all want what we can't have I suppose. The different thing, you know?"

"I guess so." I pointed to a photo of her on a horse with a collie puppy running behind with its tongue slapping around. "Oh! You had a horse and a dog." I chomped my cookie and slurped my milk and wished I had them, too.

"The horse was Buster Keaton and the pup was Ranger. My mother hated pets, but my father talked her into letting us have a dog. She didn't consider the horse a pet. I sneaked in a couple of cats, hid them out in the stable. My favorite was Miss Emma the cat." Rebekha smiled, thinking about her animals, her finger petting the horse's mane. "Mother never went into the stable; she thought it smelled too bad."

"I liked the stable that time we visited."

"Yes, I remember."

Rebekha grew up in an old plantation house near Thibodaux. There was a tiny slave house in the back that leaned in one direction where the wind had pushed it, trying to knock it down to the ground where it belonged. The slaves were long gone off, but I thought it had ghosts flying around. I was mad that people had to live in a tiny rough house while the other people got to live in the big nice house. It didn't seem fair just because someone's skin color was different. When we visited there, I'd pushed on the shack with the wind and the ghosts, but it didn't fall down.

Rebekha walked inside my head and pulled out my thoughts. "A fancy stable, with a fancy house, and a fancy mother to keep everything fancy. I hated those old slave quarters and all it represented, but my mother thought it was quaint. Quaint!" Her voice sounded like chewing on gravel. "And I blame my mother for Leona's death. She worked her like a horse. She always called her *the help*. But she was my friend."

"I liked Leona."

"I loved her." She turned the page so hard, it ripped a bit. On the next page were only two photos, one of a little red-haired girl holding a baby and another of a little girl with brown hair. Rebekha said, "Oh!" and her mouth pulled down, her eyes wide and staring, the same look as the red-haired girl in the picture. She began to turn the page again, but I stopped her.

"Wait. Who are they, Rebekha?"

She didn't answer for a spell. When she did, her voice was froggy. "That's me holding my brother, and the other girl is my sister."

"You have a brother and sister?"

"Yes, but they didn't survive."

"They didn't?"

She hitched a sigh.

"What happened?" I wanted to take back what I said about being an only child then, for I didn't want anything to happen to my brothers.

"They're resting side by side on a pretty little hill. Their names were . . . are . . . Laurence and Maria." She took a sip of her milk, then said, "Laurence died at two weeks old. Maria was born five years before me. I never knew her at all, just by photos." She pointed to the brown-haired girl who was holding a baby bunny, had pigtails, fat cheeks, and big brown eyes. "Isn't she like a china doll? She was three when she died."

I stared at the little girl and I couldn't picture how it felt to be so little and have to die. I near-whispered, "Why did they die?"

Rebekha stared way off. "A bad trick of the genes, I suppose. One of my mother's siblings died, too." She looked at the picture again. "When Maria died, my mother decided not to have any more children. Then I came along, unplanned." She rubbed her forehead. "I was sick a lot at first, but grew strong. My father wanted me to have a sibling, my mother didn't. He must have convinced her that everything would work out, since I had lived and thrived." She stroked her sister's face. "When Laurence died, too, she never forgave my father. But, she was angry with me, too."

"Why would she be mad at you? You didn't do

anything." I thought about Victoria Patterson's sour face.

"Maybe because I survived, they had Laurence and had to go through losing a child again. I made them feel safe, when they weren't after all."

"I don't get it."

She shrugged, then turned to face me. "Hon, it's why I didn't tell you about Bobby until he was almost born. I thought I'd jinx it. Like if something good happens and I feel wonderful about it, it'll be taken away from me. But if I ignore it, pretend it doesn't matter, it'll all work out. Does that make any sense at all?"

I nodded. It made all kinds of sense.

She pinched her nose. "So long ago."

"Is that why you're so sad in the picture with Laurence? Because he's sick?"

"He was dead. My mother wanted that picture." Rebekha hurried and flipped to the next page.

I couldn't even think on how it felt to hold your dead brother while someone took a picture. Thinking about sad little Rebekha with that tiny dead baby in her arms, I had goose pimples raised up all on my arms and my throat felt clogged up with eighty sobbing frogs.

She said, real quiet. "He felt so heavy. It was just the second time I got to hold him. I was surprised. I thought once his spirit left, he'd be lighter, but he wasn't."

"Maybe our spirits keep us light?"

"Well, I think you're a smart girl." She took a bite of cookie, chewed, swallowed, said, "I can't imagine why my mother thought it a good idea to take that photograph. I don't know why I've kept it all these years."

"Because you don't have another one of your brother?" I finished my cookie.

"Yes, I suppose that's it." She drank the rest of her milk, then said, "I worried about Bobby all the time right after he was born—that's why I quit working full time. I shudder to think how I almost chickened out and we'd never have had our Bobby."

"Bobby's okay now, isn't he?" My stomach did a big flop over. "He's not going to . . . to go away?"

"Oh, Hon, no. He'll be okay; he's strong like I was." She touched my shoulder. "When you children came, I was so scared. What if I wasn't a good mother? You've heard all the fairy tales about evil stepmothers." She laughed one of those cartoon bad-guy laughs and made her fingers claws.

"You aren't like that."

"Thank you. We're a family now, it feels like to me." She got busy turning the pages of her album. "Look at me. What a gawky girl I was."

I laughed at her teenager outfits and hair-dos.

"Oh, this was my prom." She laughed, then said, "Isn't that dress a pink horror of ruffles and bows? You know, I'm thinking pink is a terrible color, and there I've plastered it all over your room just because my mother did that to me." She looked at me with a crooked grin. "Tell me the truth; the pink is awful, isn't it?"

"Um, no." I wanted real bad to say yes.

"I think you're trying to spare my feelings." She pulled the picture out of the album and stared at it. "Colin Robicheaux." She smiled. "You remember those curved stairs at my parents' place?"

I nodded as I imagined her walking down them, her hair pulled back with pink ribbons. Her legs just shaved with a Sunbeam and she'd missed a few spots. Her dress swished against the new smooth as she smiled down at Colin Robicheaux, his breath taken right away off to the wind by her pretty. They went arm in arm to the prom while her parents waved and blew kisses.

"At the bottom of the stairs, I tripped and fell on my face. My dress hiked up for all to see my undies. Colin laughed." She snickered, said, "My father was laughing, too. So I sat up, giggling away, with my petticoats all twisted up. My shoes had scuff marks and there was a rip in the ugly dress my mother bought at some oo la la fancy department store."

"What did you do?"

"I stood up and took Colin's arm. I wasn't going to miss my prom. Mother was so angry. She said, 'No way will you leave this house looking like that, young lady.' I begged her, but she kept shaking her head."

We both looked down at the photo again and I

saw the torn spot I hadn't noticed before. I liked how it looked.

"It was one of the few times my father told my mother to shut up. He took our picture and hurried us out the door, while my mother huffed and fumed. She didn't speak to us for a week." She put the picture back. "It was a rather nice week."

The first time we visited Rebekha's momma was the last time.

Victoria had eyed us up and down and her first words were, "So, these are his children." She turned to Rebekha just like a bird looks at an insect. "You need to freshen up. You're a mess. Why you insist on going out in public looking like our maid is beyond me."

Rebekha lowered her head.

"I think Rebekha is especially beautiful today, Victoria," Daddy said. "She's always beautiful."

Rebekha went up the stairs and disappeared inside, Daddy following her.

Victoria turned her squinchy eyes to Micah, "Make sure you wipe your feet before you come in. The entire bottom of the shoe on both feet, understand?" She looked at my bare toes digging in the grass. "And where, pray tell, are your shoes, young lady?"

I pointed to the car.

"Put them back on immediately. We do not go around barefoot like heathens." She said immediately like *immeejedly*.

"Leave my sister alone." Micah gave her the evil eye.

"I don't abide children talking back to me."

Micah put his hands on his hips and stared at her. I ran to the car and slipped on my flip flops.

Victoria watched me put them on, her nose cat-wrinkled. "Those look like pool slippers. Don't you have proper shoes?"

Instead of answering her, I ran to the back of the house so I could breathe.

The visit lasted two hours. Micah and I were eighty-nine pouts of pitiful by then. When it was finally time to leave, Rebekha hugged her daddy hard. "Bye, Dad. Take care of yourself."

He kissed her on the cheek, then said, "Come out again soon and see us, little girl."

Rebekha next hugged Leona, who stood proud and straight in her apron, yellow cotton dress, cap covering her neatened hair, and thick stockings that must have been hot in the heat. Rebekha said, "I've missed you so much, Leona."

"Missed you, too, Hon. And, I like that boy and girl you got there, they've cast a bright light in your eyes." She smiled at Micah and me, then turned to go inside, her big fanny weaving from side to side.

I liked Leona more than the peach cobbler she'd made us. Even with the extra ice cream on top, she was sweeter. I wished she'd come live with us.

Rebekha turned to her momma. "Leona surely outdid herself this time. Don't you think she deserves a nice vacation? She's worked so hard all these years."

"What you think is none of my concern."

"Yes, Mother, I know. I was just saying. She's old and looks tired." Rebekha tried to put on a smile. She put her arms around her stiffened-up momma. "Thank you for having us over."

It looked to me as if it hurt the mean old thing to be hugged by her own daughter. Victoria opened her sourpuss mouth and said, "Rebekha Jeanne, did I raise you to marry into this mess? With children who look as if they've lived in a ditch? Do you even know where their people came from? Look at them. Next you know, the other one will be knocking at your door."

Earl put his hand on Victoria's arm, "Victoria, that's enough."

Daddy said, "Now just a darn minute here."

Rebekha stared at her momma with killer beam eyes. "This is my family, Mother. If *my family* offends you so much, we won't be back." She turned to her daddy, "I'm sorry, Dad. I'm so sorry. But just like Leona said, Micah and Virginia Kate have brought a light to my life. If Mom can't accept them, then she doesn't accept me."

Victoria turned her back, went up the stairs, and into the house. Rebekha's daddy looked from her to his wife, and back again. He put his head in his hands.

Rebekha took my hand, then Micah's. "Let's go,

Frederick." And we slid into the car and drove away. Rebekha cried while Daddy reached over and rubbed her head. She said, "We're not going back."

And we didn't. Earl came when Bobby was born, but Victoria stayed away.

The last pages of the album were pictures of Rebekha's college graduation, and then of Daddy and Rebekha looking right into the camera as they stood in front of the Atlantic Ocean.

Rebekha traced the waves. "Our honeymoon was so beautiful. The ocean smelled salty and wild. I had a sunburn so bad, but I didn't care." In the picture, Rebekha wore a flowered sundress. Her hair fell soft against her shoulders; she held a hat in her hand. Daddy wore a loose shirt flapping in the wind, his hat dipped low over his eye. They both were grinning wide enough to fit a cat inside. Daddy had his arm tight around Rebekha, and he looked happy, as if all the hurts and secrets had flown away in the wind. I couldn't remember that look, and wished he had it all the time.

She closed the album. "I need to include all the latest photos of us. Or maybe I need a new album. Yes, a new album for a new family."

I smiled, then said, "Thanks for showing me."

"You're welcome." She picked up the album. "Well, I think I need a nap. All that sugar."

On the way back to my room, I thought about how Rebekha's momma was so mean to her, and how she had only her animals to love, except when her daddy was brave enough to tell Victoria to shut up. And, mostly, I thought about her holding her dead baby brother in her arms, even though I didn't want to.

Chapter 24
Well, dummy, just open it and see
1969

I woke before daylight on my twelfth birthday, loving how it felt secret that I might be the only one awake. I stretched my arms overhead, pointed my toes, then got out of bed and looked out of my window at the mimosa. The blooms were all gone and its little fan leaves waved in the early morning breeze. I put on a pair of green shorts and a yellow cotton shirt with green trim, and then sat on my bed with my diary.

I wrote, *Today I'm twelve years old. I'm going to the library, to the Seven Eleven to spend some birthday money, and then to see Jade. I dreamed about Grandma Faith last night, she told me Happy Birthday. I can't wait for my party. Bye for now.* I locked it and put it away. I had just a few pages left of my second diary, a white one with a gold clasp.

I picked up Momma's brush to take outside with me, opened my bedroom door and listened. All quiet. I eased out the front door, closed it behind me, and sat in the rocker. The sun's first light gave everything a friendly, happy look. Hugging myself, I imagined the whole earth waking happy because it was my birthday, and the sun coming out to make everything beautiful, just for me. I brushed out my hair, beginning at the top of my scalp and working it to the ends that just hit the top of my shorts. When I had it all brushed out, I braided it, tying off the end with one of Jade's thick stretchy bands with the balls. My hair was heavy and hot, but I didn't care. I rocked and let my head fill with cotton clouds.

"What's up, Veestor?"

"Oh! You scared me half to death!"

Micah stood over me, grinning like the town idiot on *Green Acres*, his hands shoved in his pockets. His clothes looked as if he'd rolled down a wet hill. "Sorry, didn't mean to scare you out of your whirly-world." But he wasn't sorry a bit. "What're you doing up so early, Squirrel-Nut?"

"Just thinking. What about you?"

He grinned and wiggled his eyebrows, just like Daddy. When he sat, his knees bent long and his hands dangled between them. "I haven't been to bed, yet."

"What do you mean?"

"Just what I said. Me and my friends snuck out last night."

"What if Daddy finds out?"

"What'll he do anyway? Like he cares—or

notices." Micah stood up and kicked the steps. Looking down at me then, he smiled, his mood changed just like that, reminding me of the earlier dark changing to light in just that way. "Guess what?"

"What?"

"Chickenbutt!" He reached down, picked up a clod of dirt from Rebekha's flowerbed, and threw it at my leg.

"That's not funny." I wiped off the dirt.

"Since when do you care about getting dirty?"

"It's just that . . . oh, never mind." I slumped down.

"Guess what?" He waited, looking all on-purpose-serious. I wasn't going to fall for that again, so I pressed my lips together tight. He grinned. "I'm serious this time."

"You and your friends egged something?"

"No."

"You toilet-papered something?"

"No."

"You smoked?"

"Geez. No. That's all kid's stuff." He rolled his eyes, looking like Momma instead of Daddy. "I got something for your birthday."

"You remembered my birthday?"

"Yep. Hold on." He jumped up the steps like a pup, then disappeared into the house.

I sat almost holding my breath.

He soon came back holding a white paper sack.

"Here." He stretched out his long arm, letting the bag dangle in front of my face.

I took it from him, and it felt heavy. "What is it?"

"Well, dummy, just open it and see."

I opened the bag, and pulled out something wrapped in the Sunday funnies. I tore into the paper and held his gift in my hands. "Micah! Oh, it's so beautiful."

It was a thick triangle-shaped glass bowl with lots of grooves cut into it, like the special crystal glasses Rebekha had in her china cabinet. The heavy amber sparkled in the sun. The lid had a tall diamond-shaped handle, and when I lifted it, I smelled spicy-sweet powder. On top of the powder was a powder puff.

"I figured Momma's powder was gone by now. Figured you needed your own kind. You know, now that you're twelve."

I picked up the puff and put some of the powder on my arms and legs. "This is the most beautiful present I've ever got." I carefully put it on the porch and jumped up to hug Micah's neck.

He tried to pretend he didn't like my hug, but I saw through him, "I bought it with my own money I got from selling a drawing to Wayne's mom."

"You sold a picture?" I felt proud. "Wow."

"Yeah." He scratched his chin, then his arm. "Well, guess I'll get to bed."

"Wait." I didn't want him to leave. "What do you do when you sneak out?"

"Oh, just stuff." He glanced back at the door to make sure it was closed.

"What kind of stuff?"

He shrugged. "Sometimes we go out with girls. Sometimes we have a beer."

"Oh." I knew I looked like a kid who didn't know a thing about nothing.

"It's no big deal."

"I don't want you to get in trouble."

"You're an old woman." He pretended to walk with a cane. "You should have some fun; get your nose out of books and out of the sky." He pulled me into a headlock and gave me scalp-burn. I yelled at him to quit before I socked him one. He just laughed, let me go, and ran inside.

I opened the lid on Micah's gift again, drifting on more powder. When I put it back into the bag, I saw he'd drawn me riding a horse up a mountain, my hair blowing out behind me. I smoothed out the bag so I could keep it forever, then went inside to put it away. Like I put Micah away, in back of my mind where he walked around, all shadowy and secret.

Rebekha was up making breakfast; I'd smelled it as soon as I hit the door. When I went into the kitchen, she turned and said, "Happy Birthday."

"Thanks, Rebekha." I grinned.

"I'm making pancakes."

I looked into the skillet. "What are those, elephants?"

"Shoot. They're supposed to be horses." She poked at the pancakes trying to shape them better.

I was too old for animal pancakes, but it still made me smile.

She flipped the elephant-looking horses when they bubbled. "Maybe I should call Micah in here, he's the artist."

"He's asleep." I was itching to tell. But, I wouldn't.

"All these sleepy heads." She slid the pancakes on two plates. "Here, let's start on these. By the way, you smell nice."

"Micah got me some powder." Then I remembered I wasn't supposed to have seen him so I flapped shut my trap.

"How nice."

We sat at the table and ate the pancakes with lots of butter and Steen's syrup. I said, "These are really great."

"How am I going to manage Andy's astronaut's spaceship pancakes? I'll have to do the moon, instead."

When the guys woke up (except Micah), Rebekha made their pancakes. We all jabbered while we ate. Daddy finished first and headed out. Andy-and-Bobby, their names said all together in one breath, since Bobby was always glued to Andy, ran off, punching each other and making lots of racket.

Rebekha and I brought the plates to the kitchen.

I picked up a plate to wash, but Rebekha said, "No. Not today." She reached out and touched my arm.

All a sudden I thought how I'd never let her hug me, and I'd never hugged her, not once in all this time. I thought how she always had to touch my shoulder, my hand, my cheek, or just stand there and smile at me. I'd seen her hug Bobby and Andy lots of times. I'd seen her hug Micah, even though he flared his nostrils, he didn't move away. I remembered how Victoria looked when Rebekha tried to hug her. It seemed weird that I never let it happen.

She stood in her robe and slippers, strong and tall smiling down at me. "No chores, no babysitting. Go have fun, but be back for dinner. We're having a party." She grinned secrets, presents-for-me secrets. "Oh, to be twelve again, but to be it here instead of where I was when I turned twelve." She looked over my head. "I don't know why I said that. Goodness, but I'm silly sometimes."

Then I did it. I reached up and hugged her hard as I could. "Thank you, Rebekha."

She hugged me back. I felt as if I were under Grandma's quilt, safe like I never thought I would feel. I couldn't remember feeling like that with Momma, but I was sure I must have if I thought on it real hard. When I pulled away, Rebekha's eyes were all shiny. "Virginia Kate, I'm so glad you're here. You children have changed my life."

I didn't say anything; my insides were too fluffy.

I grinned like a monkey, waved, turned around, and ran outside. My feet had wings like that mythology guy we studied in school. I jumped on my bike and pedaled off as fast as I could, letting the hot wind blow on my face. I smelled like pancakes, and Rebekha's face cream, and Micah's gift.

I tore off towards the library, day-dreaming I'd become a librarian where I'd be surrounded by books and quiet all the livelong day. Or, maybe I'd work in a hospital, wearing a white coat over my suit and those comfortable shoes Rebekha wore. I turned the corner by the library and saw Daddy's car parked in front. I hid behind a clump of azalea bushes and watched him.

He stood beside his car with a woman in a very short yellow, pink, and white dress, little chain belt, and white boots. Her streaky light-brown hair had enough hairspray to hold an army of hair do's. She laughed at something he said, her hand pushing at him, and then she patted that stupid helmet of hair. Daddy raised his hands up in the air as if describing the size of something. He threw back his head and laughed when she said something back. She stared at his throat, putting her hand to her own.

I jumped on my bike, hurried and rode away. It was my birthday. I wasn't going to let Daddy and some floozy-woozy in a silly dress ruin it. I had twenty-five dollars burning a big fat hole in my shorts pocket. Mee Maw sent me twenty, and Mrs. Portier sent me five along with a letter about her new life. Mrs. Portier was happy go lucky, married to a veterinarian and moved to Georgia. She was pregnant with twins and had a real nice house to boot. I was glad for Mrs. Portier, who I'd have to remember became Mrs. Engleson. She didn't need her old husband any old day. Amy Campinelle said Mr. Portier did her a favor by diddly-dooing with Mrs. McGrander.

Last I heard of Mrs. McGrander-Baconbits, she was married to some gamillion-year-old man. I'd seen them riding around town in a fancy car. Mrs. Bacogrits had done something weird to her eyes, her hair was a frizzled mess—Rebekha said it was a Phyllis Diller Do—and she carried a look like she just ate five-hundred-year-old dog poop. Amy Campinelle told Rebekha she was an example of vanity and surgery gone all wrong. Sometimes things just worked out right for some people and it worked out right for Mrs. Portier turned Engleson, and maybe not for Mrs. Baconbits.

I didn't have a birthday card from Momma. She hardly called and sent letters or cards even less. Daddy didn't try to stop us from writing or talking to her anymore, but Momma wasn't home much. The phone would ring and ring all hollow and empty in my ear. The last phone call I had from her was three months before. She carried on about how Harold was gone. I heard Aunt Ruby in the background saying, "Who needs the asshole?" Micah and Andy wouldn't talk to her or even about her.

Only I still tried with Momma. She didn't have anybody else, except that Aunt Ruby.

Wayne rode towards me, pulled my mind off Momma. He stopped in front of me, legs to either side of his bike. I did the same. He wore dark-framed glasses and his golden brown hair was always falling in his milk-chocolate flavored eyes. He smoothed it back and it just fell right back. I hadn't seen him since school let out.

"Hey, Virginia Kate."

"Hey, Wayne."

"Where you off to?"

"To the store." I didn't want to tell him I was going to buy candy. I wanted to seem skinny and starving. "I'm twelve today." I flipped my hair, but it was in a plait, so it didn't do me any good.

He looked where my new bra was under my shirt and then looked away quick. "Happy Birthday."

"Thanks." I wondered what he saw when he looked at me there.

"How's Micah?"

"Fine. He's off . . . somewhere. How come you aren't friends anymore?"

"Maybe I like his sister better."

This was my birthday and I was tired of yapping with Wayne. "Well, bye now."

"Oh, okay. See ya." But he didn't move as he watched me get back on my bike. "You look older than twelve, Virginia Kate."

I pedaled off. Looking back, I noticed how his

calves were strong and grown up as he rode away in the other direction.

At the Seven Eleven, I leaned my bike against the wall. It had a banana seat, the old red bike with the streamers given away to some other girl. Inside, I bought an *Archie* comic book, a *Little Lotta*, *Richie Rich*, a pack of Wrigley's Spearmint gum, and two Zero bars—one for me and one for Jade.

I tore off to Jade's house. While riding, I let my mind fly around from one thing to the next. If my mind went to Daddy and the floozy, I jerked it back over to something happy. The crepe myrtles were blooming all over the place. I smelled flowers, and the fishy smell from the lake. People jogged around, even though it was hot enough to melt a ton of Zeros in one-half a second. Jade and I would have to lick all the white chocolaty stuff off the paper, but that was fun, too.

Sometimes I felt my mountain calling to me, but I had to push it way deep inside, so far inside that it was lost and away. That's just what I did as I ped-aled faster and faster and faster, away from all my thoughts.

At Jade's house, I hollered up to her window. "Hurry up and come out!"

She ran out to her bike in her shorts and a midriff top, her long skinny legs and arms looking like a boiled crawfish from her vacation at the beach. I stared at her. She'd cut her hair short as a boy's and it was turned almost white. She rode out to me. "Hey, Vee." She was the only one besides Micah that ever called me Vee.

"Hey. You're sunburned, and all your hair's gone." I gawked at her some more.

"Yeah. My mom had a fit about the hair, but I did it anyway."

"You did it yourself?"

"Uh huh. I took the scissors and went whackety whack. Mom drug me to her hairdresser to fix it." She touched her hair and then pulled on it. "It feels cool and I like it. It's sort of like Twiggy, don't you think? But, anyway I'm glad I did it."

"I think you look good with it like that." I grinned at her to show it was all okay that she looked so different.

She looked at my legs. "How come I can't be like you? Stupid white legs of mine just get red."

I shrugged. "It's in the molecules."

"Stupid molecules."

I thought her molecules looked better than mine any day. "I got you a Zero."

"Grooooooovy." She said as we pedaled off, "There's a girl in my class who looks like *The Flying Nun*."

"Yeah?"

"Yeah. Everybody calls her *The Shying Nun* because she won't talk to anyone," Jade said. "The real nuns don't like *The Flying Nun* and tell us to be quiet."

"Weird." I didn't understand Catholics, but they had some interesting rules.

We rode until time for lunch at Soot and Marco's. When we went in, Soot said, "Hey! Whatchoo doing?" They'd bought the diner and fixed it where it wasn't dirty anymore, but still smelled like fried foods and beer. Soot's hair was shorter and it swung around her shoulders like a movie star. She hugged me, gave me a kiss on the cheek. Her lips were cool and her arms were strong. She hugged and kissed Jade, then said, "Love the hair, Miss Jade." Her eyebrows cocked up, "Put vinegar on your burn. That'll take the heat right out."

"Okay, Soot," Jade said.

"It's my twelfth birthday today." I grinned up a storm.

"Well, you two setchore selves down then." Soot handed us menus.

I said, "Soot, I want a hamburger po-boy, fried potatoes, and a Cola-coke."

"And I want a cheeseburger, onion rings, and a coke." Jadesta looked at me. "Would you quit saying Cola-coke, and orange-coke, and stuff?" But she was laughing, since I was the Queen of Birthday Land and everything I said went.

Soot said, "I've never made a hamburger po-boy, but why not? It's on the house, for your birthday."

"No, I have money." I pulled Mee Maw's birthday money from my pocket, laying it on the table for everyone to admire.

"Free ice cream then, how's about that?"

Jade and I nodded our heads, grinning like downright fools.

Marco walked over, stood behind Soot, and she leaned back into him. "Look at this here, a rich woman fixin' to spee-und her money at our place."

"Go fry stuff, big galoot," Soot said.

After we ate, Soot served my ice cream with a candle in it. Everyone in the diner had ice cream, and they all sang Happy Birthday to Me. I was about to bust wide open with joy. I left her a whole two-dollar tip, putting it under my plate as I'd seen Daddy do, then Jade and I headed off on our bikes, our stomachs sticking out with all the food. We rode around the campus, went to the library (and I was sure glad I didn't see Daddy and the Mini Dress Helmet Hair), went to the lake and fed the ducks old bread Soot gave us, watched boys throw the football at the field.

When the clock on campus boinged five times, we hightailed it to my house. When I put my comic books and gum in my room, Jade said, "It still looks like cotton candy in here."

I nodded, rolling my eyes.

Rebekha had decorated the dining room in blue, white, and yellow—no pink to be found. The food was spread on top of a blue and white checkered tablecloth. There were fried shrimp, fried oysters, and more fried potatoes. The Campinelles brought jambalaya, and Miss Darla brought potato salad with extra onions. On the sideboard was a dark chocolate cake, and written in blue icing was Happy Birthday Virginia Kate.

Colored balloons were tied to the chair at the front of the table, where Rebekha pointed. "This is the Birthday Girl's chair of honor."

My face was warm, but Miss Priss sure sat in the chair. Everyone else sat down and we began filling our plates. The girls told Jade her haircut was fetching. The boys looked at her and shrugged, they didn't care—except Andy—some boys were funny about hair and some weren't.

"You cut off'n your hair. Why?" Andy asked.

Jade ignored him and talked with Miss Darla about dance. Jade had jazz, ballet, and tap posters all over her room. Her parents were always leaving stuff about piano and violin class on her dresser. Jade's father told her, "Become a lawyer like me, or get married and volunteer like your mommy. Forget all this silly dance stuff. You'll never be taken seriously." Jade put on her sweet eyes and kept her feet right in first position.

I kept catching her giving the googly eye to Micah, even though just last week, Jade and I'd made a solemn swear pact that our brothers didn't count as boys since they were brothers. Micah didn't even seem to notice her, except when he said, "Your Wonder Bread skin looks like it's got Tabasco spread on it."

306

I felt bad for Jade; she wilted right up like a crushed magnolia bloom, a Catholic one.

Andy elbowed Micah, and said to Jade, "I'm going to be an astronaut and go to the moon. The moon looks real white."

"Me, to the moon. Me, too." Bobby was ready to blast off right from his seat.

"Uh huh." Jade turned to Miss Darla again. "Did you have lots of boyfriends, Miss Darla? Or maybe you have lots now?"

"I had the cutest boys when I was a young girl. Lining up at my doorstep, they were. I remember one, named Jimmy Dodd. He was so handsome." Miss Darla sighed, then said, "That boy sure could kiss."

Jade said, "I can't wait to kiss."

I looked over at Andy to make sure he didn't do anything stupid. I said, "Well, I can sure wait."

Miss Darla said, "You won't be thinking that forever, Virginia Kate."

"Let's hope she'll be thinking that way for a long time." Daddy had the bourbon bottle and a glass bucket of ice setting on the table so the grown-ups could help themselves. Only Daddy helped himself.

Rebekha cut her shrimp with a fork. "What ever happened to Jimmy Dodd, Miss Darla? Could you look him up? Maybe he's been searching for you all these years."

"I can't, because he's gone from this earth." She

307

fiddled with her necklace. "He's in a spirits' place. You don't think black holes and space are full of nothing but darkness and rock, do you? Or astronauts flying in silly machines? No. The spirits that were once us dance on stars, or the moon, and watch over those they love. They soak up all the light they can, then, when they're ready, and when their loved ones are ready, they head into the empty black and bring their light to dark places." She stared out the window like she was looking at that place. "Anyway, once I'm on the moon soaking up my light, and if I'm allowed to see him, I'll ask him to forgive me for hurting him like I did."

Mister Husband cleared his throat, said, "The only love I'll ever have is my Amy. She's the best thing that ever did happen to me." He turned red over his already pinked-up cheeks. "I was a mess before she came around." Amy Campinelle leaned over and kissed Mister Husband on the cheek. He said to her, "We should've had kids, Amy. Think how good-looking they'd be." Amy Campinelle fed him a shrimp, and then he fed her one.

"How lovely," Miss Darla said.

Micah said in my ear, "How gross." He stuffed fifty-two shrimp and eight hundred fried potatoes in his mouth, and when some of it fell out onto his plate, he put it back in and chewed like a cow with its cud.

I couldn't help but snicker at the look on Jade's face.

Andy burped out loud a couple of times, even after Rebekha asked him to please stop. He said, "I'm sorry, they just keep popping out before I can stop them."

Bobby was already whining for cake, hitting his food with his fists.

The whole room was loud with noise and happy feelings.

I sent mind messages to Daddy, *Eat and smile, Daddy, come on, you can do it.*

Rebekha watched Daddy, too. She reached over and touched his arm and he winked at her.

After we finished eating, Rebekha cleared the dishes, and then put the cake in front of me with twelve blue candles and a white one to grow on. For the second time, I heard Happy Birthday, made a wish and blew out the candles.

I wished for Daddy to put the bourbon down the sink himself, forever and ever. I wished for Momma to call me, even though I was mad at her. In the middle of my wishes, Daddy put ice in his glass, and poured in the booze. I didn't expect the phone to ring either.

Finally, Rebekha slid a blue-and-white wrapped box with a yellow bow from under the table. Jade took a present out of her pocket and put it on the table grinning like she was so smart. The Campinelles and Miss Darla had presents for me, too. I was ready to bust open to let all my guts spill out I felt so full of everything. I ripped into Jade's package first. It was a bracelet with charms: a horse, a dog, a ballet slipper, a seashell, and a heart.

"Thank you, Jade."

"You can add your own charms to it."

I put it on and held out my wrist for everyone to admire.

Amy Campinelle made me a red crocheted hat that I put on my head and modeled.

Micah said, "You look stooopid."

Bobby said, "Nuh uh. She looks pitty." He had food all over his face. "Can I wear it?"

I said, "Maybe later, Bobby." He threw a shrimp at me and laughed.

Miss Darla's gift was a diary. Not a little girl diary, but one made of brown leather, with paper fancy thin. It had a ribbon glued inside, to mark my place. "Miss Darla, it's beautiful. Thank you."

"I know you have lots of things inside you that need to come out."

Inside the box from Rebekha and Daddy were books, *The Black Stallion Returns, The Black Stallion Mystery,* and *The Black Stallion and Flame.* There was also *The Velveteen Rabbit.* I inhaled the book smell. Underneath the books was a small white box. I took off the lid and on a bed of cotton was a Timex watch. I put it on the other wrist and held it out, too.

Daddy said, "That's so you won't be late for your birthday party next year."

Rebekha said, "I know *The Velveteen Rabbit* is

young for you, but I loved it when I was a child. I thought you'd enjoy reading it to Bobby."

Over Bobby's hollering, "Read it, read it," I said, "I love everything, thank you everybody."

"That's not all." Rebekha handed me an envelope.

I stared bug-eyed as a frog. Inside the envelope was a note, *Redeem this coupon for a bedroom remodel: paint, bed linens, pillows and new pictures.*

I jumped up and hugged her—the pink would be gone! When I hugged Daddy, his blue jean shirt felt soft against my cheek. He whispered, "Happy Birthday, Bug. I put an envelope under your pillow." His breath was hot and full of bourbon.

I went around and hugged everybody's neck except my brothers, they understood.

Jade looked through my books. "I read *The Velveteen Rabbit* before. I love that book! The stuffed rabbit becomes real because its fur is all loved off."

"Are we done?" Micah was ready to tear out of there.

"Wait, don't anyone move." I ran into my bedroom. First, I lifted my pillow to open Daddy's envelope. Inside were a note and three pictures I didn't remember seeing before. In one, I was on Daddy's lap, and Momma was beside Daddy, smiling at him. Her left hand was holding my foot. Daddy was smiling down at me, his arm across my body to hold me still. In the second photo, Daddy carried me on his shoulders, holding me by my legs. I had my chin on the top of his head. The third picture was of Daddy with us kids. We were all grinning, except Andy, he was still too little. The burning and itchy feeling behind my eyes started up, so I put the pictures back in the envelope and opened the note.

It read, *Dear Bitty Bug: I've had these a long time, they are very special to me. I sense you need them more than I do. There we are. That has not changed. Even if 'True is it that we have seen better days.' Love, Daddy.*

I folded the note and put it back with the pictures. I couldn't figure out what all the hidden words were. Daddy always had hidden words behind the ones he said aloud. I put the envelope back under my pillow and got Micah's gift to take back to the party.

I put it in the middle of the table where the light overhead made the glass sparkle all over the walls. "This is from Micah."

Amy Campinelle said, "Oh, that's nice, yeah." Mr. Husband nodded.

Miss Darla said, "Gorgeous, Micah. You have good taste."

Rebekha said, "He sure does."

Jade petted it, said, "It's magical."

Micah stared at the ceiling, his hands in his pockets. He wore blue jeans and a button up white shirt and if he looked any more like Daddy, it would be too weird.

"Good job, Micah," Daddy said.

Andy-and-Bobby didn't care: "More cake!" Bobby said. "Yeah, me, too," Andy said.

Everyone was staying put; no one was leaving, or fighting. The light that had come out so big and bright for my birthday said goodbye. I thought how it all came right around full circle from the time I first woke up in the part-ways dark room, to the end of my birthday in a part-ways dark room. It was the best birthday I'd ever had.

Chapter 25
My Sweet-pur-tater, Laudine!

We read in the newspaper, *Hurricane Camille smashed into the Mississippi Gulf Coast on Sunday night, August 17, and continued its destructive path until Monday, August 18. One hundred and forty-three people were killed on the coast from Alabama to Mississippi; one hundred and thirteen more died from flash floods and torrential rains as she made her way inland over the Virginias. There are reports of more lives lost and greater devastation, many missing and never accounted for. Hurricane partiers' lives were lost mid-drink, taken by complete surprise, as they never expected Camille to be a Category Five killer. Her winds were over 200 miles per hour with a storm surge of up to twenty-four feet. Some say it was the worst storm to hit the mainland United States.*

Mee Maw showed up the same day as Camille. Rebekha said she was a Category Five grandmother.

She blobbed in wearing a mint-green pantsuit, a lopsided page-boy wig, and a purse big enough to hold a watermelon. She stormed around the house in a whirlwind mess. She had two suitcases, a paper bag of medicines, a bag bulging with mystery, a plastic bag of licorice, two oranges, three peaches, a six-pack of Nehi, a box of dog food, and her yipping *Imper*, short for Imperial. Imper was a fluffy white poodle with wet, runny eyes. First thing it did was pee on the living room rug. Rebekha ran to get paper towels, and when she was back, she pointed to the dog, then to me, then to the back. I scooped Imperial up and put him on the back screened porch. Mee Maw and Imper didn't take to that one bit.

Daddy said, "Hello, Mother." He hugged her real quick, then went out to the front porch with his glass full to tiptop. He didn't try to pretend anymore with Mee Maw about the booze thing.

After we had Mee Maw settled in (my!) room, we girls headed to the kitchen. Mee Maw asked, "What's wrong with Frederick?"

"Oh, he just had a hard day." Rebekha laid out vegetables to chop.

"What's he know about hard? He isn't an old woman with a man who won't marry her."

"It must be rough," Rebekha smushed a garlic pod.

I chopped off the ends of the onion so I could take the skin off.

"It sure is. But, I don't need that man to take care of me, nosiree." Mee Maw squared her chin. "I got my driving license so I can come visit y'all on my own."

Rebekha sliced the onion I handed her. "Uh hum."

Mee Maw pinned me with her eyes. "You're growing up into a fine young lady. I think my birthday present will be just perfect for you."

"You already sent me twenty dollars, Mee Maw." I still had eight of it left, hidden inside a sock in my dresser.

"I know that, sweet lump, but I got you something else. From Sears." She hyena-laughed, then said, "I'm so excited about being here. I told that man I was leaving if he didn't marry me. So there. I did it. Let him see how it is without his sweet Mee Maw." She wrinkled her wrinkles into one hundred fifty-nine folds of pitiful.

Rebekha said, "Dinner will be ready in an hour, Laudine. You can get freshened up if you like."

"You're a saint. Not like that thing my son married before." Mee Maw leaned over Rebekha's shoulder. "I can cook, you know. Just let me take care of all the cooking while I'm staying here. And call me Mee Maw."

"Oh, no, you're a guest, just relax." Rebekha chopped extra hard on the onion.

I got out the tea leaves to make the dark tea Rebekha liked.

"Guest? Mee Maw's no guest," Mee Maw said. "Now, I have bunches of recipes. We'll eat something different for weeks."

Rebekha stopped chopping. "How long were you planning on visiting, Laudine?"

"Well, now, see here, it's like this. I thought I could just stay a little while. You know, a couple months or so. You know how it is." Mee Maw winked. "You got to let a man see what it's like to boil their own taters before they miss you and beg you back."

"Will you excuse me a minute?" Rebekha tore out of the kitchen hollering, "Frederick!"

"What do you suppose is wrong with her?" Mee Maw shrugged, then hummed, picked up the knife and chopped the other vegetables; pieces flying all over the kitchen, hitting the walls, the icebox, and me. I sneaked away to make a pallet in Andy-and-Bobby's room, so I wouldn't have to stay with her in my room and listen to her yammer all night.

After a supper of meatloaf, carrots, and potatoes, we went to the living room. Mee Maw clapped her hands. "Everyone! Gather 'round. I got licorice and presents." She took off her shoes and went tap-tap-tap-tap with her toe against the floor until I thought I'd go slap crazy with it.

Daddy sat in the chair across from Mee Maw. They sure didn't look much alike and I wondered what Daddy's own daddy was like, where he was and if he thought about any of us.

Mee Maw said, "My grandbabies! Growing up so fast. Mee Maw hardly recognizes any of you. Rebekha, you're doing a fine job in the place of that crazy bitch my boy married first."

I inhaled sharp, then let it out slow.

Micah and Andy snickered.

Bobby said, "Bitch bitch bitch," except he said it like *bit bit bit*.

Rebekha put her hand over Bobby's mouth. "That's a bad word, Bobby." Then she told Mee Maw, "Laudine, please don't call their momma that."

"Just calling a spade a spade." Mee Maw petted a big paper bag.

Imper barked from the back porch. He'd been barking and yipping since he got there.

"Can't you do something with that dog of yours, Mother?" Daddy stood up.

"My Imper isn't used to this. At home, he does everything with me." When Daddy went down the hall, she hollered, "Take him to wee wee!"

Rebekha sipped her tea. She had her legs crossed, everything about her looked neat and calm. She said, "That's why we put him back there, because of the wee wee."

Mee Maw sniffed, patting her wig.

Daddy came back in the room with paw prints on his britches and a Gee-Jiminy-Christmas look on his face. He gave Rebekha an I'm-sorry-to-put-you-through-this look. She smiled a that's-okay-hon look. I liked how it was them against Mee Maw.

"Poor Imper." Mee Maw dabbed at her nose with the handkerchief she kept in her pocket. "Well, now." She looked at us in turn. "My grandbabies, wonders of the universe, pride of the South, the—"

"Get on with it, Mother."

"There you go disrespecting me again." Mee Maw tossed her head as she handed a drawing tablet and colored pencils to Micah.

Micah took them, thanked her, and right away began to draw with a secret grin, holding his other hand over the page so I couldn't see.

For Andy, Mee Maw had a book on race cars. Andy said his thanks and flipped through it like a greedy goat. He loved anything that was fast and dangerous.

"I bought all this myself, nobody helped me. I drove by myself downtown in the middle of a Texas traffic jam. I carried it by myself back to my car." Mee Maw tapped her toe. "That man I left to boil his own taters didn't lift a finger! Makes Mee Maw do it all by herself."

"We're both impressed and saddened by your accomplishments and disappointments, Mother."

Mee Maw slid her eyes to Daddy. "I didn't raise you to be smart alecky, and drinking to boot. You got a wasp in your ass or something?"

Andy put his hand over his mouth and snickered. Micah laughed right out loud—he didn't care if Daddy got mad.

"Put a cork in it, Mother."

"Y'all stop it. What kind of example are we setting here?" Rebekha put her hand back over Bobby's mouth since he kept going, "Wapses in your ass. Wapses in your aaaa-aass."

Micah scribbled away and I was burning up to see what he was drawing. I leaned over and he let me see a peek. It was Mee Maw with horns sticking from her forehead and smoke coming out of her ears. I giggled. Micah closed the sketchbook, an innocent-lamb look coming over him.

"Do you grandbabies want Mee Maw's gifts or not?" She reached back into the bag and pulled out a little harmonica for Bobby. Rebekha eyes went round as Bobby squealed like a baby pig, running to grab it from Mee Maw. She held it in the air so he couldn't reach it. "What do you say to Mee Maw, young man?"

"Thank you, Mee Mawl, for the pwesent." Bobby held his hands in front of him like a little angel. As soon as she handed it to him, he blew hard into it over and over.

"Bobby, that's an outside toy." Rebekha rubbed her head. "Give it to Mommy and we'll go play in a little while." He handed it over, but not without a big pout.

"You could loosen that tight hold you got on yourself sometime, Rebekha," Mee Maw said.

Rebekha opened her mouth to say something, then closed it.

It was my turn. Mee Maw packed my present first so I'd get it last. She said, "Today, you'll take a first step to becoming a woman. If it hasn't already, before you know it, your menses'll happen."

"Good god," Daddy said.

I wished the floor would open up and swallow me whole, down to China. Nobody but Rebekha knew that it'd already happened two weeks ago. She'd gone to the drugstore for me, and then shown me how to use the pads. She'd bought books about girls growing up and said if I had questions, she was always there to answer them. I'd walked around with all that nasty blood gooshing, hating the whole business of it.

Mee Maw was screeching, still. "Can't deny it away, son, that's life."

"You don't need to announce it to everybody. Look at Bug's face, for Pete's sake."

Rebekha shook her head. "I don't think this is the place to discuss those things, Mee Maw Laudine."

"As I was saying, today we take the first steps in helping Virginia Kate become an attractive young woman." She pulled something out of the bag and held it up like a flag on a pole. "Voila! The answer to hip's prayers."

"What in hell is that?" Daddy stared at the rubbery thing as if it was an alien on *Star Trek*. Everybody leaned in for a closer look, except me. I was still trying to shrink down to an ant's size.

"What's it look like? It's a girdle for our chubbie-hipped little woman."

"Oh, my." Rebekha put her face in her hands.

Micah and Andy busted out laughing, slapping their legs with hoots and hollers. Bobby laughed to mimic his brothers and ran up to try to grab the thing out of Mee Maw's hand.

"Go put it on! Come on; let's see how you look in it. Put it on!" Mee Maw cackled like a hen.

"She isn't putting that thing on," Daddy said.

"This here's how you get a man. Smoke and mirrors."

"A man? For lord's sake, Mother. She's twelve!" Then he said, "All she has is some baby fat, and that'll go away soon enough."

Rebekha stood up. "I've had enough—"

I tore off to my room before I heard anymore, closed the door against them, and lay across my blue bedspread, feeling like Fattie mae. Rebekha came in holding the girdle with two fingers and threw it in the garbage. Andy and Micah peeked in at me with an I'm-sorry-seestor look. Rebekha shooed them off and closed the door.

She sat beside me, making large then small circles on the chenille with her index finger. "Your room looks so much better without all that pink."

I didn't say anything since I was full of pout.

"You know your Mee Maw means well. She's just, well, just Mee Maw."

I shrugged.

"I remember how my mother was always afraid I'd get chubby." Rebekha lay back beside me and our hair mixed up together. My dark hair made hers look even lighter. I wondered what it was like to have strawberry-blond hair and to be skinny and pale.

"I wish I looked like you instead of me," I said.

"I always wanted shiny dark hair and a full figure. Look at your hair, spread out on the pillow like a fairy story princess. And when I was a little girl, I had horrid freckles. I wanted to stay in my room and never go to school."

"I think freckles are nice."

"My mother was always buying me big hats and warning me to stay out of the sun or I'd get more freckles."

"Did you wear them?"

"No." She turned on her side and propped up on her elbow. "I just grew out of my freckles. Now I miss them sometimes. We grow out of a lot of things that we miss when we're older."

"I know, you're trying to tell me I'll grow out of my feelings."

"No. I'm saying you'll grow out of letting other people make you feel bad about yourself." She brushed the hair off my face. "Someone saying something about you doesn't make it magically true. You didn't feel fat this morning did you?"

"No. I don't think so." I propped up to face her. "But I do eat lots of candy."

"So, do it while you're young. My mother didn't allow sweets except on special occasions."

"She didn't?"

"Nothing except fruit. Leona would sneak me treats sometimes, though."

I smiled thinking about Leona doing that.

"You look so much like your mother. She's a beautiful woman."

"She's not chubby." I reached out and touched Rebekha's hair; it felt light as dragonfly wings flying though my fingers.

"You're filling out. You're just doing it a bit sooner than some girls, nothing wrong or terrible about that. It just is."

I hitched up a sigh.

She sat cross-legged and I copied her, our knees almost touched. "One day you'll remember this conversation and see I was right. You'll feel strong and sure of yourself."

Mee Maw busted into the room. "What's going on in here? I can't bring my grandbabies presents without everybody getting mad when I'm just trying to be a good Mee Maw." She dabbed at her eyes with a wad of tissues she pulled out of her pocket. "It just hurts my feelings how everybody treats Mee Maw."

"Laudine, I need help with the menu for tomorrow's dinner."

Mee Maw's eyes lit up.

Rebekha stood, took Mee Maw's arm, herded her out, and shut my door. I heard Mee Maw blabbing all the way to the kitchen.

I lay on my blue pillows and thought about being a girl. I pictured Momma and me, knees touching, head to head, and then her hugging me, but her face turned into Rebekha's face. I fell asleep and dreamed that Grandma Faith had the girdle on; prancing around her garden laughing like a little girl. I saw Grandpa Luke, in the shadows. He turned to me and his face became a monster, like in Micah's weird comic *Ghostly Tales from the Haunted House*. I woke up sweating and scared for Grandma. She didn't see him at all, just kept dancing around in the girdle. I got up, pulled the thing from the garbage, and put it way down in the bottom of my dresser drawer.

On the second, fourth, and sixth days Mee Maw parked her car on the grass, leaving big ruts in the front yard even though Rebekha asked her to park in the driveway or at the curb. Mee Maw just said, "Oh dear, I'm so forgetful. Oh me."

On the fifth day, Mee Maw showed up for supper with a man she met while picking out peaches at the grocery. She giggled how her tater boiling man sure would be jealous if he knew she was making time with another man. The man she toted in was a hundred and fifty-two years old and smelled like mothballs and tobacco. He said, "This here's a fine woman you got here." He pinched Mee Maw on the rear.

Mee Maw giggled, then said, "You charmer."

I whispered to Jade how I was going to upchuck.

Jade whispered, "I wish I lived here. It's fun."

I looked at her as if she grew three more white-blond heads.

Rebekha served up supper that night with a big fake smile ripping her face. That old moldy man ate three pieces of chicken, two baked potatoes, and half a cherry pie—Micah wasn't happy since he didn't get enough to eat. After supper, the old guy and Mee Maw rocked on the porch together. Rebekha said it was like they were teenagers, but when she said that; she looked like she'd eaten a fat worm. After Mee Maw drove the man back home, Daddy told her never to do that again.

Mee Maw sniffed. "I miss a man's company. Your mother needs lovin' like everybody else." We kids tore out of the room before we heard anymore about Mee Maw and lovin'.

On her ninth day there, Mee Maw moved around the furniture while Rebekha took Bobby to a birthday party. Rebekha walked in the door, holding on to Bobby with one hand, her purse and keys in the other. Bobby said, "Look, Mommy! Mee Mawl's still here."

I was with Jade on the couch that used to be where the chair was with my feet on the bare floor where Rebekha's rug used to be. Andy sat on the floor where the coffee table used to be, playing Monopoly with Dan and Neil. Mee Maw sat on a chair—without its throw because Imper had thrown up on it—telling us stories. Like how a spider could crawl in people's ears while they slept and have babies until the brain filled up with tiny baby spiders crawling around and eating brains. And how some neighbor of hers chopped off her husband's private parts and threw them in his girl-friend's window screaming, *He's yours now, whore, here's your favorite part!*

Rebekha stood in the doorway, ready to spit fire. "What happened here?"

Mee Maw hightailed it to my room, her shoes leaving a trail of dirt from walking through Rebekha's flowerbeds to pick fresh flowers to put in her (my!) bedroom. Rebekha followed her in and shut the door. I heard her telling Mee Maw she'd had enough. Mee Maw said she was old and forgetful. And on it went like that.

Jade said, "My parents think y'all are insane."

Dan was all snarky-faced. "I like coming here."

Jade gave Dan a you-back-off-my-friend look. "I'm just saying what my parents said, not what I think. I like coming here more than you."

"Shut up, I'm trying to listen," I said.

Mee Maw's voice was whiney. "I told you I was sorry, what else do you want from me?"

"Respect. That's what I want, Laudine."

Finally, on the tenth day, the clouds cleared. I answered the ringing phone to hear, "Is my sweet purr-tater there?"

"Who?"

"My sweet purr-tater, Laudine."

"Oh. Hold on." I put the phone down and snickled. I hollered out. "Sweet Purr-tater, you have a phone call."

Mee Maw hightailed it into the living room and grabbed the phone from me.

I backed away.

"Hello, Sweet Meats. Hmmm mmm, yes." Mee Maw's toe was just a-tapping. "Well, they're acting like they need a sugar tit. Uh hum. Well, you hold onto your butter buns, I'm coming home."

I almost did a jig.

She hung up the phone. "I knew he'd miss his Laudine. I knew it." She looked at me. "That's how you handle men, you listening?"

I thought it was a good thing Sweet Meats called Mee Maw back, since it looked like Rebekha was going to hog-tie Mee Maw and haul her back to Texas herself for all the trouble she stirred around.

Just a day later, on the eleventh day of Mee Maw, Imper, Mee Maw, and their mess were on their way back to Sweet Meats. Rebekha scrubbed doggie smells away, bought a new rug and throw, and we all let out a sigh. The storm was finally over.

Chapter 26
Will you adopted me, too, Mommy?
1970

Daddy called us all in the living room after supper. Rebekha was on the couch, her legs crossed at the ankles, Bobby on her lap. Daddy looked serious, so my stomach flipped around the pinto beans, rice, and cornbread, like the episode of *Our Gang* when Alfalfa ate too much and when the doctor x-rayed his belly, all the food was fighting.

"Kids, your momma has finally agreed to let Rebekha adopt you." Daddy sipped his tonic water with lemon, the only drink he'd had for three months. He and Rebekha were going to meetings. I watched him every day to make sure he didn't slip up.

Micah didn't look excited about it. "I'm too old to worry about this."

"You aren't. There are lots of legal issues to think about," Daddy said.

"This is something I've wanted for a long time." Rebekha looked at me. "I'm sorry; I know that this can be hurtful, too. But it would be an honor for me to be your mother legally."

"Don't you all want this?" Daddy could've been asking if we wanted a big bowl of ice cream.

"It sounds okay to me, I guess." I was thirteen,

too grown up to show them I was worried about who my momma was going to be.

"See, your sister is happy!" Daddy grinned.

"What about Momma? What's she got to say?" Andy asked.

"She's ready to sign the papers," Daddy said.

"I don't give a care what she thinks anyway," Andy said.

Daddy walked over to Andy and patted his head. "This will be good for all of us."

"If you say so, Dad." Micah began flipping through a *Mad Magazine*.

"I just want y'all to be happy and safe," Rebekha said. "I won't do it if all of you don't agree. It's not an easy decision for anyone."

"You all should appreciate the sacrifices Rebekha's made for you."

"It's not a sacrifice. Don't put it that way, Frederick." She straightened Bobby's collar then kissed his cheek.

Bobby said, "Will you adopted me, too, Mommy?"

"You're already my son, Bobby."

"This is what we need to do as a family. Be happy." Daddy left the room.

I wanted to follow him to make sure he didn't have bottles hidden somewhere.

"Y'all talk about it. You're old enough to make this decision together." Rebekha stood up and left the room with Bobby, who hollered out, "I want to stay with Andy."

"What should we do?" I scooted close to Micah.

Micah said, "I'll be gone as soon as I graduate high school. Why would I care who's my momma?"

"I care," Andy said. "I think Rebekha can be our momma. She's been taking care of us for a long time now."

"Yep, she has done that," Micah said.

"He said Momma was going to sign papers," I said.

Andy crossed his arms. "I'm going to let Rebekha adopt me. I don't give a goddam what you two do."

"Somebody needs to take care of things for you two. I'll be in New York and I can't take care of you both anymore."

"I've been taking care of myself," I said.

Andy said, "Me, too."

"Yeah, I guess you have." Micah looked out the window at the oak.

I felt bad, remembering how he took care of Andy and me when we were little. "I mean, me and Andy don't need to be taken care of like you had to do when we were little."

"That's right, it's better here than at Momma's," Andy said. "Won't see me back there."

"Me, neither," Micah said.

I thought to myself, that if Rebekha adopted us, we'd always have a place to go. No matter if Daddy took up to boozing again, if he left us, or if

Momma never saw us again. We'd have a home. Always. "I say we should do it."

"I do, too." Andy sat up straight and tall, his chin pointed. "Goddam right."

Micah flicked me on the ear with his thumb and finger. "Then let's do it, Veestor and Andy Bo-Bandy."

We marched into their room, caught them hugging, and after we rolled our eyes at them, we told them our decision. Daddy said Momma was flying down so she could talk to us about it herself. I stared at Daddy. I didn't know she'd be there to see how we were giving her away. My brain pinched.

"I'm so happy, y'all." Rebekha hugged each of us.

"I'll make the final arrangements then," Daddy said.

Someone knocked on my door. I said, "Come in."

Rebekha came in holding a cosmetics case. "Why, aren't you pretty, Virginia Kate."

I twirled to show off the loose A-line dress in a dark red with cream trim.

"I thought of you as soon as I saw it at Penney's."

"You look pretty, too."

"Thank you." Rebekha wore a navy suit and her hair was tucked neatly behind her ears. "I thought I could fix your hair, if you like."

"Yes, thank you." I sat on the bed

She opened the kit and took out some things. She then brushed out my hair, rubbed a dab of VO5 in it, and rolled the ends on big rollers. "We'll let that sit." From the case, Rebekha took a tube of lipstick. "What about some pink lipstick?"

"I'd like that other color instead, if that's okay."

She smiled and handed me the rose-colored lipstick.

I colored in my lips, then looked at myself in the hand mirror she held. There was my momma peeking out and I ignored it until I saw Grandma Faith, then I smiled.

Rebekha handed me a little white box. "These are for you."

Inside were silver earrings in the shape of flowers. "Oh! Thank you, Rebekha." I clipped them on and felt the pressure on my ears, a grown-up feeling.

"Silver looks good with your complexion."

We talked about Miss Darla while waiting for my hair to set. How she knew things and read signs. I didn't tell her about us knowing each other's thoughts, though.

Rebekha took out the curlers, brushed my hair into full waves.

I was ready for Momma.

Daddy was on the porch with the boys, his feet tapping over and over to match his fingers tapping over and over. It wore on my nerves. He was growing a beard and it made him look like the mysterious stranger in the movies that all the girls fall for until they figure out he's No Good.

Andy and Micah were pretend-punching each other. They both wore dark suits; Andy's already a bit dirty and wrinkled.

Bobby jumped on and off the bottom step, dressed in blue britches with a white shirt. He said about fifty-two times, "Watch me, Andy! Andy! Watch me."

Rebekha waved over Miss Darla and asked her to take our picture.

"You all look gorgeous." Miss Darla held the camera to her eye. "Say Whoopee, everyone."

Most of us said, "Whoopee!"

She gave the camera to Rebekha, walked over and handed me a small velvet bag. "This was mine when I was a young woman. It will look lovely with your earrings, too."

On a silver chain was a silver horse head with green jewel eyes. It opened like a locket and there was a folded slip of paper inside. "Oh, Miss Darla, thank you. It's so pretty." I pulled out the paper, but she put her hand over mine.

She said, "Read that later." She kept her hand on the necklace for a spell, then took it away. "Jimmy Dodd gave it to me."

I put back the paper and held the locket out to her. It was heavy in my hand. "I can't take it, Miss Darla. Not Jimmy Dodd's present to you."

"Yes, you can take it and you will. It's for a young woman, a young woman like you. I have other mementos."

I put it on, and it felt just right.

"After you read mine, you fold up your own wish and put it in there." She looked over at Rebekha. "I had signs this morning, you know."

"Signs?"

She put her hands in the pockets of her britches. "This morning two frogs were in my kitchen and I pricked my finger on a holly leaf. You'll be okay, just remember that."

I blinked a couple of times. "Okay, Miss Darla."

We all piled into Daddy's Ford and took off. He'd sold the Corvair long before to one of his students. Miss Darla waved and Sophia Loren jumped around her heels. I held myself still so I wouldn't wrinkle my dress. Micah was stiff, too, pulling at his tie. Andy looked as if he hadn't a care in the world. I remembered that Easter when we were on the way to church, Micah and I fussing about our clothes, and Andy up front with Momma and Daddy.

I had a loud roaring in my ears and a zillion dragonflies flying in my stomach.

We were at the lawyer's office fifteen minutes early, so we sat in the waiting room. A pretty woman with blond curls and a sweet face came to tell us it was time. She led us into a conference room with a big table. I saw myself upside down in it. The woman asked us to take a seat, then she squeezed Rebekha's shoulder before she left the room. I wondered if she felt sorry for Rebekha having to adopt all us kids at one whack. I remembered Momma saying how women didn't like to raise other women's kids. But Rebekha looked happy. Maybe Momma was wrong about that, maybe she was wrong about all kinds of things.

While we waited, our hands and arms smudged up the shininess of the table. I pictured Momma crying while she signed the papers to give us away and it made me want to lose all my breakfast. I could still change my mind, couldn't I? Did I want to?

A tall gray-haired man came in and said to Daddy, "Mrs. Markson is supposed to be here. She must be running late."

"Mrs. Markson?" Daddy asked.

"Let's see, says here Mrs. Katie Ivene Holms Carey Markson."

"Harold's last name is Wilkins." Daddy put both hands on the table, pressing hard.

"Just going by what it says here, Mr. Carey."

I looked around at what the man saw before he left the room. Andy swinging his feet and hitting the legs of the chair. Bobby whining that he wanted to be adopted, too. Micah was stuck on Mars. Daddy's mouth in a line.

Rebekha stared at a painting on the wall. "Isn't that Monet's *Garden at Vetheuil*?"

Micah turned to her with a surprised look. He got up, sat in the chair next to her, and they put their heads together to talk about the painting.

I kept myself in perfect posture, with my hands folded in my lap waiting for Momma and wondering if I'd change my mind. I felt like changing my mind. I changed my mind. *I'm sorry everyone, I changed my mind.*

But Momma didn't come.

Daddy stood up. "I'll call the hotel."

"I told you she didn't care," Micah said. "Besides, I bet she could've signed stuff in West Virginia. But she's got to make a show."

"And I don't care," Andy said.

"All this speculation isn't helping the stress." Daddy left the room.

While he was gone, we all were quiet, except Bobby. "Mommy, are we adopted yet? We'll go get ice cream like Daddy said? I can't wait to be adopted. Can you, 'Ginia Kay?"

I couldn't answer him. I had fifteen frogs stuffed in my throat.

"No, we're not adopted yet, Bobby." Rebekha didn't look happy like before.

When Daddy came back, he barely moved his lips when he said, "Katie is on her way back to West Virginia. She left a message at the hotel desk to tell us she changed her mind."

"What do you mean she's changed her mind?" Rebekha stood up fast, scraping her chair against the wood floor. "She said she wanted this. That it was the right thing for the children." One tear fell down Rebekha's cheek. Sometimes seeing one lonely tear is worse than seeing a whole flood of them. "I don't understand."

Daddy stood by the window, staring out at the Mississippi River. "I called Jonah to see if he'd heard anything. He said she called him to pick her up at the airport. She's not coming to see the children. She's not signing the papers. She changed her mind. That shouldn't be a surprise to any of us, I suppose."

I had let Momma get in my brain and jinx everything with my stupid thoughts.

The man came back in with sad eyes. "I'm sorry; you seem like such a nice family. But these things do happen."

I jinxed it, no matter what he said.

Nobody said anything else until we were in the car.

"I'm sure your mother is just confused." Rebekha helped Bobby into the front seat.

Bobby said, "We're not getting adopted?"

"Bobby, you're already my son."

"I wanna get adopted. We all 'supposed to be adopted today." Bobby wailed.

Andy stared ahead with his hands in his lap.

Micah said, "Figures she'd do something selfish like this."

Daddy drove out of the parking lot.

I let all the dizzy stuff whirl around in my head. I deserved to have a bad headache.

"Probably listened to Ruby, or this Markson." Daddy's hands tap tapped on the steering wheel.

Rebekha stared out of her window.

Micah said, "Momma is selfish. She'll never change."

"She just didn't want to give us away. It hurt her to do it," I said.

"Keep believing that." Micah rolled his eyes at me, then cracked his knuckles. "She's too busy running around being stupid to worry about having us brats around."

"Conversation about your mother is over." Daddy didn't listen to his own words, though, since he kept on about her. "I should have known she'd never let Rebekha adopt. I can't believe I let her dupe me."

"She doesn't mind giving me her children to raise though, does she?" Rebekha talked to her window. "She doesn't mind that, but she won't let me be their mother legally."

"Momma is crazy," Micah said. "She's a drunk, too, and everybody knows you can't trust drunks."

"That's quite enough, Micah," Daddy said.

"Talking about Momma gets Dad all fluster-blustered, doesn't it, Daddy-O?" Micah's eyes burned into the back of Daddy's head.

Rebekha sat up real straight and I felt sorry for the way her ears were like little seashells and the way her neck was long and sad.

"Micah, I said shut the hell up," Daddy said.

Micah stared at the back of Daddy's head with his chin stuck out as far as it would go. If he could've hit Daddy with it just by the force of sticking it out like that, he would've. "What's wrong, Dad? Am I hitting a nerve? Huh?"

Daddy pulled over, stopped the car, and turned around. "Get out of the car, Micah." Micah shrugged, pretending he wasn't scared. They got out and Daddy fussed, his hands moved up and down and around while he yammered hard at Micah. I heard, ". . . attitude has been appalling!"

Micah looked ready to spit chewed up nails and cannon balls at Daddy. He pointed inside the car, jabbing his finger. I heard him say, ". . . don't deserve her or anyone else . . ." Micah turned away from Daddy, got back in the car, and crossed his arms over his chest. He was breathing hard and his cheeks were high-colored red.

Daddy's shoulders dropped to the front and I thought he was going to fall forward on the ground. He rubbed his eyes, straightened up, and slipped back in the car. He said, "Let's go home. I'm so tired."

Bobby whined to Daddy. "You said we'd get ice cream. You said we'd get adopted and get ice cream."

Rebekha started up with shoulder-shaking sobs. I'd never seen her cry like that before.

Bobby put his hands on either side of her face. "Don't cry, Mommy. I don't want ice cream. I sorry."

Daddy said, "I'm sorry, Rebekha."

She didn't say a word.

At the house, Daddy parked and went inside. The rest of us stayed in the car, like if we kept ourselves still, some magic would happen to change things.

Micah leaned towards Rebekha. His face pulled down and his eyes were shiny. "Rebekha? I'm sorry."

She turned to him. "I know, Micah. I understand more than you think."

Bobby said, "Don't worry, I'll adopted everybody." He turned in his seat and grinned at me. I wished I could've hugged his squirmy little body right on the spot.

We climbed out of the car much slower than when we'd piled in. Miss Darla looked out her window, Sophia in her arms. I waved at her and she waved back, then she waved Sophia's paw. I trudged in and lay on my bed in my new clothes. I touched the necklace Miss Darla gave me and tried not to listen while Rebekha cried behind her bedroom door. I heard ice hitting glass. I sat up, my heart ready to bust right out and run out the room. But I couldn't get out of bed. I was too tired. I opened Miss Darla's locket and took out the slip of paper. I unrolled it and read, "Pieces of paper are not love, they're just pieces of paper."

I lay back down, fell asleep, and dreamed Momma pulled me away from Rebekha. Rebekha called out to me and I reached out for her while

Momma jerked and pulled me farther and farther away. Rebekha's voice sounded louder the farther I was away from her. I woke up to the real Rebekha standing over me, a plate with two lemon squares in her left hand. She sat next to me and put the plate between us. Without saying a word, we ate our treats.

When the last crumb was gone, she said, "Virginia Kate, I'm truly sorry for what happened today. I wanted it all to work out. But it doesn't change the way I feel about you, Andy, and Micah. I want you to believe that."

I put my hand on Miss Darla's locket. I believed her.

Late that night Micah came into my room. He sat on the bed. "I told Rebekha I was sorry again. I mean, I really like her."

"I jinxed it. It's all my fault."

"What're you talking about? You're the weirdest." He looked around the room. "Hey, it looks better in here without all that pink."

"I jinxed it. In my head I said I changed my mind about being adopted."

"Geez Veez, you can't change things just by thinking them. You ought to know *that* by now. If that were true, you'd be able to change bad things into good, too." He threw Fionadala at me, hitting me square in the face. "You still keep stupid stuffed animals?"

"What's it to you?" I stuck my tongue out at him, then said, "Did you really want to be adopted?"

"Doesn't matter. Momma won't ever let us go because she's too selfish."

"I guess."

"Don't let her get to you, Seestor."

"Why wouldn't she at least see us?"

"That's a good question, now isn't it?" He threw my new blue pillow in the air. "I was hoping everything would get straightened out before I leave." He hugged the pillow to his chest. "I want you and Andy to be okay so I won't have to worry over you."

"We'll be okay, Micah. I'll take care of Andy."

He flipped my hair, and then stood up. "You look too much like Momma."

"No I don't. I just look like me. And like Grandma Faith."

He stared at me. "Yeah, I guess you're like her, too." He turned to go. "Good night, sleep tight, don't let the bedbugs bite."

"Wait, Micah."

"What?"

"I'm sort a glad you're my brother."

"Like I care." But I saw by his face that he did.

Chapter 27
Then the phone rang
1971-72

It was a Wednesday morning, hotter than hot should be. I lay on my bed, kicked my feet back and forth, and read Micah's *Mad Magazine,* laughing at *Scenes We'd Like To See* and *Spy Vs. Spy.* I tossed the magazine aside and thought about the end of ninth grade, how I still hadn't kissed a boy, how Wayne ignored me when we passed in the halls, and how everything about school was stupid.

I stuck out like a piece of toast next to fresh Wonder Bread. Lots of the girls had blond hair, or forced it to be blond with cotton balls soaked in peroxide. Some wore leather headbands as if they thought they were real Indians or something. And they fried themselves in the hot Louisiana sun with baby oil and iodine, trying to get tans. There were some Cajun girls and black girls who were dark, but they stayed in their own groups. I didn't know what I was and nobody ever told me where my people came from so I could find my group.

I heard a glass shatter on the floor and Rebekha saying, "Dang it." I went to the kitchen and helped sweep up the glass. She smiled to show me she was thankful for the help, or maybe the company. I dumped the glass in the garbage. Then

I took to cleaning out the icebox. It didn't really need it, but since I was already in there, I made myself useful.

"What are you going to do with your summer?" Rebekha asked.

"Read, take photographs, stuff like that."

"Sounds like fun." She pulled pots and pans out of the cabinet, checking the bottoms to see if they needed scrubbing. "I'm increasing my work hours in the fall, now that Bobby's starting first grade." She stared into the pot as if it was a mirror.

I wondered what she saw when she looked at herself. I saw someone who more and more I thought of as a momma instead of just some woman taking care of us kids.

Since Momma had messed up the adoption, we'd all just gone along with our business. Micah took painting lessons, even though I thought he was better than his teacher. Andy had enough friends to make a football team. Bobby played kiddie baseball. And Daddy tried to go to his meetings, but didn't always.

I asked, "Maybe you could teach me how to cook better?"

"Oh! I'd love to. I have a huge collection of recipes we can start working on."

"Can you show me how to make good cornbread? I just can't get it right."

"Okay, how about we do some tonight? And we'll make okra and tomatoes to go with it." She hummed as she put the pots and pans back, and then got out her *River Road Recipes* cookbook. "Oh, and something good for dessert. This book has so many good recipes." She grinned at me, then said, "Let's meet back here at four and we'll get started." She looked happy, and I felt happy, too.

I sat on the porch with a sweet tea and watched Amy Campinelle and Mister Husband working in their yard. It never changed over at the Campinelle's and I liked how they were always the same. She huffed and puffed over and handed me a picture of her and Mister Husband at Gulf Shores, Alabama. "Look at us! Bathing beauties."

"That's a nice picture." I didn't laugh at their old-fashioned suits.

"Mrs. Portier . . . oh, shoot, I mean Engleson, anyway, she says to tell you hey. I'm just tickled over her new life." Her cheeks were cotton candy pink. "Rachel and Robin are cute as bugs on a flower. Spitting image of their parents. I'll give you a picture. I know how you like keeping track of things."

"Thanks." Things were as sweet and good as the tea I sipped.

"Where's your little white-haired friend? I need to feed that girl something, yeah."

"She's on vacation with her parents."

"And you didn't go?"

"Her parents don't like me much."

"Well, they're just stupid in the head." She wiped her forehead and said, "Whew." And then, "Okay, I'm off to get boiled crabs. Want some?"

"No, thank you." She jiggled on home, and I went in for a piece of fruit. I was trying to lose five pounds, but it kept finding me over and over.

Bobby was in the kitchen, his bat and glove grown as part of his body since he was never without them. He wore baggy shorts that made him look like one of those kids on *Our Gang Little Rascals* from the *Buckskin Bill Show*. His dark auburn hair stuck up with sweat and he had dirt all over his face and in the creases of his neck. "What're you doing, Meestor Seestor?"

"None of your bees-wax." I grabbed an orange from the fruit bowl.

Bobby puffed out his chest and his ribs poked through the thin t-shirt. Skinny, just like Micah and Andy. "Stump and I are going to play baseball, wanna come?"

I threw orange peel at him. "Why should I?"

"Stump's brother Wayne will be there."

"Why should I care?"

"I dunno." He grinned like he did. He peeled a banana and ate half of it in one bite, talking with his mouth full. "We're going over to the lake." He opened his mouth, showed me the half-eaten fruit, and laughed when I made a face.

"I'm bored so I'll go, but don't embarrass me." I went to my room and brushed my hair. I almost put it in a ponytail, but changed my mind. Bobby peeked in and made high fashion model poses until I threw my brush at him. He ran out laughing. I checked my shorts and t-shirt to make sure they didn't have holes or stains. I cleaned my teeth and puffed on the spicy powder, sad that it was almost gone. I pretended I wasn't doing any of that for any reason. I headed out, first hollering at Rebekha that I'd be back at four.

At the lake, which wasn't a real lake, but a man-made very large pond, Bobby and Stump were already playing catch with Wayne. I felt weird, like I didn't belong since I was a girl. I felt like I had something to prove.

Bobby threw the baseball to Stump, then Stump threw to his brother. Stump got his name because the pinkie finger on his left hand was half gone. Bobby said he'd held onto a lit firecracker a bit too long. Stump was so cute; I had to ruffle his hair every time I saw him.

Bobby tossed a glove to me like I wasn't a girl and that made me feel good.

I slid my eyes over to Wayne. Noticed how his shoulders were wider, his blue jean britches were filled, he didn't have on his glasses, and when he walked, I thought about a rooster in a hen house. But I pretended I didn't notice. He burned his half-closed eyes into me. "Hey, Virginia Kate. You sure look foxy in those shorts."

Bobby and Stump laughed like crazy hyenas.

I punched into my glove.

Bobby threw to me first, and I threw to Stump so Wayne wouldn't know I really wanted to throw to him. Bobby and Stump chattered about baseball players.

Wayne said, "Shut up and throw the ball, ugly baboon idjuts." He looked over at me to see if I noticed how manly he was.

I threw the ball hard as I could to Wayne, hoping it hurt when he caught it.

"Wow, that's a good throw. He almost couldn't catch it," Bobby said.

"Yeah, haha, Wayne," Stump said.

Wayne pointed his finger at his brother. "You need to shut your trap." He tossed back his longish hair like a girl.

"My brother's breath stinks. And he has a rash on his penis." Stump hollered that so loud a lady and her kids turned to look.

"You little fuck." Wayne ran over to Stump, who ran behind me. "Yeah, hide behind a girl, fuck-face. I oughta tear the rest of your fingers off."

"Leave him alone, Wayne. He's just a kid." I smoothed Stump's hair and he grinned all sappy. "He's your little brother."

Wayne backed up, gave me a smarky smile, and winked.

I decided I didn't like winkers. Winkers were silly. Did winkers think they could just wink and I'd think they were cute, even when they treated little kids like that? I decided I was tired of playing ball with Wayne.

"See if you can catch this, Wayney-poo." I threw the ball to him hard, high, and a little to the right, laughing to myself when he almost fell down trying to jump up and catch it. He stood with his hands on his hips giving me a You-stupid-girl look when it landed in the water. I said, "I'll just relax in the shade while you get the ball, Wayne." I flopped myself under the cypress and studied my toes, wondering how polish would look on them.

He took off in a hissy huff, his tight britches and boots looking silly, wearing them in the heat with no sense.

I heard Stump ask, "I thought you said your sister liked my brother."

Bobby said, "Stupid-breath, she's a *girl.*"

Stump nodded like it all made sense to him. "My brother is stoooopid. He hollers at Mom and me all the time."

"He hollers at your mom? Why? She's nice," Bobby said.

"He thinks he's so smart just because he's going to play football and be a journalist."

They plopped down by me under the cypress tree. We watched the lady and her kids throw bread to the ducks and geese. Bobby and Stump chattered about green boogers and I was just about to leave when Andy showed up on his bike holding onto something with a long colorful tail.

"Goddamn! Look what I made!" He jumped off his bike. "Come see, y'all." He held up a kite he made out of the comics, some sticks, and a tail made out of old fabric scraps. The boys oohed and aahed over it.

I said, "That's pretty good, Andy."

"Well, let's see if it flies." He took off running, his tenny shoes kicking up grass behind him. Bobby and Stump ran with him, laughing their fool heads off. When they came back, Andy said, "You try it, Seestor."

"Yeah, Seeeeestor." Bobby laughed. "She's a seestor, meestor." Stump laughed too and I noticed for the first time he had a little bruise under his eye.

We all took turns flying the kite. I wished Micah were there. He'd like to see the color flying in the sky. The four of us kicked off our shoes, and then chased each other around until our feet, knees, and the seats of our britches were green from the grass that had just been mowed that day.

I dropped to my back under the cypress, staring up at the clouds. Stump and Bobby dropped down and searched for four-leaf clovers. Andy did a couple of cartwheels just to show off, then sat beside me, and we thumb wrestled.

There was the smell of fish in the lake. The sound of the geese and ducks begging for bread while the lady's children screeched with their happy. A red-winged blackbird shrieked in the cypress next to us. Our sweat dripped while we lay around in the sweet-smelling grass. The cypress trees sighed when the wind went through their leaves. Everything felt right and good. Andy's face said the same thing. Like the sad shadows had lifted right out of our eyes and left things clear and new.

Andy said, "Seestor, your hair's got grass and stuff all in it."

Bobby said, all proud, "Seestor, you got a dirty face. You don't even look like a girl."

Stump said, "I wish I had a seestor."

We began walking, singing the song about a levee that had a Chevy in it. For the zillionth time, Andy told the story about how Rebekha killed the snake and said shitting bastards. I felt like everything was opening up like a sunflower bloom. The boys ran off to the canal even though they weren't supposed to, and I walked home. I checked the mail for a letter from Jade, nothing, and then went to the icebox for a coke. Rebekha had ingredients lined up on the counter and that made me smile. It was all lazy summer normal and good.

Then the phone rang.

Rebekha answered, and after she hung up, came to me with a look of trouble. "Sit with me, Hon."

"What's wrong?"

"It's your momma."

"What does *she* want? Like I care." I was all wound up with how she'd be crying boo hoo hoo, while I said, "Tough, Toots. So long." I saw the mountains making shadows over the house, over

Momma. She was disappearing away away under that shadow. I blinked it away, said, "She thinks she can just call here after all this time." My lower lip pooched out all the way to West Virginia.

Rebekha was at the sink pouring two glasses of water. She sat down and gulped half of hers. She said, "Your mother was in an accident." She took another gulp. All my mad feelings at my momma flew away. Rebekha stared at her glass, and then went on, "Your aunt Ruby lost control of the car." She reached out to hold my hand. "Ruby died and—"

"—and Momma?" I breathed in and out, keeping my eyes on Rebekha. The room was still—the whole world was waiting with me to know.

"She's alive, but she's badly hurt."

"How bad?"

More sipping of water. Rebekha's hands were shaking. "She asked for you. She wants you to come."

I looked down at my hands. They weren't twitching, but my stomach was boiling over like a big pot of gumbo. Momma was hurt and she asked for me. She was thinking of me. It made me mad how easy I was taken in by her again. How easy it was for me to want Momma to want me again.

"That was your Uncle Jonah. He wants you to fly to West Virginia."

I couldn't look at Rebekha. I was afraid she'd see it. See the silly girl who still wanted her momma.

"To see your mother." She drank the rest of the water in a few throat-bobbing gulps, then said, "And for Ruby's memorial."

"To see my momma."

"Do you want to go? If you don't, just tell me." She took a deep breath and let it out slow. "But I think you should go see her."

I had a funny thought, wondering if Rebekha loved me as a blood momma loves a blood daughter. A voice swam in my head like little fishes darting around—but how does a momma love anyway? How did my momma love my brothers and me? My head hurt with it all. I stood and looked out the kitchen window. Miss Darla was in her back yard, watering flowers. "What about Micah and Andy?"

"Of course they will go."

"Did she ask for them, or just me?"

"All of you."

My lips felt all stiffed up and hard. "She wants us all back."

"You can tell your brothers yourself if you like, or I could for you."

"I'll do it. But Micah won't go."

"I'm sure he will," she said.

"He won't. Unless he wants to see Aunt Ruby dead."

"Virginia Kate!"

"She deserved it!"

"No one deserves that." She rubbed her forehead.

"Your Uncle Jonah will meet y'all at the airport. You'll stay with him and your aunt Billie." She came to me and stroked my hair. "He's a good man. Y'all will be okay." She looked me in the eye. "You will, won't you?"

I nodded.

"I guess you should get some things together. Do you need my help?"

I shook my head, and then went to my room to pack. I piled clothes on my bed. A skirt, a dress, three shirts, two t-shirts, a pair of blue jeans, a pair of cotton britches, two shorts, boots, flip flops, tenny shoes, underwear, socks, and two extra bras.

Digging into the dresser for my diary I found something wadded up in the corner. It was the girdle. I had forgotten all about it. Forgotten how Rebekha came in the room and we'd talked, our knees almost touching. I stared at the thing, wondering why I'd kept it. I locked my door, took off my shorts, stepped into the legs of it, and hopped over to lay on my bed. I pulled as hard as I could until somehow I was stuffed into it. It cut off my blood and I felt trapped. I grabbed on it and tried to pull it off but it had melted right on me.

I pulled until it hurt. I rolled off the bed, teeter-stepped over to open the door, and hollered for Rebekha. When she came in the room, her eyes crinkled as if she wanted to laugh, but she didn't. "Help me get this off, Rebekha."

"Well, let's see." She grabbed the top and pulled,

grunting like a wrestler. She tried rolling it down from the top until she had it part way over my hips. It just sat there rolled and tight. "Hon, how in the world did you get this thing on?"

I grunted and pulled.

She looked around the room. "Maybe some of this powder." She got the amber powder holder and took out the puff, dabbing the powder over my hips and legs. The sweet-spicy smell took up the whole room. "Okay, lie back on the bed and suck in with everything you have."

I sucked in until I thought I would bust my gut. She was finally able to work that thing off me. Then she busted out laughing. I sat up and stared at her, until I busted out laughing, too. We both laughed so hard we fell back on the bed, holding onto our stomachs as if we were full of stupid and it was running out all over. After a while, I didn't know if I was laughing or crying, sometimes they look and feel the same. They do.

I put my shorts back on while Rebekha kept snickering. She said, "Mee Maw. Remember that visit? And that smelly man she brought?"

"Eyew. I remember."

"And that dog of hers."

"Imperial the King Dog of the Land." I giggled; it felt good to giggle, like other girls did.

Rebekha stood, looked down at my packed things. "Oh. You're taking two suitcases."

"I didn't know what to bring. It's just in case. I

wasn't sure how long. You know?" I couldn't look at her standing there with powder all over her. With her mouth still like it was laughing, before it had a chance to pull down into a frown.

"Of course you need plenty of things. Just in case you take the summer." She smiled too big, then said, "Well, your plane leaves in the morning, early. We can still cook together, if you want."

"I want to."

She left the room. I sat on my bed and stared at the suitcases. The blue and white plaid one from Rebekha. And the ugly one I'd come to Louisiana with.

Later, I told Andy, while he and Bobby were playing Chinese Checkers in Andy-and-Bobby's room.

Bobby said, "I wanna go with Andy."

"No, Bobby, I'm sorry, you can't," I said.

"Why not?" He sulled up.

"Our momma isn't your momma," Andy said.

"So? My mom wasn't yours and then she was, so why couldn't your mom wasn't and then was?" Bobby crossed his arms over his chest. "I wanna go with Andy."

Andy threw a marble at Bobby. "Hey, little brother, listen up."

Bobby kept his body stiff but turned his eyes on Andy.

"I wish you could go, but you can't. I can't

explain it. But, believe me. You wouldn't want to go to that goddamn place."

Bobby ran off with his face twisted up sad.

"I'm staying here anyway," Andy said.

"I can't go by myself."

"Why not? Why should I care to go? You go right on and tell me why, Sister?"

I didn't know. "Well, Micah won't go, so I'll be alone. Please, Andy."

Andy's shoulders drooped. "For you, but not for Momma." He jumped up and loped off.

When Micah came home, I was rocking on the porch waiting for him.

"Hey." He sat in the other chair, his long legs stretched out in front of him. "If you don't quit looking like Momma, I'm going to freak."

"You quit looking like Daddy then."

He got up and stumbled around the porch. "How's that for Daddy?"

"Stop it. He's better now."

He laughed and flopped back in his rocker.

"Micah?"

"Yeah?" He pushed back his hair and rocked as if he didn't have a care, but I saw how his body was tight, how he never looked as if he didn't have a care.

"Momma was in an accident. She's in the hospital, but Aunt Ruby's dead."

Micah stopped rocking, but he didn't say anything.

"I'm going, so's Andy."

His face was like a blank page in my diary. "You aren't expecting me to go, now are you, Veestor?"

"Why not?" I pushed with my foot so I could rock fast enough to show I was tired of him being stupid about Momma.

"I told you once I got away from there I'd never go back."

"I thought that was kid's stuff."

"No, it's not kid's stuff." He stood up and walked to the edge of the porch. "Let's take a walk."

"A walk?"

"Yeah, one foot then the other."

We walked just as we did the day I came to Louisiana. Micah had his hands in his pockets, taking lopey giraffe steps. Then he said it right out before I was ready to hear it. "I killed Uncle Ar-vile."

I stopped in the middle of the street. A car full of pigs could've driven by and I wouldn't have gawked more. He grabbed my arm to keep me walking. I said, "What're you talking about?"

He didn't say anything for a while, then, "I get nightmares. I can't go back there." He rubbed his eyes, trying to wipe out a picture in them. "I pushed him. But, it was an accident, I swear."

I remembered all the sounds and smells of that day.

"He was . . ." Micah swallowed, his Adam's apple going way up and way down. "He was trying to hurt me."

"Like how?"

"Like . . . bad things, you know?"

I thought I might, but I wasn't sure.

He looked over at me. "Did he ever do anything bad to you?"

"No."

He squeezed my arm, hard. "You promise?"

"I promise. He didn't even like me."

He stared into my eyes, nodded, wiped his face with his shirt.

"What happened, Micah?"

"I ran up the ladder to the second level to get away from him. I was going to jump out the window, and then he was there, behind me. He had his nasty drunk breath on my neck." Micah's fists were clenched. "I turned around to push him away from me and he fell off and landed on the pole. It went right through him. I heard the squishy sounds and everything. I didn't know what to do, so I jumped out the window and hid in the woods. You came looking for me, and well, you know the rest." We were back at the house by the time he finished telling me. We sat in the front yard.

I pulled grass and made a pile with it. "I didn't know."

"Well, hell, I know that. I never told a soul. You think that's something I could ever tell anybody?" He speared me with his eyes. "You can't ever tell either." His lips set to quivering. "Promise me." He took me by the shoulders and squeezed.

"I won't tell. I promise." My heart jumped right

out and landed on my big brother. "It wasn't your fault, Micah. It wasn't."

"I was just a little kid." He put his face in his hands and pressed. "Sometimes I still see him, gurgling, blood spurting out."

I touched him on the arm. "He deserved it. Rebekha said people don't deserve things no matter what. But she's wrong. He deserved it. And you didn't do it on purpose. Just like you said, you were a little kid."

"I killed someone. Doesn't matter whether it was accidental or not. Doesn't matter if he deserved it or not. It's something I gotta live with."

I remembered the drawing of the man with holes all over him. "What about if you draw the bad feelings away."

He looked at me.

"I mean, when I snap pictures, I feel like I got control over things, I guess." I shrugged. I thought I sounded silly.

"That's smart, Vee." He looked up at the oak where a squirrel ran around the trunk chasing another squirrel. The squirrels were happy like I had been at the lake just a few hours ago. Micah went on, "I can't wait for next year, so I can go to New York. I'll never come back here, and I'll never go back there."

"Why not here?"

"I don't know, Vee. Daddy I guess. I'm afraid I'll turn out just like him."

"You're you, Micah. You can't be someone else since you're you."

"Aren't you ever afraid you'll be like Momma?" I couldn't answer him.

"Maybe I'll visit Louisiana. But there's no way in hell I'll ever be able to handle going back to West Virginia."

We both looked at the house. The lights were on and it was cozy, real and normal like in magazines. The squirrels were up high in the tree and we listened to them rustling around. It was getting dark and the cicadas were humming.

Rebekha came to the door and called us to come to supper. I felt bad I wasn't helping. "We're coming in a second, Rebekha," I said.

"Take your time." She went back inside.

I turned to see Miss Darla standing in her side yard with Sophia Loren. She was smiling, but it was a sad smile. I mind-said to her, "Miss Darla, I'm scared. Help me. I don't know what to do. Everything is confusing me."

Miss Darla mind-said, "Everything will work out how it is supposed to. You're strong."

Micah called out, "Hey, Miss Darla. What's shakin'?"

"Hey, Micah. You handsome devil, you." And they grinned at each other. She picked up Sophia and went back inside. He said, "That Miss Darla is an enigma. Something about her reminds me of Grandma Faith, but I can't put my finger on it. I'm going to paint her before I leave. Maybe I'll do a nude."

I made a disgust face, then asked, "Miss Darla's an enigma?"

"Yeah, like a mystery. Someone hard to figure out because they don't act like you expect them to. They're always doing the different thing."

"Sounds like Momma."

He looked hard at me. "Veestor, go to Momma to satisfy yourself she's okay, then come right back. Don't get whirly-brained ideas, you hear?"

I shrugged.

"You won't listen. Momma has you in her spell."

"You're silly, Micah."

He stood up, and then helped me up. I noticed how big his hand was, how tall and wide-shouldered he'd become. He was like my brother and like a stranger all at the same time. We brushed the grass off our backsides and went in the house. While I set the table, Micah joked around with Rebekha like nothing bad had been said. I didn't know if he felt lighter because he'd finally told somebody, or if he was faking it because he needed to. I felt dark wings flying through me.

Chapter 28
Today

Another cup of coffee is steaming, and I'm eating stale bread I toasted in Momma's old toaster, with peanut butter spread on it. Even though I didn't sleep long, it feels as if I slept a night away, floating on a cloud. The storm passed on away while I was under Grandma's quilt, and now the sun's shining bright through the kitchen window. I finish up my breakfast, and then walk outside, cross the spongy-from-rain grass, pass Mrs. Mendel's garden, and head to her door. It's time to go see her, but I'm scared about what she might say to me about Momma.

Uncle Jonah said Mrs. Mendel found Momma. Said Momma wore a red dress, and her hair was pulled up into a long ponytail like a young girl. She was curled up on the grass beside the garden. I'll never know what Momma was doing outside that night. Maybe howling at the moon, freed and happy for the first time in a while. I imagine her spirit lighter than the mists.

I bet she danced through the grass to Mrs. Mendel's garden to sniff the flowers. Flowers look special under the moon. She danced, just as I did earlier, with the moonlight shining on her red dressed up self, holding her vodka with lemon, twirling, dancing and laughing, until she lay down and went to sleep, and dreamed of what? The beginning of her life? Or the end?

Knocking on Mrs. Mendel's door, I look up at the lonely house on the hill, wondering if it's still empty. I think of Daddy there so long ago and wish I could pull him into a hug. Tell him I don't remember all those bad days so much as I remember that he's good. I like to conjure up what I need, and sometimes a girl needs her daddy.

When I came back to help Momma after her accident, I stared up there and imagined I could live there. Thought up what colors I'd paint and what I'd plant in my own garden. I thought I'd live there while Momma stayed in the holler. I'd look down and see her passing by the kitchen window, and then I'd go down and have coffee with her.

When no one answers my knock, I turn to go back. Mrs. Mendel had watched over us kids, even when we didn't know it. And she'd watched after Momma all these years. She was Momma's only friend. I hope Momma knew that.

Behind me, a male voice says all early morning bird chirpy, " 'Morning!"

I turn to see an almost handsome man with dark brown hair and hazel eyes walking to me. I answer, "Good Morning," and the frogs are back in my throat. "I was looking for Mrs. Mendel."

"My aunt's down the road at a morning tea, if you can imagine." He grins as if he can't imagine and his teeth are strong behind firm-looking lips.

He quick-walks closer to me and studies my face. "My name's Gary. I'm Anna's nephew."

He holds out his hand and I shake it firm before snatching my hand away. I don't know why I feel so ornery, maybe because Mrs. Mendel isn't home. Maybe because I don't want to talk to anyone, especially some grinning man. And maybe because I never knew she was called Anna. Maybe I want to stay in the past and he feels like the now. I squeak like a field mouse, "I'm Virginia Kate."

"I know." The corners of his eyes wrinkle up. "I heard a lot about you from my aunt. She has pictures of you and your brothers all over the house." He runs his hands through his hair. "When I visited years ago, I had the biggest crush on a photograph of you as a teenager. You'd just gone back home and my teenaged heart was broken. Never thought I'd get to meet the person immortalized in that silver frame." Big grinning again, he has no sense. "I live in North Carolina, smack in the Smokies." Even more grinning from him (fool grinning), then he says, "I'm staying here for a while to help my aunt with some things."

"Oh, well, I need to be getting back." I back away. "Tell her I came by to see her." I must look insane, with my hair wild and messy, my clothes wrinkled, no bath, haven't even brushed my teeth. I pretend I don't care. Men are nothing but trouble and heartache—messy silly creatures, that's what they are. That's what my grandma and momma found out. That's what I told my ex-husband. That's what my daddy always was, too. Trouble.

He acts as if he didn't hear a word I said. "Yep, like I said, I'm taking care of things for a little while. Have my own business so it leaves me free. So, if you need anything, just come get me." He points to his aunt's place. "Right there, if you need me."

"I'm fine. Momma died and I'm going through her things." I hate I said something personal to him. "I mean, I don't need anything, thanks."

"I'm sorry about Miss Kate. I knew, but I didn't want to pry. I was here when my aunt found her."

"Oh."

"Aunt Anna tried to get your momma out of the house, but she wouldn't leave it, at least until that night we found her." He pushes his hand through his hair again. "I'm sorry. I talk too much."

"She was in an accident when I was fifteen. She thought her looks changed. I don't know." I wave my hand in the air, brushing away invisible flies. It irritates me how I blabber to this person standing in my way of getting back. "She didn't like getting old and she didn't like losing her pretty. I suppose that was important." I shut my mouth tight, finally.

"She was a beautiful woman."

I nod.

"I don't know if you need to hear this, but she didn't look like she was in pain. I mean, well, she looked happy. Like she found some kind of peace or something. I know that's a cliché." He slides his eyes away from mine. "She looked angelic. The moon was shining on her face . . ." He turns red as Mrs. Anna Mendel's tomatoes. "At first, I thought it was her last night."

"Huh?"

"Dancing. Out under the moon." His eyes turn right back to mine and stay there until I look away.

"Yes. Well. I'll be getting on now. Thank you." Hightailing it back, I shut the door with an extra push. Standing at the counter I take deep breaths, pressing my shaking hands into the Formica. When I feel calm again, I make another cup of coffee and sneak a peek out the window. Gary is gone and I breathe out all my air long and slow. I push myself back, back to then, away from now. But the image of Momma sleeping in the grass, near Mrs. Anna Mendel's garden, the moon shining on her while she smiles, stays with me—as it will forever.

With my coffee, I go into Micah and Andy's room. I'm not surprised to see that nothing has changed here either. Their beds are still on opposite walls with their rootin' tootin' bedspreads. Momma left everything as if they were coming right back from playing outside any minute. Inside their dresser are clothes, too. It's pitiful.

I say, "Momma, why?"

She's in the other room, ornery as the live-long day is long.

I'm trying not to picture her wandering through the house, looking at our things, touching them, just as I am. Pretending we're about to gallop in, full of kid-energy.

Under Andy's bed, there's a cigar box shoved against the wall. When I open it, I find rocks, pulverized leaves, my letters, and photos. The one of Soot and Marco is on top. Breast cancer almost took my Soot away last year, as it had her momma. I feel the same catch in my heart over my old friend as I did when I was a girl. I loved her then, and I still do. Soot and Marco married, have two kids, and still work the diner. I put the photo in my pocket.

There's one of me on my red bike, my hair in pigtails, and another of Micah and me in front of the oak tree. There's a letter from Micah talking about Louisiana. One from Daddy asking him about school. Opening my letters to my brother, I read about how I miss him, miss my mountain. All the longings of a little girl who'd been taken away and didn't understand it. I look up and out the window at the silent shadows of things bigger than me, and wonder if I will always feel as if I've been snatched up by the roots.

Underneath everything are the Texas-shaped cufflinks Mee Maw gave Daddy. I roll them in my hands, remembering how Mee Maw filled up this house and the house in Louisiana with her craziness. She's a zillion years old and I don't believe she'll ever die.

I put Andy's things back in the box and leave it on his bed to take back with me to my room. Nothing is under Micah's bed and I'm disappointed. I want to find something interesting. I touch their dresser, tracing the scars of their scratched initials: MDC and ACC. I hear Andy and Micah laughing, talking about boy-things. It makes me smile. Uncle Jonah made their dresser, just as he made Momma's and mine. My uncle sanded the wood, ran his long fingers over the warmth the sandpaper made from his pressure. The smell of mahogany, maple, pine, and oak filled his workroom. So different from Uncle Ar-vile's stinky, ugly shed. I wish Uncle Jonah had been around that summer instead of Aunt Ruby. We'd have gone there instead. What would be different now if we had?

I step inside the closet, close the door, and at first the walls move in closer, closer, the light from the keyhole shining, then I close my eyes, and I want to be on Fionadala, thundering up the mountain, sweet air against my face. I open my eyes and step out.

There is a shelf to explore. Using Andy's stool, I stand on it and reach far in the back. A rolled-up piece of paper meets my hand. I take it down and as I unroll it, my stomach churns. Micah has drawn a demon-face, with sharp black horns, a red-black mouth with jagged blood-dripping teeth, and eyes that bulge under a Frankenstein forehead. The monster has a hole in his stomach, and maggots, flies, and green goo are climbing from it in a big snarly mess. Its clawed hands are stretched out to a boy drawn in the left corner. That little boy is holding himself in a tight ball, like a babe in the womb. The drawing leaves me shaken right to my toes.

I say to the teensy boy, "It's the opposite now, Micah. You're the giant and he's the little nothing in the ground."

I start to roll it back up, but then decide if I burn it, the smoke will go up to the sky and make healing rain fall down on Micah. I take the monster drawing back to the kitchen with me, wad it up, and throw it into the sink. With Momma's matches, I touch the red tip to the side, hear the scratch, and whoosh, smell the sulphur. I place flame to paper and watch the edges curl up and over. I watch the monster disappear, and when it's gone, I scrape the ashes into one of Momma's ashtrays and take it to the bathroom. Sprinkling the ashes in the toilet, I flush them down, down, all the way down.

I say, "Bye Bye Uncle Ar-vile. Go see Aunt Ruby, you sick bastard." I flush twice. Then I wash my hands of them both. That's all I can do.

I wander down the hall—I'm not planning anything at all. I have all the time in the world. I'm strolling in the breeze. I'm a wandering woman with my thoughts all up in my head willy nilly. I'd whistle if I didn't hate whistling more than liver. I'm in no big hurry. La Tee Dah.

I stop outside Momma's room and lay my cheek against the door. I don't feel a warming tingle. I don't go in. I'm a chicken-heart. Momma snorts and Grandma Faith sighs.

My bare feet make no sound as I back down the hall and return to the living room. Even though I'm quiet as a kitten, I hear other footsteps. And laughter. And yelling. The television has a black screen, but I hear all those old television shows. Laaassie—is there trouble girl? Trouble? Lucy you have some 'splaining to do! And, I hear the radio playing old bubblegum rock, and the sound of dancing—the air moving with the bodies. I hear the sounds of ice against glasses. Ghostly memories take shape and form, wavering.

Back to the kitchen to refresh my coffee, I stop and stare at the booze. They're so straight and tall on the counter. I open the tops and pour every stinky drop down the drain. The fumes rise up and hit my face with a slap, but I don't flinch.

I slap my hands together. Another job done. I eat another piece of toast. There's a strange resting coming over me so I almost feel like humming. It's as if someone's entered my body and is guiding me around the house, trying to coax me into Momma's room. I can feel it, the way my feet want to move back down the hall. I decide a bath with Momma's Dove soap would be just right instead.

I get clean underwear, shorts, and a t-shirt from my dresser, and go to the bathroom. I put the plug in the drain, turn the faucet to hear the squeak and the rush of water, remember Momma's drunken-cure-baths. I search the cabinets until I find a bar in the back, hidden behind some washrags. Momma's secret Dove stash. The chaotic cabinet full of multi-colored towels is still the same, and I grab a well-worn blue towel and faded pink washrag. They smell like sweet mountain air. I slip into the hot water and let the tense fall out. I let the worry slide off my skin, and then up in the air inside Dove bubbles, where they swirl up and out the window. I soap my hair, still too long for hot Louisiana, but not for the mountains, no sir-ree. When I rinse, the water covers my eyes.

When I'm clean, I let the rest of my worries and cares go right on down the drain. I towel off on the line-dried towel, put on my white t-shirt and red shorts. Momma's white robe hangs on the door. I take it from the hook and wear it over my clothes. It smells like Shalimar and cigarette smoke. I can't stop the feeling that comes over me. I don't want it, but it comes anyway. I can't stop the feeling of loving her and missing her. I can't stop the feeling of all the years we both were too damn full of orneriness to see each other. I get so sad, I think I'm going to lie on the bathroom floor and never get up.

I escape out to the side yard where the maple is,

where Gary can't see me. I've walked a trillion miles since my nap. Wandered over the entire earth, except the places I'm not ready for yet. I touch the leaves, lean against the trunk. Closing my eyes, I imagine Micah comes out to sling his arm over my shoulder to tell me interesting things. And, Andy swinging, saying, "Push me higher, Sister!" I look at Momma's closed window and see her curtains hiding what I don't want to see: her empty room, her empty bed, her empty vanity.

My mountain watches me and I feel as if I could get there in three steps, run all the way to the top. I'm flying right to the mists, the trees tickling my feet on the way up. I stand and face it, and the wind makes Momma's robe billow up and out from my body. Fionadala is beside me, nuzzling me up with her soft nose. We are airborne. My face is wet. It must be raining while the sun still shines. That's what it is, it's rain that makes my face so wet.

When I hear Gary calling, "Here kitty! Come on now!" I scurry back inside.

Grandma says, "Go in your Momma's room. Even if it's hard."

I hear Miss Darla, "Oh, our girl will do it." Good old Miss Darla.

Momma doesn't say anything. I don't either. I open more bags, more diaries, more memories, anything but Momma's door. That same door that was locked against me the last day I ever saw Momma.

Chapter 29
Don't seem right that kin are like strangers

I'd never flown in an airplane before. I was a bit jittery, but excited, too. I told Andy I bet I could open the window and walk right on the clouds without falling through them. He sat quiet as a cotton field with his comic books on his lap. I guess neither one of us felt like talking much, but I didn't feel like thinking on things either.

Things like Micah killing Uncle Arville, or would Momma still be living when I got to West Virginia, and what would Aunt Ruby look like dead. How I didn't get to say goodbye to Jade. She spent most her days in the summer dancing and getting skinnier and going on trips with her parents. How Rebekha looked when she waved goodbye to us, the way she tried not to cry. Seemed like everybody and everything crowded me up with worry and hurt to carry back to West Virginia.

Then, there was Daddy. He'd come in my room as if he'd just been minding his own business and all a sudden ended up there, like, "Hmmm, how did I get in Virginia Kate's room?" I let him stand quiet while I undid my braid. I knew he had something on his mind. I wasn't sure I wanted to hear it.

Finally, he'd said, "You going to be okay, Bug?"

I nodded.

"I should come with you." He looked over my head, his eyes shining like the moon.

"We'll be fine."

"I wonder if I should go." He wasn't listening to me, not one bit.

I stared at him until he looked me in the eyes. He turned away to fiddle with the comb and brush set Rebekha gave me, then opened the music box and watched the ballerina twirl. Daddy was quiet for so long, I felt itchy. Finally, he closed the box and spit out what was stuck in his craw. "I loved your mother, Bitty Bug."

I shrugged my shoulders, what did I care if he did or not, made no difference to me, wouldn't matter anyway.

"She was the most beautiful woman I'd ever met. You should have seen her," he said. "I went to her family's old shack with those kitchen supplies in hopes of working my way through college. And there she was."

I brushed out my braid.

"She came in and sat at the kitchen table, swinging her leg as if she didn't care I was there. She wasn't wearing any shoes on those dirty feet of hers. Hair so long and tangled. Oh, 'her infinite variety.'"

I stopped brushing. "Momma had dirty feet?"

"The dirt didn't hide what she had." He smiled secret, then said, "Your smart grandma invited me to dinner. I accepted and when I came back, your momma had washed off the dirt and wore a red dress. She was breathtaking."

Daddy was telling me the love story I'd been waiting to hear all my life. But I didn't feel happy hearing it then.

"She was wild as that mountain she lived on. I thought I could tame that wild girl. I shouldn't have done that, shouldn't have tried to change her." He took the brush from me. "This was your momma's, wasn't it?"

I stuck out my chin. "I stole it."

He sat down beside me. "I thought I saved your momma and that made me arrogant. I thought I had all the answers."

"Nobody has got all the answers."

Daddy smiled, then said, "You're growing up, aren't you?"

I didn't answer.

"Turn around." I did and he pulled the brush through my hair. "Your momma was smarter than she let on. She used to sneak and read my books. I don't know why she fought against things, against us."

I was afraid of things Daddy might say. What if he wanted to go back to Momma? Would we all go back? What would happen to Rebekha? The whirly-world went round and round and I didn't know where I'd get off.

He put down the brush and stood.

I heard sounds in the kitchen and then the smell of

popcorn. That smell made me feel safe and snuggly inside. I wanted to get off the merry go round right then and stay, but I knew I had things to do first, Momma things. "What about Rebekha, Daddy?"

He kissed me on the forehead and patted my back. I smelled Eau De Bourbon on his breath. "She's been good to you children. She's been great for me. I finished school and I have a decent job. We have this nice house. She's a good woman." He was already back in his Daddy-ness, jingling his keys in his pocket and rocking back and forth on his heels.

"Then how come you won't stop talking about Momma?"

Daddy turned and left the room.

Rebekha came to my door with a big bowl. The gap in her front teeth, her pale face and reddish hair, the way she held the popcorn as if she were giving me a gift made her beautiful to me in a way Momma never could be. "I made it just the way you like it, Virginia Kate."

I looked at Rebekha standing there and I had to love her; she needed it. And I needed it, too. "Thank you, Rebekha." And I meant lots of things in that thank you.

But I had a dark-haired devil on one shoulder and a strawberry blond-haired angel on the other and they were each whispering in my ears. Grandma Faith whispered, "Listen. Listen." But there were too many voices to listen to.

• • •

The plane landed. Andy and I went down the tunnel out into the West Virginia airport. A familiar-looking man walked up to us. "Virginia Kate? Andy?"

I nodded. Andy kept looking around at everything.

The man ran his hand through dark hair with bits of gray through it. "I haven't seen you since you was a baby, Virginia Kate." I liked how his eyes crinkled in the corners even when he didn't smile, and how his nose was a little crooked. I saw Momma in his face and knew he was Uncle Jonah. He tried to take Andy's suitcase, but Andy held on tight, as if it was keeping him from flying off again.

As we walked, Uncle Jonah yapped. "I'm glad you're staying with your aunt Billandra-Sue and me. Remember her Andy?" He looked over at Andy, but Andy watched the pilots walk by. Uncle Jonah went on, "Anyway, she's cooked a feast and got rooms for you fixed up. We're sure looking forward to your visit. Just wishing it was under different arrangements."

I gave him as much of a smile as I could.

"Aunt Billie's fit to be tied silly with having you children come to the house."

After we had my things, we climbed in his car and drove deep into the country to where they lived in a pretty valley, in a trailer made to look just like a cute little house. A German shepherd came running, and Uncle Jonah said, "That there is Kayla. She likes to bark, but she won't harm a hair. She's a good old dog, she is."

Uncle Jonah had talked all the way there, and he talked while we piled out of his car, talked while we petted Kayla, and he talked on the way to the front door. He swung around his hand, pointing to all the gardens. "Aunt Billie planted everything herself."

Aunt Billie herself came out the door, wiping her hands on an apron. She was a tall woman with salt-and-pepper curls. She ran right on up and hugged Andy. She said, "Andy! Been too too long. You've shot up like a weed." She cut her eyes to me and held out her right arm for me to be hugged, too. "And Virginia Kate. Oh, it don't seem right that kin are like strangers."

Her bones felt hard and strong.

Uncle Jonah stood with his hands in his pockets, grinning at everybody. But he wasn't fooling me, I saw how his eyes kept turning to a sad place. He said, "Well, you all go on in, I'll get the things out of the car."

Andy and I walked though their living room with our arms hanging down at our sides. There was a pot-bellied stove fireplace, a horse-blanket rug, and furniture made of logs, leather, and soft-looking material. Cabinets were filled up with tiny glass and porcelain figures—ballerinas, birds, and lots of clowns. Aunt Billie took us down the hall. "This is your room, Virginia Kate, and Andy, your room is acrost from hers." She opened my door and I went inside. Aunt Billie stood in the doorway. "Make yourself at home." She closed the door.

The bed had a green cotton bedspread with four dolls in fancy dresses leaning against the pillows. There were two rag dolls on the chair, and a Barbie doll on the chest of drawers. The dolls stared at me as if they wondered what I was doing in their room. Uncle Jonah knocked, came in and put down my bags, giving me a big grin before he left. I went to the window and looked at mountains, brothers and sisters of my mountain.

I was back.

After I unpacked, I went to Andy's room. He'd dumped the things from his suitcase into the chest of drawers, shoving everything in and then closing the drawer with clothes still sticking out.

"Nice room, Andy."

He shrugged and sat on the bed with its dark blue bedspread. On the table beside the bed were carved animal figures. Andy picked up a dog and stroked it.

Aunt Billie stuck in her head. "I hope you both like your rooms. Those are Pooter-Boy's comic books, Andy, but you can have them. I thought he'd stay here, but he likes where he's been living at." She didn't say where that was and I didn't ask her. "I've made us a snack. Come on to the kitchen, kids."

We ate peanut butter and Ritz crackers with creek-cold sweet milk. Uncle Jonah told stories about bears and blasty winters, and how a man froze while riding a frozen horse trying to get away from a frozen bear.

"It don't get that cold, Jonah. You're being silly. I'm sure they remember the winters here."

"Now, woman, you let me tell my stories."

She swatted his arm and stood. "You two can go outside if you like, or if you need to, you rest a little while. We'll be heading to the hospital, directly."

"I'm going out to the workshop." Uncle Jonah stood and kissed Aunt Billie on the cheek, and went out the back door.

Andy left the room, too. I thought how men were always hightailing it out the door when there were dishes to be done.

I picked up our dishes, even though Aunt Billie said I didn't have to, and took them to the sink.

Aunt Billie poured in soap. "The woman that's raising you's doing a good job."

Sticking my hands in the hot water, I stared out the window at all the flowers—yellow, white, and pink.

Aunt Billie took the plate I handed her. "Sometimes life is vexing, isn't it?"

I nodded.

"I'm sorry about your momma and your aunt. Must be hard for you kids."

I swooshed the dishrag into the glass and thought

again about Aunt Ruby dead. "How'd it happen, Aunt Billie?"

"Oh, dear. Well, I don't rightly know."

I gave her a I'm-a-big-girl-now look.

"Well, then, I'm going to be honest, because that's how I am. Your uncle says I have a big mouth." She sat back down at the table and pointed to a chair across from her. "I'll tell you what I know." She waited for me to settle in, then began. "Your momma and that Ruby were out drinking. Ruby always did get your momma in trouble. Jonah tried to tell Katie, but she'd get that mule-gonna-kick look on her face." Aunt Billie sighed, then said, "Ruby lost control of the car, slid off the road, and went over the edge. They tumbled a few times before stopping at the bottom." She ran her hand through her curls. "Your aunt Ruby was torn to pieces. She was throwed part-a-ways out the window but was still part-a-ways inside. Your momma was throwed around inside the car, but someone was watching over your momma that day, I believe it."

I pictured Momma being scared and it made me feel scared.

Aunt Billie tapped her fingernail on the table. "Well, some soul saw the accident and stopped to help, got the police called. Your aunt was gone by then. But, like I said, your momma had an angel with her that helped keep her right alive." She fiddled with the salt and pepper shakers.

"They won't even have no funeral with no casket! Your aunt Ruby got cremated and wants her ashes on Arville's grave. She just copied off your momma, since your momma always says she don't want to be in no ground where the worms can get her."

I sucked in my breath.

"Oh, child, I'm sorry!" She put her hand across the table and patted mine. "There I go rambling like a fool. Maybe your uncle Jonah is right, I got a big fat mouth."

"I wanted to know, Aunt Billie."

"Well, I'm glad you got that Rebekha. A woman who raises another woman's children with a goodly heart is special. Especially if she treats them like her own. She treats you all good, don't she?" Aunt Billie raised up both eyebrows. "Cause if she's one of those mean ones, I'll have something to say." She took her hand away and pushed back a curl that kept falling across her forehead.

I felt proud, like Rebekha was standing there, tall. "She's good to all of us."

"Well, I had to ask. Did I tell you I have a big fat running off mouth?" She smiled at me and her eyes were all twinkly.

We sat quiet then. I heard Andy bumping around in his room. I had a sudden sly thought. "Aunt Billie? I got to ask for something."

"Sure. You need anything, I'm here."

"Can I have a bit of Aunt Ruby's ashes? I don't think Andy and me can go to the service. It'll be hard."

"I don't see why you can't have a bit. And, you two don't got to go. Not after all you been through, poor children." She stood up. "I need a nap. Take one yourself if you care to, or you can go look at our horses."

"You have horses?" If my heart could have come out of my chest, Aunt Billie would have seen it pumped up with horse love.

"Yep, up on the hill. We just couldn't bear to leave them at the farm." She leaned over and kissed the top of my head, then said, "You're a good girl."

If she knew why I wanted the ashes, she might not think I was so good.

I went to my room, took off my shoes, and in my bare feet, went to Andy's door and knocked. "Andy? You okay?"

"Yeah."

"Andy?"

"Go 'way."

"If you need me—"

"Goddamn, I don't need a thing."

I went outside and peeked in on Uncle Jonah. He was sanding a piece of wood, his hand rubbing over it after a couple of swipes. The wood could have been an animal he was petting, he did it so soft and sure. The workshop smelled clean. I wanted to walk in and watch him awhile, but his face was too sad so I left him alone.

I walked up the side of the hill behind the workshop, and there grazed a Pinto and a Tennessee Walker. I had to force myself to walk up slow and quiet so they wouldn't be scared. As I petted them, they nuzzled my shirt for treats. I'd be sure and ask Aunt Billie for some carrots or apples.

It was so peaceful, I stood under a weeping willow tree to watch the horses, listen to their huffing and munching. I let all the worries fly away into the wind. The branches of the willow were like a curtain, left me feeling all secret and away from the rest of the world. The breeze lifted the willow branches and my hair, and they mixed together where I was a part of the tree and the tree was part of me. The air smelled clean, different from Louisiana's wet-earth-moldy smells. I squatted down, leaned back against the trunk of the tree, and closed my eyes.

I dreamed I was riding the pretty Pinto. Her mane and my hair flew out behind us. I saw Momma standing at the edge of the mountain, hollering at me, her mouth just a-going, but her words were carried away by the wind. I galloped towards her, pushing the horse hard. Momma's black hair blew in the wind as she waved at me to come to her, and then, just like that, she stepped back and was gone. I screamed at her and woke up to the Pinto nuzzling me.

I stayed with the horses until I heard Aunt Billie calling me back to eat.

At supper nobody did much talking, and that was fine by me. All I thought about was what I would say to Momma when I saw her and what she'd say to me. Even Uncle Jonah didn't blabber on, and like Andy did, he pushed his food around on his plate. I guess we girls knew we needed to eat to keep our strength up to do all those dishes, since Aunt Billie and I ate lots.

After the kitchen was cleaned up, we all climbed into the Chevrolet and headed out to the hospital—to Momma. Andy and I sat in the backseat. I stretched out my hand to hold onto Andy's, and he let me. As we drove through town, I tried to remember things, to see if they were the same or changed, but I couldn't tell.

At the hospital Uncle Jonah parked the car, looked in the rearview at us. "We're here, kiddos."

I saw my rubber-smile in the mirror.

Andy studied his knees.

I had to ask what had been stuck in my craw ever since I'd heard Daddy tell Rebekha about it. I was full to the top with people not telling me things I needed to know. I asked, "Is our brother or sister up there with Momma?"

Uncle Jonah turned to look at me. "Who?"

"Momma's baby she had with Harold."

Uncle Jonah looked over at Aunt Billie, his hand still resting on the car door handle.

Aunt Billie said, "There weren't no baby. Your momma made it up so Harold would stay with her. It didn't work that way, though."

Uncle Jonah rubbed the steering wheel with his other hand. "It was tragical. He just ran off and left her alone." He swiped his face. "Even when she told him there really wasn't no baby, he still left."

I pictured Momma swigging from the bottle, wailing up a river over Harold.

"He wasn't a good man," Aunt Billie said.

"She missed you kids. She wanted to marry him so she could bring you all back," Uncle Jonah said.

"Yeah right," Andy said.

"Who knows what your momma wanted. She went here, there, and yonder with what she wanted. Changed with the wind." Aunt Billie shook her head.

Uncle Jonah opened the car door, but he didn't get out.

Andy clenched fists. "I bet there was a baby and she killed it to keep Hairy-old around."

My stomach ferris wheeled—fast, round and round.

Aunt Billie said, "Don't say that, Andy."

Andy turned to look out the window.

Uncle Jonah sounded as if he swallowed a whole cow and choked up on it. "Your momma was such a sweet little girl." He swallowed, said, "We all left our own momma, your grandma Faith, too soon, cause we had to get away from Papa. Poor Ruby just got meaner and drunker, like Papa. And your momma didn't like to think about things, so she took to the drink, too. I was lucky, I found my special girl." He reached and squeezed Aunt Billie's arm. "Your uncle Hank don't even know about his sisters' accident. He run off in the woods after Papa beat him bloody and he never come back. And poor little Ben just couldn't take things. One by one we all left our poor Momma to Papa's meanness." His shoulders fell forward. "You got to understand things, is all."

I looked at Andy and he was watching Uncle Jonah.

Aunt Billie turned to us. "Your grandpa was a mean old bastard. But, my Jonah is a good man. He just couldn't take it." She lifted her chin. "So he left and now he feels bad about it. And he shouldn't."

Uncle Jonah cleared his throat, said, "Kids, sometimes life hands over bad things. That's the way of the world, always has been. I know your momma loved you, even if she didn't always do the right thing." He put his left leg out of the car. "Now, let's get on up there before visiting hours is over."

We hobbled out of the car as if our legs were made of rubber bands. In the hospital, we rode the elevator to the second floor. Our shoes made loud squeaks down the halls. I wore a black skirt, white blouse, and black boots. I had brushed my hair until it was shiny. I had the rose lipstick Rebekha gave me, and fingernail polish to match. I was ready for Momma. Andy wore jeans and a t-shirt with black tenny shoes. The toe of his shoe was worn and it looked sad. We stopped at the door of room 226.

Uncle Jonah said, "She's bad off. You kids best be ready."

We walked into the room.

It was too cold. There was one light shining over the bed. I stood at the end and stared at the lump with all the tubes sticking out. Its face was swollen, black and blue, with a bandaged foot stuck out from under the covers. I stared at its foot so I wouldn't have to look at its face. "Are we in the right room?" I asked.

"Yes," Uncle Jonah answered.

I took up my courage and eased closer. I felt Andy's breath on my hair. The woman in the bed had a bandage on her head, there were cuts and bruises covering her arms, and at first, I thought her lips were scraped off, but it was the swelling that made it seem that way.

I turned to say something to Andy, but he was bent over as if he was kicked in the stomach.

Aunt Billie patted him, saying, "There there now, there now child."

He said, "I told you I didn't want to come. I told you."

I couldn't say anything to my brother. He was

right. I grabbed hold of his hand and took him away from Momma. Aunt Billie and Uncle Jonah were behind us.

Once outside, Uncle Jonah leaned against the wall.

"Is she going to die?" Andy looked five years old instead of thirteen. "Well, I don't goddamn care!"

"Andy, of course you'd care about your momma." Aunt Billie rubbed his back. "No matter what, we care about our mommas and we always will."

"I know how strong-willed my sister is. The doctors say she was lucky."

Andy wiped his eyes, then pulled a pointy chin. I knew then that he was back to Louisiana Andy. "She don't look the same, but she's the same inside, I bet."

"Hush, child," Aunt Billie said.

We stood there looking like a pitiful bunch. But I knew I had to go back in and see her. I had to. I did. "I want to see Momma alone, okay?"

Uncle Jonah nodded.

I went in and shut the door. I touched the hospital blanket, tugging on it a little, not ready to touch her. I said, "It's me, Virginia Kate." The cold air of the room hugged on me and I didn't like it. Grandma Faith whispered to me, but I still didn't understand her. My teeth clickity-clacked. I stayed there until it was time to go. Andy never came back in the room.

After we were back to Uncle Jonah's, I went straight to bed. Kayla followed me, her nails clicking on the floor, and she lay by the side of my bed. I leaned and petted her throughout the night.

The next day, before Aunt Ruby's services, Aunt Billie gave me a paper sack with some of my aunt's ashes. She said, "I know what I'd do with them remains. I surely do." She nodded once and left my room.

After my aunt and uncle left, I closed myself up in the bathroom with the sack of ashes. I upended the whole mess of Aunt Ruby into the toilet. Some of her floated, and some of her sank down. I flushed her, watched Aunt Ruby swirl around and around before she disappeared. I flushed twice more to be sure. Down, down she went into the nasty old sewers of West Virginia.

Chapter 30
Why are you here, Virginia Kate?

When I wasn't visiting Momma, I fed the horses sugar cubes, apples, and carrots. They'd whinny when they saw me, running up and sticking their noses in my shirt pockets. The Pinto was Starlight, and the Tennessee Walker was Big Fella. Uncle Jonah taught me how to saddle and bridle, brush and feed them, and promised I could ride soon as I learned. I couldn't wait to tell Rebekha, but then I felt weird thinking about her when Momma was so tore up and pitiful.

But, when Momma woke up and took to eating food, Uncle Jonah said we didn't have to worry so much anymore. He threw a blanket over Starlight's back and then the saddle. I showed him I could cinch the straps nice and snug. Next, the bit went into Starlight's mouth as I pulled the leather over her head and strapped on the bridle.

I put my foot in the stirrup, eased myself up, and sat tall in the saddle, just as Uncle Jonah taught me. I knew how to work the reins, keeping them firm, but not too tight.

He said, "Good job, Virginia Kate."

I was grinning so big I thought my face would split apart. Andy came out and watched with his arms crossed over his chest.

"Now, remember how the horse's mouth is tender, so don't pull in too hard," Uncle Jonah said.

I remembered everything. I pushed in with my legs, giving Starlight just a tiny kick with my heels. She walked around in a circle, while I felt on top of the world. I came to a stop in front of Andy, Uncle Jonah, and Big Fella. I never wanted to get down. It was almost as good as riding Fionadala.

"You done it real good," Uncle Jonah said.

Andy pushed his face into the side of Big Fella and breathed in.

"That's a fine horse, Andy. Gentle as a summer rain."

"I like the way horses smell," Andy said.

Uncle Jonah and I said together, "Me, too."

Andy said, "Does he mind having all this on him?"

"Well, Andy, I don't rightly know. I reckon he don't mind."

"Does he get cranky?"

Uncle Jonah busted out a big open mouth laugh, then said, "I guess sometimes, like people do." He rubbed his chin. "Would you like to ride him?"

"I guess so." But I saw he wanted to more than anything.

He helped my brother up into the saddle. "I'll ride behind Andy, Virginia Kate." He eased up in the saddle, letting Andy have the reins. "I'll go with you two a few times. If you do real good, I'll let you both ride off by yourself."

We rode off. The sun was warm and I lifted my face to it.

Uncle Jonah hummed the theme to *Rawhide*, and then we all sang it.

When we had enough practice, Uncle Jonah said we were ready to ride by ourselves come morning.

After visiting Momma, I changed into shorts and a t-shirt. Andy had been waiting for me, jumping around like a cricket. Aunt Billie packed us a picnic of peanut butter and strawberry jam sandwiches, with brownies for dessert. She put in two yellow apples for the horses.

We saddled up our horses and set out. We rode

around the valley, up the hill, and into the little patch of woods down the road. We rode those horses tall and proud. When we were hungry, we stopped under some trees to eat. My backside was screaming, but I didn't care.

The horses munched grass after they ate their apples. Andy gulped down his sandwich and started on another one before I was done with my first. Mouth half full, he said, "You ride pretty good for a girl."

"And you ride pretty good for a boy."

He threw a pebble at me and I threw it back. He said, "I ride better than Little Joe on Bonanza." He grabbed a brownie.

"Uh huh, sure you do."

He showed me the half-chewed brownie, going gah uh gah uh, swallowed the mess, then said, "Uncle Jonah and Aunt Billie are pretty okay, huh?"

"Yeah."

He jumped up and punched into the air. "It's better than at that Ruby's."

"Did she go mean on you?"

"Me? No way. Ruby Screwby was scared of me." He snickered.

"She was?"

"I played tricks on her. It was easy since she was drunk all the time."

I leaned forward. "Like what kind of tricks?"

"Like moved stuff around when she was

sleeping. She'd get up, going 'Huh? Wha'?' " He sat back down and grabbed another brownie. "I pretended like I was dead when she hit me." He laughed, pieces of brownie flying out. "You should've heard her hollering 'this here boy's done dead. Dead, aw lawd he'p me'."

I laughed with him.

He looked pleased as the cat that ate the toad. "When Momma got beat up, I got to come here, since Uncle Jonah moved out here to help Momma. Weren't no reason to go to Ruby Screwbys then."

"Beat up?"

"Yeah. Momma went looping it up and some guy beat her half silly." He did a cartwheel. "The police had to come." He pushed his face up to mine and showed me the brownie in his teeth.

I flicked his ear with my thumb and forefinger. "Were you scared?"

"Goddamn, I'm never scared." He charged to a tree and hung from a branch, swinging like a monkey. He jumped down and came over to reach for another brownie.

I grabbed the last one before he did. The brownie was warm from the sun, sweet and chewy. I asked, "Did she go on lots of dates?"

"You ask too many questions, Seestor."

"I'm just curious is all."

He crossed his hands over his chest and rolled back and forth in the grass and grunted out, "Most-of-them-I-called-assholes."

He jumped up and loped towards Big Fella, jumping on like he'd done it all his life. "That stuff was a long time ago and I don't give a rat's big hairy butt. Get that in your hard head instead of whatever else is stomping around."

"I don't know what you're carrying on about." I went to Starlight.

"Yeah you do, too."

"You're being silly." I eased up on Starlight and turned her towards the house. Andy didn't say anything else about it, just hummed the *Bonanza* theme while he did his arms like they did, saying, "I'm the good-looking one."

"Little Joe?"

"No, the other good-looking one that nobody ever remembers his name."

Two weeks later, Andy was on his way back to Louisiana and I was back in the holler with Momma. I thought she needed me. I thought I had it all figured out.

Everything seemed both smaller and bigger than I remembered. The yard seemed smaller, so did the house. But the mountains left a bigger shadow all across the house and yard, across Momma, Jonah, Mrs. Mendel's house, and me. When we drove up, I saw Mrs. Mendel peeping from her window with a big lip-splitting grin. She waved and I waved back.

We helped Momma inside and to her bed. I

opened the window for her, looked outside at the maple. It was the same as always.

Uncle Jonah smoothed down Momma's hair. "You okay, Sister?"

"Go away now. I'm spent." Momma turned away.

We closed the door to Momma's room and went into the kitchen to see what she had. The booze bottles lined up on the counter like naughty soldiers.

Uncle Jonah opened cabinets and the icebox, shaking his head. "You need food."

I didn't say anything. I felt a little scared.

He looked at me, said, "I'll stay if you need me to."

"I'm fine, Uncle Jonah."

"Well, I'll get some groceries over here."

I followed him to the door and watched until he drove away. Then I shut myself in with Momma.

I wandered around. The house was cleaner than I thought it would be. I kept imagining it to be like when Momma threw dishes all over the place. I went back in the kitchen to get a drink of water, and those bottles looked evil, like the soldiers had turned into those monkeys from *Wizard of Oz*. I poured every bit down the sink, wrinkling my nose at the smell. In the icebox was nothing but butter, jam, and a jug of soured milk. I threw the milk down the drain, too.

I then sat on the couch and thought about how

everybody in Louisiana was not happy with me for staying in West Virginia.

When I'd told Andy, he'd said, "You've lost your marbles."

"I have not. I need to help Momma is all."

He stuffed his clothes in the suitcase. "She acts insane. Daddy will make you come home."

"Daddy can't make me do a thing. Besides, he acts insane, too."

He turned around and looked at me as if he thought I might never go back to Louisiana. "You know it's different with Daddy." He picked up a pair of socks and sniffed them. "Besides, I was with Momma longer. I know how she is now."

"Momma is still our Momma."

He snorted like a horse.

"I'm just staying to help for a spell."

He closed his suitcase. "Micah's going to be real mad at you."

Aunt Billie had said her goodbyes to Andy, tears in her eyes like tiny rainstorms. We got in Uncle Jonah's car and she waved until we were out of sight. In the car, and at the airport, Andy sat without saying anything else to me. When it was time to get on the plane, he hugged my neck hard, something he hadn't done since he was little. He was boney, but he was strong. Between a man and a boy. He said, "Don't let her hurt you, Sister."

"She never hit us, Andy."

"I don't mean that goddamn way." He galloped off and was gone.

And that was that. We fetched Momma from the hospital and brought her back to the holler. Brought me back, too. And there I was, back.

I picked up the phone and called Rebekha. When she answered, her voice sounded too far away. I heard Elvis in the background. She said, "I know you need to do this . . ." and was quiet.

The devil and angel had a big fight and it gave me a headache.

I heard Bobby. "Let me talk to my seestor. Give me the phone. Give it!" His voice stabbed straight into my heart, "Come home. I won't follow you around and bug you, I promise."

"Bobby, it's not you. I just want to help my momma."

"But, my mom is your momma, isn't she?"

"I'll be home to see you later, don't worry."

"Next week?"

"No, not that soon. "

"Oh. Okay." He sounded like his goldfish died. "Bye."

Rebekha was back on the phone. "Hon, you okay?"

"I'm fine."

She sighed on the phone, said, "Virginia Kate." Another sigh, then, "Be safe, be well."

"I'm fine."

After I put down the phone, I went to my room,

smoothed Grandma's quilt with my hand, and then peeked under the bed. My Special Things Box was gone. I guessed Momma threw it out, and I tried not to care. I said, "Grandma Faith, are you here?" She didn't answer, so I went to check on Momma.

I eased open her door. She was awake and looking back at me. "Hey, Momma." I smoothed my skirt and hair, hoping she noticed since she hadn't said anything about how I'd grown up.

"Why are you here, Virginia Kate?"

I walked to her, trying to pretend she said something else. Something like, *I'm glad you're here, Virginia Kate*, especially since she asked me to stay. "I'm here to take care of you, Momma."

"Then bring me a rum and Co-Cola with lemon."

"I poured it all down the sink." I looked outside her pane at the maple.

She whooshed out her air, then said, "Call up my brother and tell him to bring more."

"But Momma, I don't think you should."

"I'm hurting all over. A little drink isn't going to kill me." With her lips dry and cracked, she said, "Go on now. Call him. You know what kind I like. And don't look like I just kicked your puppy, I need it for this pain."

I left her room, and called Uncle Jonah. Aunt Billie answered. I told her what Momma wanted. She said, "He's just walking out the door. I'll go run catch him. Hold on, okay?" The phone clunked.

I hoped she wouldn't go catch him, but then I didn't want Momma to throw a hissy fit, either.

She came back on the line. "He said he'd take care of it. By the by, your daddy called a little bit ago to check on you."

I wondered why he didn't just call here.

"That Rebekha called, too. She sounds like a fine woman. She is, isn't she? I mean, you'd tell us if she wasn't?"

"Yes Ma'am."

"You sure this is what you need to be doing, child?"

"Yes. I'm fine."

Aunt Billie said she'd baked a pie for Momma and me and then we said our goodbyes.

While I waited for the groceries, and booze, I thought about what school I'd be going to, how I'd get my license so I could drive Momma's car to the store, how I'd have tea with Mrs. Mendel while Momma rested. I took to planning out my life in the holler again without a lick of sense. And it didn't make me feel as happy as I thought it should have, so I pretended it did. The only things that helped were looking up at my sweet mountain, and hiding under Grandma Faith's quilt.

Mrs. Mendel came by to say hello, her neck wobbling like a turkey. Her hair was still in its bun on top her head, but it had gray in it and more pieces stick out all wiry. She hugged me so hard I thought she'd break my skin open. We talked about her garden until she was tired and said she had to go take a nap. "You need something, you just call."

"I'm fine, Mrs. Mendel." I watched her go off across the grass. She stopped to pick a rose from her garden before she tottled inside. It was almost as if I hadn't left at all. I stepped across time, just like that, in a big slow wink.

Uncle Jonah came with bags of things. He checked around the house, pulled on windows and doors, checked the stove and icebox, made sure the water came out of the faucets fast enough. We looked in on Momma but she was still sleeping, her head smashed in the pillow—dark against white.

After Uncle Jonah checked every little thing and the groceries were put away, booze lined up again, I said, "Mrs. Mendel said she'd help me if I needed her."

"Still, you call if, well, if things get bad?"

"I'll be fine."

When he finally left, I shut the door, glad that Momma and I had the house all to ourselves. I changed my clothes and then made grilled cheese, poured Momma's drink just right, and put everything on a tray.

She drank the whole thing down without stopping and held the glass out for more. "That'll help the outside pain; the next one is for the inside pain."

"If I get it will you eat the sandwich, Momma?"

"Well, you're the sweetest thing." She took a

little bite and chewed it slow, swallowed with a flinchy look, and said, "It still hurts to eat."

"I'm sorry."

"My special potion will help." She touched her head. "Turn on the radio for me."

I found piano music that was sad sounding, but a good sad, like when someone left but they would be back soon kind of sad. I made her another drink and brought it to her.

She sipped. I hadn't put much vodka in it and she knew it, said, "Well, isn't this a fine howdy doodly." She ate the rest of the sandwich. When her glass was empty, she held it out. "I need one more, and put more hooch in this time. And put something happier on the radio."

I didn't even fuss with her.

I read Momma's fashion magazines while she finished her fourth. When she fell asleep, I went to the kitchen, made me a grilled cheese, ate it, cleaned the dishes, and went on to my room. The night bugs called, and the frogs were all in my throat. I slipped myself under the sheets and Grandma's quilt, staring out the window at the moon's light shining on my mountain and me, on the maple, on Momma's face as she slept. The big moon grinned, shining brighter than I remembered. But I had a worried feeling that I was doing things all wrong.

I dreamed Grandma Faith was in Louisiana. I hollered to tell her I was in the holler, but she shook her head at me. When I woke up, I was alone.

· · ·

Momma stayed in bed most of the time, but soon was able to get up and go to the bathroom by herself. She stared in the bathroom mirror, saying, "I've messed up my pretty."

I said, "No you haven't, Momma," because I saw it coming back.

Uncle Jonah and Aunt Billie came by often. I liked seeing their smiles and the way everything was so simple with them. Mrs. Mendel and Aunt Billie made quick friends, walking in the garden and blabbervating on about vegetables and flowers. With my camera, we took pictures of each other. Uncle Jonah said he'd get them developed for me.

On a cool evening, we plopped on the steps with lemonade. Momma stayed inside like always.

Mrs. Mendel asked about Micah and Andy.

I told about Micah's paintings and how good he was at it, and about how Andy was a daredevil, and how Bobby loved baseball so much he slept with his bat on the other pillow. I told about Rebekha and how she had a sourpuss momma, but she was a good one herself. And about Louisiana, how moldy green, spongy-wet and hot it was, how the moss dripped down, the egrets white-as-clouds-beautiful but have a croaky froggy call that doesn't match how they look. I went on about Miss Darla seeing signs and her funny dog with a movie star name, the Campinelle's football parties. Mrs. Mendel and Aunt Billie grinned as if they'd eaten a big piece of pie and it tasted better than any they'd ever had.

Aunt Billie said, "Oh, we should all visit sometimes."

I felt as if things might not be so bad.

Then one afternoon when bloated storm clouds drifted, ready to let birth all the pressure they held, Momma took up talking ugly to everybody. The four of us were picking a bouquet of wildflowers when she stuck out her head from the window and hollered for Mrs. Mendel to mind her own beeswax. Mrs. Mendel's eyes went round, same as her mouth. Aunt Billie humphed under her breath, and Uncle Jonah turned to look at Momma.

Momma said, "I got my daughter here to take care of things, why you three have to hang around all the time? Look at her, almost grown up. Isn't she the prettiest? Huh? Prettier than her momma, don't you think?"

Aunt Billie said, "And I hope you appreciate what you got here, Katie."

"Don't be telling me what to appreciate, Billandra-Sue. You aren't the one suffering."

"I've had my share of suffering that's none of your concern."

"Uh huh, sure you have. My brother treats you like a queen. My daughter looking up to you like you're more special than me, I reckon." Momma rubbed the spot where her hair was growing back from the nurse shaving it. "But you never had your own kids, did you? Have to borrow other people's babies. You too, Mrs. Mendel. The both of you with your empty wombs and think you know it all."

I stared at Momma, my face heating up from my neck to the roots of my hair.

Mrs. Mendel pressed her hand over her mouth to stop her crying and ran in the house. Aunt Billie went after her, calling out, "Wait! Don't let her talk to you that way."

"That's enough, Sister," Uncle Jonah said. "Mrs. Mendel and Billie's been coming round helping you and you talk like that?"

Momma tossed her head and left the window.

After that, Aunt Billie stopped coming by so much, so did Mrs. Mendel. Uncle Jonah still came in to drop off groceries and check on us, but he didn't look happy about the way Momma zapped her tongue at him.

To rub my skin more raw, Jade wrote me and went on and on about her new boyfriend and how in love they were and how they'd kissed. Andy-and-Bobby sent two letters in one envelope, both saying *Come home right now* (and Andy said, goddamnit!), *Seestor*. There was a package of chocolate chip cookies from Rebekha, with a sweet note added. Miss Darla sent me another diary, in case I filled up the one I had (and I remembered I'd left my necklace in Louisiana). Amy Campinelle wrote to tell me football season would be there before I knew it, so I better hurry on home. Micah sent me a drawing of me with a stubborn pout mouth. And Daddy was quiet.

I had a big powerful ache deep in my belly, searing up to my heart.

I wrote in the new diary all the things I couldn't say aloud. I ended with, *I miss my mountain so much when I'm in Louisiana. When I'm in Louisiana, I mourn for West Virginia. When I'm here, I miss my family so much. I'm Virginia Kate and I'm a crazy girl.*

I tried to sleep and I couldn't. It was a black-blanket night. I slipped out of bed and went to the kitchen for a glass of water. Momma was at the table, the bottle of vodka Uncle Jonah brought just yesterday in front of her, almost empty. The smoke from her cigarette curled up to the ceiling. She picked up the bottle and drank from it, she stabbed out the cigarette. She held a letter in her other hand, and there were more envelopes stacked beside her.

I waited.

When she put her head down on her arm, let the letter slip from her fingers, and was still, I sneaked up and said, "Momma?" She didn't move, so I picked up the letter and read.

Katie Ivene, Did you really think I'd leave Rebekha and bring the children back to West Virginia? We had a deal. You accepted what Mother offered. Live with that decision. It would have been the right thing to let Rebekha adopt the children and you well know it. You never could stand that I left you, could you? Rebekha doesn't deserve this. The children, either. For that matter, neither do I. Frederick Hale.

I put down the letter, went to my room, and swallowed five aspirin. Laying across my bed, I tried to make my breathing come in and out slow. I remembered the adoption day and how Rebekha cried, how everything was ruined. And Momma, coming down just to fool with Daddy, not caring if it hurt us kids. And what deals and offers? My head pounded until I finally ran to the bathroom and threw up.

Momma hollered out, "What's going on in there?"

But I couldn't answer. Hate and mad and worry and sad were all emptying from deep inside of me and spilling into the toilet.

Chapter 31
Go back to that woman in Loo-see-aner

I still had a nasty sour taste on my tongue from the night before and my stomach hurt. While waiting for the coffee water to boil, I dialed. The phone only rang twice before she answered.

"Hello?" The hello sounded so full to the top with hope, I felt like bawling.

"Rebekha? It's Virginia Kate."

"Oh, Hon. Are you all right?"

"I'm fine. I'm just calling." I heard her soft breathing. "Just seeing what everybody's doing, I guess."

"You sound tired. Are you sure you're okay?"

"I'm fine." The kettle whistled and I took it off the fire. "She's been pretty sick." I added two teaspoons of sugar to my own cup first. "I give her medicine and help her stretch." A teaspoon of Maxwell House. "And I sweep the house and wash dishes." Add water, stir. "I cook things." Add cream, stir it around some more. "I made cornbread like you showed me and it tasted perfect." Sip, swallow.

"You're a hard worker, Virginia Kate."

It felt like Rebekha was far off to the moon, or maybe I was. "What's my stupid brothers doing?"

"Andy is with Dan and Neil, probably doing something dangerous." She laughed, then said, "Micah spent yesterday evening painting a portrait of Miss Darla. He's at the art supply store right now, I believe." I heard water running and I pictured her at the sink, washing the breakfast dishes. "Bobby's in his room reading. Let me get him or he'll have a fit."

I sipped coffee while Rebekha called to Bobby. I heard his running steps and felt the ache press hard.

His voice slammed into my ear. "Hey meestor seestor! Are you coming home? Are you? When? Today? I've got stuff to show you. Stump said you were a good ball thrower for a girl. He said Wayne

409

got a girlfriend, but she's stupid. You should see the lake, it's all high up from a rain and I saw a snake but I didn't kill it and Andy fell and hurt his leg, there was blood everywhere and Mom had to fix him and Micah showed me how to draw a dragon and he said I did a real good job."

When he finally ran out of air, I said, "Slow down, I can't keep up with all that." But I did.

"Are you coming home?" He asked again.

"Well, Momma's still not doing so good."

"Oh. Okay. Here's Mom." While he passed the phone, I heard him say. "Make her come home, Mom."

"So, things are okay? You are doing okay?"

"I'm fine. But I have to go, it's long distance." I put down my coffee and held the phone with both hands.

"Oh! I wasn't thinking about the long distance bills! Please, call collect. Anytime day or night, okay?"

"Rebekha?"

"Yes, Hon?"

I wanted to tell her I loved her, but I'd never said it to her before, instead I said what meant the same thing, "I miss your popcorn lots." I then said, "Tell everybody I miss them lots. And tell Miss Darla, too?"

"I will."

When I hung up, I turned to see Momma standing in the doorway with a big smarmy-smirk on her

410

face. "I miss you; oh I miss you so much." She made smacky noises, then said, "You don't have to stay here, you know. I didn't ask you to."

"But you did. You did ask me to stay and help you." I tried not to stare at her sprouty new hair. "You said you didn't want to be alone."

"Well, I reckon I did. But I thought you wanted to be with me, too. Not with *that* woman."

I picked up my cup. "Rebekha's nice, Momma. If you'd just get to know her."

"Yeah, I'm sure she's a goody goody gumdrop." She pointed to the coffee. "Did you make that for me?"

"It's mine. I'll get yours." She sat at the table and watched as I stirred hers. I set it in front of her. "Just as you like it, Momma."

She took a sip, then said, "Whew Nelly. That's hot, but good. Clears the head. Except you forgot how I really like it." She pushed on the table to stand, shuffled to the counter, picked up the dark rum, took it to the table with her, and poured a splash into her coffee. With her eyes closed, she took a bigger sip, then, "There."

I got eggs, butter, and milk, two slices of bread to toast, and from the cabinet, a skillet to fry the eggs in. I cut on the fire low, put the skillet on, and added butter to the skillet.

"Tell me all about this Roo-becker and your pick-pack-daddy-whack. Are they happy go lucky in their happy go lucky home?"

411

I cracked the eggs in a bowl. "I don't know, Momma."

"Sure you do. You live there don't you? Or lived there." I heard the splash as she poured more rum in her cup. "What's it like in Shakeslove land?"

While whipping the eggs, I added a bit of milk, salt and pepper. "Well, Micah says he's going to New York when he graduates."

"Uh huh."

I poured the eggs in the buttered skillet. "Andy makes straight A's and B's, except for a C in math."

"That's Andy and that's Micah. What about you?"

"We have a brother named Bobby. He's cute." I popped the bread in the toaster, stirred the eggs.

"I asked about you. How do you like this momma you have now? Huh?"

"But you're my momma." I took her cup and fixed her more coffee. I stirred the eggs again. I looked inside the toaster to hurry the toast.

"Don't play games. Just answer the question."

"I don't know, Momma. She's a good person."

"And I reckon I'm not?" Splash in cup.

The eggs were fluffy, I divided them on two plates. I flipped the lever to make the toast pop up. I spread butter and jam on them.

Momma drained her cup, then said, "I did the best I could. I don't know what else to say." She eased up slow and wobbled at the table.

"I know you did, Momma. I know." I helped her to her bedroom. "I'll give you your breakfast in bed, okay?"

"Whatever. Bring the rest of the rum, will you?"

"Momma, no."

"I'm the momma and you're the kid. What I say goes. Zip zippo endo."

I felt like the bird that had been trapped inside the house in Louisiana. A dark bird with bright eyes, wild with being scared. It flew from window to window, flapping its wings and making chirpy sounds. I ran and opened the front door, trying to help it out, but it didn't know what it was supposed to do. It just kept flying all over the living room. Rebekha finally threw a towel over it, picked it up, and then let it go outside. When it flew away, it never looked back, just kept going and going until it was gone.

After breakfast, while Momma took a nap, I rinsed white beans and then put them to soak. From the window, I saw Mrs. Mendel in her garden, so I went outside.

"Hey."

"There you are." She picked two tomatoes and handed one to me. "You still sound like West Virginia, but you got a little extree something thrown in there, too. Must be that Louisiana." She bit into hers, letting the juice dribble down her arm.

"I don't know how I sound." I bit into mine. It

was warm and sweet and the juice trickled down my arm same as her. I made a "mmmm" sound.

"Let's pick more for your supper tonight."

"I'm making beans and cornbread. Rebekha taught me how to cook." I popped the rest of the tomato in my mouth and squished the juice with my tongue.

We pulled more tomatoes from the vines and set them in a basket.

"That Rebekha sounds sweet." She stopped picking. "She is, isn't she?"

"Yes Ma'am." I wiped my hands on my jeans. "Well, I better go and check on Momma."

"She doing okay? Poor soul." Mrs. Mendel couldn't stay mad at Momma.

"She's fine."

She handed me the basket. "My nephew'll be coming for a visit soon. You two would get along right as rain."

"I got to go now, Mrs. Mendel. Thanks for the tomatoes."

I went inside. Momma was hollering. I ran to her room. She was on the floor, blood like lipstick on her mouth. I helped her into bed and went to the bathroom for a washrag to wipe her face.

"I fell and hit the goddamn night table. Pain pills making me woozy-loozy."

"You got to be careful, Momma."

"I need a bath and I need some ice for my drink.

Some lemon, too. And a pad and some paper. What's that on your shirt? I've never seen a girl so messy. Wipe your mouth and arm, too."

Bird's wings went a-flying all over the place.

Momma turned stronger, but she turned weaker at the same time with the booze on top of her medicine. She stayed cooped up except for doctor visits, so I had to stay cooped up with her.

Momma said, "I expect I'll see someone and they'll either be glad I'm looking like this, or they'll feel sorry for me. I won't have it." I told her she was still beautiful, but she didn't believe me. She said, "You have all the pretty now. Be careful with your pretty, Virginia Kate. Men act stupid over your kind of pretty."

If I called Rebekha and Momma found out, she'd get a poochy pout mouth. If I didn't call, I felt lonesome. At night, it was dark and lonely. I wanted Fionadala. I wanted Grandma Faith. I wanted my brothers. I wanted my sister mountain to sing to me. I wanted to see what came next without being scared.

When Uncle Jonah picked up Momma for her doctor's visit, as usual, she wore a red scarf, big sunglasses, and sat scooched down in her seat.

Her doctor scolded her, "Stop sucking down the alcohol. Do you know what this is doing to your body?" He looked at me. "Not to mention your family."

Momma said, "What do you know?" and stormed out.

On the way back to the holler, Uncle Jonah tried to talk sense into Momma, too, but she got mad at him, told him to mind his own, and to stop at the next store. She said, "Brother, my check hasn't come in the mail yet, I'll need to borrow some money, okay?" She handed me a piece of paper. "Virginia Kate, here's the list of things I want."

I knew what the list read without looking: red fingernail polish, red lipstick, Pond's Cream, and four bottles of her favorite booze. I wanted to throw the note in the trash, but I wanted more to go inside and look around to buy something for myself.

Uncle Jonah said, "Why don't you come in and see if there's something else you want?"

Momma ignored him.

With my own money, I bought myself a pair of silver dangly earrings, Flex Shampoo and Conditioner, a bottle of lavender-scented bath salts, a new fashion magazine, and two Snickers bars (they didn't have Zeros!).

Back at the holler, Momma asked me to do her nails. She sang along with the radio, a cheese and Ritz casserole bubbled in the oven, and Mrs. Mendel's tomatoes were on the counter next to Momma's best-friends-in-a-bottle.

While I painted red on her nails, Momma yapper-vented on about how evil Mee Maw was. How she used her money to lord it over everybody. She said Rebekha was playing like a goody two shoes know it all. I wanted to take up for Rebekha, but I kept quiet. It didn't do any good to get Momma all up in a state.

She next carried on about her daddy, how mean he was. She talked about the wreck, and Aunt Ruby. "I saw my sister, Virginia Kate. I saw her eyes all wide and all that blood with her face half torn off. Torn up, torn up. I saw my momma, burned up to a crisp. It was terrible, terrible." It took me an hour to get her settled down.

While she napped, I took the casserole out of the oven to cool, and picked up around the house. It wasn't hard to keep up as long as Momma didn't have a hissy fit or want to cook anything. When she tried to cook, she'd think it was funny when things didn't work out right. I'd watch her flopping around the kitchen, throwing things in bowls and pans. She'd laugh, but I didn't laugh knowing I'd have to clean it up while she was sleeping it off.

I could usually get her out of the kitchen to watch television. She liked *Mission Impossible*, but could never keep up with what was going on. Dean Martin made her laugh. She'd hold her drink in her left hand and a cigarette in her right and say, "Just what do you think is in his cup, hmm?"

After we ate our casserole, she stood in front of me with a big looped-up grin. "I want to make some cookies."

417

"I'll do it, Momma. You go rest."

"I just got done resting. Go fix the radio on something good and I'll make the bestest cookies ever."

I found a station playing the greatest hits.

She sang along while the dough went flying. Her hair was in a ponytail so the growing-out spot didn't show much.

While the cookies baked, she danced around, trying to get me to dance with her. But I wasn't much in the mood, knowing I had all that sticky dough and all to clean up.

"You sure are a stick in the dirt. What did that woman do to you over there in Loo-see-aner?"

"Nothing, Momma. I'm just tired."

"You're too young to be tired." She twirled around and her housedress twirled with her. Even with her scars and what the booze did to her, she was still the Queen of West Virginia. "I think you'll do better living here, won't you? Learn how to loosen up some." She grabbed my hands and pulled me off the couch. "Come on, Virginia Kate. How can you not dance?"

I danced with her, taking in her Shalimar floating around the room with the liquor-smoke smells. She wore her new apple-red lipstick, her ponytail bounced around, her eyes moon-shined, and she laughed showing her strong teeth, except one pointy one missing from the accident. We twirled around. I was little again and in love with my momma. Then she was on the couch and asleep, just like that, boom bam, done. I turned off the radio, put a blanket over her, and cleaned up the mess in the kitchen.

And it was that night when the house whispered to me. I heard Grandma Faith sighing. The open window let in cool air and the serious moon was big and bright. I wandered around picking up things Momma left around. I felt like good things were right on the other side of my mountain. That if I could just get there, everyone would be waiting for me and I would bring them to me so we could all be together. The whispering grew louder, "Virginia Kate. Virginia Kate. Virginia Kate."

The phone rang and I hurried to answer it before it woke up Momma.

"Girl, this is Darla calling."

"Miss Darla!" I grinned into the phone as if she could see me.

"I got the number from Rebekha; hope you don't mind me giving you a ring." Sophia Loren was barking in the background. "Silence, Sophia."

"I don't mind at all."

"You okay there?"

"I'm fine."

"Sometimes you do things because you feel like you have to."

"I guess so."

"Sometimes we have to do things. But sometimes we don't have to do things that make us very unhappy."

"I'm fine, really."

We both breathed in our phones. I thought hard, hoping she could hear my thoughts, like she used to.

"Your momma is a strong woman. She'll do whatever she needs to do to survive. But you're a young woman, with all this life ahead. Everybody has their burdens to carry. I think you've carried your Momma's enough."

I leaned my head against the wall. So tired. I was so tired.

Then, just like that, we talked about other things. The crepe myrtles. The mimosa lost all its blooms, but was thick and green as it waved in the hot wind. How everything was boiling, wet, and moldy. The cicadas were louder than ever. How Miss Darla had to rescue the house geckos that Sophia Loren liked to chase. She told me Micah was hardly home anymore, but only because I made her tell me about my brother. We hung up and I let the sound of Miss Darla's voice stay warm on my ear. I went to my room and even though I said I never would ever again, I cried until my pillow was wet and snotty.

I didn't hear Momma come in. "What do you have to cry about?"

I looked up at her. Momma had put on lipstick and she missed her lips some, so that her mouth looked like it was bleeding. It was on so thick it left a big lip print on the glass she held. I said, "I don't know."

"I'm the one who ought to be crying." She gulped her drink, then said, "I'm the one who lost her whole goddamned family. All my babies. Even you. You're here, but just part of you is here. I've lost you all. My Frederick, my babies, my pretty. All gone."

"I'm sorry, Momma."

"You setting in here crying. Well, you see me doing that? Huh? I don't have nobody, but I'm not wasting my breath blubbering over it."

I didn't sass back and say that she cried a lot. She probably didn't even remember it. I wiped my face with Grandma's quilt and took breaths.

"If you don't like it here, then why don't you go back? Huh? Why don't you go back to that woman? She's your momma now, not me."

I shot out of bed. "No, that's not true."

"Sure it is. All you kids were going to let her adopt you and leave me in the cold with nobody."

"But, Momma, I—"

"—all my babies, and that daddy of yours, too. One thing I couldn't do was give her the last bit of you I had. Then I'd be nothing, not a woman, not a momma, nothing."

I went to her. "I'd still be your daughter, no matter what." I wrapped my arms around her, took in her booze, smoke, and Shalimar. "I won't ever leave you, Momma. Ever. You need me."

"So, you feel sorry for me? Is that it? My daughter thinks I'm pitiful?" Momma pulled away, turned around, and headed to the kitchen. I followed her. She opened the freezer, reached in the bowl for ice, and threw three pieces into her circle glass. "I don't need you feeling sorry for your own momma." She grabbed the vodka, poured to the rim, put down the bottle. She drank half the glass down in a gulp.

"Don't, Momma. Please. I can't take it again." I pressed my eyes with my palms, then dropped my hands and looked at her. "Please, Momma."

Over the rim of her glass, I saw something change in her eyes.

I took a step to her.

She put up her hand, said, "You're young. Everything ahead of you. I remember that. Well, sort of." She turned to the window. "I expect I never got to be a kid, not really. They wouldn't let me. Damn men thinking they can take what they please without caring about the mess they leave behind. Thinking young girls are like grown women. And a Daddy who'd rather whup us silly than hug us."

I went still.

"Your grandma tried to make things better, but she had her own hurts, I reckon. That day, I knew what to do when your daddy came around." She drained the glass, turned to the counter, and poured another. "I'm glad I left home when I did, but it wasn't enough." She waved her hand over the room, and me. "All this wasn't enough for me.

Husband and babies. I wasn't ready, do you see? Do you understand?"

I nodded.

"No, you don't. You think you do, but you don't. You're still untouched, aren't you?"

I lowered my eyes and felt heat rising in my face.

"That's what saved you, isn't it? Away from me, from here. From momma to child, momma to child, momma to child. Maybe you broke the chain? Huh?"

I looked at her, took in my momma like a big breath, she filled up my lungs and body and all a sudden I couldn't breathe.

She pushed her hand through her wild hair. "Mee Maw sent me money in trade for you kids. I thought it would just be for a while, that's all. I thought I had it all planned out." She tossed her head. "I found Harold because I thought I could get you all back. But he hated kids."

I gawked at her. My voice box clicked clicked.

"When it all fell to shit, I figured maybe you were better off. Or maybe, maybe I just wanted to be free." She poured another drink, took a big swallow, then said, "When Harold left, I married Melvin; he wanted babies and he loved kids. He said he'd try with all of you."

"He wanted us?" I sat at the table, my legs wouldn't hold me any more.

Her chin pointed out to me. "He wanted me to quit drinking, smoking, and being me, and that's not what happened." She made a sour face. "He wanted me to go to church and tell that Jesus I was a sinner. Well, nobody tells me what to do, not even Jesus."

I stared at her. All a sudden, I hated the way her mouth curled up at the ends. Hated the smell of her liquor-smoke breath. Hated the way she worried about her own self first. I had to hate her right then. I had to put hate over the love so it wouldn't hurt so much.

"I don't need someone to take care of me." She wasn't soft anymore. "All you do is remind me of everything I lost. That's all you do. Remind me. Remind me. Remind me of it all. All I don't got."

"Why are you saying all this to me? Why, Momma?"

She pointed her right finger at me. "I don't want you, you hear me? I want you to go back to Loo-see-aner-faner-bananer-fuckaner." She bent over and coughed up eighty cigarette-smoking toads, straightened up, said, "I'm happy here all by myself. I can do what I want when I want. Maybe I want to have some men over. Can't do that with you here. Not with those looks. They'd be all over you instead of me."

I jumped up, turned and ran to my brothers' closet, slammed the door behind me, pressed my palms to my face, tried to ride up to what was good and true, but all I could do was breathe and breathe and breathe, in and out in and out, hard and fast.

Later, back in my room, Momma didn't come check on me, or come tell me she was sorry. She didn't come tell me everything would be okay. Or that she was just drunk and didn't mean it. All I heard out of her was the slam of her door and the lock clicking in. I let the headache come on, buzz buzz went the hornets. That pain was better than the heart pain.

I fell asleep and dreamed Grandma Faith was holding out her arms. I was little again as I ran to her. She held me tight and stroked my hair as I cried into her dress. She let me stay there a long while. I smelled the bread and apples even after I woke up.

The next morning, I knocked on Momma's door with coffee and toast. "Momma? Breakfast is ready."

"Go away. I told you last night." I heard something crash on the floor. "Call my brother and tell him to pick you up and take you away from me."

"I have hot coffee, just as you like it."

"I'm not unlocking this door and I'm not coming out and I don't want any fucking coffee. You aren't wanted, you hear? Never ever ever do I want you back here. I never want to see you again as long as I live. You damn kids have ruined my life. Well, from now on, I don't have kids. I don't have a daughter. Now *Git..*" Something thundered against the door and I jumped, spilled some coffee.

I put the tray by the door and went to the kitchen

on rubber legs. I looked out the window at Mrs. Mendel working in her garden. Her hair was under a funny straw hat with flowers pinned all over it. I drank a cup of coffee and let the wind blow on me. After I drank every drop, I went to the phone and dialed up Uncle Jonah. When he answered all I could get out of my frog throat was, "You got to come now, Uncle Jonah. Momma's acting stranger."

He was there so fast; it was as if he flew over on a bird. He couldn't get Momma to come out, either. She cussed up a big black storm cloud. She told him she wanted to be alone. She said she didn't need a brother right then either and I saw by his eyes that it cut Uncle Jonah to the core.

After we went back and forth to her closed-up door for two days, and after she vowed not to eat until I left, we finally believed her. I packed up and went back to Uncle Jonah and Aunt Billie and Starlight and Big Fella. I stayed there until I quit crying. I did lots of crying on the back of Starlight, and she'd never tell anyone. The last day of my crying, I told Uncle Jonah I was ready to go back to Louisiana

When I called Rebekha to tell her, she said, "We'll meet you at the airport."

I flew to Louisiana and let all the hurt from Momma's words fly away to the wind as if it never even happened. I tucked her away like an old photo of old relatives no one remembers but their face is familiar.

Daddy and I rocked on the porch drinking tea, at least mine was tea, I wasn't sure about his, or maybe I decided I didn't care. He put his glass on the porch floor, took out his wallet, and handed me a photo of Momma he kept secret. In the photo, Momma stood with her left hand planted on her hip, the right one behind her back, as if she was hiding something there. Her dress pressed against her, so it must have been windy that day, and her hair tumbled all around her shoulders, pieces of it blowing across her face.

"You kept it all this time?"

He looked like a little boy caught sneaking cookies before supper. "Yes."

"Well, you should have Rebekha in there."

"I have Rebekha, see?" He flipped open his wallet and showed me Rebekha's gap-toothed grin. I thought she was pretty; she looked sincere, too.

"You shouldn't keep Momma in your wallet." I couldn't let it go; it was bugging me like itchy ant bites.

"That's why I'm giving it to you. I feel a release." He sighed, as if he really were releasing something.

I put the photo in my britches pocket.

He smiled at Rebekha's picture, and then folded and stuck the wallet back in his pocket. He said, "You must think me foolish."

I didn't say how I'd been doing the same thing when it came to Momma casting a spell on us. I looked out at the giant oak and asked, "Am I ever going to see Momma again?"

"I just don't know. I wish I did." He rubbed his hands on his knees. "Things will work out just fine, however they're supposed to." He opened up his Shakespeare book of plays. I looked at the page he was on, read with him about stormy seas and people being shipwrecked and pitiful lonely creatures named Caliban.

Chapter 32
He always hated goodbyes
1973

We celebrated Micah's high school graduation with a trip to New Orleans. A storm came up and we held our breath all the way across the spillway, but by time we checked into the Monteleone, the storm passed. In the French Quarter, we drank café au lait and ate beignets, shrimp and oyster po-boys, muffalettos, and Bananas Foster. We put money in hats and guitar cases, and tapped our feet to the street music. The street kids danced their hearts out. I thought they had sad eyes behind their big huge grins, but maybe they were just getting tired. How could I know for sure the mind and heart of other people?

When we had our palms read and did the tarot cards, Micah just rolled his eyes and said all he saw in our future was less money in our wallets. In

Napoleon House, we kids slurped cold Coca-Cola in frosty beer glasses, and Rebekha and Daddy had Pimm's Cups. We took a carriage ride, the mule's feathers bouncing. I watched the Mississippi River, muddy and quick and full of deep dark secrets. Drunk people swarmed out at night, so we stayed inside after dark. New Orleans was like a circus, except a circus that stayed around all the time and the people came to it, instead of the other way around. I used up three rolls of film.

It was the only time we had a real family vacation. We drove back tired and happy and ready for our own beds.

Micah shook me awake.

I propped up on my elbow. "Hey. What's wrong?"

"Hey. Nothing." He cracked his knuckles.

"How's it feel to be out of high school?"

"Unbelievable." His teeth shone in the dark as he stood looking down at me. "Remember I told you I would go to New York soon as I graduated?"

I nodded. I never really believed he would go. I thought he'd just dream about things, as I did.

"Well, I'm leaving tonight."

I sat up. "Tonight?"

"We're going to hitch."

"Hitch?"

"Yeah, we figured it'd be more exciting that way." He looked excited, his face swirling like his paintings.

"But, I bet Rebekha would buy you a ticket, or let you use the car."

He blew out his breath, then said, "I don't want a car and I don't want a ticket. What's exciting about that?"

"But what about college?"

He walked back and forth by the side of my bed, itchier than ever. "I'm going to be an artist. Who needs college?"

"I'm going to college when I graduate. It's what we're supposed to do." I crossed my arms over my chest. Miss Primmy Priss.

He stopped at the side of my bed again. "That's you. I can attend art school or something. More opportunities in New York than here, Sister-bo-blister. You should get out when you can."

"It's not that bad here."

"Geez, come off it."

"Our family is here."

"Families can break up; you should know that by now."

"You think our family will break up?" I heard my mimosa scratching.

He kneeled by my bed, the silly moon touched his face. "I'm just spouting off. Look, this is what I want to do and how I want to do it. I'm just saying don't let Louisiana suck you in forever."

"I do miss my mountain all the time."

He rolled his eyes. "Come on. You can dream better than that."

I shrugged.

"Stop being so scared of everything and take a chance."

I flopped my head back on the pillow.

He jumped up and stretched. "Time to flee, Vee."

I lay like a whiney lump. "But I'll miss you."

"Aw, don't worry; I'll write."

"Why can't things stay the same?"

"Why should they?"

"What did Daddy say?"

"I wrote a letter and stuck it on the fridge. It's easier this way." He stared down at his feet as if he wanted them to start moving—all the way to New York. He said, "This is a good thing. Don't look sad."

"What about Andy? Did you tell him."

"Yes. He said, 'Goddamn, Micah.'"

I closed my eyes tight, tighter, tighest, to stop the burning, and when I opened them, Micah was gone. He always hated goodbyes. Life was all about goodbyes, seemed to me. I hated goodbyes, too.

Rebekha found the note the next morning and went wild with worry. She and Daddy made calls, talked about going after him, until Daddy finally said Micah was old enough to make his own way. Rebekha looked sad, but she just nodded.

Andy moved into Micah's room, and decorated it with fast cars and pictures of girls in bathing suits. Bobby re-did his room with everything baseball.

We kids started school again in the fall, and the house settled into the ground, groaning and creaking like an old man getting in his easy chair. We all settled with it, settling in our bones, getting used to the changes. Daddy and Rebekha argued here and there, but even their arguments sounded so regular they weren't even scary anymore.

Jade said that at least arguing meant people cared, not like at her house where it was a mausoleum and everybody walked around with sticks up their butts. She said she felt like running away herself, that maybe next time they went on vacation, she'd slip away to a new place and start a new life like Micah.

I wondered about people running away. Wondered if secrets or worries stuck to them like a tick sucking out blood. Wondered if Micah was running away from old things, dark wing things. Wondered about Jade wanting to run away from her family and it seemed like her own body, too, she was so skinny. I thought about these things all the time and they were weighing my shoulders down.

I thought maybe some things shouldn't stay secret. Secrets are lonely. Secrets have to be buried in dark places. That's what I thought about while I pretended I wasn't going to tell anyone the secrets I held, when I pretended I was just minding my own business, strolling in the breeze, walking around humming as if I had nothing at all on my mind, no secrets, no promises to hold secrets. *La la la tee dah*, I'm trailing in the breeze. Running my hand along the table.

Rebekha sipped tea and read a magazine. I stood behind her to see what she was reading, she smelled like Flex Shampoo, and she was reading about how to save marriages.

She closed the magazine. "Hey. How was school?"

"Hey. It was fine." I sat across the table from her.

She turned to the back of the magazine, pointed to a recipe for a seafood casserole. "I'm going to try this. I want to experiment with different recipes. What do you think?"

"It looks great."

She stood up to pull two cookbooks from the shelf. "This has some fancy French cooking in it and this one is Italian. I can't wait to try them." She flipped through the cookbook, stopping at different recipes. She said, "And you, won't be long before you'll be off to college. Do you know where you want to go?"

"Not yet. Maybe here." I heard Micah sigh, all the way from New York. I sighed, too.

She closed the cookbook. "What's wrong? There's something wrong."

"It's different stuff, I guess."

"You know, we all tiptoe around until something either explodes, or goes away." She traced her finger on the table's wood grain. "But, I can see by your eyes that something isn't going away. If you need to talk about it, any of it, I'm a good listener."

I tried to smile at her.

"Releasing makes us lighter. I'm finding that out myself."

Before I lost all of my nerve, I let the frog croak out, "I tried my hardest to make Momma happy, but I couldn't. She didn't want me anyway, no matter what I did."

"I'm sorry, Hon."

"Why don't people want things to be happy? Why does everything have to be so crazy-mixed up?"

"She must be in a lot of pain and doesn't know how to deal with it."

"You always take up for her, but she doesn't take up for you."

"That's just how it is sometimes. I mean, what would it solve for me to go around saying bad things about your mother?"

I shrugged.

"I really believe your mother loves you. She just doesn't love herself, I suppose." She tucked a stray hair. "Mothers—they have so much power. A few little words and a few un-thought out actions can nurture or destroy a child. It's a power I always said I'd use wisely. I sometimes feel as if I've failed."

"But you haven't. You're a good momma."

"Thank you. That means a lot to me." She sipped

her tea, then said, "I suppose people make strange alliances, and pacts, and weird accommodations they become accustomed to."

I nodded, even though I wasn't sure I understood.

"People can love each other and not know how to handle things. They become confused and chaotic, like those paintings Micah does, where you think you see what the painting is about, and suddenly it changes into something else. You have to keep looking at it. It's fascinating how they seem like one thing and then another. All those hidden meanings. Just like people."

I went still. I said, "Are you going to leave Daddy?"

She stared at me, sighed, then said, "I'll be honest with you since I promised I always would. I don't know what will happen; things seem to be going smoother lately." She reached across and squeezed my hand. "I mean it when I say that you children are safe here, this is your home. I'm not leaving and neither are you. Unless you want to, okay?"

I nodded. I believed her.

"You still look troubled."

I was tired of scratching at things until they bled; scabbed over, scratch again, over and over. "I miss Micah, I guess."

"Me, too. I miss his paints and brushes all over the place. I was always after him and here I go missing the very thing that irritated me."

"I wish he'd call or write."

"I imagine he's taking on the town and not paying attention to time."

"I guess so."

"Oh, I bet he's painting up a storm and living large."

The sour nasty boiled up, burned and pushed, and then spewed, "He ran away because he's full of his secret."

She leaned forward. "What do you mean by that?"

Out it spewed, like vomit. "Micah pushed Uncle Arville and killed him. He was trying to get away from him is all. It was an accident. Uncle Arville fell and the pole went through him. Micah said he has nightmares all the time. He made me promise I wouldn't tell anyone." I panted.

Rebekha's left hand was over her mouth while I told her, her right was clenched in a fist.

My heart thundered. "You can't tell him I told, Rebekha. You can't. I never tell on Micah. Ever."

She clasped her hands tight. "Oh, god. So much makes sense now."

"It's supposed to be a secret."

"So terrible. Poor little boy."

"I had to tell. I had to." My face felt hot.

"You did the right thing telling me. This isn't a secret to keep alone."

I went to my room where it was quiet. I stared in the mirror and it was as if every time I looked in the mirror, someone else looked back at me. But I was not my momma. I was Virginia Kate Carey.

I slept hard that night, so hard I had a gallon of drool dribbled on my pillow. Grandma Faith came to me with her hair blowing around, saying, "All will be okay. All of you." When I woke up, I thought about people that I loved.

I saw little Micah pulling away from me in Daddy's silly little car when Daddy took him from West Virginia. Then grown Micah when he stood by my bed and told me he was leaving for New York. And I wondered if I'd ever see him again, and I knew I would because I had to. I pictured him heading to his dreams, painting everything he saw, inside and outside of him.

I knew Andy would be okay, he was always laughing with his friends, telling the world to go goddamn. He was as slap happy as could be, with all his tears dried up. He never said a thing about Momma. I never said a thing back about her. But she was there all the same between us.

And how Bobby lost the baby sickness that made him seem like a ghost of a boy, and grew strong and tall. How one day he wouldn't tag along behind anyone, since that's what kids did to grow up, they set out to find their own way instead of tagging behind someone else. Andy-and-Bobby would be Andy and Bobby.

I saw Rebekha just as she always was. The same

every year that passed. Her quiet ways. The way she made me feel safe. The way she took us in and gave us a place to call our own. Home. I saw her like a momma and like a friend.

There was Grandma Faith in the clouds. I wondered how it felt to stay around the earth instead of dancing around on the moon and stars. I didn't want her to leave, so I kept her with me.

And then, I thought of my daddy and how he kept trying to do what he should even though he messed up. Sometimes in my dreams, I saw him getting smaller and smaller. I chased him, but he kept away from me, for every step I took, he went farther away. His Shakespeare plays fell out of his back pocket, and I picked them up and ran faster, the wind slamming against my face, until I caught up with him, and then he took my hand and told me what everything meant.

I thought how I had friends who saw me as solid. The Campinelles, Ms. Portier-turned-Engleson, and especially Soot, Miss Darla, Jade. I saw all this while between asleep and awake. I wondered what kind of man I'd one day marry and how many babies I'd have and what their names would be. I decided I wanted a husband who'd smoke a sweet-smelling pipe and I'd see the smoke in the air like happy spirits.

I was sixteen and I was wise as the moon.

My last known thought was of me riding Fionadala up my mountain with the smell of earth tickling my nose, the leaves brushing me as I passed the trees, and mists all around me, while the moon stained my face. I felt the wind rush against me, as I fell up, up, up into sleep. There was a release on the rise of the mountain, and I reached for it.

Chapter 33
Today

If Grandma makes the wind knock my stuff around one more time I'll let out a scream and put up a big stomp hissy fit. I know it's time to go into Momma's room. She doesn't have to keep on with her poking and blowing and being filled up with ornery busy-body-tell-me-what-to-do tricks. I know I can't leave here until I finish, and I'm not finished until I go into Momma's room. The curtains snap at me, and I know Grandma is losing her patience in the face of my stomp.

As I move down the hall, the wind flies through all the open windows, blowing in and out and through. I roll my eyes and say, "I told you I'm going."

I look at Momma's door, and then take a little side trip to the kitchen to get a big glass of water, slugging it all down in five gulps. I wipe my mouth and say, "I just needed a drink of water."

Micah would bop me upside the head and tell me to stop being whirly brained and get down to the business of Momma. Andy would clomp right on in Momma's room and shrug his shoulders. He'd say, "What's the big deal anyway?" Bobby would tell them to give me time. He'd stand close by until I was ready.

I pull my family to me by the power of my want. By closing my eyes, I see them how they are now, instead of how we were then. I like knowing the ending of us kids, the ending so far anyway. It makes all this remembering easier, the knowing how things have turned out.

I know that Micah ran so hard from himself, he ran right into himself. I was at his first art show, wearing a fancy red dress, my hair pulled up into a french twist, my fingernails and toenails painted red, and Miss Darla's locket shining on my chest with a note inside that read, *Let Micah's night go well, old spirits*. Micah was all sassy and full with his own self. He swaggered over and said, "I told you! I told you this would happen." He did the things he said he'd do, that's my older brother. But I also know the addictions that plagued him, ones I hope he's released, released.

Andy has his bookstore that smells like old books, coffee, and incense. He gives me books saying, "Read this, you'll love it," and I usually do. Andy owns fast cars, plays blues and jazz, and writes his own music. He takes chances sometimes, still. His jittery jitters. I was at his wedding to Beth Anne, and then when their son Benjamin

Hale came squalling into the world. Ben is just like Andy was when he was a kid. All fearless and spitting at the world if it gets in his way.

And I was there when Bobby graduated from medical school, an orthopedic surgeon right smack in the middle of our family. He looks handsome in his white coat and wire-framed glasses that don't hide the twinkly eyes. I ate wedding cake as I watched Bobby dance with his new bride Angela. And I passed out bubblegum cigars when their three children came along quick, one two three—Rebekha Kate, Robert Dean, and Frederick Andrew. Their house is full-up to the top with noise and laughing. Now my brother has all these kids tagging along after him, just as he followed after Andy. And if he has secrets, he's not telling.

I touch Miss Darla's locket that I wear all the time. It's empty right now. I didn't know what I wanted to wish for when I came tearing up here to get Momma. Didn't have time to think on it anyway. I was there when poor Sophia died, and I helped Miss Darla bury her in her backyard. She has a Boston Terrier named Marilyn Monroe to keep her company now. On hot Louisiana evenings, we still plop ourselves down on her swing and sip sweet tea and we don't need to say anything at all. I want my Miss Darla to live forever. Silly me.

And Jade. She dances her way to eating disorders and too many men, but I love her.

And I was there when Adin came needing a momma, since her own Momma didn't want her anymore. I was there when she cried all night for her own momma, holding on to a stuffed animal with chewed on ears. And later, when she asked me if she could live with me, I was scared, but now I don't know what I was scared of anymore. She came right after my marriage crashed and burned into a big fiery smoke of ugly. He found someone he loved more, someone who could have his children. But I don't care. Not one speck do I care that he found someone else, has five kids, and lives in a big house he built in California. I don't care. I have Adin and I have my family. I wish they were here in the holler right now, but I know they can't come.

I open my eyes wide open, put down the water glass I've been holding in the air. I say in a clear, loud voice, without frogs, "You're stalling, Virginia Kate." And I sound like Grandma Faith. And I sound like Momma. But, mostly, I sound like me.

Back at Momma's door, I turn the knob, open the door. There's her new radio. There's her favorite cross-stitched pillow. There's her scatter rug. Crossing over and into the room, I open her window and let come the wind. It rushes in and knocks over her little glass swans. I think back to so very long ago when she sat at her vanity and brushed out her hair one hundred strokes plus two to grow on.

I turn and am flabbergasted into a big open mouth stare when I see two of Micah's paintings on her wall. One is of all of us kids, grinning out of the painting like prime fools; we have our butts parked on the top of a cedar trunk that I imagine holds all our yesterdays. In the other one, he's painted Momma at her most beautiful. She has on her lipstick and her shoulders are bare from the gypsy top she wears. Her hair spills down her back, but pieces of it fly in the invisible wind all around her. Her eyes are so dark I could fall in and never be found again, just explore around in them to figure out her mysteries until the end of time.

My cheeks are wet and I wipe them dry. I'm too silly for my own good with my silly little girl tears. I open her closet and there are her dresses hanging like shades of the day and night sky, and the sunrise and sunset, except for her favorite red one she died in. Pulling out a blue one with a cinched in waist, I press my face into it, taking in Momma's smells. Up on the shelf are two shoeboxes and a hatbox. I take them down and look to see that they are filled with photos, letters, pieces of paper with Momma's writing on them, Micah's drawings when he was a little boy, rocks from the creek we used to bring her, our school papers, and ribbons she put in my hair. I put them aside to take them back to my room.

I turn and there's Momma at her vanity, brushing out her long dark hair. Shalimar fills up the room on invisible clouds. I catch my breath in and out and in and out. Her beauty is always evident. Even though she was an old woman when she died, I will never see her in any way but young and alive, and wanting. In my memory she will remain younger than I am, always. But I can't help wondering what she would have been like as she aged, what our days together may have been like as she grew older and I grew older with her, until finally the spaces between us didn't make a difference anymore.

I walk to her vanity dresser and pick up the silver-framed photo of when I was born, the one where Momma holds me, posing for the camera with parted lips. I know that on the back, in Daddy's handwriting, are the words: *Baby-Bug Carey, born August 14, 1957. What Dreams May Come to her*. Fifty-one years flown by. And so few of them were spent with Momma. Beautiful-wild, Momma's face reposes in still life. I never untangled the mystery of her need. Neither did she, or anyone else who loved her. The realities are only weaved from the evidence.

I trace my finger over our faces. All my life before me as I snuggled in her arms. I set the picture down beside a rose from Mrs. Mendel's garden. Maybe Mrs. Mendel gave it to her to cheer her up. I pluck a petal and fold it inside Miss Darla's locket. There, now I have what I want inside the locket, a rose petal the color of Momma's lips.

I then notice the envelope with my name on it

tucked in the mirror frame. Hands trembling, I open it, read,

Dear Virginia Kate, I'd hoped for you to come. If you are reading this, then you surely did come home. Guess that means you don't hate me, that you might even still love me. Means I'll see you from wherever I am and can touch your hair soft and sweet like I did when you were little. Well, I'm not too good with words, but maybe now that you are grown you see what I had to do? Maybe now you can forgive me so I can rest. Be sure to find all the things you need to find while you're here. Then you can rest, too. Love, Momma.

I blink back the stinging in my eyes, finish reading her instructions, fold the letter and put it in my pocket. I stare at the painting of Momma. I think of Grandma Faith and Momma, how maybe they let their children go to keep them from fates too sad to imagine. I know I'll read everything I found in the boxes from her closet, and on the story will go.

The room cools and warms. The Shalimar becomes strong. I'm startled by a wind ruffling my hair, soft and sweet. I never question the ghosts. Why should I do so now?

I call out, "Momma?" There's no answer, just a short burst of wind to pull the curtains in a dance and she's gone, floating up up and up until I can hardly remember the feeling, even though it was just here. But I do remember. I do.

I take all the things I want back to my room. I go back to Momma's room one more time and turn around in a full circle. One full slow circle, and then I leave and shut the door behind me.

On my bed, the piles of memories have grown. I pass my palms over all the past; my hands become warm and tingly again. Which one? *Where to now, Grandma? Now that you led me where you knew I needed to go.* I hear voices and sounds. I close my eyes to wash away old dust. I press my palm on what I can't see.

Ghosts call my name, stronger, closer, louder. The voices are so real; I think I'm going insane. I've been too lonely here. Someone is walking through the house, calling out to me.

Not ghosts or mountain spirits, but real voices.

"Vee? Hellooo?"

"She's in here somewhere."

"Is this where y'all lived?"

"Hey, it looks almost the same as I remember."

Shoes clomp on the floor, closer, closer, until here they are, filling up my room. And I can't believe they came. All three of them. (Even Micah!) I jump up to hug on brothers. I say, "I can't believe you're here!"

My brothers make faces, pretending they aren't glad I'm happy to see them. We step back and grin at each other. They look around the room.

"What the hell is all this stuff, Vee?" Micah points to the mess on the bed and floor. "You've been scooting down memory lane, getting all whirly brained again?"

"She never could leave stuff alone." Andy looks like a kid again. We all look like kids again—the house is pulling us all back. "You're kind of a mess, Seestor. What's with the robe and wrinkled clothes?"

"Huh?" I check myself in the mirror and see a silly grinning girl instead of a middle-aged woman.

"So this is your house, and your room." Bobby looks around. "I always tried to picture where y'all lived."

"Yep, Bobby. This is it." I swing my hand around, including Momma in the sweep.

Andy says to Bobby, "Come on, I'll show you our old room." I hear their grown up shoes clomping down the hall, like Daddy's had.

I smile at Micah, say, "You're here."

"Yeah. I'm here." Micah pushes aside some of the mess and flops down on the bed.

"I can't believe it."

"What's to believe?"

I look at Micah as if he's made up of solid stupid. "You said you'd never come back."

"I did?"

I flop beside him. "You know you did."

He shrugs. In the next room, my brothers are laughing up a storm.

"I guess I thought nobody was coming."

"Well, here we are." He pushes through a pile of

photos and picks up a picture of Momma and Daddy. "Dad's here, too, Vee."

"What do you mean, here?"

He doesn't say at first. "You're right, I didn't think I'd ever see this holler again. But hell if here I am." He gets up and goes to look out my window. "You always loved that mountain, but have you ever been on it?"

"Yes."

He turns to eagle eye me.

Andy's stomps retreat to the other end of the hall, and Bobby's follow. I imagined it just as it happens, I hear Andy bust into Momma's room and say, "This is my momma's room," and then walks out, as if it's nothing at all.

Micah says, "Dad's not sure if you want him to come to the memorial."

"Why did *you* come?" I unflop myself from the bed.

"I came for you." He stares over to the picture of us in the Popsicle frame. "Well, maybe I came for all of us, even Momma."

"I'm glad."

He shrugs, again.

"I never knew you sent her those paintings. They're good, Micah."

"So, she didn't throw them out."

"No, she didn't. They're in her room."

He looks around my room, as if he's seeing things, or wanting to see things.

The screen slams. Andy's showing Bobby the maple and where the old swing was, I bet.

A breeze lifts up Micah's hair.

I stand closer to him and lean my head on his shoulder.

A slam, and shoes clop towards my room again and then Andy and Bobby are standing in the doorway.

Micah goes to Momma's urn and touches it. "It feels warm; I thought it would be cold."

I turn to straighten up the things on the bed. "Mrs. Mendel said she was all dressed up when they found her. Had her hair done up in that high ponytail she liked when she was young. Red lipstick and all."

"Well, that's Momma. There's no trying to figure her out," Micah says.

Andy and I nod.

Bobby says, "Y'all had this life here I always wondered about."

"We wondered a lot of things ourselves, Bobby," Micah says.

Bobby nods, looks away, and Micah reaches over to pat his shoulder to let him know all is well.

"I thought we'd have the memorial under the maple tree," I say.

"That's good." Andy nods.

"All of us have to take a part of her with us and spread her out. It's what she wanted." I take the letter from my pocket, rub it.

"What's that?" Micah asks.

"She said she wanted to go different places she'd never been. Guess this is one way for her to do that." I tell them Momma's wish she wrote in the letter, how she wanted her ashes to go here and there and yonder.

Bobby says, "I wish I'd have known her."

Micah, Andy, and I look at him. It's as if he's always been here with us all through time, as if we all came from the same place.

Andy says to Bobby, "Let's go get some food."

"Good luck finding anything much," I tell them, but they're off again, clomping.

"I'm getting hungry, too. You want a peanut butter sandwich, Micah?"

He grins sheepish, then says, "I have something to tell you first."

"What?"

He pushes back his hair until it sticks on end. "I bought the house on the hill."

"Huh?"

He points to his right. "The one up to the hill on the other side of Mrs. Mendel's." He grins, shrugs. "Where Dad's waiting to see you."

My mouth falls right onto my lap and stays there. I have to pick up my chin and work it back. "You bought the lonely house on the hill?"

"Uh huh." He puts his hands in his pocket and jingles his keys just like Daddy. "I remember how you always thought it was such a mystery. I did, too. I used to watch Dad go up there." He stares at Momma's urn. "I guess I bought it for reasons I haven't figured out yet."

I rub my eyes. "But what about Momma's house?"

Micah looks away from Momma. "Leave it here to rot?"

My head spins.

"Come on, let's get out of here. I hate talking about this in front of Momma."

In the kitchen, my brothers have found a box of crackers, the half loaf of stale bread, a jar of black-berry jam, and the peanut butter. They have the circle glasses out and Bobby is making ice water. They all gather around the table and start gobbling and slurping it all down. I almost expect them to open their mouths and go, "gah uh gah uh," showing me the half-chewed food. I eat a peanut butter and jam sandwich with them. We're quiet for a while. I'm thinking about Daddy on the hill, won-dering why he isn't coming down, but knowing why just as much.

Andy asks, "Where's Momma's booze?"

"I poured it all out."

"Good," he answers.

I finish my sandwich quick as a hungry dog. All a sudden, I don't want to stall, I want to see Daddy as bad as ever. I want to see him with the holler below me. See what it feels like to stand on the hill with him and look down as he used to. "I'm going for a walk," I tell them.

They all nod and chew. They know.

I walk to the house on the hill. I see Daddy standing up there, his tall, wide shoulders that stoop just a little under the weight of his age, and the dark hair that has turned white and sparse. When I reach him, I gather him up in a hug. I smell Old Spice and sun-drenched cotton, but I don't smell the bourbon. Not today.

"Daddy, you're here."

"I am."

"And Rebekha?"

"She didn't think it right to come."

I nod. I remember how she sat in the car, waiting for Momma to give up Micah. "I'll call her later to fill her in."

"She'll like that."

I look down at the holler, and at Momma's house. I can see through the kitchen window a bit. Micah sticks out his head and waves. I wave back. I ask, "Why did you always come up here, Daddy?"

"It's the perspective. Look, you can see so much from up here."

I look across the holler, over the next hill, and to the distant mountains.

"There's something I want to show you." He walks towards the corner of the house, stops to kneel down, and puts his hand to the ground. "It's here. Right here I buried it."

"What, Daddy?"

"I buried everything the hospital gave me. It was all I had, all I had of our little one."

I can't think of what to say. Little lost babies that Momma and I never knew or held.

"I had to have a place for it. I had to have somewhere I could come to. And facing the house below, like some kind of strange taunting."

"Why'd Momma do it?"

"Do what?" He looks at the ground, and not at me.

"Nothing, Daddy." I watch his face tense and release and tense again as he lets himself remember what he has to remember. He stands up and scrubs his face with his left hand.

"Let's go to the house, Daddy, okay? I'll send the boys to the store so we can cook some supper."

"Seems strange to be back here, Bug. I'm tumbling back, like I'm off-balance."

"No Shakespeare quote for me, Daddy?"

"I suppose I'm not in the mood."

I take his hand and help him down the hill. When we get back to Momma's, he's sucked up by the house, same as I am.

Over a supper of stewed chicken and cream potatoes, we all don't talk much. The ghost mists are swirling about and everybody feels tired and spent with feelings. It's strange having us all at the table again, but without Momma. It's strange, and sad, and just like a kid, I wish for things I can't ever have.

After supper, everybody finds a place to rest. Daddy goes to town to stay at a hotel, says he'll be back early. Daddy couldn't stay in the house overnight. Ghosts.

I get under Grandma's quilt and wish her to me again. I want to be coddled like a baby-girl. I wait and wait until I fall asleep without her.

The next morning I get up early before it's full-out light. Micah and Andy are sleeping in their rootin' tootin' beds, their long adult legs flopped off the end of those kids' sized beds. Bobby is sleeping on the couch, looking much more comfortable than his brothers do.

After putting water on to boil, I go to the window and see Gary and Mrs. Mendel in the garden. I wave at her, but she can't see me. Gary waves back, and I want to shout out, "I'm not waving at you. I'm waving at Mrs. Anna Mendel." I'll see her at the memorial and hug her neck then. She's bent and her movements are slow and deliberate. She walks with a cane now and wears thick supportive shoes and stockings. But she is timeless. I laugh when I remember how as a child I thought her old, when she was younger than I am now when I lived in the holler.

When I get the coffee made, I sneak past sleepy Bobby, and open the screen, the *scrangy* sound loud in the morning quiet. I settle myself down under the maple and sip. I'm there for days, months, and years. I'm there until the sun is full-out strong. I'm there even after I hear a car pull up, and then another one. I keep my back to the maple and sip my hot sweet coffee without a care. And then my daughter is slamming out the back running to me like Fionadala galloping. She hollers out, "Mom, are you okay?"

I'm grinning happy stars. I hug her and she smells like Jean Naté. "I thought you couldn't come."

"I tried to call your cell to let you know I'd be here after all but you never answered. What is it about you never answering your cell?" She asks. "I finally reached Uncle Jonah and he picked me up from the airport. I rode out here with him and Aunt Billie." She pushes back her hair. "They won't let Aunt Billie drive anymore and they argued about that all the way here. She said they let old men do anything they want to up until they fall over dead, but women have to fight for every scrap of every-thing all their lives." She laughs.

I laugh, too, but I know it's true for my momma's generation more than now.

She inhales deep deep. "It smells good here. It's so pretty."

"Yes, it sure is."

"I'm starved, Mom."

We go inside where my brothers are all talking at once, their hair standing on end. I laugh at the sight of them. Daddy has come, hanging back as if he doesn't think anyone wants him here. I hug Uncle

Jonah and Aunt Billie and they both feel like they have bird bones. They turn from me and give Adin big hugs.

Aunt Billie and I get breakfast on the table. Everyone looks at Mee Maw's marks on the wall. We talk about how Mee Maw is playing Queen of the Nursing Home, driving the staff wild and sinking her claws into all the men who still have a pulse. It was her decision to go there once her last husband, the one following the tater boiling man, died from what surely was sheer Mee Maw-induced exhaustion.

We pull in chairs and somehow all fit around the table.

My brothers stuff eighty pounds of biscuit with gravy down their gullets while talking about work and family and all the things that make up their lives now. I know we're all getting older, but now that we're all here, I can't see the gray in Micah's hair, or the way Andy's crow's feet fan out from years of squinting in the sun, or how Bobby's hair is thinning on top. They still look much to me as they did when we were children. I wonder if I look like a young sister to them. It's this house; my eyes wide open makes us all go backwards faster and faster until the lines and gray and talk about mundane things fade away and what's left are barefoot kids running in the grass.

I look to Daddy. He's still quiet, but he smiles around the table at us all there together.

After the breakfast dishes are done, I go to my room to get Momma, and Micah is right, the urn is warm. I bring her outside, search the faces of my brothers, wondering if my eyes match theirs, and if our eyes are saying Momma is never coming back.

Mrs. Mendel sniffles in her hankie while Gary holds onto her elbow. He looks at me with something I can't fathom, and then away. I appreciate him looking away.

We all stand in a circle around the tree. I pour out a little of Momma's ashes and let her fall. We say nothing. It feels right to be as quiet as butterfly wings. The wind picks these pieces of her and carries her up and around. She dances as the breeze pushes and pulls her. Then each of us kids take our part of Momma to spread to all our places, just as she wanted. Daddy doesn't take any of her, since he released what he could of her long ago. He's here for the last of his release, I guess. Or maybe he's here for me. I let that thought sink to my bones.

Daddy says, "Katie Ivene Holms Carey. She was loved and she did love. 'Rough winds do shake the darling buds of May, And summer's lease hath all too short a date.'"

Aunt Billie and Uncle Jonah say, "A-men."

There is nothing more to say about Momma.

Back inside, Daddy and my brothers talk about what route home is best and what fast food place has better hamburgers. Adin is making sandwiches, gabbing away to Micah about art.

I think how maybe I've been holding onto the heavy things that make me slow instead of lightening my load so I can run up my mountain free and clear. It's hard to let go, but maybe it's time. Is that what Grandma's been asking?

I head back to my room, shut the door, slip under Grandma Faith's quilt and lie against the feather soft. I decide that I'll take my vial of Momma's ashes with me to my mountain and leave her there. I'll wear red lipstick and my hair will blow around like a living thing. I'll say, "Feel that wind, Momma!" And she'll say, "Wheeeee!" And off we'll go. When I get there, I'll smell the earth and feel the tickle of leaves under my bare feet and against my face. The wind won't let the tears gather at all. And I'll let Momma dance in the wind as I pour her out.

All a sudden the voices in the other room fade and fade as my childhood room becomes bright with light. I smell apples and fresh-baked bread stronger than I ever have before, and then I see Grandma Faith standing at the foot of my bed, smiling down at me. She's whole and real, she's Here.

I feel drowsy as a little girl when I say, "Grandma Faith, you're here."

"Yes, Virginia Kate," she says. "You've done well, now comes the release."

I pull up from the heaviness of the quilt and reach out to her, but even as I do, I feel a slipping away, a parting from me. A wind flies out with a sigh; the curtains twist and dance, and then are still. The room's glow dims. I lay back on my pillow, looking beyond.

I'm happy and that thought slams against me.

Feeling the release, I let go.

Aye to the proof. I let Momma go. Down sweet sister mountain I ride on Fionadala's back. We are not in a hurry now. Easy. Easy. I smile. The release decides for me, where I will next go. Where my life will lead me. The release sets me free.

The Recipes of *Tender Graces*

Katie Ivene's Salt Rising Bread

To make the sponge:
3 between sized potatoes
3 tablespoons of meal
1 teaspoon sugar
Pinch of soda
4 cups water that's come to the boil

The next day:
2 cups of sweet milk that's warmed a bit
1 cup of water that's come to the boil
2 teaspoons salt
⅛ teaspoon of soda
2 tablespoons of shortening (and best not be using any petal puss pig lard in my recipe!)
Flour

Makes three loaves unless it makes four or two, sometimes I change the recipe so you best check it twice. The day ahead, while the kids are still outside playing before supper, peel and slice up the potatoes and add the meal, sugar, soda, and water that's come to the boil. Put all that in a glass bowl or big jar if you still have one that's not broke, and cover it up with a good weight-sized dishrag. Let it stand in a warm place all the night and don't let the kids play around to knock it over or else you got to start over again. The next morning there should be a foam risen up top of it. Get the potatoes out of the mixture, and then add milk, water, soda, salt, and shortening. Add flour just enough to make the dough stiff enough to knead up until it's right. Keep the kids out of the dough with their dirty hands or else you got to throw the nasty dough away and start all over. While kneading, think on things that's been bothering you and soon the answer will come. Shape the dough into loaves. Put the loaves in greased up pans, cover with a dishrag, and let them rise again until twice the size. Then bake the loaves in a 400 degree oven until it's done, maybe 40 minutes or so. Give the kids warm bread with apple butter and send them outside so you can think straight. Serve the bread to your husband so he can see just what you can do when you set your mind to it even if you can do more than bake bread at least the bread gets his attention.

Grandma Faith's Apple Butter

Pull together:
5 pounds of tart apples
3 cups of apple cider that's been made another
   day
4 cups of sugar

3 teaspoons of cinnamon unless you like more
1 teaspoon of cloves unless you like more
A pinch or so of salt to bring out the sweet

Peel the apples, remove the cores, and cut the apples in quarters—if the grandkids are visiting, this will keep their hands busy, but watch the young ones with a knife. In a heavy pot bring the apples and cider up to the boiling. Don't let this burn by leaving the kitchen to do other things, make your time for it! Cut the heat down and simmer for about twenty-five to thirty minutes. Then take the mixture and put through a sieve or a colander. Mix in the sugar, salt, cinnamon, and cloves. Taste it to make sure it's perfect. Give the grandkids a taste to see if it is good to their tongue. If everyone is happy, pour the mixture into a dish and bake for two hours at 300 degrees. While this bakes, clean up your mess in the kitchen so that's all done and let the kids take the peelings and cores out to the pig. You can check your mixture before two hours to see if it's gone thick enough for your tastes. Then, when it's done how it should be, pour into canning jars. Make extra for selling—hide those in the secret place. Put the rest up for the family for later. Good on cornbread or biscuits.

Rebekha's Pralines

Ingredients:
1 cup of white sugar
1 cup of packed light brown sugar
¾ cup of cream
¼ teaspoon of salt
2 tablespoons of butter (real butter, not margarine!)
1 to 1½ cups of pecans (leave them in halves, not pieces)
1 teaspoon of vanilla

This is a good recipe to teach children about passing down traditional recipes, measuring, and soft ball versus hard ball stages. Take a heavy 2-quart-sized saucepan and butter the sides—a child can do this part easily. Add the sugars, the cream, and the salt to the saucepan and cook over a medium heat, stirring constantly, until the sugars are dissolved. Keep stirring with a good heavy wood spoon and continue to cook until the mixture begins to come to a boil. It is not a good idea to let younger kids help with this part, as the mixture gets very hot and can cause bad burns. Turn down the heat and cook until the soft ball stage, about 234 degrees on a candy thermometer. When at soft ball stage take off the stove and add the butter and vanilla. Again, be careful that the children do not burn themselves; this should be the adult only part of the recipe. With your wooden spoon, start stirring to cool and add in the pecans. Keep stirring until the candy has become thick and isn't shiny anymore. Be fast now! Take a teaspoon or tablespoon and spoon out the mixture onto waxed paper—some newspaper under that wax paper is a good idea. Let the candies cool completely before you let the children at them, or else they'll eat them before they are ready. Wrap them up in wax paper with a ribbon and share with neighbors!

Acknowledgments

How do I possibly thank everyone who has encouraged me in the process of writing this debut book? I think a first book creates layers upon layers of support, which is why you may see a first-time author's acknowledgement page 50-galleven pages long, and the second book one page long, and by the third book, a simple "To You, thanks." When I described my angst, someone said, "Geez, it's not the Academy Awards!" No, but still...I believe in giving thanks, because I am sincerely grateful.

There are people who always have an encouraging word—such as the twinkly-eyed post office worker. Charles at Calandro's supermarket in Baton Rouge. The Hart Theater, especially The Regulars: Charles, Mark, Frances, and Christy Bishop who came by one really cold mountain morning and took beautiful author photos. My Rose & Thorn colleagues. The "LSU & FPC people."

Then there is the cyber layer—how could I leave out the wonderful community of blog friends who have supported me and cheered me on. My WDC friends who've been cheering me even before the thought "novel" was thunked. The forums of Bestsellers & Literature and NABBW. Mountain Writers Alive for which I keep promising JC and Sonja I will soon attend. And the supportive Backspacer's group.

As the layers progress, those lovelies who read TG and then so beautifully wrote blurbs for Tender Graces—their names are visible for all to see and you have my thanks. And my "Readers" who volunteered their time—John & Tere Robinson, Kim Vickers (who also works doubly hard to create my website), David Blackwell, Kyndra Goodman, Margaret Osondu, Patresa Hartman and Ruvena Snellings. There are my friends far and near who supported in some way special: Adnan Mahmutovic, Mike, Stephen Rowe, Cherie, Marta Stephens, Dr. Boudreaux, Sarah & Margaret, Sonja, Michael Manning, Pam, Connie, Lorelle Bacon, Mrs. Barbara Gray and Robin Becker.

The layers grow ever deeper still; my beautiful NAWW friends: Poet and Ancient Soul Marilyn Shapely, Jazzy Blues Poet Cynthia Toups (who went an extra mile or two or three with her eagle eyes), In-Your-Face-World Poet Alaine Benard with her bird's wings soaring, Author and Wonder Woman Deb Leblanc (who gives of herself freely to help writers), Literary Writer and Couch-enthusiast Mary Ann Ledbetter (see the Reader's Guide at the end), Scent-sory Perceptive Marie L. Broussard (she reminded me how Librarians are cool!). And I've saved a special mention for last: VK's "Godmother" Angie Ledbetter—she poked me until I wrote this book. There is a lot of Angie in Rebekha, or is it the other way around? Angie holds the NAWW sisters together, even when we spin outward and beyond. My NAWW friends are strong and beautiful and talented and I love them. They helped me in all their ways to see Virginia Kate's way Home.

The layers develop further, ever deeper. For there is my Family. Surrounding me, cheering me on. My Good Man Roger, who is an "author widower" and never complains. Roger lets me have the space I need to write; he brings me food (the ultimate act of love) and wine and quick hugs. He is a rock. My gifted son Daniel taught me how to be a mother who raised a good son. He is wise and has grown in to a kind man and I am proud of him. Carol Magendie, who drove all the way to New Orleans to bring me needed gifts. Mom and Frank—thank you Mother for taking us in, sheltering us, and keeping us together. Dad and Noreen—my daddy has been sober for near-fifty years—he wants me to give that gift to Frederick, and maybe I did— thank you Daddy for always wanting us. Robin and Rachel—your daddy was special, never forget that, ever. Nephew Christopher Snellings. My brothers: Tommy, (David), Mike, Johnny—I know you are proud of your seestor, and thanks for being the bestest ever brothers even when you tortured the heck out of me and teased me even though I was a saint and never did a thing to y'all and I probably was the most even-tempered un-moody sister EVER. My (adopted) family members in Arkansas—I miss that farm and the simple ways.

And to my "lost and found" biological mom (who I'm glad I've come to know the beautiful woman she is), "half" sister and, "half" brother (who are wholes), uncles and other family in West Virginia—I hope you read this and are proud. And to Adrienne (Zetty) and Jon Bryce Magendie— thank you for accepting me.

Of course to Bellebooks/Belle Bridge books – thank you for taking a chance on Virginia Kate, and me. Thank you for what you see and what you saw.

To everyone who picks up this book and reads it—you have my gratitude. I wrote it while thinking of who would hold my words in their hands and come to love Virginia Kate. This book is a love letter to you all.

About Kathryn Magendie

Kathryn Magendie is a writer and freelance editor, and Co-Managing Editor/Senior Newsletter Editor at *The Rose & Thorn* Literary Ezine.

Kat's essays, poetry, short stories, book reviews, interviews, and photography have been published or are forthcoming in places such as: *New Southerner* Magazine, *Vagabondage Press-Battered Suitcase*, *Sotto Voce*, *Western North Carolina Woman Magazine* (including a first place win in WNCW's 2008 Short Story contest); *Mocha Momma Literal Latte*; Baton Rouge Sunday Magazine; BoomerWomen/Our Stories; *Cantaraville Three*; *OCEAN* Magazine; *A Cup of Comfort for Writers*; *Moondance-Celebrating Creative Women*; C/Oasis: *Writing for the Connected World*; *The Rose & Thorn*; *Jubilee Anthology*-Nicholls State University (*Tender Graces* novel excerpt); *Halfway Down the Stairs*; *Drollerie Press; Lunch Hour Stories*; *L'Intrigue*, the *Wild Magnolia of Literature*; and has had feature stories, a literary column, restaurant reviews, and interviews in publications *The Indie*, and The Mountaineer Publishing Company's *The Guide*.

She is a member of organizations such as:

Backspace, *NABBW*, *NetWest Writers*, and various sites for readers and writers. She has a successful blog, writes with three other *Rose & Thorn* writers in a year of gratitude blog (YOG), and participates in the *Roses & Thorns* staff blog.

Visit Kathryn at www.kathyrnmagendie.com

Tender Graces
Reader's Guide

Tender Graces is haunted by many ghosts. How does the spiritual world aid both the young and the adult Virginia Kate?

The supernatural is a very real presence in *Tender Graces*. What psychic power does Miss Darla have? How does she help Virginia Kate, physically, emotionally, and spiritually? Explain the significance of the green-eyed-jeweled horse pendant she gives to Virginia Kate.

How does Virginia Kate bear hardship? What extra-sensory power does she have? What is her quest? Has Virginia Kate broken the spell of her mother and grandmother's lives?

What kind of person is Grandma Faith? Instead of running away, she uses her money to purchase material for a red dress, among other items, for Katie Ivene. Why do you think she does so? How do you think she died? Discuss her continuing presence in the book as a guiding spirit.

Virginia Kate often refers to her West Virginia mountain as her "sister." What do you think she means by this appellation? Does Virginia Kate ever move emotionally from her mountain, as she moves physically and, if so, how? Additionally, explore the idea of mountain as character.

Katie Ivene is a tremendously complex character. Despite mocking her husband's knowledge of Shakespeare, she studies his books in secrecy. Why did she give away her children, one by one? During her recovery after the accident, does Katie Ivene finally realize the single most loving thing she can do for her daughter is to send her away for a second time? What evidence proves this theory?

Why does Micah remain silent for so many years about the truth of Uncle Ar-vile's death? How has Micah dealt with the event? What prompts him to tell the truth to Virginia Kate? Is Micah set free?

Andy seems to be the child least affected negatively by Katie Ivene's actions. How does he retain his resilience and good humor, even after being tricked into abandonment in Louisiana? Why is he a risk-taker? Does he constantly test himself against some imagined challenge?

Frederick remains a puzzle until nearly the end of the book. Does Virginia Kate ever gain insight into her father's drinking, his leaving, and his womanizing? What ties him to such a destructive personality as his mother? What does he do to signify he is at last able to break free from not only his mother's legacy, but from Katie Ivene's "spell"?

What makes Laudine so downright "ornery"? Discuss Laudine's relationship with Katie Ivene, Frederick, her grandchildren, and with Rebekha. How does she compare with Grandma Faith?

How is Rebekha capable of such unselfish love? Why is she so different from her own mother? Do you see her as a force of salvation? If so, explain who she saves and how.

Why did Rebekha's mother insist on taking a picture of the young Rebekha holding her dead infant brother? What does this action say about her? Is Rebekha correct in her assessment that her mother blames her for Laurence's tragedy?

Discuss Bobby's adoration of his "half" siblings, particularly Andy. Do you think he is "the lucky child?" What is his important role in his "half" sibling's lives?

Why is Aunt Ruby evil? Or is she completely evil? Discuss her abuse of her sister Katie Ivene's children. And why are Arville's and Ruby's deaths so satisfying to the reader? Discuss the universal human longing for evil to be horrifically punished.

How is Uncle Jonah untouched by the "taint" of some that are his kin? How did he escape his past?

What is Anna Mendel's significance in the novel? What drives Anna Mendel as a force for good?

Though the reader encounters Mrs. Mendel's nephew Gary only twice in the book, he is in Virginia Kate's consciousness by the conclusion. How does Virginia Kate respond to his presence?

What role does Amy Campinelle and Mr. Husband play for Virginia Kate? What about Soot and Marco, Mrs. Portier? Are they symbols of stabilizing presences in Virginia Kate's life?

Discuss the friendship between Virginia Kate and Jade. Why does Virginia Kate at first resist friendship?

The color red figures significantly in *Tender Graces*. Think of Katie Ivene's red lipstick, nail polish, and dress, for example. What does the color appear to mean?

How does Virginia Kate think of the moon? Does she personify it as she does her mountain? Does it illuminate more than physical space?

Tender Graces lifts family celebration to an almost spiritual level. What are some of the events celebrated in both West Virginia and Louisiana? What part does food, music, and dance play in these celebrations? How does family celebration contribute to character development?

Fire is an important element in *Tender Graces*. What might Magendie be telling us with her uses of fire and ashes? Think about the fire that consumes both Grandma Faith's body and her house. Think, also, of the cremation of Ruby and Katie Ivene, and remember that cremation was an unusual burial method in the novel's time frame. Why do you think Magendie chose to dispose of the two women's bodies this way? Virginia Kate burns Micah's drawing of the bloody man with holes in him. Why didn't she simply throw away the disturbing picture? Is Magendie referencing Celtic mythological wildfire in her novel and in what ways?

Obviously, Fionadala's name is Celtic. Why do you think Magendie chose this name for Virginia Kate's imaginary horse? Is the horse imaginary? Is there a possibility that Virginia Kate sees the horse as real?

Who do you think are Grandma Faith's mother's kin? What part do you think heredity plays in the development of Magendie's characters? Does environment play an equally important role? Does the utter isolation of mountain hollers affect character development? How about the humid, Spanish moss-hung locales of south Louisiana?

Photographs figure prominently in *Tender Graces*. What is Magendie trying to show us about their power? What is Virginia Kate trying to clearly see?

What does her beloved sister mountain symbolize allegorically? How about the moon? Fionadala? Discuss *Tender Graces* as allegory.

What exactly are the tender graces referenced in Magendie's title? Do all characters receive grace? Which characters are open to unearned blessings?

Look over Magendie's Shakespearean allusions. What layer of meaning is added to *Tender Graces* by literary allusion?

Does Magendie write about religious hypocrisy? Think about Grandma Faith's very name. What is its significance? Which characters exhibit unwavering faith—in themselves, in God, in both dead and alive loved ones, in a divine intellect? Does their faith help them in their life journeys, and, if so, in what ways?

Many characters in *Tender Graces* are on quests of different kinds. What is Virginia Kate's quest?

Does Katie Ivene have a deliberate quest? Is there something for which she aches and searches? Why does she only appear to be a bad mother? Can you locate proof that one of her quests is indeed motherhood, though on the surface she seems to have her sights sets on far less worthy ideals?

What is Frederick's quest? Why does he marry Rebekha? What role does education play in Frederick's life? Does he hand down his passion for learning to his children? Why does Frederick so inconsistently deal with his addiction to alcohol? Does he find peace?

What is the "releasing" Magendie references at the end of *Tender Graces*?

(Reader's Guide created by Mary Ann Ledbetter, teacher, writer; Baton Rouge, Louisiana)

Center Point Publishing
600 Brooks Road • PO Box 1
Thorndike ME 04986-0001 USA

(207) 568-3717

US & Canada:
1 800 929-9108
www.centerpointlargeprint.com